SCG

This book should be returned to any branch of the
Lancashire County Library on or before the date shown

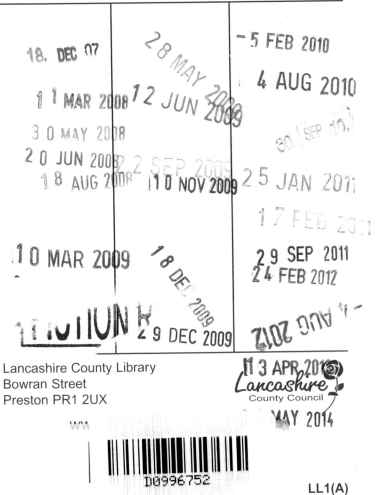

THEFT
OF THE MASTER

Edwin Alexander

Garev Publishing
International

First published in the United States in 2008
by GAREV PUBLISHING INTERNATIONAL, INC.

ISBN 978-0-9707558-5-8

Garev Publishing International, Inc.

North American address:
1095 Jupiter Park Drive, Suite 7, Jupiter, FL 33458, USA
Tel: 561 697 1447

European address:
50 Highpoint, Heath Road, Weybridge, Surrey, KT13 8TP, England
Tel: (44) (0) 1932 844526, Fax: (44) (0) 1932 820419

Web: www.garevpublishing.com

Cover and typesetting: SMK Designs

Garev Publishing
International

ACKNOWLEDGEMENTS:

David Burrowes MA (London Greig Ensemble, Royal Philharmonic Orchestra)
The cellist who so generously allowed me to use his recording of the Bach Solo Cello Suite No. 1 BWV 1007 to add atmosphere to the web site.

Debra Godshall
Publisher of the wonderfully named Half Moon Bay Review & Pescadero Pebble who gave me permission to use the name. 'Tiny' Larsen is constructed entirely from my imagination and, so far as I know, bears no relation to the present or any previous Editor.

Efrem M Grail, Reed Smith LLP
Gave me a professional critique of the Jim Otte interview chapter.

Dr Andy Hershey PhD, Military Historian
Apart from detailed information in his specialist field, provided a meticulous critique of the entire text.

The late Bud Moorman, Coroner of San Mateo County, Ca.
Bud explained the working procedures used by Coroners and other officials in California.

Duane Preimsberger, Ex Deputy Sheriff of Los Angeles County
A big man in every sense and a prize-winning author himself, was endlessly helpful in commenting on everything relating to US law enforcement.

Brian Sewell, Art Critic of the Evening Standard
Introduced me to the work of Veit Stoss.

Mark Warner, Lloyd's List
Went to a deal of trouble to provide examples of shipping movements.

Mark, Proprietor of the Café 3-0, Half Moon Bay Airport
Gave me lots of background on the airport (and some great food).

A Philosophy Professor at The Pedagogical University of Tallinn (whose name I have sadly mislaid)
Gave me valuable insights into the history and psychology of the Estonian people.

Because this novel contains much that is fact, footnotes are included for those interested in pursuing details.

"To my wife – sine qua non"

PROLOGUE

ARCHEOLOGY OF A MURDER

January 1493. Martin Luther is ten years old, Michelangelo is eighteen. In Milan, Leonardo is designing a flying machine. Richard Plantagenet, smiling villain, is dead, the Wars of the Roses have ended and Henry VII rules Tudor England. Alexander Borgia - Pope Alexander VI – thief, adulterer, multiple murderer and Vicar of Christ, rules the One True Church. Estonia, remotest and wildest of the Baltic States is in the two hundredth year of foreign domination which will persist for five centuries more.

In Tallinn, Estonia's capital, icicles drip from the eaves of the Church of the Holy Spirit. Inside, breath smoking in the frozen air, Heinrich Schenk, trader in amber, Leader of the Town Council, kneels before the altar. The cold stone floor is hard on ageing knees but, strong in the faith, he makes no complaint. He is tall and sturdily-built, rather worn by his sixty years but with grave presence. His round fleshy face, heavy brow and deep-set eyes mark his German ancestry. An austere man, his one weakness is for elaborate and expensive dress. In acknowledgement of the evening's ritual importance he wears a floor-length robe of burgundy silk-velvet deeply pleated across the chest and with balloon sleeves. He prays for a safe journey; prayer is his travel insurance. He will follow the familiar yet hazardous route of the amber trade but his purpose this time will be different. On behalf of his wife Maria, he will commission a masterpiece.

*   *   *

A month's arduous journeying later Heinrich arrived in Krakow, then capital of Poland. In the town's finest private residence he followed a young serving girl through rush-strewn corridors to the Spartan workroom of one of Europe's greatest sculptors. It was long, narrow and undecorated, furnished only with a small writing desk, two chairs and a side table bearing the remains of a meal. Giant logs smouldered ineffectually in an enormous fireplace. Stone-dust and the smell of sweat hung in the smoky air. The servant nervously announced 'Herr Schenk from Tallinn, sir' and backed out quickly, her wooden-soled tread receding to leave the room in thick silence. On the hearth a large and shaggy-coated dog got to its feet, looked at Heinrich curiously, stretched its muscular body then, with a groan, rearranged itself for sleep.

At the far end of the room a block of raw stone was set on a heavy wooden table and Veit Stoss[1] stood before it, his back to the door, in operatic pose - erect, right foot half a stride ahead of the left, head thrown back, hands clasped behind him, motionless as the stone itself.

Heinrich waited. Despite meticulous preparations, he had suffered a particularly taxing journey. Scarcely a dozen miles from Tallinn, fording a swollen river, he had almost drowned. Then, after surviving the routine hazards of bears, wolves, bitter weather and sketchy navigation to reach Warsaw, an uncharacteristically rash encounter with a street vendor's mutton pie had delayed him by three days spent mainly on a commode. And finally, in deep forest only a few miles short of Krakow, he had narrowly escaped an attempted kidnapping by brigands. Perversely, these experiences had produced in him an inner calm which enabled him to view his host's calculated rudeness with amused detachment.

At last Stoss turned and shuffled to confront his visitor. He was a bulky, round-backed figure dressed in an ankle-length, shapeless grey smock which flapped around him as he moved, like a mainsail close-hauled. Despite the chill of the stone floor his feet were bare. His face, grey as his smock, was coarse, heavy-jowled, the eyes deep and angry. On each cheek was a purple scar, branded there by the authorities of his home city of Nuremberg, a punishment for counterfeiting. Yet he could count himself fortunate since a less prominent man would have been castrated.

[1]Veit Stoss (c. 1445 - 1533). Perhaps Germany's finest ever wood-carver. In St. John Cantius, Chicago, there is a one-third size replica of his St. Mary's Church Altar, Kracow.

"Schenk. That is a good German name." Stoss spoke with a strong south-German accent.

"My family originated in Hanover." "I had a servant from Hanover... an idle cur. But you have journeyed from Tallinn."

"I am Estonian."

Stoss gestured derisively. "Nothing of value has come from Estonia. A subject people, without culture." He began a slow tour of inspection around Heinrich, muttering under his breath, now in Polish. Having completed his circuit he faced Heinrich once more.

"Why are you here?" Heinrich's amused detachment was wearing thin.

"I have come to commission a carving." Stoss turned away, went to the side table, poured himself wine and sat down.

"Do you know my fee?"

"No."

"Hmm..."

Stoss tilted back his chair, stretched out heavy legs and stared across the rim of his cup at his dirty naked feet. "I have many commissions," he said morosely, as though the work were a burden.

This was enough. Heinrich, now neither amused nor detached, crossed to the table, poured himself a beaker of wine, dragged a heavy wooden chair to face Stoss and sat down.

"I wish for a carving of Christ, seated, preaching.[2] It is to be carved in wood. Can you make such a thing?"

Stoss shrugged. "I can make anything," he said, calmly. He drained the beaker and refilled it extravagantly, splashing wine onto the table, then drank, the liquid seeming to fall down his throat as into a drain.

"This carving, it is to be large?"

Heinrich gestured to indicate the height.

"Hmm... Seated, you say?" He refilled and drained the beaker once more, set it down and looked questioningly at Heinrich who said nothing. "Preaching while seated?" he muttered, doubtfully. Heinrich's response was firm: "As the gospel teaches, 'Seated, he taught them - sedens docebat eos', John, Chapter 8, Verse 2."

---

[2] Strangely, although John does describe the Sermon on the Mount as having been delivered seated, I was unable to find any statue or carving showing this.

Overwhelmed by biblical authority Stoss wiped wine from his chins and pointed to the table in the bay.

"I have a very fine piece of Straccicario marble…"

"Wood," said Heinrich.

"Wood," repeated Stoss, solemnly.

"And," Heinrich continued, "a text. To be inscribed in German on the base: 'The Truth will make you Free', John, Chapter 8, Verse 32." Stoss sat up, picked up his beaker, made to refill it then put it aside and instead seized the bottle by its neck as if to throttle it.

"Very well, my much travelled Hanoverian friend." A gurgling drink from the bottle then, to Heinrich's surprise, a warm smile. "I will create for you a masterpiece."

On the final word, delivered in an echoing bellow, he stood up abruptly, tipping his chair to the floor with a crash. The sleeping hound raised its tousled head and stared at him reproachfully. Suddenly Stoss appeared more than a little drunk. Swaying, clutching at the table for support, he drained the bottle as a libation to his own magnificence.

"Stoss, ego ipse," he proclaimed, jabbing a solid forefinger into his chest while gesturing splendidly with the bottle, "Christum Sedentem bellissimum sculperam."

Six months later, sweltering in the August heat, Heinrich sat alongside his wife Maria, daughter of one of Estonia's oldest families, in the Schenk family pew in Tallinn's Church of the Holy Ghost. Maria's great-grandfather's great-grandfather died in the 1343 St. George's Day Uprising and at last the family and the nation have a memorial, a national icon. Now, before a passionately nationalistic congregation, the Bishop consecrated Stoss's masterpiece. On its base was carved the text 'Wahrheit macht Frei'. At the insistence of the Tallinn authorities, Maria had reluctantly agreed to the use of German.

And so this masterpiece, itself commemorating an ancient slaughter, five centuries later will become the trigger for bloodshed and betrayal…

PART I

March 1992

SETTING UP THE PIECES

In the dusty morning sunshine, as his taxi labored through rush-hour fumes and ill temper, Karl Heinz Fiedler eased his broad frame forward, away from the clinging leather seat and stared at the letter, trying once more to convince himself that it was genuine. In Erden, in the security of the Schloss, when he had raised the possibility that the letter might be a trap set by Israeli Intelligence and Josef Brandt a fiction, the Baron's cool logic had reassured him – 'this letter is naïve, Karl, the Jew would be more subtle'.

However, now, in this squalid, lawless town on the other side of the world, the threat reasserted itself and he had never felt more alone. He wouldn't be the first of his kind to finish up strapped to a chair being asked questions to which no reply was acceptable.

Distractedly, he ran a hand through the bright blonde hair kept, in token rebellion, just a little longer than the Baron preferred. An athletic man in his late thirties, his conservative suit and leather document case could have belonged to any middle executive of Siemens or BMW sweating out a tour of duty as a punishment for some corporate misdemeanour or a rite of passage to the South American desk in the Export Department but Fiedler's world was rather more dangerous than corporate Germany. Fighting down rising panic he ran shaking fingers across the embossed heading. Twenty-four hours of travel, a sleepless night in a dismal hotel had shredded his nerves and the morning's alcohol intake had failed him as it did increasingly often of late. Forcing his eyes to focus, he read the letter yet again. The writing was stylized, once the jagged, aggressive hand of authority, now wavering and uncertain. The content was uncompromising.

March 2nd 1992

Baron Edelmann,

My name is Josef Brandt. From 1942 I was a senior official in the administrative department of the SS. Since 1945 I have of necessity resided in Paraguay.

I am aware of the work of your New Templars in preparing for the Fourth Reich and intend to contribute to the cause. I am an old man and in poor health. I shall soon die. You therefore need to send most urgently a legally qualified representative to make the necessary arrangements.

Heil Hitler

Brandt

The extensive files in the Templars' Research Department had shown that no Josef Brandt had ever existed in any senior capacity in the SS administration. Discreet soundings among Asunción's German community had returned only the unhelpful information that Brandt was a near total recluse. An approach to the diplomatic staff in-country had been considered but vetoed by the Baron – 'traitors and communists'. So on the meager and uncorroborated evidence of this single page, here he was, errand boy sent to a crumbling, filthy country in the heart of a barely civilized continent. He returned the letter to the file, sat back, closed his eyes and tried to understand how his life had come to such a pass.

Two years earlier he had been invited to a meeting, in effect an interview for a senior post with a secretive organization calling itself the New Templars, based in a remote Schloss near Erden some thirty kilometers northeast of Nuremberg. Enquiries among colleagues in Hamburg's legal world – he now wished to God he'd never left it - had indicated that this was a privately funded organization dedicated to the preservation of the German cultural heritage. Preserving Goethe manuscripts no-one will ever read, as a fellow prosecutor had described it. Before declining he had spoken with his friend and superior, Hamburg's Chief Prosecutor who mildly suggested that, as he would at least have a good meal and some interesting conversation, he should attend. So, on this gentle recommendation he had agreed to the fateful meeting in the Berlin apartment of one Baron Edelmann, the New Templars' founder and head.

To his surprise he had found that the Templars' creed summed up all he had come to believe yet had never properly articulated. They too despised the new Germany, its sentimentality and lack of discipline and the creeping erosion of national sovereignty to the Common Market, to the French for God's sake. And the Baron had been urbane and persuasive. He had navigated an entire evening selling extreme nationalism without a mention of Jews, National Socialism or immigration. True, the job would mean an initial loss of income but a young man with – the Baron had reached across the table to lay a hand on his arm - personal commitment could expect rapid promotion. And, he added, as insurance, senior Templars were men of influence, many in the legal profession like himself, and he would be 'looked after' should he choose to return to 'the outside world' – a flat lie as he would discover.

Brandy was being served and Fiedler was nibbling the bait when the Baron's sister arrived, ostensibly unexpected. Erica, tall, soignée, around thirty, wearing a crimson ankle-length gown and a year of Fiedler's salary in diamonds, swept in, kissed the Baron on the cheek and took the glass from his hand. Already just detectably drunk, she complained that the party had been 'simply awful' and demanded to be introduced to 'your beautiful young man'. Fiedler's infatuation was immediate. Within weeks he was living in a private apartment in the Templars' absurd Schloss, brother-in-law and personal assistant to the Baron, immersed in fund-raising, floating on a cloud of sex and enthusiasm.

He was not told and knew better than to ask what was to be bought with the money he so energetically raised. That was the preserve of his seniors, the Baron and the six anonymous Knights who controlled the organization. But he was not blind. There were documents accidentally seen, conversations abruptly halted when he entered a room, and visitors' names discreetly withheld. It was the dark side of patriotism and Karl had to work hard to shut it from his mind.

His taxi and a chauffeur-driven Cadillac, side-by-side, inched forward together at a junction. Suddenly Fiedler was rammed back into his seat as the taxi forced its way across the bows of the Cadillac then braked sharply for a left turn provoking a barrage of blasting horns and threatening gestures. Catching his eye in the mirror the driver grinned triumphantly. Fiedler looked at his watch. Ten forty-five. She would be in Berlin, her usual suite at the Adlon – 'always a pleasure, Frau Fiedler' – a comfortable taxi-ride from the Ku'damm and reassuringly expensive, then dinner with one of her young women.

Why Erica? He'd tortured himself endlessly with the question. Hamburg's social circuit had been a smorgasbord of beautiful, intelligent women and over the years he'd had more than his share. One in particular, an Italian lawyer, he recalled fondly, would have married him but he hesitated and she flounced off to Milan with some outlandish overweight Count twice her age. So, why in God's name, Erica? He tried to summon images of their first weeks together, the wonderful body writhing beneath him, the convincing cries of ecstasy but now even the memory had deserted him. In three days he would be thirty-five years old. His marriage was a wreck, he was effectively bankrupt and he hated the Templars and everything they stood for. The Baron and his spendthrift lesbian sister had dismantled his life.

"Hey, Americano!" They were stopped at traffic lights. A girl of perhaps twelve or thirteen, with wide dark eyes and a knowing, insolent grin, jumped down from the guard rail she was sitting on, pulled her black satin dress tight around her and stood, hand on hip, displaying her half-formed body for his consideration.

"Me very pretty, yes?"

He hunched his tall frame forward in the seat a little to meet her eyes. He held her gaze, saw the smile fade and the fear and desolation that remained, until the driver shouted and gestured threateningly at the waif who stuck out her tongue, turned and with a defiant sway of her hips strolled coolly away.

In seven years as a prosecutor in Hamburg he had dealt with every form of criminality from public nuisance to multiple murders. Over hurried working lunches, Bratwurst sandwich in one hand, magnifying lens in the other, he had scrutinized crime scene photographs which had made court officials sick to their stomachs. Yet this casual public display disturbed and irritated him. Why wasn't this child at school? As the Mercedes pulled away from the lights the driver half turned and in atrocious German made some remark about cheap tarts. Fiedler ignored him. The irritation had already evaporated; he was no better than she was, worse rather. With only a pretty face and a blossoming body, she had been born into her trap. Given everything she lacked - intelligence, education and a civilized country – he had leapt enthusiastically into his.

His slide to disaster had started early. Within a couple of months Erica had quit his bed and the visits to girl-friends in Berlin had resumed. The bickering over her absences and reckless extravagance had exploded five days ago into a violent argument. Newly returned from one of her trips and drunk enough for the truth, she had told him in explicit anatomical language that 'my Rosa' was more fun than he was, in or out of bed. Seeing his stunned expression she had added maliciously that she had married him on her brother's instructions and had agreed only in return for an increase in her allowance, her 'bride price' as she scornfully described it, and why else did he think she had been present at his interview. The Baron, it seemed, felt that a young married couple alongside him would assist fund-raising and further polish the Templars' facade of respectability.

Blind with anger he had lashed out, in street language matching hers, screaming that she had proclaimed herself the best-paid tart in Germany and that the number, gender, even the species of her lovers was of no interest to him provided she contained their costs within their resources, emphasizing the point by cutting up her credit cards. She had thrown a glass ashtray at him and returned to Berlin, delaying only long enough to gather up her jewellery.

Then there was the money; my God, the money. He had closed his mind against the spectre of yet another review of his finances with the icily polite Herr Jurgens at his bank. The excuses were exhausted. Maybe this time they'd put the knife in. Well, he'd thought, with a surge of anger, if they thought he could pay a hundred thousand off the overdraft they could damned-well wait for it. But the bravado had evaporated rapidly as he pictured the resulting interview with the Baron.

Following the fight, he had spent the evening in the apartment with Johnny Walker for company and at ten o'clock called the Hamburg Chief Prosecutor at his home to ask for his old job back. After listening in silence to a maudlin tirade against the Baron, the Templars, and life's inequities in general, the old lawyer had said 'Go to bed, Karl, sleep it off. If you still feel the same in the morning I will consult the other Knights but we seldom release people of your rank'. Only then had he understood the Baron's observation during the interview that he had been proposed by a 'very distinguished legal gentleman'.

At noon the next day he had crawled out of bed with a grim headache, stumbled downstairs to find he was out of whiskey and poured himself a schnapps breakfast. Overwhelmed by loneliness and desperation, he'd sat naked on the sunlit wooden floor staring at the slowly shifting shadows of the leaded windows, wondering how much schnapps it would take to kill him.

"Señor." It was the taxi driver, pointing to the meter.

CHAPTER 2

The Mercedes purred away leaving him alone in the silence and swirling dust of the empty street. Behind high steel gates and stone walls set with glass shards, only the tops of palm trees were visible. He poured an unsteady measure into the silver cap of his hip flask, tilted back his head and swallowed. The fierce spirit hit his stomach like acid. At last, with a deep breath, he squared his shoulders and pressed the bell. It was eleven o'clock exactly.

"Yes?" The voice was harsh, of indeterminate sex. "Karl Heinz Fiedler to see Herr Brandt."

"Herr Brandt sees no-one without an appointment." So whoever this was, had not been told of his visit. Brandt was careful.

"I have an appointment."

The loudspeaker clicked off rudely. After a delay of two or three minutes the pedestrian gate opened and he entered Herr Josef Brandt's private paradise. He found himself at the foot of a rising, undulating lawn spread with flower beds, tall palms and banks of delicately colored bushes. The smells and dust of the street had gone, replaced by a fine, flower-scented mist. The only sound was the soft rustle of wind through palm fronds. He leaned back against the gate, closed his eyes and relaxed for the first time since leaving Erden, such was the angst of his life and the peace of this place. Suddenly he became aware of the first jarring note. Every dozen yards up the tiled path, half hidden among the vegetation, he noted the very latest security cameras, heat sensors, motion detectors, all the paraphernalia of the fearful. The house, when he reached it, was modern colonial, in the same gentle, luxurious mould as its surroundings. In the porch stood a tall woman in her fifties dressed entirely in black, rigid with hostility. As he approached she swivelled on her heel like a sentry to take up position holding the door. Inside he followed her as she marched across a spacious hall and up a flight of wide, polished wooden stairs flanked by intricately carved balustrades. He noticed that as she climbed the stairs her step became lighter until, as she paused at a solid-looking wooden door, she was moving as stealthily as though about to peer in at the keyhole. She knocked deferentially.

"Herr Brandt?"

"Come."

He followed her into a comfortably furnished bedroom.

"A visitor, sir." As she turned to leave she whispered:

"The Master is a sick man. You must not tire him. I shall come for you in twenty minutes."

In an ornately carved wooden bed a grey, wizened man sat shrinking into a mountain of pillows, his face leaden, wisps of white hair smeared across his sweat-dampened forehead. Repelled by the sight of this near corpse, Fiedler hesitated. Moist, red-rimmed eyes sought him out and Brandt beckoned with feeble urgency.

"Here! Over here, young man."

Although the voice was thin and piping, the words were harsh, abrupt, delivered with a strong Prussian accent. As Fiedler reached the bed he held out a hand and started to speak but the old man shook his head and beckoned him yet closer. As he bent to listen, a thin bloodless hand seized his arm and drew him down.

"The music. Turn on the music."

Music? Was the man raving? Then he followed the watery-eyed gaze to an ancient wireless set cased in bakelite standing on a marble washstand and felt himself propelled towards it by a surprisingly energetic push. A few experimental twists of the knobs produced some rather crackly Beethoven.

"Louder!" Obediently he turned up the volume until the room was filled with orchestral noise. More furious beckoning. "Chair!"

Setting the chair by the bed he leaned over the old man once more.

"They are listening. They listen to everything."

Fiedler was aghast; paranoid delusions were hardly a good beginning.

"Who is listening, sir?"

"Who? Why, Ortega's men of course. Internal Security. Damned amateurs! Fools! But I'm a step ahead of them."

Fiedler tried to get control of the conversation:

"Herr Brandt, I have come in response…"

"Brandt?" The old man tried to laugh but emitted only a high-pitched squeaking before falling into a violent coughing fit. In response to still more gestures of command, Fiedler helped him drink from an infant's feeding cup on the bedside table. Recovered, he proceeded as though Fiedler hadn't spoken.

"Identification." Fiedler took out his card case and offered his card.

"Karl Heinz Fiedler, sir.' The old man pushed the card aside.

"No, no, you idiot. The letter, my letter."

Silently Fiedler handed over the file open at the original of Brandt's letter. At last the old man became less agitated and sank back on the pillows.

"Good. Good. Now listen carefully, young man. I don't have much time and I'm not repeating anything just because you're too stupid to pay attention."

He leaned forward, urgent, confiding. "You couldn't track down Brandt, could you? You even tried over here. You couldn't find him because he was nothing. The only worthwhile thing he did in his life was provide me with an identity."

He paused; gathering himself to continue, then drew Fiedler close to him and breathlessly muttered something only half intelligible.

"Did you say Department 'D', sir?" The old man, shaking his head in furious irritation, pulled from under the bedclothes a leather briefcase bearing the double lightning-strike insignia of the SS. "It's all in here." He offered it but when Fiedler took hold of it there was a hesitation and the old man looked up, pale moist eyes suddenly wheedling and pathetic.

"My whole life is here."

As suddenly as it had come, the humanity disappeared and he thrust the case at Fiedler with a barrage of instructions.

"First, you lock the door. When that old witch comes to throw you out, ignore her. Next, you study this file, every item, every page, especially the inventory. I hope you can absorb things quickly, I have little time. Then draw up my will. There's a blank form in the file with some notes in German – you don't speak Spanish, I suppose? I thought not. Don't speak it much myself, woman's language. Feeble. The will's easy, the whole collection goes to the Templars, the Templars, mind you, not the damned Baron or whatever he calls himself. This is for the Reich not for yachts and rent boys for some ersatz aristo. Understand? The woman will be witness. Now get on with it, and be quick. Use the table in the window."

The old man twisted painfully in the bed to turn his back and made a cowl of the sheets about his head.

The case held two folders, newly-labeled 'Inventory' and 'Will' together with a typescript of some fifty yellowed, curling pages whose title page, dated March 1944, read 'My Life' by SS Gruppenführer Richard J. Gluecks.[3]

The first page contained only a badly faded photograph annotated 'Berlin 1942' showing a stocky man in SS uniform, an Alsatian at his heel. The picture had been taken in bright sunshine on the lawn of a fine country house, its tall terrace doors thrown open, curtains blown into soft billows by the breeze. Fiedler studied the picture minutely. The uniform was of a senior SS officer, Gruppenführer probably, but the face was surprisingly rounded, soft-fleshed and jovial. Could this be the face of the wheezing fossil behind him? Decades of decay of both image and original made it impossible to say. He turned the page and began reading.

'Early Life.

I was born on 21st of April 1899 at my parents' home in Danzig. My father was a Major-General, my mother the daughter of Count von Schellendorf.'
The prose was icily correct and monotonous, the narrative dull – the routine story of a privileged childhood. With a sigh he turned to the index, ran down the headings and selected chapter eleven: 'Götterdammerung'.

'May 1st 1945 Berlin.

Berlin is a dying city in a world gone mad. The Führer dead by his own hand, we who are left must run, to freedom if possible but at any cost to escape the Russians. The Wehrmacht is fighting its final battle. The Red Army is dismantling the city street by street. There is bombing every night. My plans are ready. Marta and I leave tomorrow night.'

These yellowed pages continued Gluecks' desperate story: his murder of a subordinate for his identity, Marta's disappearance and presumed death, days on the run north to the Danish border and the temporary safety of a British naval hospital in Flensburg. Then, by the infamous rat-line of the ODESSA[3], the Nazi escape organization, through Sweden, Italy, Argentina and at last to Paraguay and the safety of the villa.

In his final entry Gluecks reflected on his extraordinary escape.

'July 20th 1945 Asunción.

I have indeed traveled like a rat, for sixty-four days. Funded by an unsecured loan of one thousand US dollars from the Vatican Bank I passed through Malmo, Stockholm, Rome and Buenos Aires seeing nothing of any of them. I was locked in a barn, an attic and a monk's cell, transported crammed into the boot of a car, in the stinking hold of a fishing smack, in a hot and noisy cabin in the bowels of a freighter and at last in the curtained rear compartment of a chauffeur-driven limousine. I posed as fisherman, priest and Red Cross official, slept on a camp bed, a hammock and a medieval four-poster, ate stale bread and fine Italian cuisine, relieved myself in a bucket, on the floor and over the side of a boat. I was helped by secret Fascists, honest mercenaries and criminal Papists. And through it all my mood swung from elation to boredom, from panic to resignation, sometimes in the space of a day.

I am fortunate. Pohl[4] chose well - the villa is magnificent. I will establish here a small world of order among the filth and chaos of this country. As for the art, I understand it is worth a great deal but it is fortunate that Pohl also provided adequate cash. Disposing of his collection would be difficult. He was a fool, investing so much effort in the destination and so little in the journey. I doubt he will make it and I know he lacks the courage to die like

---

[3] ODESSA. Organization Der Ehemaligen SS-Angehörigen = The Organization of former SS members.
[4] Pohl (1892 – 1951) Captured by the British in Berlin and, after much unnecessary debate, hanged.

an officer. I suppose they will hang him. I owe my life to ODESSA; perhaps one day I will repay the debt.

So now, Richard Gluecks, ex-Red Cross official, ex-priest, ex-fisherman, ex-Head of the Inspectorate of Concentration Camps, Gruppenführer of the SS, by strength of will and superior planning, has closed behind him the gates of this paradise built in hell and removed himself from the face of the earth. Here, as Josef Brandt, Health Records Officer, he will die.'

Fiedler closed the manuscript and took up the inventory, a stapled booklet of some fifty pages between plain black card covers. He opened it at the cover page: 'Inventory of Art Objects in the Collection of Oswald Pohl 1944. Revised 1992.'

He began reading, at first casually then with concentration, clutching the booklet in both hands, staring, re-reading the pages several times, gradually hunching over it as though seeking to hide it from the figure behind him. He turned a page, then another, before slowly setting it down. Thoughtfully he ran a hand through his hair then, abruptly decisive; he stood up and returned the papers to the briefcase. Crossing briskly to the bed he placed a hand on Gluecks' shoulder. The old man came awake with surprising rapidity and, with a grunt of effort, twisted to look up at him with startled eyes. Fiedler noticed a hand slip under the pillows.

"Yes. What is it? Have you finished?"

"No, I have not finished. The work will take some time. I will need to take the papers away and work on them in my hotel. I will call on you at the same time tomorrow."

He was hustling, foreclosing the argument. To his surprise, none came.

"Oh, very well. if you must. Eleven tomorrow."

If Fiedler had expected that her master's acceptance of him would help relations with the harridan, he was mistaken. Marching heavy-footed along the garden path she led him to the gate, ushered him out and slammed it shut, all without a word. During the taxi ride back to his hotel, he kept a firm grip on the SS briefcase.

CHAPTER 3

His hotel room was a furnace. The manager's assurance that the air conditioning would be 'fix very quick' had proved as unreliable as the device itself. Fiedler locked his door, threw off his sweat-soaked suit and shirt, opened the French windows and settled on the bed with a whiskey to study the inventory. His initial excitement had become the controlled exhilaration he used to feel on first opening the file of an especially interesting criminal case.

Opening the booklet at random he found a slightly faded photograph of a painting and on the facing page:

Item:	Painting
Title:	'Panel No. 4 for Herr Benjamin Sachs'
Date:	1914
Artist:	Kandinsky, Vasily 1866–1944
Nationality:	French (b. Russia)
	Naturalized German 1928, French 1939
Materials:	Oil and gouache on canvas
Size:	162.5 x 80 cm
Provenance:	1914 Sachs' apartment, Berlin
	1936 Surrendered to the Reich in settlement of tax debt
	1937 Berlin apartment SS-Obergruppenführer Pohl
	1944 Paraguay villa, SS-Obergruppenführer Pohl
Value:	$250,000 (estimate updated at January 1992)

He stared at the photograph in amazement. A quarter of a million dollars for this daub, these spatterings of color with neither form nor meaning. He flicked through several more pages glancing at the dollar values, then set about it systematically, page by page, adding the figures in his head with increasing incredulity. When he had finished he set the booklet down, picked up his drink, went to the window and stepped cautiously onto the crumbling balcony.

Six stories up he was mercifully insulated from the din of traffic and street musicians below. Across the rooftops he could see to his right the oozing brown river with the start of the Chaco desert on its far shore, to his left the grandiose presidential palace, legacy of the Stroessner era of torture, disappearance and death, and, pressing hard upon it, the viviendas temporarias, Asunción's slums. As he watched, the sun darkened abruptly. A skinny cat sprawled on an opposite balcony raised its head, then with a howl leapt to its feet and, tail erect, ran the length of the balustrade and bounded inside. Fiedler was wondering what had so disturbed the creature when seconds later the rain started with such sudden ferocity that by the time he had retreated into the room and slammed shut the balcony windows, he was already alone in a private world screened by an impenetrable grey curtain.

He refilled his glass, thinking he really must eat something soon. He was moving and drinking now with slow deliberation. Twenty-eight million US dollars. It was a sum he could not properly comprehend. The Templars' total debt, an amount that made even the Baron anxious, was scarcely five million. Now the Baron's only problem would be how best to spend the surplus. He sipped the whiskey and at last faced the prospect that had simmered in his sub-conscious since his first sight of the document, that he might have in his hands a secret passage to a new life. The task was daunting but he started with the good news - this was almost certainly the only copy of the inventory and so far only he and Gluecks knew of its existence. So he was free to select for himself a world-class trinket or two. But at this point the difficulties began.

The drinking had slowed almost to a stop as questions twisted in his brain. Gluecks was decrepit but not senile; he would most probably be planning to cable the inventory to the Baron to protect against pilfering en route. Which meant... he hesitated, the brutality too much for him. He gulped at the whiskey. The mere thought made him shudder but there was no escaping it: if he was to steal from the collection then he must silence Gluecks.

Hands shaking he again refilled his glass. Then so be it – he would kill the old man. Damn it, he thought, Gluecks was half dead already; it would be a kindness.

He seized the inventory and began again, page by page, Degas, Matisse, Monet… but always the question that doomed him, how to convert his prize into cash. How would he find a dealer – a Trade Directory? And then what, a telephone call?

'Good afternoon. I see from your advertisement you deal in art. Would you be interested in a painting of a girl holding a basket of flowers? It's by someone called Monet'.

He was beginning to despair at the unfairness of it, everything he wanted out of life in front of his eyes but out of his reach, when he came to the final page and at last an unfamiliar name. The photograph was so dark as to be almost unrecognizable but the text was clear:

Item:	Wood carving
Title:	'Christus sedens' (Der sitzende Christus)
Date:	1493
Artist:	Stoss, Veit c. 1450-1533
Nationality:	German national (b. Nuremberg)
Material:	Dark wood
Size:	45 cms (height)
Provenance:	1493 Commissioned Heinrich Schenck of Tallinn, Estonia
	1493 Consecrated Church of the Holy Spirit, Tallinn
	1943 Reclaimed for the Reich
	1943 Berlin apartment, SS-Obergruppenführer Pohl
	1944 Paraguay villa, SS-Obergruppenführer Pohl
Estimated value:	US$1,000,000?
Remarks:	Value uncertain due to the specialist nature of the piece.

It was the only carving in the collection and the only work which, with luck, could be sold back directly to its true owner. And a million dollars would solve all his problems. He smiled at the irony - Christ would be his salvation – then laughed aloud as he realized the perfection of his revenge. The carving, by a German artist, was the one work Edelmann would wish to keep; the French and Italian works would be sold. His confidence inflated by the whiskey, he set aside concerns about the difficulty of smuggling the carving out of Paraguay.

Having secured his future, he turned his mind to the Templars. How could he extricate the rest of the collection from this ramshackle country where the law was unavailable to the poor, unnecessary for the rich and a tool of the government? Did Brandt... no, he must learn to think of the man as Gluecks... did Gluecks really believe that a valid will could be drawn up by a visiting German lawyer with no Spanish and no local help? In Paraguay even a valid will would mean nothing if Internal Security were to claim the estate without troubling the lawyers. Clearly Gluecks' collection must leave Paraguay by the side door. He picked up the telephone.

The Baron, apprised of the situation, was overflowing with bonhomie and dismissive of difficulties. One of the Knights was Chairman of an air charter company specializing in irregular customs procedures. Fiedler was to expect a call within two hours.

He put down the phone and stretched out on the bed. Basking in the warm glow of whiskey and anticipated wealth he planned a new life of luxury and release from the shadow of the Templars. He became euphoric. He felt as he had not felt since the Hamburg days when scintillating court performances had put him, son of a nobody, at the top of smart invitation lists and on the front page of the local press.

But the next morning, the moment he entered Gluecks' room, Fiedler's plan began to miscarry. The bedridden invalid of the previous day now sat erect in a chair, looking twenty years younger, a rug over his knees, a bottle of schnapps and two glasses on the table before him. Suddenly Fiedler's legs felt weak. Gluecks' death would have to look like natural causes; any sign of a struggle and the harridan would raise hell. As things were, his only hope was that the old man would return to bed before he left.

Gluecks gestured to the chair opposite and Fiedler sagged into it gratefully. Taking the will and his working papers from the SS briefcase he laid them on the table. Seeming not to have noticed, Gluecks poured two glasses of schnapps with his left hand, his right hand remaining beneath the rug. With no apparent sign of pain or stiffness, he passed one glass across the table, drained the other and sat back. His eyes, so pale and rheumy yesterday, now glittered in an intense, unblinking stare.

"Tell me something of yourself, Karl," he said abruptly.

Fiedler eased himself in his chair. His throat was dry and he felt himself flushing. Reaching clumsily for the glass he spilled some of the contents onto his papers then swiftly downed the remainder.

"Well, sir. As you know, I'm a lawyer. I am from Hamburg…"

"Where you were an outstanding prosecutor, I am told."

Fiedler started. In Germany this was no secret but, in these backwoods… "I was quite successful, yes."

"But you never killed anyone."

Fiedler gaped. "Killed? Of course not. Why…"

"Why indeed?" Gluecks smiled venomously. "I have killed three men." He said this without emphasis, as another man might claim to have won a tennis match. "Personally, that is. Of course, as an officer of artillery there were thousands but only three like this…", he gestured, back and forth between them, "…man-to-man."

He splayed three fingers of one hand across the table like a poker player showing winning cards. Fiedler knew he was lost.

"It is often said that with practice, killing gets easier but for me it was never difficult." He shifted his decaying frame in the chair. "You are intelligent, Karl. You have seen the opportunity, maybe even that the Stoss would be your best choice, the piece you could dispose of. But there is a problem. The dying old fool might tell your Baron what was being sent."

Fiedler listened, paralyzed, as his plan was dissected.

"So you thought you could solve the problem, eh? With a pillow, perhaps?

'Quietly in his sleep' as the obituaries say. But when it comes to it you can't do it, can you?"

If there was an adequate answer, Fiedler couldn't find it. With slow deliberation Gluecks brought out the pistol from beneath the rug and pointed it at Fiedler's abdomen. Fiedler was familiar with lethal weapons from swordsticks to assault rifles and he recognized it at once as a Browning 9 mm automatic, its Waffen SS markings showing it to be one of the many thousands produced in the Belgian Fabrique Nationale factory during the Nazi occupation. His expertise however did not extend to the firing of a pistol and most certainly not to being threatened with one. He stared at it in horror.

"I, on the other hand," Gluecks slowly raised the weapon until he met Fiedler's eyes across its sights, "could so easily kill you."

In the silence that followed, Fiedler waited. He recalled a forensic pathologist explaining why you would not hear the shot that killed you. A trickle of sweat ran like a tear down his cheek.

"But sadly," Gluecks laid the pistol on the table, "my time is short and you are necessary to me." He paused as though assessing the wisdom of this judgement then dismissed the issue with a brisk shrug. "No matter."

Fiedler, overwhelmed by this devastating defeat at the hands of a dying man, stared at the papers spread across the table, the meaningless will and above all, the gun. "Why?"

The monosyllable was no more than a scraping sound in his dry throat but Gluecks understood and eyed him with naked contempt. "Why waste time with all this?" He indicated the papers spread across the table. "A weak man's question; I did it because I have the power." Suddenly the voice was strong and his eyes blazed with an old passion. He leaned towards Fiedler who started back instinctively. "Look at me, Karl. What I am, Germany is; what I was, Germany will be. The Führer dies, the Reich is immortal. That is why the Templars exist and why you will ensure my gift arrives safely." He sat back and his tone became one of cold command. "You will arrange immediate transport for my collection to Germany. An export permit will be required. At the airport you will see Herr Weber in Customs, a reliable German who arranges such things. You will tell him the consignment is the property of Herr Brandt. He will ask five thousand dollars, you will pay three. In Germany the consignment will be checked by the Baron's staff against the inventory I will send to him under separate cover. Is that clear?"

Fiedler, sweating with fear, could not speak. Gluecks seized the schnapps bottle and emphasized his words by hammering it on the table.

"Do... you... understand?"

"Yes, sir, yes. The airport... I..."

Pinned by the gaze of this horrifying relic of a dead regime he had almost lost the power of speech. Gluecks sat back in his chair and waved a dismissive hand. "Now get out."

He must have pressed some hidden button because Fiedler heard below the housekeeper's heavy tread.

In the street, he slumped against the wall, the slamming of the gate echoing in his ears. He was trembling with relief and fright.

"Hey, señor."

The waiting taxi driver was sitting on the pavement, his back against his car. He drew on a small cigar and exhaled slowly, watching the smoke drifting on the breeze.

"You OK?", he asked, without concern.

Unsteadily, Fiedler crossed the pavement and climbed into the car.

Inside the villa the housekeeper, who had run up the stairs, entered Gluecks' bedroom to find him semiconscious in the chair. With much muttering and head-shaking – her protestations against the cocaine injection had been ignored - she removed his dressing gown and half carried him into bed. As she was about to close the door she heard him mumble, "Edelmann will destroy him."

Three days later, Herr Josef Brandt died in his sleep. According to a will dated 1985, his entire estate – the villa and a small amount of cash - went to the astonished housekeeper. The following morning, her eight year assignment completed, she handed over to her immediate superior the cash and the keys to the Brandt villa and returned to her duties as a desk officer in the Security Office of Paraguay's Interior Ministry.

On the same day, at the private airport of the Erden Flying Club, the defeated and disconsolate Fiedler stepped from a chartered aircraft to a hero's welcome and champagne reception while Templars' staff unloaded a consignment which added almost thirty million dollars to the paper value of the Schloss Edelmann art collection. The bourgeois dross would be gradually and discreetly disposed of through friendly channels. But in the place of supreme honor, on a plinth in the Great Hall, the Baron ceremonially placed the Templars' most prized possession – the Veit Stoss masterpiece 'Der Sitzende Christus'.

C H A P T E R   4

Three months later, still broke and back on the fund-raising treadmill, Fiedler was in Berlin when the Baron's secretary called at 6 a.m. to say that there was a serious problem and he was to return to Erden at once. The usually imperturbable woman had sounded shaken. Mystified but filled with the ill-defined unease of the guilty, he had scrambled to pack and catch a Nuremberg flight and been ushered straight into the Baron's office to be told that the Christ had been stolen.

Fortunately, the Baron had been so consumed by anger that he had failed to notice Fiedler's state of near collapse at the news.

'You should see the place, Karl – everything secure, alarm still set, not a sign of damage.'

White with fury, he had pounded a fist on the arm of his chair.

'Quarter of a million for a security system and they use my Schloss like a public lavatory - walk in, do their business and leave.'

Then, fingers curling around an imagined throat, 'I want to know who helped them; and the parting words, 'You can start with that security guard. They're working on him downstairs. Report to me in forty-eight hours.'

Back in his own office he'd locked the door and slumped behind his desk, struggling to grasp the implications of this crushing news.

The theft had closed off his planned escape from his financial and marital problems, but what really concerned him was the appalling coincidence that the carving should have been snatched away when negotiations with his buyer were under way.

Instantly, he remembered the prosecutor's rule: coincidence is evidence. And now he saw the worst possibility, that somehow, by some inconceivable process, his own actions had triggered this catastrophe. But at least, he had thought, the Baron couldn't know... Yet what if, by some ghastly miracle of clairvoyance, he was to find out? Then, by God, he'd find out first hand what they did in that damned basement.

Panic gripped him. Suddenly the office had seemed uncomfortably hot. He'd loosened his tie, unbuttoned his collar. Sweat had trickled down his forehead, stinging his eyes. He'd brushed at it with his sleeve, leaving a greasy smear on his white shirt cuff. He had to get out, to the apartment. Maybe she would be up there, he didn't know but it made no difference, he desperately needed time to think.

Now two days later, his investigation completed, he sat waiting anxiously in the Baron's outer office, nauseated at the extent of the risk he had taken. What was it about that damned carving? And how much did the Baron know?

Meanwhile the Baron, who knew a great deal, adjusted his tie and brushed his dark hair flat against his skull. With a last approving look at his impeccably suited figure in the full-length mirror, he closed the doors to the built-in wardrobe and dressing table, returned to his seat and pressed a switch. Outside a buzzer sounded and the light above his door changed to green.

"The Baron will see you now."

Did the secretary's voice have an edge he'd not heard before? He looked at her sharply but she did not meet his eye. With a last nervous realigning of his papers, he knocked and entered. He was greeted with a smile and made his way, knees shaking, to the offered seat at the desk.

"Coffee, Karl?"

Fiedler nodded, unable to speak. The Baron poured coffee for them both.

"How are things? All well at home?"

He cleared his throat. "Very well, thank you, Baron."

Fiedler did not mention that his Berlin trip had included a despairing and futile attempt to talk with Erica, to see whether anything could be rescued from the wreckage of their marriage. But the question was merely a part of the ritual; Edelmann already knew his appalling domestic situation and was interested only in the Templars, Edelmann Metals GmbH[5] and his current lover.

[5]Gesellschaft mit beschränkter Haftung = Company with Limited Liability

Fiedler licked at dry lips. "My report, Herr Baron..."

He proffered the document but to his astonishment the Baron waved it away. "Later, Karl, later."

Fiedler sipped at the coffee, trying to understand why the report which had been commanded in such a paroxysm of anger two days earlier and which had cost him most of two nights sleep now seemed unimportant. He was reminded of a dinner in Hamburg with an industrialist friend newly returned from China where he'd spent three days meeting senior government officials. Asked how the meetings had gone, he bitterly observed that he had felt the parties were attending concurrent but unrelated meetings in the same room.

"Tell me about Gluecks."

Gluecks! This was the last thing Fiedler was expecting.

"I don't understand, sir. The man is dead... we have his donation..."

The Baron bared his teeth. "Do we?"

Fiedler, appalled at this gaffe, floundered. "What I meant to say, sir..."

The pale eyes glittered. "Of course, of course." He repeated his question.

"Tell me about the late Gruppenführer."

Fiedler's worst nightmare as prosecutor had been running into what chess players call a prepared variation, what the layman would call a trap; to sit listening to the defense pursuing an apparently pointless line of questioning, gradually realizing that they knew something he didn't. Having no notion of where the Baron was headed, he stonewalled.

"I'm sorry, Baron, but I believe you are already fully informed of my dealings with the Gruppenführer."

"That is what you believe, is it?"

Fiedler's stomach contracted - the words meant nothing but the tone was the same silky, arrogant, prosecutor's voice he'd used himself when closing for the kill. He managed to croak something vaguely affirmative. The Baron stared at him for an impossibly long time then, without shifting his gaze, opened a drawer, took out a document and slid it across the desk. With difficulty Fiedler broke eye contact to look at it. It was an uncyphered and

therefore obliquely worded cable, dated the day Fiedler and the Gluecks'
collection left Asunción:

Baron Edelmann

*Confirming arrangements agreed with your representative today. Raw
materials as per inventory sent under separate cover will leave here via your
transport soonest. Your representative will deal with local formalities as I have
instructed. I am sure the attempt to secure a substantial commission for his
services was not authorized by you. In any event, no commission was paid.*
Brandt

He read it quickly, then again more carefully. Commission? The old fool must
have been raving. He looked up to see Edelmann staring at him, waiting for
an answer to his unasked question. Then the subtlety of it hit him like a blow
to the stomach. Gluecks had seen that an accusation of intended murder
would never be believed but this calculated, plausible, irrefutable lie was
fatally damaging, the coup de grâce from beyond the grave.

"I am at a loss, sir. I made no such request. I…"

The Baron retrieved the cable, returned it with deliberation to the drawer
and sat back.

"I am relieving you of your duties. Leave your papers with my
secretary. Gunther Neubauer is taking over the investigation. He will wish to
speak with you. You will remain in your apartment until you are sent for."

In the empty apartment Fiedler poured himself his now customary half-
tumbler of whiskey and stood staring out of the leaded window. The evening
was beautifully clear. In the steeply angled sunlight he could see across
densely wooded hills to Nuremberg and the outline of the Kaiserburg castle
etched onto the horizon. As the neat spirit took effect, the immediate
paralyzing fear receded and he replayed the meeting in his mind the way he'd
taught himself as a young lawyer. The irony of it was agonizingly clear – the
Baron had him on a counterfeit charge he couldn't defend, while his real crime
was, he felt sure, undetected. What was baffling him was the charade, the

preposterous 'investigation' he'd been thrown into when the Baron had had Glueck's letter for so long. If it was an attempt to force him, as a warning, to watch what they were doing downstairs, then it had failed. Nothing less than physical force would have induced him to enter that basement. He'd simply told the interrogators to feed him whatever Tommi gave them.

He took in the whiskey without enjoyment but with steady determination, puzzling it out. The bottle was almost empty when realization came to him in the chilling words of the dying Gruppenführer: 'I did it because I have the power.'

Too late, he saw himself as Gluecks and the Baron saw him. To these past and future Nazis he was just another underling over-reaching himself. Self-pity engulfed him. Why in God's name had he left his perfect life in Hamburg? He felt a lump form in his throat then pounded a fist on the leaded glass as self-pity was overtaken by revulsion.

Almost in tears he turned away to look around the room, taking in the opulent, oak panelled environment he had so thoughtlessly taken for granted. He sighed, wishing to God she were here; even in an argument would be preferable to this echoing emptiness. He worked out preposterous terms for reconciliation: she spending less of his money, he tolerating her women friends. As the whiskey crept into his brain he tried again to conjure her from the air but he could not obliterate the image of the basement and the ever-smiling Tommi with his large, peasant frame and stolid obstinacy.

On impulse he drew a chair to the bureau, took pen and paper and, after some thought, wrote:

'Erica'.

Ten minutes and a new bottle later he took a fresh sheet and began again:

'Darling Erica,
So little time. Do I drink or run?'

For a long time he sat, pen poised, staring at the page. At last, with a sigh, he methodically tore it into small pieces which he allowed to fall like confetti through his fingers to the floor.

Once more at the window he stared down, toying with cartoon images of knotted sheets and death-defying dives. He had long regarded as quaint, even risible the Baron's insistence on the rituals of the drawbridge and the punctilious cleaning and refilling of the moat, yet now, staring down into the courtyard fifty feet below, he appreciated for the first time how effective these archaic devices could be against both invasion and escape. The sheer stone cliff of the wall, the moat too deep to ford, too shallow to dive into, the hundreds of yards of open meadow beyond, made unauthorized exit almost impossible. He saw again the cold eyes of the dying Gluecks – why did everything come back to that grotesque old Nazi? With a final, half-focussed look down into the deserted courtyard he seized the bottle and headed unsteadily for the bedroom.

CHAPTER 5

PART 2

June 1992

OPENING MOVES

On the coast, twenty-five miles south of San Francisco's Golden Gate Bridge there is a five mile long crescent-shaped bay. The shore here is hard and rocky and the Pacific rollers smash onto it so that even on a quiet day the sea-mist drifts and swirls over the coastal plain giving the light a special quality, sometimes silver and dazzling, sometimes eerily grey and sinister. The waves here are as big as those of the Hawaiian beaches but they are colder, darker and more menacing, drawing world-class surfers from around the Pacific to hazard their lives riding the waves they call the Mavericks.

God fashioned this bay for the smuggler; its isolation, its rocky coastline punctuated by dozens of small inlets, many difficult to reach by land, its dangerous shoals and fierce currents inhibiting all but the most determined sailors. Guns, booze, illegal immigrants, drugs - whatever the need of the age, some reckless renegade would come forward to turn danger into opportunity.

For thousands of years, a village has existed at the heart of the bay. To the Costanoans it was Shagunte, to the Mexicans, San Benito, to the Yankees, Spanish Town, but for Geoff Hughes, for whom it was a refuge, it was Half Moon Bay.

Geoff pulled over and stopped the car. Meg looked at the sign across the street. "Capablanca[6] – didn't he play chess?"

Geoff smiled. "Didn't Shakespeare write plays?"

"A chess café. Geoff, really!"

"Look, forget chess, it's just a great place. Full of interesting people…"

[6] Jose Raoul Capablanca (1888 - 1942) 'The Mozart of Chess'. "With his death, we have lost a very great chess genius whose like we shall never see again." [Alexander Alekhine]

"Full of smoke and dirty old men."

"I'll only be forty-five minutes and you'll get the best coffee in Half Moon Bay."

"Why do you have to go at all? Can't it wait?"

"Sorry, the guy's flying back to New York this evening. You can wait in the car if you'd rather but honestly, the Capablanca's better than it looks."

Meg grimaced. "Alright, Geoff. But coffee or no coffee, I wouldn't hang about here for anybody else. If you're not back in an hour I'll take a taxi and see you at the house."

As she turned to close the door behind her he grinned at her. "Forty-five minutes, I swear by the laws of physics. Bye, muppet."

With a sigh she watched the car disappear. Her godfather's unpredictability was part of the charm of life in the beach house but she could have done without this on a Friday evening.

She'd just finished the first week of a twelve month contract with Ceramic Magnets Inc., her first job since graduating from university, and they were already getting their money's worth. She'd spent the entire week trying to write a training manual on superconductivity, discovering in the process how much she'd forgotten about it. On top of wrestling with the problem of finding a flat in San Francisco near the new job, it was too much.

She had her evening planned - hot tub, dinner on the balcony watching a Pacific sunset and an early night. She hadn't mentioned work problems to Geoff, of course; he'd never understood why she'd chosen to spend the year working with great hulking magnets when she could have been with him in ILT, the family firm, with nice friendly lasers, as he'd put it. She sighed. It had better be good coffee.

She paused at the curb as a sports car, the only vehicle in sight, growled towards her. The young driver, with courtesy exaggerated even by the standards of small-town America, slowed and waved her across. When she smiled and waved thanks he stopped altogether, his eyes following her small trim figure, the dark hair flowing behind her, with frank admiration before he reluctantly drove on. Reaching the café, she pushed open the door then hesitated on the threshold, peering into a fog of cigar smoke.

Chess débris lay scattered across unoccupied tables: empty cups, cigar butts still smoking in dusty ashtrays, chess boards, most with games in play, a chess computer, the image of the white king flashing a patient 'check' to an absent opponent. Even International Master Gregorovitch, a good Ukrainian who would not play against or even speak to a Russian, had removed his monstrous, creaking bulk from his private armchair in the corner and vanished with the rest. And where was Miguel, the proprietor, once Havana's most feared blitz[7] player, Miguel who never played against his patrons and claimed stolidly to have given up chess when he left Cuba? Café Capablanca was as still and silent as the saloon of the 'Marie Celeste'.

"Queen b7 check and mate in three."

The voice rolled from the foxhole, a curtained-off area at the far end of the room in which were two tables usually reserved for serious – that is, high stakes – games. The name was an in-joke referring to the fate awaiting weak players, rabbits, rash enough to enter.

After a short, calculating silence Meg heard the death rattle of a toppled King followed by a chorus of "Yes!" and a surge of applause. Then the crowd erupted through the curtains.

"Man, did you see that? He's not for real. How come he never plays for money?"

"Would you play him for money? Anyway, he's got too much already."

Beyond the displaced curtain the object of their veneration now sat alone, his back to the wall, upright and still. He was of medium height but his powerful physique and unusually erect posture made him appear taller. He looked tough, fit and younger than his years, the glassy bald head accentuating the severity of his long, hard-boned face. His complexion was sallow, his slightly slanted, deep-set eyes were very dark, changing color like opals with the light or his mood. In repose his gaze was open and child-like

---

[7]blitz. German = lightning. For non chess players, the blitz version of the game is played to completion in a very short time, typically 5 minutes.

but in contention, across a chess board or elsewhere, the eyes would burn with menace. He projected threatening power, closely restrained.

On the two tables pushed together before him were three boards, concealed from him by cardboard screens. And now Meg saw the reason for the excitement: this man had, without sight of the boards, defeated three opponents simultaneously. As she stared in unembarrassed amazement she realized he too was staring and before she could disengage, he beckoned, slowly crooking his right index finger, a schoolmaster summoning an offending pupil. As she later said in some exasperation to her mother, she felt herself drawn, unwilling but unresisting, to stand, as it seemed to her, at his feet.

"We will play for the price of a cup of Miguel's excellent coffee. I will give you the white pieces, rook and knight."

The voice was quieter, less triumphal than when delivering the final checkmate but it still drew Meg to look into the dark eyes and to shiver a little inwardly at what she saw there. She wanted to explain that she'd come only because her godfather had dropped her there to wait for him, that she wasn't a serious player but instead she sat down. She reached to remove the cardboard screen concealing the board from him but froze as the index finger moved again, side to side, a priestly gesture of admonition. An image of her father came to mind, arriving home late, drained and exhausted after a match and his heartfelt comment that chess, real chess between strong players, was as brutal and unyielding as a martial arts contest.

"Honestly, it will be a waste of your time."

"Do you mean you believe I will win?"

She gestured with silent eloquence at the screened-off boards with their fallen kings.

"And it is your view that chess is merely about winning?"

"No, that is not my view. It's just…"

"Then…". He gestured to the board.

As she set up the pieces she was thinking about his accent. It sounded like that of any of the dozens of interviewees in Moscow streets and state-rooms filling western television screens in these high days of glasnost and perestroika, yet there was something different.

So they played and as he swept aside her poor efforts, his eyes never left her except to flash a warning to any who dared sidle up to watch.

"Now we shall have coffee."

As Miguel poured their coffee he took down the screen, reset the pieces and took her through the game, charming her with his animation and good humour.

"Here, your sixth, it's not good... ecclesiastical authority is nothing without mobility; this poor bishop is entombed. And here, your tenth, you missed the threat from my knight, yes? That was because you were not focussed; your eyes were all over the board, looking at everything, seeing nothing."

Now her attention was not on the board but on the voice and the compelling intellect behind the eyes. "And you're not focussed now!"

She started at the sharpness in the voice, flushing a little until she realized he was teasing her. "Yes," she smiled, "I'm sorry. I was thinking how much my father would enjoy a game with you."

"He is stronger than you?"

Meg laughed aloud. "We've been playing since I was five and I've never won a game."

"From so young and he never allowed you to win." He nodded approvingly. "Good. I should like to try his strength."

He took his cup and sat back, cradling it in large hands and studying her with frank interest. "Your father, he is a professional?"

"Chess player? Good heavens no. He played for his university..."

"Ah! He is a professor?"

He saw that the thought of her father languishing in some academic backwater amused her. "A politician, then? A member of your parliament, yes?"

Now she laughed aloud at the idea and at the absurd guessing game. "He's a physicist. He has a laser optics company, International Laser Technology."

She was about to ask whether he knew of it until she realized that she had no idea what his interests were. Maybe he didn't even know what a laser was.

"Here in America?"

"My father is based in London but there is a subsidiary here, in San Francisco."

"London, I see. Then we will play by correspondence."

"Maybe not. He and my mother will be coming over soon for the company's Fourth of July party. They'll be staying with me, at Geoff's place. Geoff's my father's business partner and my godfather."

Stefan was nodding his approval of these domestic arrangements. "Excellent. Please give your father my card." He took a card from an inside pocket and passed it to her.

Looking at it she asked: "Stefan Vanosivich. Is that a Russian name?"

"It is."

"But you have lived here for a long time?"

"You may tell your father I can offer him English tea and perhaps a challenge worthy of his skill." He stood up. "And now if you will tell me your name, I will ask you to excuse me."

"It's Meg, Meg Gilchrist."

"Meg. A fine English name, a diminutive of Margaret."

"Wrong, both times. I am English but the name is Welsh, short for Megan."

"Ah, yes, Welsh." He spoke as though it was remiss of him not to have known. "So your family is from Wales?"

"My mother. My father is English."

She heard a step behind her and turned to see Geoff.

"Hi. Told you I'd be back in..."

She watched his smile fade as he recognized the Russian. He took her by the arm, nodding perfunctorily to Vanosivich.

"Let's go."

Startled at the barely disguised hostility, Meg glanced quickly from Geoff to Stefan and back, tried to say something but found herself guided firmly towards the door as Stefan's parting words rolled through the gloom.

"It was a pleasure to meet you, Megan."

In the car Meg protested. "What on earth was that about?"

"Nothing much. I just don't like the guy."

"So I noticed. What did he do? Beat you?"

"No, I drew. It was the others he beat."

"The others?"

"There were three of us. It was an exhibition not a contest. Simultaneous blindfold."

"Oh! That's what he was doing today."

"It would be. From what I hear he plays mostly on the Internet these days. Drops into the café occasionally, makes them look second-rate three at a time then slithers back to La Honda."

Meg pictured the Russian, silent, immobile, dark eyes brooding over a keyboard. "Slithers… You see him as a snake then?"

"Don't you?"

"I see him as… pure."

"Pure?" Geoff pondered the idea. "I'd call him dangerous."

Meg gathered he didn't mean only across a chessboard. "Do you think Dad could beat him?"

"Hard to say. Peter doesn't play to his strength these days, lack of match practice. Even I had a draw against him the last time he was over. Hypothetical question though."

"It's not, actually. Mr Vanosivich gave me his card and invited Dad up there for a game."

"Did he now! And you were invited, I suppose."

"Yes I was."

"I see."

Meg looked across at Geoff who was determinedly concentrating on the road. "See what?"

"What his game is and I don't mean chess." His tone was flippant but the message was clear enough.

"Oh, really! You sound like my mother." He said nothing and she went on in a quieter, more serious tone, "You're wrong, Geoff. It just isn't like that at all.

He's...", she hesitated, needing the precise words, "His life's joyless. He needs a friend. Maybe he likes young people."

"Hmm."

Meg had said her piece; she refused to rise to the sceptical grunt.

A few minutes later they turned off the Pacific Coast Highway onto the track through the dunes to Geoff's house. Meg lowered her window as she always did, to let in the smell of the cypresses and the ocean and, as she always did, she thought it was her favorite place in the world.

She'd been still at school in England when she read the realtor's blurb that Geoff had sent to her parents with an uncharacteristically terse note: 'Thinking of this for week-ends. Miriam says it's awesome! What do you think?'.

The lyric prose sprawled across two pages: *stunning ocean views, formal entry, breakfast bar, open fireplaces, vaulted ceilings, hardwood floors, Italian tiles, sun deck with hot tub, private mooring...* She'd thought it was the most romantic house she'd ever seen. Geoff had come to the same conclusion and bought it, determinedly shutting his eyes to the full implications of *Victorian gem'* and *'Opportunity for refurbishment to buyer's specification'*.

It took him two years of lost week-ends and more money than he could really afford but he'd never regretted it. Even after a booming ILT moved from the poky Palo Alto office to the two upper floors in California Street with an apartment for his use, most evenings he still drove from San Francisco just to overnight there. Miriam had shared many of the DIY week-ends but a few weeks before the work was finished, remorseless nagging from her strictly Jewish Orthodox mother finally achieved its purpose and abruptly one Christmas Day – Geoff was sure the date was symbolic - she failed to turn up for lunch and it was over. He had not formed a lasting relationship since. Christmas had never been the same either.

Geoff pulled up at the 'formal entrance', classical columns in rendered fibreglass on either side of a pair of tall wooden doors, switched off the engine and sat for a while. As he got out of the car, he said: "Analytic Englishman versus passionate Slav. That's a game I'd like to watch."

CHAPTER 6

Meg, in a swimming suit, headed through the dawn light for the kitchen, moving quietly to avoid disturbing Geoff. As she passed the door to his study, she heard to her surprise the faint rattle of a keyboard. She wondered why he would be up and working so early. In the kitchen she threw stewed fruit, yoghurt and honey into a bowl and brewed a cup of tea for Geoff, his own blend obtainable only from an oriental herb shop deep in San Francisco's Chinatown.

Juggling precariously with her bowl and his cup, she elbowed the door handle and stepped quietly into the study. It was a spacious, L-shaped room and the desk was not visible but, as the door clicked shut behind her, she realized that the dawn typist was not Geoff. The sound she heard wasn't his ragged hunting and pecking but the fluid rhythm of a professional. She hesitated, recalling that Geoff had said something about a software engineer who worked very odd hours, mostly from home but occasionally here at the house.

The typing stopped and a man's voice said, "Geoff?"

"I'm not Geoff."

A chair scraped, footsteps approached and the professional appeared, stopping abruptly as she came into his sight. "Well!" he said, "I can see you're not Geoff."

He was a tall, lean young man wearing Californian software engineer's standard issue sneakers, shorts and a T shirt on which, in startlingly clear type, was printed 'Windows is less stable than the walls of Jericho – it falls over without trumpets'. The morning sun made a halo of his shoulder-length blonde hair.

Disconcerted by his frank interest she tried to hold his gaze but couldn't.

She felt herself blushing. "I brought the tea for Geoff."

"That's fine. I'll make my own."

"Oh! No! I mean it was for Geoff. I heard the typing... I thought you were him." Annoyed with herself, she took a deep breath, trying to regain her composure. "You're quite welcome to it, only it's a bit odd. The tea that is. Geoff's own blend. He's very particular about his tea."

"And his women."

Before she could respond to this presumption, the stranger had taken the cup and walked back past the desk with its scattering of working papers and ponderous, unintelligibly-titled manuals, out onto the balcony. Meg, irritation overcoming her confusion, followed; stopping as close to him as she felt wise and in her sternest English voice began: "Hold on a minute. You've got the wrong idea. Geoff's my father's business partner..."

"And you're Megan, his goddaughter, I know. Do you like Greek food? How about I pick you up here at eight? I know a really great place."

She drew in her breath preparing to put him in his place but he reached out and put a light hand on her arm.

"Don't say no, please. You'll really like the food, I promise." Seeing her resistance weaken he pressed on. "Terrific. Now I have stuff to finish up and you have twenty-five lengths to swim. I'll be back to pick you up at eight. Oh, my name's Jim by the way, Jim Otte. That's o-t-t-e."

He smiled then stepped past her into the room, resumed his seat at the desk and began typing. An hour later as she was drying her hair she was still wondering how much more Geoff had told him about her.

*　　*　　*

"Care for some breakfast?"

Geoff's voice came from the pool area. Meg went through the lounge and out to join him. Although it was a Saturday morning he was sitting at a glass-topped table, his stocky body already wrapped in a business suit, busy with tea, toast and several newspapers.

"Yes, please."

She took a mug of tea, buttered some toast and relaxed into a deeply padded cane chair.

He glanced up at the sky. "It'll be a good day. Any plans? Care for a ride up to town?"

"No thanks, Geoff." She would have very much enjoyed a wander around San Francisco's tourist traps but the new job was showing up gaps in her knowledge. "I really must cram up on this superconductivity stuff."

"That sounds like fun!" He finished his tea and poured himself another. "Did you meet Jim?".

"Who? Oh, him!" She grimaced. "Yes."

Geoff looked at her quizzically. "And?"

"And what?"

"How did you get on?"

"Get on? He was rude, that's how we got on. And he stole your cup of tea."

"I see. Not a nice chap at all then. You'll be glad not to see him again."

"Yes, I will."

"And you turned down his invitation. What was it? Dinner? Sailing?".

"It was dinner. Greek. And stop it, Geoff."

He paused, hands raised in mock surrender. "I was only making conversation. I mostly get complaints for lack of small talk."

"And while we're in the complaints department," she continued, trying to sound aggrieved, "why did you tell him so much about me?"

"Because he asked. He'd seen your photograph on my desk."

"Hmm…"

"And," he went on with a knowing smile, "you're pleased I did, aren't you? You find him… interesting. I thought you might."

"No. Well, yes, maybe. It's not easy to tell with him. He's very presumptuous but…"

"It's tough to stay mad at him?"

"Yes it is. But he is a bit odd."

"He's reasonably civilized for a software engineer."

"Working all night in someone else's home?"

He studied her face for a few seconds. "You really did like him," he said, quietly.

"I think perhaps I could. Tell me about him."

"What would you like to know?"

"Everything. How well do you know him? What's he doing here?"

Geoff leaned back in his chair. A nostalgic smile, a pursing of the lips then, unexpectedly, "Did you ever see a film called 'The Day the Earth Stood Still'?"

Meg sighed. She could usually handle Geoff's circuitous narrative style with its frequent diversions and allusions to movies - he was something of an expert on movie history - but right now she wasn't in the mood. "No Geoff, I can't say I did."

"Shame. Great movie, Sci-Fi, 1951. Michael Rennie plays a rather superior alien who drops to earth to save us from blowing ourselves up. He calls on a physics professor who turns out to be away, but sees on his blackboard a problem that's got the prof baffled and solves it at a glance. Well, Jim was my superior alien. It was 1985. ILT had just opened over here. You remember? A tiny office in Palo Alto, with me, a secretary and a couple of engineers. One Saturday morning I was having breakfast in Printer's Inc. working on a software problem we'd been struggling with for a couple of days. I left the table for fresh coffee and when I got back, this young guy's sitting at my table looking at the work. I was about to ball him out when he coolly asked if I would give him a job if he solved the problem. In a rash moment I said yes, so he did it, right there." Geoff was shaking his head, still bemused at the recollection. "He started the following Monday and worked with us off and on for the next two years - evenings, vacations or sometimes just when he didn't feel like attending class – he was supposed to be taking a masters in Software Architecture at Stanford. He was the best software engineer I've ever seen. Still is."

"So you know him quite well?"

"Yes I do. We've worked together a lot. He really helped us get ILT established over here. And, after hours, we'd go out for meals and drinks and stuff. He'd talk about his home, his ambitions. His ambition, that is.

You remember 'Goodfellas', the opening line? 'As far back as I can remember I wanted to be a gangster'? Well, Jim felt the same about sailing. Funny really, because he was born in the mid-West, about as far from the sea as you can get. But his family moved to Boston when he was young. He watched the boats on the Charles River and from then on, everything else in his life came second. He did what little sailing he could but the family weren't well off, then his old man ran off and things got even worse.

So when he was about ten-years-old he made a decision; he put sailing to the back of his mind and concentrated on raising the stake money. He figured that his best way to do that was in software and the best place to do software was Stanford University so he worked like a lunatic to get himself accepted. That's how we met."

Meg looked puzzled. "So how old is he?"

"Going on thirty, I guess."

"And he still hasn't made it?"

"Well, there was a problem."

"What kind of problem?"

"A female kind of problem. He'd hardly bothered with women, he hadn't had the time, but he fell for this girl, woman rather, Kathy. She worked part time in the Stanford library. We were all pleased at first. She seemed nice, rather quiet, shy even. It seemed like she'd be good for him. They were married within a month and within two the trouble started."

"What sort of trouble?"

"It turned out she had a long history of mental instability, depression mostly. But she would have sudden spells of really wild behavior. Running out into the street naked, banging on neighbors' doors, shouting threats and obscenities. Then she took to bothering the police, complaining she was being followed, she'd been raped by the Mayor, God alone knows what, but it was the knife attack that finished it."

"Knife attack?" Meg stared in disbelief.

"I'm afraid so. Jim was in the front yard washing the car when Kathy rushed at him with a kitchen knife."

"So what happened? Was he hurt?"

"Not a scratch. The defense psychiatrist said that she hadn't really meant it. You know, a cry for help and all that mumbo-jumbo. But Jim told me she tried to castrate him. He had to hit her, hard. Knocked her out cold."

"So she went to prison?"

"Sure. But only for a few months. The day she came out she went back to the house, packed a bag and vanished. Jim tried to find her but it was hopeless. He hardly spoke to anyone for months. Started drinking, his work went to hell. I had to fire him in the end. After that I heard nothing from him for a year or so. Then suddenly he pops up, walks right into my office looking like an Olympic athlete and asks if I have any more tough problems!"

He looked at his watch and got to his feet. "Out of time, muppet. I'm due in the office. See you later."

"Maybe. Don't wait up! And I've told you about that silly name!"

"Sorry, sweetie!" he called over his shoulder.

Meg smiled. She couldn't stay mad at Geoff either. She was starting to clear up the table when he put his head around the door.

"Oh, one last thing. You'll be one up this evening."

She looked blank.

"I forgot to mention to Jim that you speak Greek."

CHAPTER 7

They were driving towards the Santa Cruz mountains along the edge of the Stanford University campus on Page Mill Road, a seemingly never-ending street in Palo Alto; Meg noticed a mailbox numbered 16448. As far as she could recall, nowhere outside of America had she seen a house number above 500. Jim slowed, made a turn then another.

"You'll like Greek food," he assured her as he swung the elderly Corvette into a parking lot.

"I'm sure I will," Meg replied gravely.

The building was a windowless, single-story concrete construction whose principal architectural feature was an industrial-scale air-conditioning unit on the roof. Meg's immediate reaction was that in her cream linen trouser-suit she would be over-dressed, whereas Jim's jeans and T-shirt – the latter admittedly so new that its retail creases were clearly visible – would be just right. A tall gantry in front of this unprepossessing building bore an illuminated sign brashly announcing in pseudo Greek lettering: 'Vlahakis Greek Restaurant. Established 1978. Nikos Vlahakis prop.' Inside they were greeted by a swarthy, bustling man, beaming professionally.

"Jim! Good to see you again. How are you, my friend?" He turned to Meg with a Mediterranean smile: "And how is this most beautiful young lady?"

"I'm fine, just fine," said Jim. "This is Meg. Meg meet Nikos. He serves the best Greek food in Northern California."

"Jim, what do you mean? I serve the best Greek food in the whole damn state. West of the Rockies, I tell you." Turning back to Meg he shook her hand then held it in both of his, saying in Greek, half under his breath: "Ah, to be young again."

Meg, waiting unhurriedly for the return of her hand, smiled and said, also in Greek: "Cretan men are forever young."

He stared at her nonplussed. "You speak Greek!", he cried at last in English, then, returning to Greek: "The voice of civilization in a land of barbarians! And you know Crete, also." He turned to Jim with a wink: "A very special lady. You will take best care of her, OK?"

"I plan to, sir," Jim responded, looking at Meg in astonishment.

Gesturing to a waiter, Nikos said in Greek, "Table five for my friends." The waiter hesitated then mumbled something, pointing vaguely towards a small table in the middle of the room. Nikos swept aside the man's objections. "Table five! And an apéritif with my compliments."

The room was small, seating no more than forty. The décor was American commercial Greek with richly panelled walls and masses of more or less authentic Greek bric à brac but among the plaster busts and plaques of the Parthenon, Meg noted a sprinkling of apparently original photographs of archeological digs and in particular, in a cracked wooden frame, a faded sepia print of the Lion Gate at Mycenae. Table five turned out to be in a partially curtained corner booth.

As they settled themselves, a waiter appeared bearing a plate of olives, a bottle of ouzo, a carafe of water and two tall, thick glass tumblers bearing a logo in the form of an outline of the island of Crete. The bottle boasted: *'Sans Rival - Gold prized at all expositions. Especially prized at the World Exposition of San Francisco 1915*[8]. He poured the syrupy liquid, and offered Meg the carafe.

"With Nikos's compliments," he pronounced magnificently.

Meg topped up her glass judiciously, enjoying the familiar aroma and swirling white clouds. The waiter watched anxiously as she took her first sip.

"Superb. Please thank Nikos and tell him this is my favorite ouzo," said Meg, again in Greek. Now beaming, the waiter departed to convey this compliment. Jim, having observed the ritual without comment, followed Meg's lead.

"Hmm. Not a bad drink. What's the flavor?"

[8] Verbatim from the label.

"Aniseed. It's a sort of Greek Pernod," she added, realizing too late that this conveyed nothing to him. 'In America, Mickey Mouse is a cultural icon' – her father's flippant observation wasn't entirely unfounded', she thought.

As a further token of their special status, Nikos himself came and fussed over their order. This included an intense debate, conducted in Greek with occasional translations for Jim's benefit, over the merits of the kleftiko versus the stifado, resolved eventually in favor of the former. There was a further lengthy discussion about the wine before Meg selected a red, which Nikos proudly explained 'comes from Vlahakis vines in Chania, planted with my great-grandfather'. When Jim ordered a Bud Lite, Nikos looked pained but strode off to the kitchen saying nothing.

Jim fixed Meg with a long thoughtful look over the rim of his glass. "Well," he said, failing to appear unimpressed, "how come you speak Greek?"

Meg smiled inwardly. In truth, her Greek was quite limited. Not a natural linguist, she had capitalized on a good ear and a retentive memory, picking it up over years of visits. Although she was very comfortable in shops and restaurants, that was as far as it went. She was not about to say as much to Jim, though.

"We spend holidays in the Greek islands quite often, Crete mainly. It's one of the benefits of living in the Old World, you know," she added, mischievously.

"And," he pressed, "how could you tell he was Cretan? A guess, right?"

"Clairvoyance," she said.

He sat back, head on one side, studying her. He wasn't accustomed to being caught on the back foot. For a while Meg stared back evenly but eventually couldn't keep a straight face.

"His name," she explained. "Names ending in 'akis' are usually Cretan families."[9]

"I see." Jim was keen to get onto a more serious subject. "Why did you come?"

Meg stared into her ouzo before answering. "I never turn down a free meal. Why did you ask me?"

[9] -akis, a diminutive suffix applied derisively to Cretans by the Turks during their long occupation.

"Because you're amazingly beautiful."

Meg blushed. "And you invite every beautiful girl you meet to dinner?"

"Only the intelligent ones."

"And I'm intelligent?"

"What would you call a girl with a First Class degree in Physics from London University?"

So he knew about that too; she began to wonder what Geoff hadn't told him.

Gradually tables began to fill. A swarthy man of about twenty-five appeared clutching an electric bouzouki which he plugged into an amplifier in one corner and began quietly tuning up.

"Geoff tells me you're a sailor."

"Right now I'm a software engineer," he said, gloomily. "But I will be a sailor one day."

"What's stopping you?"

"I'm waiting for the right shipmate."

The waiter reappeared and spread out plates of tsatziki, made of cucumber, yoghurt and a touch of garlic, hummos, the well known dish created from chick peas. and taramosalata, fish roe blended into a creamy spread, plus a Greek salad and a basket of bread. The task of opening the wine, however, was too important to be delegated; Nikos himself drew the cork and waited for their - Meg's - judgement on the Vlahakis family wine.

"Excellent, thank you."

Nikos, with a quick sideways glance at Jim, said in Greek that he was sure she would enjoy it and withdrew.

"What did he say?" asked Jim.

Meg hesitated. "He said 'Enjoy!'"

The electric bouzouki began plinking the inescapable 'Never on a Sunday'.

"So why the software engineering?"

Jim gestured over Meg's shoulder. "You see the picture?"

On the wall of their alcove was a faded black and white photograph of a rather weedy looking man with intense eyes and an extravagant Victorian moustache, formally dressed with a silk top hat and an overcoat. The coat, lavishly trimmed with dark fur, was monumentally too large, entirely engulfing his arms. He looked like a member of the Crazy Gang. In heavy script across the bottom were some indistinct words in German and a date - 1861.

"His name's Heinrich Schliemann. He's a hero of mine."

"So you're interested in archeology?", Meg asked, surprised.

"My father was. When I was small, he told me how Schliemann saw a picture of Troy when he was only nine and told his father he would find it one day. He didn't even start looking until he was quite old but he found it."

"What's that got to do with your boat?"

"It's about discipline. Old Heinrich had the Troy obsession from the age of nine but he knew it would need a ton of money to satisfy it so he spent the first half of his life making money to be free to spend the second half finding Troy. That's why I'm doing all the software crap. Then one day I cast off and go find Troy. And I'd have made it by now, if it hadn't been for... difficulties."

A look of despair passed quickly over his face.

"Your wife."

"So Geoff told you. I wondered if he had."

Meg put a hand on his arm. "Yes, he told me."

He grasped her hand, held it tight and looked at her intently. He was about to speak when the waiter reappeared.

"I should bring main course now, yes?"

They separated like guilty children.

"What? Oh, yes please," Jim said.

The moment was gone; Meg hovered between relief and disappointment.

Suddenly, there was tension between them. The main course was accompanied by rather awkward small talk. When the waiter left them with the dessert menu, Jim launched into explanations. "You'll find that Greek desserts are all the same - nuts with honey, honey with nuts, ground nuts with honey..." He stopped. "Well, I guess you know that already, huh?"

"I do actually," she acknowledged, without sarcasm.

Their waiter reappeared, pointedly looking at Meg. "Coffee? Dessert?"

Jim got in first. "I'll stick with the Bud, thanks."

"Ena sketo, parakalo," Meg responded.

"What's all that?", Jim asked.

"It means 'without sugar, please'", she translated.

And while the waiter was busy with the spirit stove and the copper pannikin, Meg explained the Greek coffee ritual. Jim ordered another beer.

It was almost midnight when they drove up to the house, Jim switched off the engine and turned towards her. "That was a great evening."

Meg leaned across and kissed him lightly on the cheek. "Yes, I enjoyed it too. Thanks."

"I'm taking the yacht out tomorrow."

"That sounds nice."

"It'd be nicer if you came along."

"Is that a Californian invitation?"

To his credit he looked abashed. "I guess it is. Sorry. Will you come?"

She pursed her lips thoughtfully. "Well… I had promised my tennis coach he could take me to lunch."

"You have a tennis coach?"

"I haven't played tennis since school."

He looked puzzled. "Then why…" Light dawned. "Ah! OK, you got me. But you will come?"

"I'd love to come."

"Great. Tomorrow morning then. Pick you up here."

"I'll press my sou'wester."

"You won't need it. Tomorrow's going to be a perfect day."

"How can you be so sure about the weather?"

"I wasn't talking about the weather."

"Jim, you're outrageous."

"I do my best!"

Suddenly he took her by the shoulders and kissed her firmly on the lips then, before she could respond, leapt from behind the wheel, sprinted round to her door and helped her from the car.

"See you tomorrow morning. Is eight o'clock OK?", he asked.

"Eight o'clock will be fine."

"She's called 'Spirit of Troy', by the way."

"I'll look out for her."

He seemed on the point of saying something else but suddenly turned, slid behind the wheel and drove off, revving furiously, spinning the Corvette's wheels. She watched until the tail lights vanished among the cypresses.

CHAPTER 8

Meg's parents, Peter and Helen, had changed out of their regulation Californian shorts and T-shirts into somewhat smarter wear for the 'Great Game' as Geoff had christened it, and were stretched out in padded chairs diligently watching the sunset. Meg, wearing a white sleeveless dress, a younger version of her mother, was sitting cross-legged with an overweight volume – *Fundamentals of Superconductivity'* - on her lap but Helen could see that whatever she was daydreaming about, it hadn't much connection with superconductivity.

At forty-five Peter was still effortlessly handsome - fair hair, blue eyes, fine features. He sat up abruptly. "Geoff, come and take a look at this!"

He was looking seawards, watching a power-boat, perhaps half a mile off-shore, running south, parallel to the coastline, throttles wide open, sitting back on her stern, her bow pointed skywards, not cutting through the water but planing over it, gliding from wave-top to wave-top. Geoff, having finished setting out the board and chess clock, was in the kitchen pretending not to hear.

"He's hitting sixty knots," Peter added. "Hope he knows what he's doing."

As they watched, the pilot – sailor seemed too prosaic a word for the commander of such a glamorous and athletic machine – began a dramatically late turn to cut a sweeping arc towards the mooring. The slender hull leaned steeply, fighting the g forces like a racing motorcycle.

"He seems to be headed here," Peter added.

"That'll be Jim. And right on time for the celebration," announced Geoff, appearing with a tray of glasses and champagne in an ice bucket.

"Jim?" Meg, forsaking champagne and even superconductivity, made for the steps to the mooring.

The cruiser, now about three hundred yards off, had straightened its course and, still at speed, the pilot no longer visible behind the steepling bow, was headed directly for the narrow inlet which sheltered the beach-house mooring. As she left the swell of the open sea for the calm waters in the curve of the bay, her twin bow waves arced gold against the sunset.

Helen was out of her seat. "Celebration? Oh, Geoff. You haven't swapped 'Light Fantastic' for that, have you?" She was smiling but the reproach was half serious.

Geoff, cheerfully unrepentant, handed her a glass of champagne. "I'm getting too old for all that winching and tacking business. Here's to 'Star of the Sea'."

He filled a glass for Peter and one for himself. Peter took his and watched the bubbles rising before taking a first taste.

"Thanks, but Helen's right. That thing belongs in St. Trop. Was the eager young starlet included or do you have to find your own?"

Geoff grinned. "You guys can scoff as much as you like but I've done my years before the mast. It's naked luxury from now on. Come on down, take a proper look at her. You probably won't admit it but you'll be impressed." Geoff was already bounding down the steps.

As Meg watched from the jetty, the cruiser slowed, her bow dipping gracefully, the sound of her engines subsiding to a rumble as she slid alongside. A last brief burst of power, a twist of the wheel, and the long delicate prow nudged the dock fender, while Jim, mooring rope in hand, was miraculously already ashore to make her fast.

"Not too shabby, eh?", he said, then adrenaline still running, he seized Meg around the waist, swung her around and set her down.

"Agile young man," Peter remarked, to no-one in particular, as they reached the dock.

They were shown around the elaborately equipped machine, not by Geoff but by Jim who, it turned out, had recommended her to Geoff – suitable for the older man, he explained, straight-faced. Meg noticed that Jim was especially attentive to her mother who later admitted to being much more impressed by the guide than the tour.

When it was time for Jim to leave, he and Meg kissed, more decorously than they would have preferred, then he began organizing his own boat for departure. Helen, characteristically keeping track of time and social obligations, caught Meg's eye.

"Meg darling, someone should be upstairs when Mr Vanosivich arrives," she said, "especially since we asked him to play here rather than at that estate of his." She was expecting a protest, as Jim was still preparing for departure and had not yet even started the yacht's auxiliary motor but to her surprise Meg, with a final wave, set off at once to climb the steps.

This was how she came to be the only one watching when, punctual to the minute, the dark Mercedes came rapidly down the track. From the door, she was struck by the steady precision of the Russian's movements as he parked, climbed out, opened the rear door and picked up a large leather-bound case. He locked the car with a remote control then tried the driver's door to confirm it really was locked. Although he must have been aware of her presence, he acted the whole time as though she were not there. Only as he approached the house did he acknowledge her:

"My dear Meg!" He affected a tone of surprise. "It is good to see you again."

"And you, Mr Vanosivich. Do come in."

"Ah, that name," he sighed, "so many syllables. Stefan, please."

Inside he removed the heavy coat – how odd to wear it on such a warm evening, Meg thought – and when she offered to take it, he quietly insisted on hanging it himself.

"Come through. Everybody's down below seeing Jim off."

"Down below?"

"Yes, there's a mooring at the foot of the cliff. Come and see. She led him through the lounge where Geoff had set out the board, pieces and clock. "This way."

Putting his case down by the table he followed her onto the balcony. Below, at the mooring, her parents and Geoff were watching Jim skilfully maneuvre his boat away from the mooring then raise her sail as soon as he was in open water.

"Isn't it a beautiful view?" She loved the swathe of sea and sky, the way they merged into a smudge of indigo at the horizon.

But Stefan was staring at the scene below. Without looking up he said: "The woman, she is your mother?"

"Yes."

"You are very much alike. And Jim, he is the young man in the boat?"

"Yes. He's an engineer who does some work for Geoff."

"A fine boat and he handles her with skill."

"Yes, he does," Meg responded with enthusiasm. "And he's the only person Geoff trusts with his new boat."

"You have sailed with him?"

"Once."

Stefan watched the scene in silence for a while. "I prefer trees. In winter," he said at last. He sounded abstracted.

"Why trees?"

He paused before answering and when he spoke it was with the same grave precision he'd shown with the car. "When I was young we had many trees, deep forests, very dark and safe. Especially in winter." He turned to her suddenly, smiling. He looked quite different when he smiled which she'd noticed in the café too. "But it pleases me to see how much you like the sea." Still smiling he held her gaze. "And the young man, too. He is fortunate, I think."

He was already heading back into the room. "Come, we must prepare." He paused at the door, looked around, then picked up the carefully laid out board and clock, handing them to her and replacing them with his own plain wooden board and pieces, rather worn, and a clock, exquisite in ebony chased with silver but also well-used. And as he dismantled his host's careful preparations in favor of his own, Stefan said nothing, seeming already absorbed in a contest which had not yet begun.

"Your family, Stefan, are they here in America too?", she asked.

Her words had come without thought but when she saw his face darken – was it anger or sorrow? – she quickly sought a way to soften the question or remove the need to answer it altogether. To her relief, voices on the steps from the mooring solved the problem.

Half an hour into the first game, Meg could no longer contain herself. "Is he doing as badly as it looks?" she whispered to Geoff.

Her interest in chess was almost completely vicarious. Other than the basic rules she knew practically nothing of chess theory but when she was young she had been fascinated to watch her father playing, and the strong players she'd met all seemed impressive characters, though frequently eccentric and occasionally downright weird. Vanosivich she thought especially formidable but the game seemed not to be going terribly well for him. Her question was breathed gently into Geoff's ear but Stefan looked up sharply. Geoff motioned to her and she followed him out onto the balcony. He closed the doors quietly behind them.

"The short answer is, he's throwing it away. He's played a gambit called the Wild Muzio and he knows as well as anybody that against decent opposition, it's a dead loser."

"Wild Muzio? Sounds like an Italian fighting bull."

"Bull's the word. Strong players use it only against weak opposition, exhibition games, that sort of thing."

"You think Stefan feels he's up against weak opposition?"

Geoff shrugged. "I think your friend Stefan's an egomaniac." He put an affectionate arm around her shoulders. "Come on. I want to see this." At the door he paused. "By the way, I take it you noticed – you were the one who spoke but it was me he glared at."

Meg smiled sweetly. "Maybe he just prefers women."

"I think he just prefers you," was Geoff's response.

Inside the game was moving to its predictable conclusion and after twenty-eight moves, the Russian resigned.

"Interesting choice of opening," Peter observed.

"Now you will be white," Stefan responded, already setting up the pieces.

A dozen moves into the new game Geoff grinned and winked at Meg. When she shrugged interrogatively he steered her back to the balcony.

"Magnificent," he chortled.

"It looked to me as if Dad was making the same mistake Stefan made," she said, although she hadn't been paying close attention.

"Peter's playing the same opening but it's not a mistake."

Meg was lost. "What are you talking about?", she said in exasperation.

"Look, Stefan plays a losing opening which makes Peter's win meaningless. Then your father does a judo throw, turns his opponent's strength against him. Stefan threw the first game with a dumb opening; your father does exactly the same in the second. So it will be one game all. Then they'll play a proper game as a decider. You watch, there won't be a fighting bull in sight in the decider."

"I'm sure you're right, Geoff. Enjoy it. I'm going up to find Mum."

Geoff was right. By midnight they were twenty moves into a closed variation of the Queen's Gambit Declined. Geoff's offer of drinks was turned down by both players, neither looking up from the board. By one o'clock they were in the endgame with a slight positional advantage to white which even Geoff could see would be tough to convert into a win. It was almost two o'clock when Stefan slowly sat back, ran a hand over his glistening bald head and offered his hand.

"It is late even for chess players. We could seal the position but I always find restarting a game most unsatisfactory – one can never recapture the intensity of the original struggle. A draw?"

To Geoff's surprise Peter thought for several seconds before taking the offered hand. "A draw."

Within minutes Stefan had gathered the board, pieces and clock and collected his overcoat. At the door he turned to Geoff. "Please say goodnight to Meg for me."

As their visitor climbed into the Mercedes, Geoff locked up and returned to the lounge. "Coffee?" He poured for himself and Peter. "The last time I saw a

Wild Muzio it was that Scandinavian guy, forget his name, playing a simultaneous blindfold in New York. Some spotty teenager tried to wrong-foot him with it and was demolished in eighteen moves."

Peter took a cup and sipped it appreciatively.

"It surprised me too, I admit. Then I realized he was hedging his bets. If he wins he's a genius, if I win it's not worth much."

Analysis of Stefan's gamesmanship was halted when Helen and Meg appeared wearing dressing gowns and conspiratorial expressions, the product of female confidences and a glass or two of wine. Their talk had followed a ritual as old as motherhood, a conversational minuet in which each perfectly understood the steps which both transparently pretended did not exist. By this means they had been able to have a discussion on the topic of real interest – Jim – while truthfully claiming that neither of them had initiated it.

"Thank the Lord he's gone," Helen said, sinking onto the sofa next to Peter. "Odious man."

"Mother!", Meg protested, "You've scarcely met him."

Introduced to Helen, Stefan had shaken her hand with a perfunctory 'How do you do?' then turned to Peter to suggest they get the game started.

"And I plan to keep it that way."

"So you won't be joining us, then," Peter suggested.

"Joining who, for what?"

"Meg and me for the rematch, at La Honda."

"At his place? No thanks."

"What do you make of him? As a man, I mean," Geoff asked Peter.

Peter thought about it. "He's a mystery. All the signs of wealth: private estate, expensive car, and did you notice the English overcoat? Savile Row, I'd bet. When Meg passed on his invitation I asked around. You remember Yusupov, the Russian who organized that inter-varsity tournament in Moscow?"

"The one where you lost twice and we finished second bottom?" Geoff prompted, innocently.

"Oh God, yes. Don't remind me. Anyway, I spoke to him. He knows his way around the Russian chess world and he said nobody of that name had played serious chess in Russia in the last thirty years. So he's a pretty strong chess player but invisible. And then there's the money. Nobody knows where that comes from. There's vague talk about multi-national business but I couldn't find any record of share ownership, nothing in the financial press, nobody I asked in the City knows anything."

"How long has he been over here?", Helen asked.

"The realtor who sold me the house said she sold him the estate – well, she dealt with his lawyer, never actually saw him – in 1971. But she said the local gossip was that he moved here from somewhere on the east coast."

"So he probably left Russia in the sixties if not before," Helen pointed out.

"Sure," Geoff said. "And that's Vanosivich. Everything a bit off-center but always a reasonable explanation. It's just when you put it all together..."

"And looking like Savenkov doesn't help," Helen added.

"Who's Savenkov?" Peter got the question in first.

"A Russian revolutionary. Another bald fanatic."

"Good heavens, Mum!" Meg protested.

But Peter was pondering the idea. "Well, he's certainly fanatical about chess. I've never seen such intensity across the board, even in serious competition. Winning mattered to him."

"Oh, come on, Peter. You used to wear yourself out playing matches," Helen objected.

Peter shook his head. "Yes I did but I never played against anyone like him. Stronger players perhaps, but nobody with that... ferocity."

Meg recalled the look in the dark eyes in the Café and said nothing. She was wondering why she reacted so strongly, so instinctively, when Stefan was criticized. She could see that most of what was being said was true but there was something about him, some hidden vulnerability that made her feel protective. She smiled at the thought; Stefan needed protection less than anybody she knew.

"What's funny?", Helen asked.

"Oh, nothing really. I was just wondering whether he's as tough as he seems."

"Well, he's certainly got a soft spot for you, Meg," Geoff pointed out.

Helen stood up with an air of decision. "Peter's got his 'I'm still not happy about the pawn sacrifice' look. I'm going to bed. Good night all."

Peter sighed, got up and put an arm around Helen's shoulder. "She's right, Geoff. See you for a late brunch maybe. Good night, Meg."

CHAPTER 9

Geoff's Fourth of July parties had started largely by accident in 1984. He had just moved to the west coast to run the newly-formed ILT US subsidiary and had invited a few friends for drinks at his apartment near the small Palo Alto office. As the party broke up somebody said 'see you next year' and sparked a tradition. Within a few years the party had expanded to accommodate the sixty or seventy people who seemed to appear, some by invitation, and now it had moved to Geoff's home and sported a five-piece band imported from San Francisco and the best barbecue for miles around.

It was already after eleven and a fine, balmy, starlit evening. On the floodlit terrace at the side of the house the band had slowed the tempo and most of the couples had drifted back inside. By the barbecue, Peter, Helen and the ILT Head of Legal Affairs were at the height of an animated argument about the merits of a written constitution when Geoff appeared, eyes fixed on Helen.

"My dance if you don't mind, Peter," he said, taking her hand. "I wait a whole year for this."

They stepped onto the terrace as the band began a slow, romantic version of 'Misty' led by a breathy soprano sax… 'I'm as helpless as a kitten up a tree'.

Helen was delighted. "Geoff," she said, "you'd think they knew…"

"They do," he grinned, "it's costing me a round of drinks."

Neither of them could remember when the two of them had adopted this tune as their own. They were each lost in reminiscences, dancing very slowly, scarcely moving. The music brought back to Helen vivid memories of a hot June night in 1969. Even without what was to follow, that Saturday would have been hard to forget. The weather forecasters maintained that the hot dry spell had lasted only four weeks, but it had felt like forever. Day followed enervating day with no respite; the final exams had been held in a merciless glare of sunlight through the uncurtained windows of the Central Hall but now there was the reward of the going-down party on a Thames riverboat, a last orgy of camaraderie, a rite of passage to the real world. Helen had been looking forward to it as a magnificent last fling. She was ecstatically happy about her engagement to Peter and well into preparations for the wedding at the end of July.

The evening had begun inauspiciously with a phone call from Peter, already overdue to collect her. "Helen, you won't believe this. It's my stupid shoulder again. I'm in the emergency room at the hospital, Paul drove me. He's still here. Guess he feels responsible, but I'll beat him one day if it's the last thing I do."

In the background Helen heard Paul's voice. "Bull. You're too damned slow and not fit enough, old chap."

"Piss off, Paul. Sorry, Helen, did you say something?" Peter completed the account of the disastrous squash game. He'd spent the last three years trying to beat Paul but although he'd come close, he'd never managed it. Nor had anyone else in the club. Not surprising since Paul was to turn professional within a year.

"Oh, Peter. You're impossible. What about the party?"

"No problem." Peter had an inborn ability to find a way. "I'll call Geoff. He's going anyway. He'll be glad to pick you up."

So it was that Geoff came to be Helen's escort.

By ten o'clock, a slight breeze rose on the River Thames and the dancing, not to mention the drinking, became fast and furious. Afterwards, Helen couldn't remember exactly what had started the laughter as she and Geoff walked slowly back along the Embankment in the moonlight. They didn't seem to need a reason. Even when they reached her flat just behind the Tate Gallery, they had to make an enormous effort to control themselves as they stumbled up to the second floor, and once inside the hallway, Helen remembered collapsing against Geoff's shoulder, tears of laughter streaming down her face and onto his shirt.

"What we need is a shower," he said with mock severity. "Would it make too much noise? Hell, it's nearly four o'clock. You'd better go first and I'll make the coffee."

How they finished up sharing the shower - water saving? noise reduction? – again, she couldn't remember but it seemed the most natural thing in the world. They hadn't bothered to get dried and Geoff had carried her, dripping, through to the bedroom. She could remember every detail of the gentle but confident kisses Geoff lavished all over her body and the pleasure she'd felt, deeper than she'd ever done with Peter.

The next morning had been difficult. They sat for a long time on the sofa Geoff should have slept on, drinking coffee, saying little, agonizing over whether to tell Peter, at last agreeing to say nothing. And it had been the right decision. In spite of Geoff's devotion to her and the complete ease she always felt with him, she knew it wasn't enough for her. She wished Geoff could find the right woman; he deserved to be happy.

A month later he was Peter's best man at their marriage.

'I'm too misty and too much in love.'

As the saxophone whispered into silence they became aware of the few other couples - the older ones, they noticed with a smile - who joined them in appreciative applause for the band.

"Same time next year?", asked Geoff.

"It's a promise," Helen replied and they kissed spontaneously.

*   *   *

Peter was on the telephone and didn't see the police car arrive. Helen went to the door.

"Peter!"

The brittle tone and the panic in her steps twisted Peter's stomach and he cut short the call and hurried into the lounge. Helen, dark-eyed from lack of sleep, hands clenched at her sides, was staring at the tall, capable looking policewoman whose uncomfortable expression had already broken the news.

"I think maybe you should sit down, Mrs Gilchrist."

Peter took his wife's arm and helped her into a chair. It was Helen who croaked out the question.

"You've found her? She's alright..."

"I'm afraid not, ma'am. The body of a young woman was found on the beach about an hour ago. I'm terribly sorry..."

"You mean..."

Her voice cracked; Peter took up the question. "Are you telling us my daughter drowned?"

"Well, sir, at this time we have no identification but..."

Slowly the spirit drained from Helen and she slumped forward, hands clamped to her head.

"You take care of your wife, Mr Gilchrist and I'll fix something."

"Please. Can you make tea?"

"Hot tea? Sure I can. My husband drinks it all the time. He worked in London..."

"Thank you. I'll show you..."

She was already at the door, relieved to have something practical to fill the time. "That's OK. I'll find it."

*　　*　　*

'We brought nothing into this world, and we can take nothing out.'

Unseasonable black storm clouds raced along the rim of the South Downs and rumbles of distant thunder echoed slowly around the gravestones. Between Peter and Geoff, Helen stood perfectly still, staring sightlessly ahead. She had cried just once, more in shock than grief, when the Half Moon Bay policewoman broke the news, but within hours distress and outrage had congealed in her, her emotions were suspended and her life became cold and motiveless.

And now this. He would have preferred the minimum formalities required by law for the disposal of what remained of his daughter but Helen, incapable of offering a considered view, had deferred to the wishes of her mother, a life-long High Church Anglican much given to quoting scripture.

So here they were. Someone, the funeral professionals Peter imagined, had arranged the wreaths and flowers in a mound by the graveside, far more of them than he had expected. Apart from the white roses from himself and Helen, an enormous arrangement of lilies from Helen's mother, pink rosebuds in the form of an 'M' from Geoff and numerous bouquets from her friends at school, college, her Swimming Club, the staff of ILT and, surprisingly, Peter thought, from Ceramic Magnets with the message 'We're sad not to have had time to know you better'. And among the sea of white and pink, one wreath stood out - a circle of cornflowers with a card: 'For Meg whom I had hoped to make my friend. Stefan'.

'The Lord gave, and the Lord has taken away, blessed be the name of the Lord.'

The minister was a tall, distinguished looking man in his sixties with leonine features, white hair and a leading man's voice. He had the perfect graveside manner, dignified, compassionate and empathetic. Peter detested everything he symbolized. He had ceased believing in the Lord when he was ten years old. What he wanted was punishment for the man who had taken away his daughter. And not some watered-down punishment, a prison sentence served in conditions monitored by the American Civil Liberties Union, but a slow and agonizing death.

'Man born of woman has but a short time to live.

Like a flower we blossom and then wither.'

Wrong, wrong, wrong. Meg did not wither, she was cut down.

'In the midst of life we are in death;

to whom can we turn for help, but to you Lord...'

To whom indeed? He didn't know what he would do but whatever it was, he didn't intend waiting for the Lord or anybody else. He'd waited too long already. It would be soon, today, now... the minute this damned farce was ended.

*'We have entrusted our sister to God's merciful keeping, and we now
commit her body to the ground; earth to earth, ashes to ashes, dust to dust...'*

Peter watched as Helen's mother, leaning heavily on her stick, sprinkled the
ritual earth onto the coffin. Helen stood quite still.

'...in sure and certain hope of the resurrection to eternal life.'

'Sure and certain'. He'd once fired a Marketing Manager who was given to
mouthing similar repetitious platitudes.

As the four of them walked in silence to the car, Peter reflected that he now
had only to get through the funeral tea at Helen's mother's home before he
and Geoff could immerse themselves in final preparations for the Ancona
conference. He would have preferred to leave it all to Geoff but Helen
had insisted on him going, saying she'd be better off alone with her mother
for a while.

CHAPTER 10

Against Peter's expectations, the hectic two days of travel and business had allowed him to push the horrors of recent weeks out of his mind. But now, heading home from Heathrow Airport, the lights of the highway gliding rhythmically across the hood of the taxi, the nightmare returned, sharp as crystal. Helen's voice through the party chatter, straining to be calm, asking had he seen Meg... He wondered how Geoff was coping, waiting alone in the impersonal calm of the First Class lounge for his flight back to the west coast. He had been like a third parent to Meg.

"ILT 'ouse, sir."

They were outside a darkened six story building just off the Hammersmith ramp. With difficulty Peter refocused his mind on the present. "Wait, please. I'll be ten minutes."

As the driver watched Peter's tall, slim figure taking the steps to the front door two at a time, the combination of obvious wealth, fitness and authority were too much for a balding overweight cockney; alright for some, he thought, sourly.

Peter peered through the misted glass of the main doors, scanning the reception area, looking in vain for the night-man. Damn him, he thought, skulking in the kitchen again. He rammed a thumb irritably onto the night bell-push and kept it there, reflecting briefly on the irrationality of treating door-bells as though a harder push produced a bigger noise. Maybe that was how bells ought to work. Now that really would be a worthwhile design project. Get the damned boffins to create something useful for a change, he thought, with more than his usual cynicism. After a full minute of deafening racket, Fairclough, the security man on the ten 'til six shift, a small, plump red-faced man in stockinged feet appeared from the elevator lobby. He was preceded by a stream of invective which, as he saw Peter, abruptly became a fawning "Oh! It's you, Mr Gilchrist. Sorry, sir. Thought it was them damned kids again. Bane of my life they are, little bastards. Beggin' your pardon, sir."

Peter strode rapidly across the chromium and marble foyer, Fairclough trotting noiselessly at his heels. The lift smelt of curry and disinfectant.

In his office he switched on the desk lamp, sat down gratefully, slipped off his shoes and reached for the 'In' tray, piled high as always. Despite personal assistants and secretaries, he still had trouble delegating. The GP's diagnosis was accurate; he reflected gloomily - a tense and meticulous personality. Between that and the wrangles with the Non-Executive Directors, he was striving for an early grave. Helen was right; he should spend more time relaxing and less time 'in the damned office' as she put it. As she regularly pointed out, after over twenty years of grinding effort he had reached a point where he could both afford and needed some time off. Peter would grunt his assent and do nothing.

He skipped through the mail seeking only one item. On the day of the funeral, finally stirred into action by the horror of watching the coffin descend into the ground, he had placed an advertisement in the personal column of the San Francisco Examiner offering a reward of ten thousand dollars to anyone who could, *provide information explaining the death by drowning of his daughter Megan Gilchrist'*. And there it was. A fat, official-looking envelope with an impressive but bogus heraldic emblem and, embossed in silver, the legend *'VIP Mail Forwarding (California) Inc. – Your Security is Our Business'*. He slit open the package and dumped its contents onto his desk: three envelopes, two typed, the other hand-written, clearly by a woman. He opened this first. It was from an address in Shiprock, New Mexico and read:

Dear Friend,

A friend has told me of your advertisement. I see that you are in travail. I bring you succour. Be not afraid. Your daughter's spirit is with the Manitou. I am a chanel. I can help you reach out. Just send me some small item of hers

*and I will tune in to her wavlength. I earnestly beg you to Have Faith. Many
have been helped.*
Yours.
Elvira Begay

With a grimace he turned to the second, addressed by means of a neatly
typed label:

Dear Sir or Madam,
*The Hershey Partnership has served the Bay area for many years. We
undertake investigations of all kinds, specializing in serious criminal work.
From your ad I understand your daughter's death to have been in suspicious
circumstances. Investigating such situations is our speciality. Our fees are
reasonable and our service is discreet, honest and professional. Please let me
know if we can be of service.*
Sincerely.
Al Hershey (Prop.).

After some thought, Peter put it to one side.

The last envelope was white, expensive, edged with green. Across its flap by
way of a seal was embossed 'From the Inner Temple of the High Priest of the
Church of the Sacred Flame'. Undeterred, he opened it:

To a Brother or Sister in Need
*The High Priest has instructed me to offer our condolences on your recent
sad loss and to invite you to seek Redemption through the Lord.*
*The Drama of the Ages enters its Final Act. The prophets are fulfilled. Men's
hearts fail. Perversion and violence overwhelm us. The People sink beneath a
tide of filth purveyed by a mass media serving a Godless ruling élite:*

'But watch therefore: for ye know not what hour your Lord doth come.'
(Matthew 24, 42)

*'And take heed to yourself, lest at any time your hearts be overcharged
with surfeiting and drunkenness and cares of this life, and so the day shall
come upon you unawares.'*
(Luke 21, 34)

*Yours, seeking Salvation
George Christos
(Servant of the Flame)*

Printed in green at the foot of the page was an invitation to write for a free
leaflet titled: *'Salvation Can Be Yours'.*

It was, he thought soberly, disappointing. But then, disappointment was
predictable. On this unsatisfying contradictory note, he put the Hershey
Partnership letter into his case, swept the remainder into the trash and,
hoping to relieve the ache in his legs, took the stairs to the foyer. In the
reception area he delayed long enough to tell Fairclough, with ferocity
deriving more from his state of mind than from the gravity of the offense, that
if he thought his nocturnal culinary adventures went unnoticed, he was damn
well mistaken and that if he valued his job he'd better watch his step.
Fairclough assured him that 'it wouldn't 'appen again sir. Definite'.

He climbed back into the cab. "Jubilee House. It's in Saffron Street, just by
Tower Bridge."

"I know where it's at, sir."

As Peter sat back, trying to relax, it started again, replaying over
and over...

"Peter, have you seen Meg?" Helen's voice, too casual, strained.

Then himself, stupidly: "Seen her? Last time I saw her she was talking to the
whiz kid, the Berkeley guy, sociologist or something."

"That was ages ago. Then she went for a walk on the beach. Said she'd be
back in half an hour. Something's wrong, Peter..."

Now the taxi's arrival at the flat caught him unawares a second time.
Fumbling for his wallet he remembered how often he'd cursed slow payers in

taxis blocking his path; 'Surely they know they've almost arrived. Why can't they have the money ready?' He decided he would be more tolerant, a resolution he made frequently and just as frequently broke.

C H A P T E R   I I

PART 3

July 1992

MIDDLE GAME

From habit, Peter unlocked the door quietly until he remembered that Helen was not there. He would have telephoned her but it was far too late. Mechanically, he went through the late-home routine: leave shoes beneath telephone table, raincoat in the hall cupboard, to the kitchen to brew a large mug of hot chocolate with two spoonsful of sugar, then to the study to check his email.

His computer had been set up by Robert from Research and Development, a deeply serious young man of immense height and a pale, shiny complexion. Slow and ponderous, socially maladroit, he reminded Peter of a maths master at his prep school of whom some unkind but penetratingly accurate commentator had written - on the old man's own blackboard - *"Did you ever see a dream walking? Mr Quinn, Room 31."* Yet Peter, himself quite competent technically, recognized in Robert an extraordinary ability to communicate with machines.

As a result of his ministrations, the computer had taken on a life of its own, waking itself at unlikely hours, establishing telephone connections to the various networks Peter worked through, despatching, collecting his mail and other information essential to the business. There was the usual assortment of routine messages from the west coast office and various American universities but one item caught his eye at once. To begin with, its source was Finland where ILT transacted no business. But it was the title that really struck him: 'No accident'. Intrigued, he opened the message:

'Meg's death was not an accident. I'm not after the reward. Keep looking.'

Dumbfounded, Peter sat gazing at the words until they swam in front of him. Of course some part of him had always known that Meg's death was neither accident nor suicide, not only because she had been an exceptionally strong swimmer but also because he felt that it was just not her destiny to go that way. Yet his austere intellect had buried his instinctive feeling under plausible alternatives, cramp maybe, a freak current. Now, for the first time, shimmering at him on the screen from an unrecognized source somewhere in the digital half-world, was proof that his suspicions were shared. And yet the message raised more questions than it answered. Why 'Meg'? The advert had not given that name and all the press reports had used her full name: 'Megan'. How had the sender made the direct connection to Peter? Above all, how could he so confidently make so explosive an assertion? And why 'he'? Could the sender be a woman? Peter studied the message header carefully but it was unhelpful; the electronic identity of the sender was quite unfamiliar to him.

From a desk drawer he took out the Staff Private Telephone List, located a number and dialed it. The response was almost immediate: "Yes."

"Robert? Peter Gilchrist. Sorry to bother you at this hour but I've got a problem."

"Oh! Mr Gilchrist. You're back in London. What's the problem? Your mail getting bounced again?"

"No, no, it's incoming mail. It's from an odd address and I really need to know who sent it. It's important or I shouldn't have bothered you."

"Oh, incoming. OK. What's the originating address?"

"jsmith@alpha.cx2.fi"

A delighted chuckle: "Oh that. It means the message was routed via an anonymous mail system."

"You mean people make a business helping anonymous letter-writers?"

"Well, it's not a business. They don't charge for it."

Peter thought this bizarre but let it go.

"The Finns specialize in it." Robert continued. "Alpha.cx2 is a Finnish computer system which forwards mail anonymously."

"And jsmith is just a notional name - John Smith - as used in Brighton hotels down the ages?"

"Brighton? No, no, that server's in Finland. The fi means Finland. Where does Brighton come into it?"

"Forget it. What if I contact the people who run this operation and ask for the sender's details?"

"You won't get them."

"And what if the police ask the same question? With a subpoena maybe? What if there's some criminal activity involved? They'd be obstructing the police."

"The battle's been going on for years about that. Privacy versus the government's need to protect society and all that. But the people in Finland wouldn't necessarily know."

"I don't follow. They must know where the message originated. The system can't work if they don't."

"Not necessarily. There's a trick. If the sender's clever enough, then he can do it." Robert was clearly fascinated by the ingenuity of it. "He would use a chain of anonymous servers and a method of coding the messages - PGP they call it, stands for Pretty Good Privacy. Neat name, isn't it? It's not easy to explain on the phone but it's like Russian dolls, messages wrapped in messages if you see what I mean."

Peter didn't. "OK, skip the details. What you're telling me is that anyone determined enough and knowledgeable enough can send email messages completely anonymously. He could even defeat a police investigation."

"That's it, Mr Gilchrist. Exactly right."

"I see. OK. Thanks, Robert. That's all I wanted to know. Sorry to disturb you."

"No problem. Anyway, I wasn't in bed. I'm working on that automatic mail forwarding problem you mentioned. I've designed a really elegant method…"

Peter cut him off as gently as he could and went back to studying the message on the screen: *Meg's death was not an accident. I don't want the reward. Keep looking.*

The simplicity and the absence of rhetoric were persuasive. It seemed he had an ally; he wondered who and where.

Staring into the mug's turgid chocolate recesses he realized that what he needed to do could not be done from London. He stood up, crossed the room, opened the doors to the balcony and poured the remains of the drink into the oily blackness of the River. As he watched the milky smudge drift seawards on the slow tide he heard, barely audible on the westerly breeze, Big Ben chime three o'clock and felt a surge of elation. The shadow life he had been leading since Meg's death was over; tomorrow – today, in fact – he would return to California to find the man who had murdered his daughter.

Barely three hours later, Peter was awakened by a confusion of noises. Distant shouts, fiercely revving engines and screeching seagulls. He could still taste chocolate and wished he'd cleaned his teeth. He felt awful. His eyes seemed to have been superglued shut, his neck ached and his stomach was full of marbles. He forced his eyes open. Across the room a giant cobra reared menacingly on the dressing table. Concentrating hard he recognized a Bauhaus table lamp. It was a present from someone, maybe his mother-in-law. The bedside clock showed 5:55am.

Struggling to his feet, he found his way to the bathroom, splashed his face with water as hot as he could stand, then scrubbed furiously at the chocolate residues on his teeth. Consulting the mirror, he thought dispassionately that he looked much better than he felt. Face and teeth cleaned, he telephoned Helen, bull-dozing his way through her mother's objections that she was still sleeping, and told her his plan.

She said she thought he was insane and in the same breath insisted on joining him. She would be in London by noon. Although she didn't mention it, Peter suspected that by now she'd had enough of her mother's biblical homilies. A 6:30 a.m. call to the home of his endlessly patient secretary set off a whirlwind of arrangements for flights, to Accounts Department for a float of US dollars, a car to the airport and messages – to the Deputy Chairman to hold the fort and to Geoff to meet them off the plane.

Back in his bedroom he crossed to the window, opened it wide and stepped out onto the balcony for his morning isometric routine. He had to work hard to keep in shape, increasingly hard of late, he reflected ruefully. He was in the gym twice a week and played serious squash whenever he could.

On the river below he saw the cause of the cacophony which had woken him. The river police were carrying out some kind of exercise involving a great deal of high speed maneuvering by police launches, blue lights flashing, much agitated gesticulation and raucous shouting of instructions from presumably senior officers on the police jetty directly beneath the flat, the instructions having no effect that Peter could discern. From a barge moored in mid-stream, more policemen were letting off flares generating a huge cloud of sooty orange smoke which was carried downstream on the breeze obscuring everything in its path. Three bright yellow life-preservers, bobbing gently, drifted slowly on the incoming tide towards Tower Bridge. The harbormaster's launch hovered anxiously, its occupants leaning on the rail gazing at this frenetic scene with silent but palpable derision.

Peter watched fascinated for several minutes, endeavoring vainly to discern some pattern or purpose to it all, then gave up. Small wonder we spend so much on policing to so little result, he thought, and began mentally composing a letter to 'The Times' about it. He did this quite often, usually by way of complaint about the incompetence of some public body or other but he'd never actually got around to writing one, still less sending it.

Before he left the balcony he paused to take in the view of the Thames with Tower Bridge close by and St Paul's on the skyline. It was that view which had sold him the flat and he'd never regretted it.

Turning away, he shifted focus to the problem of what to do about his informant. It was now 7a.m. - 11p.m. on the west coast, he thought. Why not try Hershey? The letter was in his briefcase but Peter's memory, uncertain in some areas, was freakish with numbers. He could recall pi to sufficient decimal places to specify the distance between the earth and the sun to within a ten millionth of an inch, a feat which would no doubt some day come in useful in an emergency. He concentrated for a few seconds, recalling the image of the letter then punched the number into the telephone.

Peter's image of Hershey was pure Hollywood – tall, granite-faced and laconic, a three fingers of bourbon man. All, as it would turn out, entirely wrong. The phone rang twice then anti-climactically a youthful-sounding woman's voice said: "This is the Hershey Agency. We aren't able to come to the phone right now but please leave your name and number and we'll get back to you. Your message is important to us." Peter hung up.

By eight o'clock, he was in his office where he spent the first hour mechanically dealing with administrative trivia, showing unusual ruthlessness. Junk mail, which he normally opened compulsively, went to the trash en masse. At 10 am, senior colleagues joined him in his office for the weekly meeting. This usually leisurely and good-natured ramble through the agenda was despatched in 45 minutes, upsetting several people in the process. As they filed out of his office he overheard someone grumbling that the Old Man had turned really sour since his daughter's death. He was back at the flat at two o'clock, tickets and cash in his briefcase. By seven in the evening, he and Helen were enjoying British Airways' hospitality, wondering in their separate ways how the adventure would end.

C H A P T E R   1 2

Albrecht 'Al' Hershey parked in the underground bay marked 'ILT Visitors' and, as he often did even after a decade of ownership, turned back to admire his car.

It was one of his very few indulgences, and an odd choice since he was no connoisseur of cars. In New York in 1981, just out of the army, he had needed a car and was intrigued by the sleek yet muscular shape of the local Ford dealership's 'Pre-Owned Special of the Month'.

The young salesman had talked confusingly about how Al would look 'cool, like Steve McQueen, the man' behind the wheel, but Al just liked the shape and the paint job - Highland Green, he would later discover - and the way it seemed to know how to get round corners better than he did. Besides, he was finding civilian life unsettling enough without trailing around car dealerships, so he bought it on the spot.

It wasn't until months later when Holly, his first wife, had taken him to see her favorite movie and he saw Steve McQueen hurling 'his' Mustang around San Francisco streets that he understood. Owning a cult car wasn't at all what he'd planned but by then he was stuck on it and anyway Holly had loved it, most of all when she could persuade him to drive fast with the windows wide open. But the present Mrs Hershey disliked it, complained about the uncomfortable ride and the noise of its exhaust and on those occasions when they traveled together, it was always in her Toyota, which he was not allowed to drive.

With a last satisfied look at the burnished paint, he turned and headed for the elevator and the first interview of the new case, a job, which to his surprise, had come from his letter. 'Ambulance-chasing' his wife called it, responding to the advertisement placed by the dead girl's father.

~ CHAPTER 12 ~

Short, barrel-chested, slim in the hips, in 1968 Al had been the ideal Tunnel Rat, small enough to maneuver, durable enough to survive. Three Vietnam tours and the divorce from Holly had made the grey eyes watchful but the face was still young and his movements were lithe and energetic. At his wife's insistence he was dressed to meet an English gentleman - sharply pressed slacks, a dress shirt and, to his particular disgust, a tie.

The US headquarters of Integrated Laser Technology was the top floor plus the penthouse of one of the smart but anonymous buildings at the eastern end of California Street in downtown San Francisco. Leaving the elevator, Al held the doors for a young woman hurrying across the foyer and she caught his eye the way Holly had. Sure, this girl was different in every respect, small, plump and bustling where Holly's svelte, tanned body had moved like molten chocolate, but the large mouth with its pale, full lips smiling Holly's smile, reminded Al of how things had been.

At the reception desk, an oriental woman in a tailored suit and a tie monogrammed 'Pacific Property Services' smiled and looked up ILT on a computer terminal.

"36th floor. No smoking in the building, please," she said, gesturing vaguely upwards to eliminate any confusion as to the location of the 36th floor.

The ILT reception was unmanned. A telephone on a black and chromium desk bore a notice advising him to please lift the receiver and dial the extension number of his visitee or if he did not know the number, to dial zero and assured him that he would be attended to momentarily. Before he could follow this advice a slender young man appeared. He wore pale mauve slacks and a matching T-shirt with the words 'There's more to life...' across his chest. He looked Al up and down approvingly and asked whether he could do anything for him. He made it sound like a proposition.

"I have a meeting with Mr Geoff Hughes."

"Oh." He sounded discouraged. "Dial 2000" he said and went out.

The back of the shirt read '...than boy meets girl'.

The voice on extension 2000 was cool and professional. "I'll be right with you, Mr Hershey."

A few seconds later a secretary entered, wearing a beige outfit that might have been designed in Paris. She led Al along to the end of a corridor, knocked and opened a door labeled 'President' then ushered him into a comfortable office decorated in soft shades of green and grey. At the farthest point from the door, Geoff was seated behind an executive desk. Over his shoulder, through a floor-to-ceiling window, was a picture-postcard view of a cable-car struggling up California Street. Geoff got up and came to greet Al, hand extended.

"Good morning, Mr Hershey. It's good to see you. Have a seat."

"Thanks."

Al had resigned himself to how long it took the English to call him by his first name. Geoff handed Al his card which confirmed him to be Geoff Hughes, President, Integrated Laser Technology (US) Inc.

"A coffee? A soda?"

"No thanks. Maybe later."

"OK."

When they'd seated themselves at the conference table, Al took out his notebook.

"I guess you know I've been hired to investigate Miss Gilchrist's death?"

"Of course, Peter told me. I…", he stopped awkwardly.

Al waited.

"Before we start, I feel I should tell you I don't agree with what they're doing. Peter and Helen I mean. Look…". He clearly didn't much like the sound of this and began shuffling. "We've known each other for twenty-five years, since university. They're like my family, but…"

"But you think they're wrong to hire me?"

"Yes… that is, not you personally, of course. I mean to hire anybody."

"Because you think there's nothing to investigate?"

"That's right. Meg's death was clearly an accident."

Al sighed. Why was there always somebody who knew the outcome of an investigation before it began? "Look, Mr Hughes, you're allowed an opinion, I'm not. I get paid to find out what happened."

Geoff nodded apologetically. "That's fair enough. Sorry if I spoke out of turn. How can I help?"

"First, you can tell me about Miss Gilchrist."

"Where would you like me to start?"

"How about at the beginning?"

So Geoff, gently steered by Al's questions, told Meg's story, birth to death.

"And what sort of a girl was she?"

Geoff took a deep breath. "Meg was rather special, Mr Hershey. Beautiful, sensitive, intelligent. She was the best London Physics graduate for years. And a decent athlete, swimming mainly, but she was pretty good all-round. And she was quite unassuming." Geoff paused, sighed, then added: "I still expect to see her... when I get home from the office, at breakfast... It's horrible, and her parents, well it's all 'stiff upper lips' but it's a nightmare, for Helen especially. Peter has the business but Meg was Helen's life. I'm worried about what it's doing to her."

Al pressed on. "What can you tell me about...", he glanced at his notes, "Jim Otte."

"Jim? Oh, he's a great guy. Software engineer. Quite brilliant. But a bit, well, erratic. Bohemian lifestyle, lives on his boat a lot of the time. Not a 9 to 5 man."

"Where can I find him?"

"Hmm. Hard to say with Jim. Come to think of it, I haven't seen him since Meg... died. Upset by the accident, I should think. You could try his mobile but he may have it switched off. I can give you his number. If I hear from him, I'll suggest he calls you."

"Thanks. How long had they known each other?"

"Oh, no time at all, a couple of weeks. She was staying with me at the beach house – that's in Half Moon Bay – while she was looking for a place near her new job and Jim was working at my place from time to time. He doesn't like offices, too many interruptions and he prefers to work all night. She often stays... stayed with me during vacations."

A flash of melancholy as he corrected himself.

"And Otte, how old is he?"

"About thirty. A bit peculiar, as I say. But then, aren't they all? Software chaps, that is. Live on another planet. And the better they are, the more peculiar. Don't you find?"

"I've not really had much to do with them," Al said, truthfully. "Was he violent?"

"Violent? Good Lord, no. Wouldn't harm a living thing. Buddhist, well sort of. Bit of a mystic, the way they are over here. On the west coast I mean. His wife was the violent one!"

"Wife?"

"Ex-wife. He was divorced a year or so ago. Nastily. Well, it's never a light-hearted business of course, but this was particularly unpleasant. She attacked him with a knife. In the street, in front of the neighbors."

Al thought he made it sound as though the public nature of the assault was its worst aspect.

"He was damned lucky actually. Young, fit, strong, good reflexes or he'd have been in hospital at least. She's gone now, fortunately. Detroit I think." For the first time since they'd met, Geoff smiled. "She'll fit in alright there though, won't she? Running around the streets knifing people."

Al also allowed himself a smile. "Otte was at the party, I believe?"

"Yes. Well, just. He'd told Meg he would be a bit late but in the event, she thought he wasn't coming at all. Upset her a bit, I think, and that's why she went walking on the beach." He added thoughtfully: "Shows just how keen on him she was, I suppose."

And again Al saw the fleeting sadness in Geoff's eyes.

"So when he arrived, she'd left the party?", Al prompted.

"I guess so. Which," Geoff added bitterly, "is what started all this."

"What time did Otte arrive?"

"About one."

"You're sure of the time?"

"Fairly. We had the firework display at midnight. Later I saw his boat arrive while CNN's one o'clock news was on TV."

"Boat? He came by boat?"

"Oh, sure. He usually comes to the house by boat. He has a car but always uses the boat when he can."

"And what time did he leave?"

"Hmm... Can't say, really. I guess he left when he found Meg wasn't there. He's not a party man. He only came to see her."

"I see." Al put away his notebook. "Only one thing more - could you let me have a list of people attending the party?"

"Well, " he smiled, "I can give a list of those invited, but gate-crashing my party's become part of the tradition, I'm afraid. And this being California, we get all kinds of interesting people." He hit the intercom. "Barbara, can you let Mr Hershey have a copy of the guest list for the Fourth of July party, please?"

"Certainly."

Barbara turned out to be the lady in the Paris suit. She came in as though on castors and handed Al a printed sheet which he folded and slipped beneath the band securing his notebook.

Back in the car, he tried Jim's cell phone but it was off the air. Ten minutes later, he headed for home, the Mustang echoing to the sound of the Goodman band's 'Sing, Sing, Sing', looking forward with more than just professional interest to talking with Jim, if he could find him.

CHAPTER   13

Early the next morning, there was little traffic on Route 92's sinuous descent to the Pacific and Al was having fun in the California sunshine. The Mustang leaned and the V8 howled with delight at this unaccustomed opportunity to show off, and when they reached the junction with the Pacific Coast Highway both car and driver were ready to turn right around and do it all again until Al reminded himself of his age and the reason for the trip and settled for a gentle cruise along Half Moon Bay's Main Street. He'd not been to this quiet, minding-its-own-business, coastal town for some time but he knew it well and, like most who knew it, was fond of it.

He parked in the square, patted the gleaming hood in congratulation and crossed to the Station House. At the desk Police Sergeant Duane Zimmerman, ex-Marine, ex-professional boxer - fought 10, won 6, lost 3, drawn 1. A large man with tattooed arms, a fierce scar across his right cheek and appraising, cynical eyes, he was leafing through paperwork. As Al approached, he didn't look up. "Yeah?"

Al stood looking silently at this friend from another life. When at last Duane did look up, he hesitated, then a huge and surprisingly warm smile took over his war-worn features.

"Well damn it. Al! How are ya, buddy?"

The smile and rumbling voice summoned an image of a party, the style of party peculiar to Marines on active service, given in this instance to celebrate Al leaving Da Nang at extremely short notice. This abrupt departure had been arranged by a friendly Colonel after Al had volunteered his unambiguous opinion of the moral worth and command capabilities of one Captain Belmont, a Southern gentleman whom he had forcibly prevented from raping a young Vietnamese girl in a village near the camp. The entire command knew the truth but the military work only one way and Al was fortunate to be shipped out to join Captain Thornton's newly-formed tunnel-fighting unit before Belmont's friends could organize something worse.

"Fine. You?"

"Terrific. Hey, you had breakfast?"

He was already out from behind the desk and calling to the back office in a voice that rattled the walls: "Hey, Jablonski, I gotta go out. If that tramp from the hardware store comes complaining about her husband, tell her. . . Ah, forget it. Just tell her to come back. I'll handle it."

As they left the building he was muttering fiercely: "She makes me puke. Screws around town like a ten dollar whore then complains when her husband gives her the back of his hand."

Duane wouldn't have been sympathetic to the question of whether the back of the hand came first.

Half a block from the Station House they turned into a lane trapped between windowless buildings. A girl who should have been in high school was sitting on a pile of garbage sacks painting her toenails. As they passed she looked up at them with raw hostility. She looked like she didn't belong in a nice town like Half Moon Bay, but Al had yet to see a nice town without people that didn't belong. A short way down the lane Duane heaved open a sagging fire door and they entered, dragging the door shut behind them. Inside, the corridor was almost completely dark but Duane seemed to find his way by instinct. At the end of the corridor he pushed open another door and they were hit by a blast of warm air rich with the smells of the Great American Breakfast. At a grill, the lone occupant of the kitchen, a tall man with a flamboyant red bandanna around his neck called, without looking round: "Hi Duane. The usual?"

"Make it two. Al, meet Jake. He's ex-Navy but he's OK. Jake, Al."

Jake left two eggs sizzling on the griddle and came over to Al, wiped a hand on an impeccably clean apron and greeted him warmly. "Any friend of Duane's..."

"Yeah, two breakfasts," said Duane "your best."

As he passed, Duane put an arm around Jake and hugged him; Al's ribs contracted in sympathy. They took a table near the window.

"I guess you heard what happened to Belmont after they posted you?"

Al said he hadn't.

"He bought it a couple of weeks later."

"Us or them?"

"Them," replied Duane. "But there was a line of Marines waiting the chance, the lousy shit. Still, what can you expect? He was from Louisiana."

Al knew the futility of trying to talk to Duane while he was eating, so they started on their eggs, bacon, hash browns and pancakes in silence. At last Duane pushed away his empty plate, placed a giant hand delicately in front of his mouth and belched. A woman two tables away looked across disapprovingly. Duane smiled at her and selected a toothpick.

"OK. What's the pitch, Al?" he said evenly. "And don't give me any crap about passing through. You want something. Private Dicks always want something, always for free and it always ends up with trouble."

"How are things in Half Moon Bay, Duane?" Al asked innocently.

"Well, the Chief's a pain in the ass, the Mayor thinks we should be nicer to faggots and my feet hurt."

All nodded gravely to show his concern. "Is that right? What about murder?"

"Murder?" Duane studied a morsel of bacon impaled on the toothpick, trying to decide whether it was too small to eat or too big to throw away. "Who's asking?" he managed finally.

"A friend."

"Whose friend?"

"Mine. A client. English. Name of Gilchrist. His daughter was drowned off Half Moon Bay, on the Fourth."

"Yeah, I remember. Not nice, but it happens. Night swimming in these waters. This ain't Florida. The water's cold. Anyhow, nobody swims good when they're loaded."

Al's professional detachment slipped and his voice rose in protest. "Whoa, buddy! First off, she was walking, not swimming. Second, who says she'd been drinking?"

"The way I heard it, she was at a party."

"She was an athlete. She had one glass of champagne."

Duane grunted. In his estimation, anybody who attended a party and left sober had wasted an opportunity. "OK, Al, say she *was* murdered. Where's the motive? No assault, nothing stolen. You telling me the Half Moon Bay strangler was prowling the beach at two in the morning?"

"Maybe she was just unlucky - wrong place, wrong time."

Duane chewed on the toothpick thoughtfully. "Accidental witness, huh?"

"Right. And what's the favorite night work on these beaches?"

Duane had to admit that smuggling had been an honorable occupation on this coast for centuries. "Narcotics, you think?", he suggested cautiously.

"Maybe. It would have to be hard stuff. Can't see a homicide over a bale of grass."

"And now," Duane got in first, " you want to know who. Am I right?"

"It would help."

"When I find him I'll send a car right to your office."

"That's nice."

Duane finished his coffee. "Any more favors I can do you?"

"Who's the Medical Examiner?"

"Alberto Fermi. He does most of the autopsies around here."

"Is he straight?"

"As they come." Duane nodded to himself, approving this solid citizen, then went on: "His brother, mind you, he's a piece of crap." Duane sucked his teeth with relish. "Giorgio Fermi. second generation Italian. A couple of years younger than the Doc. Six three, 240 pounds, his main line of work is frightening people. Father has a small farm up in the hills, a decent family, mother very religious, but Giorgio was right out of diapers and into trouble.

Petty theft, then not so petty, cars mostly, he's car crazy, and always quick with the fists and boots. By the time he was 21 he was Half Moon Bay's answer to Don Corleone - pimping, dealing, breaking bones. So far as we know, he hasn't killed anybody yet but we figure he's working on it. He's slippery but we got him once and we'll get him again. We get them all sooner or later." Duane's tone was matter-of-fact. "1985. Highway Patrol clocked his Porsche at a hundred and fifteen." He breathed a long nostalgic sigh. "They put him away for three beautiful years...".

"For a speeding ticket?"

"Yeah, it turned out the owner didn't know Giorgio had borrowed the car."

"And now?"

"Last I heard, he was in business up in San Francisco, fancy place, more or less legit, selling imported cars, the kind the Chief would have if they doubled his salary. It keeps him in whores but he's a crook at heart. For sure he'll be up to something but we just haven't found out yet. Narcotics most likely."

"Could he have been on the beach?"

"I doubt it. Giorgio's vicious but not stupid. The prison rehab program taught him just one thing - make sure it's the hired help that gets caught. And her baby boy in prison near killed his mother."

Duane looked at his watch and stood up. "I'm out of time. Where next, Al?"

"I'm going to talk to the ME."

They parted in the square, agreeing to a private reunion over a rib dinner and beers when Al had finished his investigation. That would be in a week or two, Al guessed. A considerable underestimate, as it turned out.

CHAPTER 14

The office was a pleasant white and green clapboard house in a quiet cul-de-sac off Main Street. A crisply-painted board in the front garden read: Doctor Alberto Fermi, MD while a printed notice inside the glass panelled door gave his Business Hours: Tuesday and Thursday 9:30 a.m. - 12:30 p.m. and 2:00 p.m. - 5:00 p.m.

Pushing open the door, Al entered a rather fine Victorian residence, converted to double as a home and consulting rooms. The panelled hall had become a Reception, witness a hideous desk in rosewood formica, two orange leather armchairs drawn up to a hexagonal glass-topped table bearing a Wall Street Journal, a selection of glossy magazines calculated to interest well-heeled clients and a cheerful porcelain pot containing five symmetrically arranged silk lilies. A bottle of nail varnish stood open on the desk, its aggressive smell hovering in the air. Of the owner of the nails there was no sign. Behind the desk was a door marked Private. Al knocked and, not waiting for a reply, entered Fermi's consulting room, the sometime drawing room. It was a large and elegant room expensively but conservatively furnished, a surprise in view of the brash décor of the Reception. An antique desk was placed in a vast bow window which looked out onto a conservatory leading to a formal garden with a small pond and a fountain. The room was empty but Al heard a voice from the garden.

"Good boy! Fetch. Good boy!"

Knowing that it's better to discover than be discovered, Al moved swiftly across the room, through the conservatory and out into the garden.

On the lawn was a slightly built man whose dress, at some expense, had been contrived to look casual. As Al watched, he threw a ball, calling encouragement to a dog.

"Fetch it, boy!".

Al was no dog lover but even he could see that this was no ordinary dog. It was a tall, svelte but deep-chested hound with long elegant legs, a silken cream coat and a magnificent wand of a tail which it brandished excitedly as it ran. The man had his back to Al so the dog saw him first. As it scrambled to a halt, seizing the ball, it stopped in mid-stride, one front paw raised, delicate as a dowager with a teacup, and fixed him with a look he'd never seen from a dog, not threatening, not even hostile, simply superior. It made him feel what he was, an intruder.

"Doctor Fermi?" he asked.

The doctor turned sharply, hesitated. "Yes. Do you have an appointment? Where's Josie?"

"There was no one in Reception. My name is Hershey," said Al, offering a genuine card. "Fine dog. What breed?".

Begin with the easy questions, thought Al.

"What? Oh! He's a saluki," replied Fermi absently, studying Al's card. "Arabian gazelle-hound. Desert Arabs use them to hunt gazelle with falcons, in the er... desert."

Al wondered why he was talking too much and too fast.

"What do you want, Mr Hershey?"

"I understand you're the Medical Examiner for Half Moon Bay."

"One of them."

"And you recently carried out an autopsy on the body of a young Englishwoman called Megan Gilchrist."

The doctor hesitated then abruptly turned to the dog. "Come!"

The dog advanced warily, head down, eyes fixed on the intruder. Fermi reached down and took it by the collar, then turned back to Al. "What is your interest?"

"I've been retained by the family to enquire into the circumstances of her death."

Fermi frowned. "Circumstances? I don't understand. The verdict was accidental death. She was walking at night, slipped on the rocks, fell into the sea and drowned."

"You are aware that she was an excellent swimmer?"

"No, I did not know that. But my conclusion would have been the same. The strongest swimmers have drowned off this coast, Mr Hershey. The currents are strong and unpredictable."

"Were there any marks on the body?"

"Of course there were marks. The body had been in the water for some hours. Some bruising is inevitable in such circumstances."

"Bruising? So there was bruising? Where on the body exactly?"

"Several places."

"The arms, for instance?"

"Among other places, yes."

"Bruises consistent with a violent struggle?"

Fermi colored. "That's quite enough, Mr Hershey. I must ask you to leave."

"There's no need to raise your voice, doctor. I'm simply doing my job."

Fermi looked Al up and down, considered trying to eject him physically but decided against it. Instead, calling to the dog to follow, he strode past Al into the house and picked up the phone. "Either you leave at once or I'll call the police."

Al followed, a hand raised in a placatory gesture. "You won't need the police. I have all I need for the present."

At the door, he turned. "I should tell you, doctor, that Mr Gilchrist is a wealthy and exceptionally determined man. He is quite sure that his daughter did not die by accident. He will not let this drop."

Fermi had been following Al as though to escort him off the premises but Al's parting words stopped him as though he had been struck.

As he closed the consulting room door, Al saw that the receptionist was now at her post, complete with nail file and Olympic standard nails. Hearing Fermi's raised voice, she had swivelled her chair to have a better view.

She studied Al, nail file poised, piqued at this interruption to her duties. A natural blonde with a long, fine face and neck, cool, grey-green eyes and elegant legs, she sat as though posing for an office furniture catalogue, head very erect and shoulders pressed back emphasizing her breasts. Her legs were crossed extravagantly, the brief skirt hitched almost to invisibility. The 'Basic Instinct' pose, Al thought.

He paused at the desk. "Excitable man, the doctor."

"That depends."

"On what?"

"On what you ask him."

"What makes you think I asked him anything?"

"That's what people like you do. But he didn't help you much."

"Not much."

She swivelled the chair around, extracted a square of pale violet paper from a fluorescent green plastic holder on the desk and, glancing at a watch with too many jewels around it, wrote briefly but expensively with a gold pen.

"Then try me," she said ambiguously, passing him the note. She got up, adjusted what there was of the skirt, turned briskly and, looking every inch as good from the rear, went into the consulting room.

As he closed the front door, Al noticed that one of its glass panels had recently been replaced. In the street he read the note: Rod's Place 5:30. Screwdriver.

*   *   *

Al let the car drift along the almost empty road while he mulled over the encounter with Fermi. The doctor was worried. A five minute conversation with a total stranger seemed to have threatened his world. But why? He sure could use a few more facts. Well, collecting, interpreting and, when necessary inventing facts, that's the journalist's job. It was time to renew acquaintance with Tiny.

Tiny Larsen, Editor-in-Chief of the Half Moon Bay Review and Pescadero Pebble[10] – Serving the Entire San Mateo Coastline Since 1896 - was

[10] This name is used with kind permission of publisher, Debra Godshall.

proud to be known as the only teetotal, non-smoking editor in Northern California and spared no expense in maintaining his reputation. Al knew better than to call at the Review's office at lunchtime but headed up the Pacific Coast Highway to the Café Three-Zero[11] at the airport, the only place in the area which would put up with Tiny's idiosyncrasies, notably, running up huge bills, late but unfailingly paid, monopolizing space conventionally reserved for a party of four and treating the only phone as thought it were the Review's switchboard, and the proprietor his operator. In case this wasn't sufficient aggravation, Tiny had so violent an aversion to smokers that Café Three-Zero became a no-smoking zone as soon as he entered and remained so for the duration of his stay. Against any stranger unwise enough to breach this totally unauthorized embargo, Tiny would unleash a blistering verbal barrage which never failed to restore what in Tiny's world-view, constituted order.

Al paused in the doorway; gradually, like a slow fade-up in a theatre, a scene emerged from the gloom. Tiny was in his booth at the far end, head resting on his hands, his fingers entwined in the untidy mass of hair, greyed prematurely, he claimed, by the remorseless pressure of the job. The table was littered with editorial bric a brac: the Review's current edition, heavily annotated in thick blue pencil, a pink folder conspicuously marked 'Confidential', a child's pencil box with 'Snoopy' motif, overflowing with pens, pencils, elastic bands and other administrative trivia, an empty plate and, readily accessible, a huge mug of coffee with the motto 'Journalism largely consists in announcing 'Lord Jones Dead' to people who never knew he was alive.'

As he pored over these elemental constituents of his life's work, his face was lit by a fine brass desk lamp, Tiny's treasured personal possession which was kept, like some priceless relic, in the Three-Zero's back office to be brought out, on pain of incurring Tiny's extreme wrath, only when he himself arrived for one of his daily sessions of work and feasting.

As Al approached, Tiny looked up, already filling his lungs for an outburst. Notwithstanding that he chose to set up office in a public eating place, he

11 See http://www.3-zero.com/toppage11.htm for more information.

found interruptions irksome. Then a great glow of recognition spread across the craggy features.

"Al, my friend. Great to see you! And in such great health too," he boomed, and, pointing to the booth's other bench, added "Step into my office. Coffee?"

"Black." said Al.

"Mark! One editor's coffee," Tiny bellowed in the direction of the kitchen then turned back to Al with a knowing smile. "So... surprise me. You came down from the Bay for the pleasure of my company?"

"Not exactly, Tiny," Al said.

Tiny's tall, thin face was overdue a retread but the eyes were sharp and inquisitorial, sharpened by half a lifetime of scrutinizing doubtful people, potentially libelous stories and over-enthusiastic expense claims.

"Uh huh."

Tiny was seldom criticized for reticence, but as a good newsman, he knew when to keep his mouth shut.

"Do you remember a story about an English girl who was accidentally drowned?"

"Sure I remember her photograph. Very pretty girl. Left a Fourth of July party in the small hours to walk on the beach, body found next morning. Death was alcohol-assisted, no doubt."

Another one! Al bit back a sharp response. "Her parents believe her death was not accidental," he continued.

"Is that right?" His tone was non-committal but he was interested. An accidental death is an incident, anything else is a story.

"What can you tell me about the ME?", he asked.

"Doc Fermi? Oh, he's a good doctor. Folks like him."

"Including you?"

Tiny thought about that one. "I'm pleased I'm not married to him," he responded knowingly.

"So he's married?"

"He is when he's in San Francisco. Sicilian wife, two kids, nice apartment in the Bay. He has his other practice up there."

"And when he's down here?"

"He has a receptionist."

"You mean the blonde, Josie? I met her earlier."

"Ah! Well, she's the reason he's not married when he's in Half Moon Bay."

"Funny, I got the feeling they weren't best buddies."

"What gave you that idea? Last I heard, they were sharing a pillow."

"Nothing specific. Just something about the way she looked."

Tiny grinned knowingly. "Oh that! The special look she reserves for anything in pants."

Al recalled grey-green eyes appraising him, liking what they saw and showing it. He shook his head. "No, not that look. I mean the look she had when her boss's name came up. Kind of sour."

"So..." Tiny mused, "he's dumped her then. I wonder what brought that on."

"Maybe he traded her in for this year's model."

"There'd be a job for you on the Review if you got that story first," Tiny said, sceptically. "But why the interest?"

"Just routine."

Tiny could smell a story. "You know something," he accused.

Al ducked the question. "Give me what you have on Fermi."

Tiny didn't need to drive to the end of the street to recognize a dead-end. He sipped his coffee then twisted his face in disgust. "Mark! This coffee's cold. What's with the service here? I'm gonna take my business elsewhere."

Mark appeared from the kitchen carrying, as if by second sight, a pot of fresh coffee. He was in his late thirties, medium height, lean and sinewy. He wore glasses tinted an unusual shade of pink. "I should be so lucky." He grinned at Al.

Tiny made an introductory gesture. "Al, Mark. Short-order cook, amateur pilot and lifelong airport bum. Claims he owns the place."

Mark's thin hand gripped hard.

"How come you put up with this guy?" Al asked.

Mark grinned even wider. "I need the business. Besides, he keeps the riffraff out." He put the pot on the table. "Plenty more where that came from."

As he headed back to the kitchen he waved acknowledgement to the pilot of a scarlet biplane, a Pitts Special aerobatic plane, Al recognized, taxiing by the window.

Tiny paused to collect his thoughts then gave Al the Fermi family history, identical to Duane's version but with even more emphasis on Giorgio's relationship with his mother. In Tiny's version, she doted on the baby of the family and went deaf if anyone offered a bad word.

"How does he make his money?" Al asked.

"Officially? He imports European cars. The real money comes from the retail trade. White powder, hundred dollars a gram."

"So, if there's bad stuff happening on the beach, Giorgio's a good bet?"

"Not with my money he isn't. Smuggling's dangerous and unnecessary. The Colombians make the deliveries. Like I said, he's a retailer."

Hoping that both Tiny and Duane had it wrong, Al pressed on. "And with his brother taking care of the autopsy..."

Tiny frowned. "Damn it Al, you're speeding. The Doc an accessory to murder? Where's your evidence?"

"Don't be difficult, Tiny. I've got the conclusion - all I need is a little help with the proof."

Al waited, diplomatically sipping the ferociously strong coffee. Tiny heaved himself into a more upright position and laid his hands, fingers splayed, flat on the table.

"What's the deal?"

"A free run at everything I get."

"Done," he said gravely, and, as if in celebration, sank a great gulp of coffee. There was silence for a while.

"So..." said Al. "Where do I go next?"

Tiny thought for a moment. "Well, you could talk to the receptionist." He grinned lecherously. "Even if she won't tell you much, it might be a worthwhile experience."

Al nodded. "Already got the invitation."

Tiny raised his eyebrows but said nothing. They drank more coffee.

"Is that it?", Al asked.

"No, there's one more thing. Have a word with Fermi's..." he looked at Al oddly, "...assistant, name of Fuzzy. You'll probably find him on the jetty, fishing he calls it. Very tall, wears a green woollen hat."

"Fuzzy? That his real name?"

"No idea. You could ask him but I'd bet you won't."

Al shook Tiny's hand and extricated himself from the booth's confines. As he reached the door, Tiny's voice followed him, thundering along the rows of empty tables. "And go gently. Fuzzy bruises easily," he warned.

CHAPTER 15

Al headed south along the coast road. Although it was high summer, clouds hung heavy over the Pacific and the horizon was a blur of slate sea and cloud. The wind was brisk and on-shore, pushing the breakers ahead of it, flicking the wave-tops into foam. He slowed to watch a woman on the beach, well muffled in scarf and windbreaker, throwing pieces of driftwood for a dog. He noticed with a smile that the dog would retrieve the stick only as long as it stayed on the beach but nothing would persuade it to go into the sea. Looking at the water, Al figured he was watching a pretty smart dog.

A few hundred yards further on, he found the jetty and parked the Mustang. Tiny had implied that there would be no difficulty identifying Fuzzy and there wasn't. Even hunched almost double on his canvas stool, Fuzzy was clearly, immoderately tall. His oily brown hair was tied back in a pony tail. He wore tattered jeans shrunken to reveal skinny ankles, an antique oilskin jacket, once yellow, and on his head the promised green woollen hat with pom-pom. Standing erect he would resemble a giant lollipop. On a piece of string around his neck was what appeared to Al to be the remains of an octopus. He was fishing. That is to say, he was sitting next to a fishing rod propped on a stand with the line dangling feebly in the water. His jacket was open and his shirt buttons, assuming there were any, were unfastened almost to his waist. He might have been sitting there since time began. As Al approached, he was not surprised to see that Fuzzy had caught nothing - the whole set-up suggested that a catch would be a rarity.

"Hi there," he said as he came within earshot.

As a matter of professional courtesy, Al seldom surprised anyone unintentionally but Fuzzy's mind was elsewhere. He tried to look over his shoulder, twisted awkwardly, lost his balance and collapsed in a peculiar, slow motion fall, finishing up on his back with one leg tangled in the stool. Al smothered a laugh with difficulty and held out a hand. Fuzzy however, chose to ignore the offer of help which, given the maladroit squirming needed to extricate himself from the stool, was both churlish and ill-advised. When he finally got to his feet, he glared at Al angrily.

"Sorry," said Al, cursing himself. What a way to start an interview. "I didn't mean to startle you."

"You didn't startle me," Fuzzy spluttered, truculently.

This, thought Al, will be tough going. "My name's Al. Al Hershey. I'm a private investigator. I'm told you're a doctor. I need your help. Can I buy you a cup of coffee?"

The crude flattery worked better than Al could have hoped. Fuzzy's expression froze, then a slow smile of pleasure crept over his long thin features.

"And a donut?" he said. Given the skinny frame, his voice was remarkably deep and sonorous but his delivery was treacle-slow and carried so little inflection that, as Al was to discover, conversation quickly became tedious.

"Sure," said Al. All the donuts you can eat, he thought.

In difficult circumstances, the Waterfront Café was trying hard to be cheerful, with freshly painted exterior plus nearly new plastic everything. Al ordered coffee and donuts for both and began by mending fences repair to his approach. "How long have you been a doctor, Fuzzy?"

Behind eyes clouded with mental effort, Fuzzy groaned through the computations. "Six years," he said, at length. But Al could see that Fuzzy himself found this answer less than satisfactory. "Er, no, not six, 'cos Francine came after I'd started and she's been gone three years and then it was Mike. No, he was before. Next was Betsy and she was two years, no three years and now Josie who's been… er… so that makes five. Yes, that's it." His voice rose triumphantly. "I was wrong. It's six years. Six years I've been with Doctor Fermi."

Observing Fuzzy's tortured progress through this chain of illogic, Al now understood Tiny's hesitation when seeking a title for him. Fuzzy looked expectantly at Al, waiting for congratulations, but before Al could think of anything suitable, he spoke again. "He's a good man," he added, seriously. "A very nice man."

"Yes, I gather everybody hereabouts likes him," Al responded.

"He's very kind to Ahmed," Fuzzy added, mysteriously.

"Who's Ahmed?"

Fuzzy looked puzzled. "Who's Ahmed?" he repeated, carefully. "Ahmed's the dog. He's a very nice dog." He paused thoughtfully then added, as if by way of justification, "He doesn't bite."

A miserable looking waiter brought coffee in bright red plastic mugs and a plate of doughnuts. Al, struggling to find an interviewing technique appropriate to the situation, ignored the dog. "So, you help Doctor Fermi with his work?"

"Oh yes," said Fuzzy, enthusiastically. "I help Doctor Fermi with his work."

"What kind of things do you do for him?"

"Everything. I help with everything."

Al was about to elaborate the question when he realized that Fuzzy was still composing.

"I bring in the mail. I keep the place nice and clean. I fetch things for Doctor Fermi. But mostly I help with the dead people," he announced eventually seeming at once proud and troubled by this job description.

"You mean with post mortems," Al encouraged.

"Post mor-tems." Fuzzy repeated the words painstakingly. Then, proudly, "Yes. I help Doctor Fermi with post mor-tems."

"So you helped him with the young English girl? The one who was drowned?"

Fuzzy looked mystified. "Drowned," he mused, as though unfamiliar with the word. "Drowned," he said again, his jaw working convulsively.

"Yes, drowned. She'd been walking on the beach at night and she was drowned," said Al, patiently.

Fuzzy was suddenly enthusiastic. "English girl," he exclaimed. "I remember her. Margaret. She was very beautiful. She had beautiful brown eyes," he added, now overcome with sadness.

"That's right, Fuzzy," Al heard himself speaking like a teacher encouraging a child struggling with the alphabet. "But her name was Megan. Megan Gilchrist."

Fuzzy took a drink of coffee, then spluttered and grimaced. "It's got no sugar in," he complained. Al gently pushed the bowl across the table, turning it around so that the spoon faced him. "So how did the post mortem go?"

Fuzzy studiously measured four spoonfuls of sugar into his coffee and began stirring it slowly, clearly unable to continue speaking while this was going on. After at least a full minute's stirring, he carefully placed his wet spoon in the sugar bowl then, with evident and noisy satisfaction, took a long slow drink. He put down his cup, dragged out a donut from the bottom of the pile, took a large bite and looked at Al. His face was perfectly blank; he obviously had no recollection of the question.

"How did the post mortem go?" Al repeated, evenly.

"Go?" Fuzzy frowned. "Where?"

"I mean, what did you and Doctor Fermi find when you did the post mortem on Megan?" Al explained, then to cut off Fuzzy's imminent question, "Margaret, I mean."

"I don't know," said Fuzzy regretfully. "I wasn't there."

"But I thought Doctor Fermi always needed you at post mortems."

Fuzzy could see there was a problem and he assumed a serious expression. "Yes. He always needed me..."

"But not this time. Not for Margaret?"

"Not for Margaret," Fuzzy repeated woodenly.

"Why not, Fuzzy? Were you sick? On vacation maybe?"

"I never get sick," he said firmly. "Only that time when I fell off the jetty into Tom's boat. I had to go to the hospital. The nurses were very kind. They said I was an ex-treme-ly for-tun-ate young man. I might have been killed." Fuzzy looked upset at this thought but recovered quickly, adding happily. "Only I wasn't."

Al took a deep breath. "So why did you not help with Margaret?"

Fuzzy was suddenly agitated. He paused with a chocolate donut half way to his mouth. "Because he sent me away."

"Doctor Fermi sent you away? Away where?"

"He sent me to Grandma Humboldt's house. It's a long way." he added, pointing vaguely over Al's shoulder.

"And what did he ask you to do there?"

"He told me to tell her she should come see him."

"And did you?" asked Al. "Give Grandma Humboldt the message I mean?" he added hastily.

"No. She wasn't in. I knew she wouldn't be in. She always goes to see Mickey, Monday afternoons. He's her son. Everybody knows that."

"Did Doctor Fermi know that too?"

"Oh sure. Everybody knows."

"So how come he sent you to see her if he knew she would be out?" Al spelt out carefully, but he knew the answer already.

"I asked him that when I got back." Even now Fuzzy sounded aggrieved.

"And what did he say?"

"He got upset. I can tell when he's upset, his face gets red. He told me not to ask stupid questions. But it wasn't a stupid question, was it?" Fuzzy asked anxiously.

Al said "no, it wasn't a stupid question". Actually, he thought, it was an excellent question. "Have you told anybody else about this?"

Fuzzy's incomprehension was painful. Al waited. At last Fuzzy, smiling roguishly, wagged a long index finger at Al. "That's a trick," he accused. "Doctor Fermi told me. We're in a priv-il-eg-ed pos-it-ion. We never talk about doctors' things. So I don't." He paused for a few seconds. "Anyway, people mostly never talk to me about anything. They cross the street when they see me coming. They think I don't know but I do." His face crumpled and his old man's eyes slowly filled with tears.

As Al drove off, he watched Fuzzy in the mirror, standing at the door of the café energetically waving one skeletal arm above his head in a farewell gesture more appropriate to the departure of a close relative. He kept on waving for as long as Al could see him. Tiny was right, thought Al, he does indeed bruise easily, and often, by the look of him.

*   *   *

Above Smugglers Beach, the parking lot was empty apart from a desolate looking camper van. Al left the Mustang and picked his way down to the deserted stretch of lichen-covered rock and coarse sand where Meg's body had been found.

The walk took him fifty yards through a steep-sided gully, just wide enough for a vehicle but rock-strewn and deeply rutted, Al noted.

At the foot of the gully he stood watching the three foot waves breaking hard on the gently shelving shore. Al knew something about boats and it seemed to him that bringing a small craft in to this beach would be a risky business. Then he remembered that according to the weather report for the night of the fourth, which Mrs Hershey had thought to check, conditions had been ideal, a light wind and a wave height of under one foot.

He retraced his steps slowly, hoping against the odds to see something – a tire mark, a paint scrape on a projecting rock – but was not surprised to find nothing. As he jotted in his notebook, he consoled himself with the thought that such proper attention to procedure would keep him in good standing with his wife.

On his way back north he called at a place he'd known that had served decent food, only to find it transformed into a drive-thru burger joint. Disgruntled, he skipped lunch, which annoyed him even more and would have upset Mrs Hershey, too, had she known. Instead, he set off to renew his acquaintance with Skyline Drive and the hills inland of Half Moon Bay. He took his time but still found himself back in town too soon for the 5:30 appointment.

He made a pass to the far end of Main Street returning via the coast road. Both were almost deserted. The Waterfront Café was still there, as fresh and as empty as when he and Fuzzy had entered it. Fuzzy had gone but oddly his stool and bag were still in place. Al wondered if Fuzzy ever took them home and for that matter, where, even what, his home was. One more circuit and he was downtown by 4:15. He decided Rod's was as good as any other place to kill the rest of the time and by 4:30 he was sitting in the semi-darkness of the bar toying with a scotch he'd bought to rent some space, updating his notes, trying to think. He preferred conversation to introspection and waiting was the part of the job he liked least. On the other hand he reflected stoically, he'd had damned sight worse experiences than framing the world in the bottom of a tumbler while waiting for a beautiful woman.

CHAPTER 16

At 5:35 the door swung open. Josie paused in the doorway, her figure framed in the light from the street. At a nod from Al, the bartender threw ice into a glass and reached for the vodka. As the early evening drinkers became aware of her presence, a wave of silence rolled down the twin rows of booths. Only when it was complete did she allow the door to close. Al watched her as she swayed down the aisle to his table; a bravura entrance, he thought and felt like applauding. She gave the impression she could have done it naked with no less aplomb. He enjoyed the admiring stares as she sat down opposite him. As the murmur of conversation resumed, the bartender arrived with the screwdriver and a refill for Al.

"Your cocktail, Miss," he said, staring greedily at Josie and enviously at Al.

Josie dismissed him with a nod, took the drink and sipped it expertly.

Al waited. Between the army and private investigating, he'd had a lot of practice waiting. But Josie was in no hurry and the screwdriver was three-quarters gone before she spoke.

"He really is an asshole."

Al had been expecting verbal preliminaries, so her words and the quiet bitterness of her tone surprised him. He wondered what Fermi had done to justify it and guessed he was about to find out. First, more waiting. She finished the drink, putting down the glass pointedly. He ordered another and it, too, was half gone before she went on.

"I came down to this dump at two o'clock one wet Monday in April last year. I'd seen his ad in the Examiner. It was lust at first sight. He interviewed me all afternoon and screwed me all night. I didn't even go back, just closed up my apartment in San Francisco, sold most of my stuff and moved in. He was Mr Wonderful, intelligent, thoughtful, sensational in bed, and generous."

She pulled back the sleeve of her jacket to show Al the watch he'd noticed as she wrote the note. "Five thousand dollars," she said, savagely. "We were living in never-never land, the perfect couple except when he was up in town with his wife. Then one day, it was over a lunch - I'd thought it was odd, a sudden lunch invitation - he's not like that normally, not impulsive, he's careful, a planner. That's why he's so good at his work. Anyway, over dessert he just says it, straight out. It's finished, Josie. Bang. Just like that. At first..."

"Just a minute. Can you remember the date?" Al interrupted.

"I can tell you exactly. It was the first weekend he'd managed to get away from his wife for months – four weeks ago yesterday - sixth of July." She raised her glass in a toast. "Happy anniversary."

"Cheers," Al responded. "You were saying..."

Josie hesitated.

"At first...", Al prompted.

"Oh yes. At first I didn't know what he meant. I couldn't believe he was talking about us. Then I realized he was. And it wasn't a joke. I remember thinking of things they do in the movies. You've seen them, tipping a drink in his lap, saying something really smart or shouting obscenities then walking out, very dignified. But I couldn't do any of that. I just sat there with a plateful of cheesecake in front of me, thinking I might throw up and how I'd never seen any leading lady do that. I moved out of the love nest that day."

She finished her drink. Al made to speak but Josie got there first.

"So how come I'm still working there? Because I can't bear the thought of leaving. You're looking at Old Man River - tired o' livin', scared o' dyin'. He can't stand having me around but he hasn't figured out how to fire me. I can see it in his eyes. It's not that he hasn't got the balls, it's just that he hasn't managed to work out a plan... yet. He will, one day, and that'll be it. Finito. Maybe when he finds out I've been talking to you..." She stopped, hunched over, clutching her empty glass, suddenly pathetic. Al ordered her another which the bartender produced instantly. It seemed that when Josie was in town he kept screwdrivers ready-made.

"And what will you do then?" Al asked, as gently as he could.

"Do? Same as always - the next thing. New job, new town, new man... Have you ever been to New York?"

Al shook his head. He had, of course, but this was an invitation not a question. Josie shrugged. With an effort she sat up, put the half-finished drink aside and smiled a thin smile. "So how can I help you?"

Al smiled back and made his pitch. "I'm enquiring into the death of a young Englishwoman called Gilchrist, Megan Gilchrist. She was drowned here in Half Moon Bay last month."

"You are? Why?"

"Insurance. I've been hired by her insurers to investigate the circumstances of her death."

She looked at him hard. "Bullshit," she said, evenly.

Al sighed inwardly. Why is it, he asked himself, that everyone involved in this case is either dumb as a rock or smarter than Nixon's lawyer.

"OK. I'm working for someone who has a close interest in the girl's death."

"Who?"

"I can't tell you that."

Josie tilted her head in a gesture of acknowledgement. "None of my business. What did Alberto tell you?"

"Zilch. But he didn't much enjoy my asking and it's my guess he's up to something."

"Like what?"

"I'm hoping you can tell me."

She shrugged. "If Alberto is up to something then you can bet his brother is mixed up in it."

"Giorgio?"

"Ah, you've heard about Giorgio."

"I keep on hearing, none of it good."

Josie drank the rest of her cocktail in one swallow. She looked angry and frightened. Al caught the bartender's eye. He figured if Josie was as good at her job as she was at drinking vodka she'd be one hell of an asset.

"Well if you want good, I can't help. He's a fat, greasy, vicious low-life who gets off on hurting people. Alberto can't stand him. They hardly ever see each other; just as well, there's a argument every time they do."

"You're saying they're mixed up in something?"

"No I'm not. All I do know is that a few weeks ago Giorgio stopped by the house in the middle of the night. There was the most God awful argument."

"The night of the Fourth of July?", Al ventured.

She looked surprised. "Yes it was. How did you..."

"Not important. Go on. There was an argument."

Josie wasn't happy with this answer but she could see it was all she was going to get. "I could hear them from upstairs. I don't scare easily but I was scared that night. I thought he might hurt Alberto. I was on my way downstairs when I heard the front door slam so hard the glass broke."

When the bartender brought Josie's refill he almost tripped over himself as he peered down her cleavage. She chose not to notice.

"Could you make out any of the conversation?"

"Not really. Only what Giorgio shouted as he was leaving, 'that whore upstairs' and then something about 'it'll be your fault if she dies'."

"Did you know what that was all about?"

"I guess the whore upstairs was me..."

"'If she dies' - if who dies?"

Josie shrugged. "The mother, I imagine. She has a heart condition."

Josie was drinking vodka as if it were club soda.

"He dumped me the next day. It must have had something to do with his brother's visit but I can't get him to talk to me. And he's so miserable all the time."

Her teeth clenched in fury. "I'd like to strangle him."

Al took it she meant Giorgio.

"Tell me about him."

"I told you, he's a bastard. What more is there?"

"How long have you known him?"

"I first met him a few months ago in an Italian restaurant in Washington Square. We were having a quiet dinner and Giorgio came in with a redhead. She looked like something he'd just scooped up off the street. He came over to our table and he and Alberto went through all that Italian business, hugging each other, then everybody got introduced but Alberto didn't invite him to join us. After they'd gone to their own table, Alberto got the bill and we left. We hadn't even finished eating. I started to complain but he got really angry, not just angry, upset too. I couldn't get him to explain..." she trailed off. The vodka was beginning to play tricks with her concentration. "Oh, there was something funny... Alberto said something about his brother never needing to pay."

"For the meal?"

"Yes. I figured maybe he owned the place or something."

Or something, Al guessed.

Noisily, she took in more vodka. Al could see her grip on reality loosening by the minute but before he could continue she came over all kittenish.

"Are you married or anything?"

She was slurring her words a little. Al sighed inwardly. He knew this routine too well.

"Married. And my wife will give me hell if I screw up this job."

"Yeah. I was married once..." her brow furrowed in concentration. "Did I tell you that already? He didn't need a reason. He just gave me hell because he enjoyed it. He was a pig."

Josie sipped her drink wearily. "OK." She shrugged off bad memories. "What else do you need?"

"Autopsy reports."

"What about them?"

Before Al could ask the next question he saw that Josie's attention had been diverted to something behind him. Looking over his shoulder he saw, navigating down the aisle towards them, a bulky, middle-aged man wearing a blue and purple checked shirt and jeans clamped too tightly around his protruding belly by a broad leather belt, with a buckle the size of a saucer depicting crossed rifles and the flag of the Confederacy. He was perfectly bald and his eyes loomed threateningly through thick glasses. From the studied style of his walk, the whiskey in his hand was not his first of the evening. He drew up at their table, swaying gently and put a heavy hand on Al's shoulder to steady himself. Blinking rapidly, he gave Josie what he imagined was a winning smile.

"Hi, Miss Clayton. You don't know me but I'm a big fan. I've been to all your concerts. I think you're just terrific. Would you mind..."

He fumbled in his hip pocket, pulled out a wallet and dropped it. Mumbling something about an autograph and holding firmly onto the table he doubled over with unexpected agility, recovered the errant wallet and, clearly unwilling to release his grip on the glass for even an instant, began a fumbling attempt to take something from it with one hand. Josie decided the pantomime had gone far enough.

"You've made a mistake. My name isn't Clayton." Her slight wooziness had vanished.

Check-shirt looked puzzled, then disbelieving. "Aw, honey! Don't give me that. I seen ya a million times. An' I got all your albums. Just a teensy-weensy autograph for your top fan. Come on, sweetheart!"

Al stood up and took a firm grip on check-shirt's shoulder. "Look, you heard what the lady said. You made a mistake. Let's don't make it an argument, OK?"

Check-shirt's face reddened dangerously. He turned to face Al, squared up to him and for a perilous few seconds stared blearily into his face, weighing up his chances. Then a deep instinct for self-preservation overcame him. He stepped back, threw up his hands in exaggerated friendliness, splashing a good measure of whiskey over himself in the process. "OK, buddy. Sorry. My mistake. No harm done, eh?"

He patted Al on the arm soothingly, turned a puzzled look on Josie, mumbled: "You sure as hell look like her though. Damned if you don't."

He wandered unhappily away, heading in exactly the wrong direction until a large man with a huge bushy beard, slightly less drunk, wobbled across to rescue him.

"It happens," Josie said. "I do look like her, some."

Al doggedly returned to his questions. "I was asking about autopsy reports. Do you do the typing?"

But Josie's mind was still with check-shirt. "You'd have hurt him, wouldn't you?" she said.

"Maybe."

"You're good at it, aren't you? Hurting people."

Al could see Josie found violence exciting. He'd seen it in women often before, had even exploited it with enthusiasm when he was young, but now he found it repellent.

"When I have to be, yes. The government trained me for it," said Al patiently but keeping his voice level. "Can we go on?"

She smiled ruefully. "Sure. What was the question?"

"About autopsy reports. I asked whether you do the typing?"

A real smile this time. "Well, Fuzzy sure doesn't."

Al smiled back encouragingly, pleased to see her looking less miserable.

"I do some of them. Alberto dictates into the tape system at the morgue. Sometimes the office there types them."

"Did you type the report on the Gilchrist girl?"

"Yes."

"How come you're so sure? There must be quite a few."

"There are. But I remembered that one, maybe because she was English, the name..."

"Did anything strike you as odd? About the report."

She looked puzzled. "Odd? Odd how?"

"Anything unusual? Different from the normal run?"

She frowned. "No. Can't think of anything."

Al was about to speak.

"Wait a minute. There was one odd thing. Alberto did it alone."

"How do you know that?"

"Alberto always adds a note of those present. I told you, he's very careful. There would usually be a couple of others present - somebody from the DA's office and Fuzzy. Fuzzy was always there - God knows why. I'd have thought he'd be a damned nuisance. But he always was, except that one time."

"Why not? Where was he?"

"He'd gone out somewhere. An errand for Alberto I think. I remember he was pretty upset when he got back. Fuzzy, that is. I didn't take any notice." She spread her hands expressively. "You don't with Fuzzy."

Al said that he could see how you wouldn't. "And the DA's man?"

"He wasn't there either."

"Unusual?"

"Depends. If it's just a straightforward thing - some old man with a history of heart problems drops dead - they might not bother. But a drowning, and such a young woman, I'd have expected someone to be there."

"But you have no idea why no one was there that time?"

"None at all. Sorry." Suddenly she drained her glass. "Look, if that's all, I have to go. I have a date with my masseur. Thanks for the drinks and the company."

"You've been very helpful. If you think of anything else or if anyone hassles you on account we talked, call me. OK?"

He handed her his business card. She put it into her purse, drained the dregs of the last screwdriver and slipped gracefully out of the bench seat.

"This... what you're doing...", she was looking anxiously down at him, "it won't mean trouble for Alberto, will it?"

"Only if he's been bending the rules."

She looked hard into his face, an unsubtle look he knew well. Her exit, as her entrance, was to the silent admiration of Rod's male clientele. As the bar conversation resumed, Al sat, leafing through his notes, pondering Josie's information and, if he were honest, Josie herself.

CHAPTER 17

They were standing by his car, three of them. Al saw them as soon as he turned the corner to the narrow street where he'd parked. He took a deep breath but was careful not to slacken stride. Check-shirt was lounging against the driver's door. On the sidewalk stood his two buddies, hands on hips, trying to look tough but Al could see they were conscripts, not volunteers; check-shirt had shamed or bullied them into it.

He kept walking, heading straight towards check-shirt, neither hurrying nor hesitating, with Jay's voice sounding in his mind. Jay, short for Jumbo - Al had never known his real name - had been Al's unarmed combat instructor when he first joined the Tunnel Rats. Apart from his martial arts skills, Jay was best remembered by his students for his teaching methods. To open his first lesson he conveyed his view of the army's training methods by tearing in half a copy of the inch-thick manual with no apparent effort.

It was not until much later, when Al also had made Sergeant, that during a drinking bout of Herculean proportions, Jay revealed that the manual had been baked in a slow oven until, as Jay put it, his granny could have torn it. But, tricks or no tricks, by a combination of a maniacal fitness regime and diligent training in the brutal arts, Jay saved lives, Al's included. He could hear the gentle, insistent voice like a tape-recording in his brain.

"Lesson one: the soft answer turneth away wrath," Jay had announced solemnly to an incredulous class at the start of their first session. Despite or maybe because of his strength and skill, Jay held to the Zen principle that the best way to win a battle is not to fight it.

Check-shirt's face was flushed and his eyes were blood-shot. Al decided against the soft answer.

"Lesson two: Divide and conquer. Three guys is hard work. One guy three times is easy."

Al felt he could probably handle these three simultaneously if he had to, but not without taking a few himself and Mrs Hershey preferred him not to return home looking like he'd fallen off a train. Also, the Half Moon Bay police didn't like civilians beating on each other in their town so it would be better if he could make it clean and quick. Fortunately, they were making it easy. The two guys on the sidewalk were big but they were much too far away. Novices, thought Al. They think they're going to wade in once the fight starts. He made one last sweep of the area to be certain there was nobody else waiting to join in. As he covered the last few yards he turned his mind to the details. Now he was just a couple of yards from check-shirt and, as expected, the conscripts were still comfortably out of range of the action. He stopped.

"Lesson three: Don't get mad. Get the other guy mad."

He fixed his gaze on check-shirt's face and spoke without raising his voice.

"Listen fatso. You're a big guy but you take too much booze and not enough exercise. I'm trained for this stuff. Why don't you just get the fuck away from my car so I don't have to mess up your shirt?"

A careful observer, seeing the tension of Al's body contrasting with his expressionless mask of concentration, might have warned check-shirt, as one would warn a child poking a snake with a stick, but check-shirt was reacting, not observing. He gave a grunt of anger and lunged forward, not swinging as Al had anticipated, but with arms extended, intent on getting Al in a bear hug. Given the man's upper body strength, Al figured this would not be a comfortable place to be but avoiding it was not difficult.

"Lesson four: In war, kill if you can; in peace, kill if you must."

At the last split-second he side-stepped and as his opponent lumbered past off-balance, he spun on his toes driving an elbow into the back of check-shirt's ribs. The impact made a surprisingly loud noise. Check-shirt fell heavily, face first, without a sound. Blood began pouring from his nose and mouth. In the same movement, Al recovered his balance and turned towards the other two.

They had started around the front of the car but, seeing the ferocity of Al's attack and its horrific results, they stopped like cartoon figures, almost tripping over themselves. He took a threatening step towards them but he knew it wasn't necessary. The bearded one held up a hand:

"Hey,mister. We got no beef with you. It was Chuck. He's OK mostly but when he hits the booze".

His voice trailed off as he watched with horror the blood slowly spreading from his friend's inert form.

"Then why don't you just pick him up and clear out? He needs a doctor."

"Sure, sure. OK, mister."

"Final Lesson: When it's over, watch the dead guys. There's plenty got it from dead guys who came alive sudden."

His eyes on the trio, Al backed to his car, got in, reversed clear and drove off. The last thing he saw in the mirror was check-shirt's friends still standing in operatic pose over their leader.

A mile down the road he stopped, locked the car doors and cracked the driver's window open. His heart was racing and his mouth was dry. He scrabbled in the door pocket, retrieved a can of Coke and took a series of mouthfuls interspersed with slow deep breaths. The feeling was always the same, a buzz of professional satisfaction allied to disgust at the futility of it. He found it hard to believe now, but when he'd left the service he really had thought that he'd done with violence. Check-shirt would suffer for a long time. And why? In the bar he'd had the sense to quit while only his ego was hurt. He'd sensed that Al was better left alone. But in the street, a few more drinks later and with odds of three to one, caution had been swept away by alcohol and a lot of misplaced confidence in numbers.

CHAPTER 18

Al shivered. Through the Mustang's screen, sea, cliffs and sky shimmered and merged in the early Pacific mist. He took out his notebook and made a heading for the coming meeting: 5 a.m. July 21st, cliff-top parking lot, 'The Distillery' restaurant, two miles north of Half Moon Bay.

The restaurant claimed to be haunted, *'Home of the Mysterious Woman in Blue'*.[12] Peering into the murk, Al thought it probably was. He sat gratefully drinking Mrs Hershey's coffee and waited. She'd got up with him as she always did, whatever the hour. He leaned back against the head rest and thought of the contrast between his present life and the time with Holly, of their final desperate months together, lives slipping out of synch, as she slept deeper into the day and drank later into the night. He'd been hitting it pretty hard himself until the day the janitor had found Holly curled in a drunken ball at the foot of the stairs and carried her to their apartment. When Al arrived home he had found her, the ghost of Christmas yet to come, face down on the floor by the bed in a pool of vomit. It had brought him up short.

In the billowing mist the car seemed suspended in a void. Through a slightly open window - a jungle fighter fears ambush more than anything – over the cries of gulls and the pounding of breakers on the beach below, he felt, rather than heard, a muffled vibration. He tilted his head towards the window and listened, concentrating hard as the source came nearer, emerging gradually as the characteristic beat of helicopter rotors. It would be headed for the satellite tracking station up on Pillar Point. He recognized a Huey, the Jeep of Vietnam...

"Al Hershey?"

The voice came from right outside the passenger door. Damn it, he thought, so much for combat awareness.

[12] See http://www.mossbeachdistillery.com/ghost.html

"Yeah, that's me. Jump in."

Al unlocked the door and Jim slid into the passenger seat.

"Do we talk here or someplace else?" Al asked.

"Here's just fine. Anything in the thermos?"

Al passed it over; Jim drained it in a couple of gulps.

"Thanks." He peered into the rear of the car as though expecting to see someone hiding there. "I don't have much time."

"Where's your car?" Al asked.

Jim looked puzzled. "My car? It's parked in Half Moon Bay. Why?"

"So how did you get here?"

Jim smiled a little. "Oh! I see. Boat. I always use the boat if I can."

Now Al was puzzled. "And you climbed the cliff? It looks sheer."

"It is. But there's a path. Old smugglers' route." He gestured at the mist. "Boat's anchored off shore. I used the dinghy to get to the beach." The worried look again. "Can we get right on with this? I'm not comfortable on land just now."

Al nodded. "I understand. Thanks for getting in touch." He took up his notebook and waited.

For a moment Jim hesitated. He looked blank, as though he'd forgotten why he was there. Then a terrible blackness settled on him and suddenly he was older and weary.

"I knew from the start I shouldn't have gotten involved." He sounded resigned, a man come to terms with his own weakness. "But it was $5,000 cash for a couple of hours work. And I figured if I didn't do it, one of the fishermen would. They've all got two jobs minimum. Who makes a living from fishing in Half Moon Bay? And who gets hurt?" He laughed, a choking, humorless noise, at the irony of it. "Well I found out who got hurt!"

Jim's head was sunk onto his chest. For a long time he said nothing then slowly he turned to look at Al. His face was pinched, his lips thin and white. Al had seen the expression before, but never since Vietnam. It was the outward sign of the corrosive anger of a man with nothing left to lose. When Jim finally spoke his voice was expressionless.

"There were two of them on the beach. It would be the big one who did it. When the fuss dies down, I'll find him and kill him."

Al had heard a lot of threats in his life, in and out of the service, more than a few directed at him. They were mostly meaningless but not this one; if Jim did find the big man, one of them would die. "Tell me the whole story, Jim. I need to know everything."

"Sure, I understand. I rang Geoff. He told me Meg's father hired you to investigate her death. Whatever the coroner said, all that legal crap, it wasn't an accident. And I'll help all I can." He spread his hands expressively. "That's why I'm here." He paused to collect his thoughts, took a deep breath. "It was the second of July. I got a call on the cell phone. A man, at least I'm pretty sure it was a man."

Al raised an enquiring eyebrow.

"He was using a device to distort his voice. You know?"

Al nodded.

"He said if I wanted an evening's work, well paid, no risk, to call him in an hour from a payphone. Then he gave me a number and hung up." He sighed. "And that's when I made my first mistake."

"You called him?"

"I called him. I still can't figure out how I could be so dumb."

Al reckoned never to argue with a man telling you he's no good. "So, you called?"

"Sure I called, and the deal was simple. Pick up a package off shore and drop it on the beach. Two and a half thousand up front, same again when the job was done. No questions, no names, tell nobody. He didn't say what would happen if I did tell anybody but it didn't sound like I'd win a cigar. I said I needed to think about it but he said it had to be yes or no right then."

"And it was 'yes'?"

Jim nodded.

"And then?"

"The last thing he said was 'Go straight back to your boat' and hung up. It took me less than half an hour but when I got back there was a holdall in the cabin with the down-payment, a box of electronics and a page of instructions."

"'Straight back'. So they knew you'd come from the boat," Al mused.

"Yeah, I noticed that. They must have been watching."

"And somebody was waiting to make the delivery."

"Right."

So they were pretty confident Jim would accept, Al noted.

"Anyway, the box was a custom built radio transmitter-receiver. I was to steer to a point two and a half miles off the coast then switch it on. The box does two things – first it triggers an explosive charge to detach a sink-weight so the package floats to the surface, then it starts scanning, listening for a signal from the package to home in on. Neat, or what?"

Despite everything, the engineer in Jim just had to admire this effectively perfect scheme of concealment; short of blind luck or prior knowledge, discovery of the package without the radio would be impossible.

"And then what?"

"Well, the instruction said to throw the radio overboard as soon as I'd made the pick-up."

Damn, Al thought. He'd been hoping for some help from an examination of that radio. He tried anyway. "Any manufacturer's name, model number…?"

Jim shook his head. "Not a thing on the exterior, so I figured if I had to junk the thing, at least I'd take a good look at it, so I opened up the box."

"You opened it up?" Al, who left technical matters like programming VCRs to Mrs Hershey, was incredulous.

"Sure. The day it was delivered. My course included a semester on hardware – it's no big thing if you know the trick."

"And?" Al said.

"No markings."

Al's incredulity shifted to puzzlement. "You expected markings?"

"Of course. Most electronic components have some kind of manufacturer's identification code but in that baby everything had been scraped off or painted over. It would have taken hours just to do that."

"So whoever built it really didn't want it traced?"

"That's right."

Al wrote 'METICULOUS!!' in his notes. After a moment's thought, he underlined it. "Is there anybody around here could do that kind of work?"

"Not as far as I know... well, I guess maybe some guy in Stanford or Berkeley..."

Al wrote 'Try Colleges.' "And this was all supposed to happen on the fourth?"

"That's right, at midnight."

"And you weren't contacted until the second?"

Jim had seen the point. "Last minute, huh? After all that planning. I can't understand it either. Anyway, that wasn't my problem. I guess they chose the fourth because the whole of Half Moon Bay turns out for the celebrations and every cop in the county is tied up directing traffic and trying to stop the drunks from killing each other. It was bad news for me though. I'd agreed with Meg to go to Geoff's party - he has a big bash every year at the beach-house. But I figured I could still get to the party not too long after midnight and anyhow I wasn't about to request a postponement. So I figured to set off about eleven, make the pick-up and delivery by midnight, then it's only a few minutes to Geoff's mooring."

He laughed grimly. "Hell, I'm an engineer; I should've known. The damned motor wouldn't start. Just a flat battery but it took me an hour to go find a guy I know in Pacifica and borrow a spare so it's after midnight before I even cast off." He heaved the 'if only' sigh Al knew from screwed-up operations in Vietnam. "Anyway, I get to the pick-up point, the radio does the job, I grab the package and I'm at the beach by one o'clock. Two guys are waiting with a four wheel drive – a Jeep, light colored. The big guy, who acts like the boss, balls me out for being late, the little guy takes the package and hands me an envelope and I hit the throttle and make a run for the party."

"But you were too late."

Jim nodded heavily. "Helen said Meg had gone for a walk on the beach so I took off to try to find her."

"And did you?"

Jim shook his head sadly. "Well, there was only moonlight and I didn't know which direction she'd gone…". He shrugged helplessly. "After maybe twenty minutes I quit looking, sailed up to Half Moon Bay harbor, left the boat and drove home."

"When did you find out what had happened to her?"

"Next morning. I was having breakfast when I heard it on the radio. I couldn't take it in. I just took off, - ran away, I guess - in the boat, north, past Golden Gate to where the coast gets really wild and there's nobody around. Next day I moored her in a quiet creek I know and walked into Bodega Bay. The TV said she'd been accidentally drowned while night swimming off Half Moon Bay during an all-night party. It made it sound like she was smashed for Christ's sake!"

"Makes a better story," Al said, packing the flask into its case, giving Jim time before he went on. "OK, Jim, I'm nearly through. Can you describe the package?"

"It was about a couple of feet cube, wrapped up tight in black waterproof material."

"Heavy?"

"Heavy enough – it was a heave to get it on board."

"Any markings?"

"I didn't see any."

"What did you think was in it?"

Jim scratched his head. "I've lost a lot of sleep over that one. Drugs would be the obvious – that much heroin would be worth a stack of bills."

"But?"

Jim shook his head firmly. "The cartels have their own transport department. They don't drop out of the sky on an amateur like me for one shipment."

True enough, Al thought. Unless somebody's plans had got screwed and Jim had been the last-minute solution.

"So, if not drugs then what?"

"I don't have the vaguest notion, sorry. I guess it would help a lot to know?"

"Probably, but don't sweat it. Tell me about the second man."

"Oh, he's around five six, solid, bodybuilder's shoulders. Blond hair, cropped like a marine. And stupid."

"Stupid?"

"Yeah, his eyes, you know... Vacant Lot signs."

"You could see his eyes?"

"Sure. I put my spotlight on so I could see the beach. The big guy nearly exploded so I killed it fast. But I'd seen enough."

Indeed you had, Al thought, which was why you did it. You just weren't comfortable working with anonymous silhouettes.

"Did they use any names?, Al asked, without hope.

Jim shook his head.

"Something puzzles me. Why you? With so many fishermen around?"

"The problem was that transceiver. It had to be somebody who wouldn't get panicked by the radio."

"Don't the fishermen have radios?"

"Sure they do, but it's just 'press to talk' engineering and they've been practicing for twenty years. You don't need to be Phi Beta Kappa to catch fish. If it's not silver and slippery, they panic."

Recalling Mrs Hershey's attempts to teach him to use the word processor, Al knew the feeling. "Do people round here know you're an engineer?"

"You bet they do! When you're freelancing you don't keep your résumé a secret."

Jim looked at his watch. "Are we all through?" He cast an anxious look around the car. "Sorry... but you know how it is." He was shaping up to leave.

"Yes I do. But do you know how it is?"

"What does that mean?"

"Jim, look at it from the DA's viewpoint. A girl dies a violent death. The coroner decides it's accidental but her parents are making a fuss. Her new boyfriend, at the very least a material witness, disappears the next day and he's still missing. What would you think?"

Jim nodded slowly. "Yeah. I can see it must look bad but…" he looked despairingly at Al. "I loved her, Mr Hershey. You can't think…".

"What I think doesn't matter."

"It matters to me."

"Geoff Hughes doesn't think you did it."

Jim made to speak but Al silenced him with a raised hand. "Why don't you just come forward and put yourself on the right side of the law here?"

"I mean to, truly I do. But I'm hoping you'll sort things out first."

Jim climbed out of the car then, holding the door open, looked closely at Al. "You are going to get them, aren't you?"

"I'm going to try."

"And not just the dummies on the beach, I mean the smart ones who planned it all."

"Especially them," Al said. But although he meant it, they both knew he would be playing against a stacked deck.

Jim nodded acknowledgment, quietly pressed the door shut, and, after a careful look around, set off briskly towards the cliff edge.

Al lowered the window and called after him. "It was you who sent the e-mail to Peter, wasn't it?"

There was no reply. Jim had already disappeared into the morning mist.

CHAPTER 19

At eight-thirty Al called the Review from the car and got through to the editorial office. He could hear Tiny's elephantine booming in the background.

"If that's for me, I'm out unless it's the White House."

But he relented when he heard it was Al. "What is it? And no bullshit."

"Where can I find this Giorgio?"

"I knew it wouldn't be long before you'd be asking me that. His office is near Candlestick Park. Euro Imports, a car showroom on Third, just a few blocks north of the 101 ramp. Not an upscale area - take something to hit people with."

"Thanks, Tiny. I owe you."

"Sure you do. And you know where to find me."

*   *   *

Al parked the Mustang and walked the last block to get a feel for a part of San Francisco he'd only ever passed through, or rather over, on the freeway. It was a run down suburb struggling to make its way back up. He was surprised by the scale and high style of Euro-Imports. Clearly a new development, the showroom was cool and spacious, floored with a fake lawn and dotted with palm trees and flowering shrubs. It reminded him of the approach to the Getty museum. The cars, displayed on stands set at perilous angles, were Italian, wild and exotic, looking as though they had been hauled there in cages. Each bore a label telling the reader everything about the creature except its price. Al guessed that the visible stock was standing somebody upwards of a couple of million dollars. The receptionist switched on her smile.

"Good morning, sir. How can we help you?"

Al held out a plausible business card. "Giorgio around?"

The smile flickered, then reasserted itself. "I'm afraid Mr Fermi isn't here at present..." she glanced at the card "...Mr Ponti."

Al affected disappointment. "Not here? That's not so good, I only do business with him."

"Well, sir, if you're interested in buying a car, I'm sure Mr Iacopi will be able to help. He's our Vice-President of sales."

Without waiting for Al's agreement, she pressed the switch on a microphone. "Mr Iacopi. Customer in Reception. Mr Iacopi, please."

The sing-song voice echoed around the building. Almost at once a man appeared at the chromium plated rail of the mezzanine floor and held up a welcoming hand in Al's direction. "Hi! I'll be right down. A cup of coffee for our visitor, Arlene."

"That's OK, I'll come up," said Al, and took the stairs two at a time, moving too fast to permit any protest. At the top, he handed the card to the disconcerted Iacopi. "Is there somewhere private?"

Iacopi was a squat man with an immense nose and salesman's eyes. He was in uniform – sharp, dark, grey business suit, white shirt, Italian silk tie and, for additional authority, Cuban-style, leather boots with two inch heels. He shook Al's hand warily. "I guess you'd better step into my office, Mr Ponti," and he led the way.

He remained standing while Al sat down, tilted his chair back and stretched out his legs.

"I need to talk with Giorgio. When will he be back?"

Iacopi smiled professionally. "Mr Fermi's out of town right now. But I run things when he's away. What is it you're looking for? Ferrari? Lamborghini? Or maybe a sedan, a Rolls Royce perhaps?" adding earnestly, "We can obtain any vehicle."

"I'm not here to buy a car. It's..." Al lowered his voice almost to a whisper, "...a family matter."

Iacopi looked concerned. "Is it his mother?"

"No, she's fine. There's no problem. I just need to speak to him. It's confidential, capische?"[13] Al tapped the side of his nose with a meaningful finger. "When will he be back?"

A momentary flash of anxiety crossed Iacopi's fleshy features. "Well, I'm afraid I really can't say. Like I told you, he's out of town."

Al nodded sympathetically. "Look, Giorgio told me he'd be away. From the Fourth, he said, for maybe a week. I called his home a few times but he hasn't been there. So that's why I'm here."

Iacopi shifted uncomfortably. "Look, Mr Ponti, your guess is as good as mine. Maybe better. All I can do is give him your message as soon as I see him."

Al got to his feet. "I guess that'd be best." At the door he stopped suddenly. "So you haven't seen him since the Fourth?"

Iacopi's face hardened. He said stolidly, "Like I said, I'll make sure Mr Fermi gets your message."

*   *   *

Hoping to get still more help from Tiny, Al reached the Three-Zero shortly after eleven. Mark was standing at the door catching a little fresh air.

"Hi, Mark. Tiny around?"

"Not yet. He gets in around noon usually."

"OK. Maybe you can help."

"Always happy to help a customer," Mark said, levelly.

"Oh… right. Am I too late for breakfast?"

Ten minutes later, he was working his way through an All-day Breakfast Special: eggs, Canadian bacon and a huge helping of Three-Zero home-made hash brown potatoes, onions, and bell peppers laced with garlic.

"More coffee?"

"Please, and a minute of your time?"

Mark poured the coffee, gestured expansively at the empty tables and sat down. "Guess I can fit you in."

"You know a guy called Fermi?"

[13] Italian (correctly 'capisce') = 'understand' or 'get it'

"Sure, two of 'em. You'd want Giorgio, the wise-guy."

Al smiled ruefully. "That's how I spend my life."

"I take care to avoid him but he comes through here sometimes, uses a private charter company belonging to a buddy of mine… weekends in Vegas, Reno, wherever. He's a high roller, they say."

"Well, I'm looking for a friend of his. About five six, solid build, blonde hair cropped short."

"Oh yeah, that would be Nick. He's a car freak, hangs around Giorgio all the time waiting to be told who to hit. Cheap muscle, strong and stupid."

"Nick? Do you have a surname?"

"'Fraid not. I just know Fermi calls him Nick."

"Where can I find him?"

Mark pursed his lips thoughtfully. "Giorgio will know," he suggested.

You bet, Al thought. "Yeah, but that's my problem. Giorgio's gone AWOL. I'm hoping Nick can help."

"Let's see… he's a work out freak. You could try the gyms."

"OK, thanks." Al pushed his chair back. "Great breakfast."

"Best at any airport around these parts."

At six bucks including information and the tip, Mark's breakfast was pretty good value, Al thought. Back in the Mustang he called the Station House on the cell phone. Duane answered.

"Duane? It's Al. How you doin'?"

"I've been worse but not often. Who do you want?"

Al smiled to himself; Duane had been around.

"Blonde muscle, associate of Giorgio, Nick something or other."

His deep chuckle rumbled down the line. "Oh, sure. Nick Angelino, angel-face. Now there's a sweetheart. You want somebody's legs busted?"

"I just want a few words, Duane. You got a home address?"

"Hold on."

Al heard podgy fingers banging painfully on a keyboard, the occasional oath.

"OK. I've got an address but it's not too recent. He was last arrested April of eighty-seven. He gave an address in Redwood City - 1256 Lavalle Street, Apartment 29."

"Thanks, Duane. Appreciate it."

"Appreciation sucks. Just make sure I get the collar."

Redwood City was only an hour's drive. As Al got out of the Mustang a skinny black kid of no more than 14, beer-can in hand, sitting on the steps to 1254 eyed the car speculatively. Al turned towards him, looked at him hard and drew a forefinger across his throat. The kid looked Al up and down, his stare flickered, then he took a slow defiant drink from the can but he'd got the message.

At first sight, 1256 appeared to have been built more recently than its neighbors. The stonework was immaculate. Plastic tubs on every ground floor window-ledge overflowed with geraniums and trailing ivy. The basement area was free from the usual urban detritus. The front door was freshly painted and each bell bore a neatly hand-written label. Getting no response from prolonged ringing at apartment twenty-nine, Al tried the supervisor. The response was immediate: "Yes?"

"Can you help me, please. I need to speak with Nick, Nick Angelino."

"Who ask prease?"

The unmistakably, strangulated English of the Japanese.

"Name's Hershey. I'm a friend of Nick. I have a message for him. Can you tell me when he'll be back?"

"I come."

The supervisor was a small, slight man, with a neat fringe of grey hair surrounding his ample bald patch. As they shook hands he bowed slightly from the waist. "Tagaki. Sorry, Nick no here. Since one month."

"Do you know where I can reach him?"

A grave shake of the head. "Sorry, don't know. Maybe Gorden Rady."

"Who?"

"No who. Is crub."

"Crub…. Oh! The Golden Lady Club on the Highway."

"Yes," Tagaki confirmed patiently, "Gorden Rady crub. Nick membah."

"A member, I see. Thank you, that's a great help."

Al knew the Golden Lady, a real clip joint. If they got caught serving real champagne, the manager would shoot himself. Fortunately Al didn't drink champagne, he didn't like it much and anyway Mrs Hershey kept the books.

They shook hands and this time Al bowed too. Tagaki looked pleased.

The black kid watched with steady hostility as Al drove off. As the Mustang turned at the lights, he slowly crushed the can in one hand and carefully threw it into 1256's basement area.

*   *   *

Encouraged by a ten dollar bill, the Golden Lady's doorman confided to Al that Mr Angelino had not been seen at the club for a few weeks. For a further ten dollars, while swearing that he had no idea where Mr Angelino was to be found, he recommended an early-morning – 'I'd say about six-thirty, sir' - visit to the 'Muscle Bound' gym on Jefferson.

So it was another early start, fuelled as always by Mrs Hershey's coffee.

At six-thirty sharp, as Al watched from across the street, Nick's Corvette swung into the almost empty car-park, looking and sounding like he had to work long and hard to support it. He parked it chauffeur style in the center of a two-car bay, leaving no room to park either side, then retrieved from the trunk a long leather sports bag. Closing the lid gently he walked briskly through the gym's gold-trimmed glass doors. As soon as he was inside, Al crossed the street, waited until an over-bronzed young man with noticeable pectorals left the reception desk then slipped quietly in.

Nick was alone in the changing room, bent over a washbasin. He turned quickly as Al entered, his street-warrior's instincts telling him Al was trouble, made a dive for the sports bag, skidded on the wet floor and fell, hitting his head hard on the corner of a wooden bench. Al grinned to himself. This was his lucky day; Nick was strong and fit and had probably gone a few rounds, mostly without the expense of a referee. Al rummaged in the bag and pulled from it a neat little snub-nosed .38, dragged a set of metal lockers against the door and sat on the bench next to Nick, who was slumped against the wall, apparently dazed, blood trickling from a gash in his forehead.

"And when it's over watch the dead guys."

As the slumped form suddenly tensed, Al jammed the .38 hard into the thick neck. Nick weighed his chances for a second then collapsed in a terrified heap.

"You'll never get away with it. Not here." His voice cracked with panic. "There's armed security…"

"Easy, Nick. All I want is a quiet talk."

"I didn't touch your fuckin' package. It was Giorgio… I told him…"

"Nick, shut up and listen. I…"

The lockers rattled as someone banged at the door. "Nick? It's Jazz. What's going on, man? You got a chick in there or what?"

Nick opened his mouth to answer but the look on Al's face and the .38 stopped him.

"This facility is closed for maintenance, sir,' Al called, 'We'll be through momentarily."

There was a final disgusted thump on the door then footsteps receded down the corridor.

He pressed the muzzle of the .38 against Nick's throat. "Get dressed. We're walking out together, nice and friendly, to my car. OK?"

Nick hesitated, still hoping for an angle, then nodded. Al could see the fight had gone out of him. He dragged the lockers away from the door and stepped out, a comradely arm around Nick's shoulders. As they passed through the foyer a placatory voice came from the concierge's office:

"I assure you, sir, there is no maintenance crew in the building at this time."

CHAPTER 20

'Go directly to the warehouse. Alone. No stopping, no diversions.'

The control unit on the passenger's seat flashed red as it triggered the warehouse door to admit the Jeep and again as it rolled down behind it. The big man switched off the engine and pressed his left arm against his body, feeling again the bulk of the Colt. It helped, but not much. Not for the first time that eventful night, he wished he'd turned the job down, that he hadn't been so desperate for cash.

'Drive in, turn off all lights and release the rear hatch. Stay in the vehicle.'

Keeping the vehicle's doors locked and its headlights on, he waited, scanning the darkness beyond the pool of light, seeing nothing, hearing only the creaking of the cooling exhaust manifold. He grasped the door handle, changed his mind, lowered his window an inch, then fully.

When at last he reluctantly extinguished the lights, the darkness was absolute. Minutes passed. He leaned out of the window, straining to catch the sound of breathing or of movement, perhaps of a vehicle, but heard nothing. He realized he was gripping the wheel so hard his fingers hurt and he forced himself to relax. Now his eyes were dark-adapted yet he could see only questionable outlines in the moonlight filtering through the sagging roof.

As he groped for the door handle he recalled another instruction he wished he'd ignored: *'remove the bulbs from the interior lights'*. He opened the door wide and waited, still listening. Nothing. At last he swivelled his bulk on the seat and slid to the ground. Still no sound. Breathing more easily now, he took the flashlight from his pocket, switched it on and, its beam probing the darkness in front of him, made his way to the tailgate and opened it.

'The package is my business. Your job is to deliver it unopened.'

Heart racing he set down the flashlight and drew the package to him.

It moved easily over the thick carpet. The still damp black outer wrapping was cold and slick to the touch. He stood staring at it for a while then, in a sudden burst of excitement, took a clasp-knife from his pocket and began slashing into the wrapping, peeling it away. Beneath it was a layer of heavy waterproofed canvas and, beneath that, a varnished wooden case, its lid set into a thick rubber seal and secured with screws. He cursed under his breath then remembered the tool kit.

The screws removed, he levered off the lid and set it aside. Almost there. To go to so much trouble for one small box… Whatever it was, it had to be valuable. He tore off a thick layer of cotton wadding then gazed in disbelief.

"Is it worth dying for?" The voice came at him from the darkness.

For a second he froze before making a grab to extinguish the flashlight.

"Even a creature like you has the right to know why he is going to die."

He had just got his hand on the butt of his pistol when the Parabellum round passed through his left knee, shattering the kneecap and kicking the leg from beneath him. He collapsed, sprawling on his back, coherent thought obliterated by the unspeakable pain. The voice continued, steady, implacable, washing over him.

"There are two reasons."

Now he could hear the soft crunch of feet on the earth floor and the voice came closer.

"First, because you know what's in the package."

In the blackness the big man could see nothing. With a supreme effort he fought back the pain to croak a protest: "Who gives a shit? I don't even know who you are, for Christ's sake."

"Second," the voice continued as though he hadn't spoken, "because there's a special place in hell for men who enjoy killing women."

The big man's final act was a reflex twist of his head away from the voice so that the second bullet entered at the base of his skull, removed the better part of his face and ricocheted off the floor to bury itself in the planking of the warehouse wall. He was dead before the echoes of the shot faded to silence.

A figure, confident in the darkness, took the Jeep's Owner's Manual from the glove compartment, tore a page from it, wrote rapidly three words and a simple sketch of stick figures, then tucked the page behind the bloodied silk tie and left, the bulky package balanced on one shoulder, closing the warehouse door behind him and throwing the remote control unit far into the trees. Outside, still moving freely through the dim moonlight, the figure collected his car from behind the building and, without lights, set off down the hill, driving fast, the package strapped securely into the passenger's seat. He had almost reached the highway before he removed the night-vision goggles and switched on his headlights.

At the warehouse, the regular occupants, scattered like refugees by the roar of gunfire, crouched listening among the undergrowth until at last, led by the boldest, they began creeping stealthily back towards the irresistible allure of the scent of blood.

*   *   *

Roughing people up was not Al's favorite occupation but it came easier with some than others and with Nick, Al almost enjoyed it. It took a few minutes to extract the story, but Nick eventually admitted how, contrary to instructions to leave Giorgio to deliver the package alone, he'd followed the Jeep up the coast but quit when it turned off the Highway. That was all Al needed.

"OK. You drive. Keep the speed down and no funny business," he pointed with the pistol, "or you lose a kneecap."

Al detested being driven, especially in his own car through morning rush-hour traffic, and it was an uncomfortable trip to the coast. He was relieved when Nick swung the Mustang off the Highway and onto a dirt road. A decrepit, crudely painted sign said 'Jem's Artichokes 200 yards. Parking. Cold Drinks.'

As the track wound into the hills, Al could see that at night it would be a dangerous drive with lights off and even more dangerous following Giorgio with them on. They bounced past a deserted Jem's place, then on for about a mile, climbing steadily. Below them the sun silvered the Pacific wave-tops; Al thought how much he'd prefer to be swimming. A tight left turn, a last steep climb, then the track leveled off and petered out among trees in front of a rusting, windowless sheet-metal warehouse, one storey high with a brand new roller-door. The building bore no identification marks. It might have dropped from the sky.

The roller-door was locked but Nick pushed through a gap in a thicket of bushes at the side of the building towards a rear door sagging on its hinges, partly open, the hasp recently broken. A couple of paces from the door, Nick stopped. "Oh shit!" He threw a hand over his nose and mouth and swung away, retching. A second later Al caught it too, the characteristic smell of decaying flesh.

"OK, Nick. Give me the shoes."

Nick looked at him blankly. "Huh?"

Al gestured with the pistol. "The shoes. Take them off."

Swearing under his breath, Nick struggled to balance on each foot in turn, removing the tan colored Italian slipons. When Al threw them into the undergrowth, Nick howled with rage. "Fuck, man, that's two hundred bucks..."

"Shut up and wait in the car." Al reckoned that, even if Nick wanted to make a run for it, he wasn't the type to go far over rough ground with only silk socks on his feet.

Ignoring the mumbling protest, Al squirmed through the half-open door, switched on his pocket light - Mrs Hershey wouldn't allow him to leave the house without it – then paused to give his eyes a chance to adjust. The smell was so strong it seemed he could feel it; he covered his nose and mouth with his handkerchief and, sweeping the beam around him, edged forward, straining to see. He found a light switch but it did nothing. Something ran over his foot.

At first, it seemed the place was occupied only by the stench but then the torch picked out a parked vehicle, a Jeep, just inside the roller door at the far end of the building, the tailgate standing open. What remained of Mrs Fermi's favored son was sprawled at the rear of it, arms flung out, a large caliber bullet wound at the base of his skull, his upper body surrounded by a congealed black lake. Scratches in the dirt showed the last reflex scrabblings of his big hands. Getting closer, Al could see that the face had gone and there was a second mass of blood around the left knee. A piece of paper, blood-spattered and grimy, was lying beside the body. Acting on a detective's reflex and with only a momentary thought for what an outraged Duane would say, Al pocketed it.

Starting from the rear, Al completed a slow circuit of the Jeep. The vehicle was almost new and its interior immaculate but, oddly, the Owner's Manual lay open on the passenger's seat. The rear compartment was empty but the deep pile carpet showed the imprint of a large, heavy object and closer inspection revealed shreds of black plastic film littering the compartment. At the wide-open driver's door he leaned in, studying the interior for some time before cautiously backing out, leaving everything as he had found it.

Back in the Mustang, Nick still looked queasy. Al sighted the pistol at Nick's groin. "You get just the one chance to tell me about the girl."

Nick's voice was quavering and miserable. "Oh man! None of that shit was in the plan. It was gonna be such a simple job, just pick up a package and we're on our way. But Giorgio was twitchy... anybody else I'd have said scared... so right off I'm gettin' a bad feelin'. Then the sonofabitch in the boat is late and when he does arrive he stays off the beach a little ways. Well, Giorgio ain't about to dampen the Guccis so I get to wade in."

Al grinned inwardly; Giorgio might have been vicious but he wasn't lacking in style.

"The man in the boat. Who was he?"

"Who was he?" Nick's voice rose in a querulous crescendo of indignation at this outrageous behavior. "He was a fuckin' idiot that's who. He puts his fuckin' searchlight on and suddenly it's like we're in the circus. Giorgio went crazy, hollerin' to put it out. I just get my hands on the package when I hear splashin' and there's Giorgio wrestling some guy. I'm up to here in the water strugglin' with the damn package and wondering where to Christ the guy came from.

Wonderin', is it a cop? But now there's screamin', it's a woman and the whole job's gone to crap. I get the package onto the beach but by then he's holding her under."

"And you rushed in to save her."

Nick flared angrily. "Fuck you, pal. Giorgio's a psycho. He enjoys it. Nobody messes with Giorgio."

Somebody did, Al thought, picturing the scene in the warehouse with satisfaction.

"Go on."

"OK, so now we hit the next problem. The order is to wait five minutes after the pick-up before we leave the beach. Five minutes! With a dead body right there in the water? No way. Giorgio's busy wringing out his socks so he tells me to back the Jeep up to the highway, then we're gone, him in the Jeep, me in the 'Vette."

Now, Al wondered, why would they have been instructed to wait five minutes? You'd have expected the orders to be get the heck out of there fast. It needed thinking about. Nick was talking quickly now, the way the guilty talk once they've got started.

"Giorgio's supposed to make the delivery alone but I figured as sure as shit happens he would open the package, so I follow him. First it's his brother's house. I can't figure it, Alberto's a fuckin' saint so how come he's in on the job? But then the package stays in the Jeep so I figure maybe he ain't. I'm sittin' ten minutes at the end of the street thinkin' maybe I ain't no choirboy but I never got mixed up with murderin' no woman before, then Giorgio comes out steamin', slams the door so hard I hear the glass fall out and takes off like he's late for Mass. I stay with him back to the highway then he takes this track so I quit."

"And then what?"

"No fuckin' money, is what! Giorgio's a sonofabitch but he never ripped me off before so I know somethin's up. I keep ringin' him, at home, the showroom, but nothin'."

"So you come up here and find him."

"What's left of him." Nick shuddered. "And I figure I'm next so I quit the apartment and make like the invisible man."

Al took the opportunity. "I think you split because you killed him, Nick."

Angelino's eyes widened.

"You blew him away to get the package. What was so good about that package to kill your buddy for it?"

Nick's face reddened and the veins on his forehead bulged. The wound reopened and a trickle of blood ran down into his left eye. He brushed at it angrily with a fat fist and began measuring the distance between himself and Al.

Al raised the .38. Nick eyed it uncertainly then his anger slowly subsided. "Giorgio was my partner." He was mumbling, wheedling. "I never did nothin' without him. When I found him he had no face, man. And the package was gone. The guys who shot him took it."

"So why did they shoot him?"

Nick shrugged.

"Say they killed him for the package. What's in it to kill for, Nick?"

Nick sighed heavily, almost a groan. "I tell you, I just don't know."

There was no doubt in Al's mind that this was the plain truth but he tried one more tack. "You carried it up the beach. What did it feel like? How big was it? How heavy?"

Nick had had enough but he forced himself to reply. "It was so big." He indicated a couple of feet. "It weighed sixty-five maybe seventy pounds."

A weight-lifter's estimate, Al realised. "And the wrapping?"

"Some kind of black shiny stuff."

Al could see that this was the most technical description Nick could manage. "Drugs?"

Nick's anger flared again, briefly. "For fuck's sake, man. I told you. I don't know what was in the fuckin' package."

Al adopted a soothing tone. "Easy, Nick. Just one more question. Why did

Giorgio take the job if he was so scared?"

"Money. The car business was in deep shit. Twenty grand for a night's work was good news."

"But it still wasn't enough, which is why he opened the package."

"What's enough? And it wasn't just the money, he was crazy to know what was in there. That's why I followed him. I knew he'd open it."

He did open it and they killed him for it. These are serious people, Al thought. He reached for the cell phone then paused. "Why would Giorgio take the lightbulbs out of the interior lights in the Jeep?"

Nick's gaping incomprehension was all the answer Al needed. He dialled the Station House. "Duane? It's me. About that collar. Off the highway, end of the dirt road past Jem's Artichokes. It's my summer sale - two for the price of one. Bring a body bag and a gas mask."

Half an hour later, ignoring Nick's grumbles about his missing shoes, Duane shoved him into the back of a Black and White.

Tiny was as happy as God allows an editor to be. As he said, a sexual angle would have been an improvement, but you can't have everything and first on the street with a nice gory murder, like aerobic exercise, aids the circulation.

CHAPTER 21

The foyer of the Holiday Inn in San Francisco's Chinatown is spacious and anonymous, its potted plants and ornate wooden pillars creating a maze of discreet alcoves. To Peter, it seemed to have been designed for illicit lovers, dubious businessmen, undercover policemen - every variety of San Francisco's secret citizens among whom, for this occasion, he uncharacteristically numbered himself.

He sat in a corner near the entrance, the same vantage point he had used five days earlier while waiting to meet Al for the first time. Now he was nervously reading, or rather peering over, a Wall Street Journal. Al's brief telephone report the previous evening had suggested that the business was getting out of hand; faceless, decomposing corpses of murdered gangsters were not part of Peter's life. Feeling exposed and unsure of what he was looking out for, he nonetheless scrutinized everyone who came and went by his post.

At 9:30 exactly, easing his way through the bustle of Chinese around the entrance, Al arrived. He was scarcely five and a half feet tall and his slightly crouched walk made him look still smaller, but no amount of crouching could make him look insignificant. He advanced, hand outstretched, a broad smile capturing his face.

"Hi, Peter. Good to see you again."

"Hello, Al. You too. Coffee?"

"Coffee's great, thanks."

They chose an empty alcove and sat down at an elaborately carved mahogany table supported by leering wooden dragons. Peter looked around and a waiter magically appeared and took their order.

"Why here, Al? Why not the ILT office?"

"Just a precaution. I'm a percentage player, never take an avoidable risk."

He grinned. "It works too. I'm alive, a few of my clients aren't."

Peter grinned back. "That's comforting."

Al looked concerned. "Say, you don't have to worry. The kind of guys I'm talking about had it coming. I couldn't be too choosy about who I worked for when I started out."

"No problem." Peter would never come to terms with American immunity to irony.

"OK, let's get to it. Verbal report now, written version later, after Mrs Hershey's worked it over with that word processor of hers. You know, that thing cost a thousand dollars. Can you figure that? I mean, why can't she use a typewriter for Chrissakes?"

To Peter this was equivalent to recommending a bicycle as a replacement for a Cadillac but he said nothing.

"If it's OK with you, I'll tell you what I've done first, then I'll give you my guess as to what it all means."

Peter said this was fine with him. Al took his notebook from an inside pocket and flicked over the pages, wetting his thumb as he went, but before he could begin his report the waiter returned with the coffee. Peter poured for them both as Al set to work.

"Well, I started off talking to your partner, Mr Hughes, but he couldn't help much. Matter of fact, he's convinced it was an accident."

Peter would have made a comment but Al was intent on his notes and his story. "Like I told you, I lived in Half Moon Bay for a while before I met Mrs Hershey. So I went around calling in a few markers from my old booze and poker buddies - cops, press, the guys who know stuff the citizens don't." He turned to his notes. "First I talked with the local police. The desk sergeant's Duane Zimmerman, a great guy I knew in Vietnam. He gave me the story on the ME."

"ME?"

"Medical Examiner. The doctor who did the autopsy."

"Ah yes, Fermi. I met him at the inquest. Seemed a decent chap."

"Decent chap." With a grin of appreciation Al rolled the phrase around, trying to copy Peter's articulation. "Yeah, that would be right. Alberto Fermi, solid Italian family, he's second generation. Straight, at least he was. But there's a brother, Giorgio, a wise-guy, John Gotti wannabe."

"Who's John Gotti?"

"You don't know John Gotti - the Dapper Don? He was big time mafia, New York, capo of the Gambino family."

"I see," Peter said, politely.

"Of course, brother Giorgio can't even make it as head of the Fermi family but he has ambitions so he does the overcoat and the swagger." He turned a page. "I call on Alberto first, I ask a few straightforward questions, he gets excited and throws me out."

Peter struggled with the image of Al being thrown anywhere but didn't interrupt.

"So I tick the box marked 'something to hide' and move on. Next is Tiny Larsen - the man-who-knows-everything: editor of the local paper, master of the slick headline. He gives me the same story: Alberto's so clean if he ran for Pope he'd win in a landslide but young Giorgio's crooked from his slicked-back hair to his hand-made shoes. Oh, and Tiny also says to talk to Fuzzy." Al took a drink of coffee, flicked over two more pages and continued. "It seems when Fermi took over old Doc Black's practice, Fuzzy came with the deal. He's dim, slow as Christmas molasses but he thinks he's a doctor, attends every autopsy. God knows why but that isn't the point, the only one he misses out on is your daughter. And why? Because the Doc sends him on a wild goose chase."

Peter was puzzled. "He was relying on a man like that to keep his mouth shut?"

"Oh absolutely. Fuzzy's religiously stupid but he's devoted to his boss, sees him as a God. God must have a reason, so follow orders and keep your mouth shut. And anyway, nobody talks to him if they can avoid it. And they usually can. He only talked to me because I treated him as though I noticed he was alive and bought him donuts."

Peter was having trouble adjusting to Al's world, and the idea that witnesses could be bribed with donuts didn't help but he just nodded. "And then?"

"And then I get lucky. I find the spy in the enemy camp, Fermi's receptionist, Josie - Mata Hari in a mini-skirt. She and Alberto were shacked up, then the day after your daughter died he called it off without explanation. She doesn't know why exactly, but she swears he was forced into it by his brother. And listen to this. According to Josie, Giorgio called at Fermi's place in Half Moon Bay in the small hours of July fifth and the brothers had a hell of an argument."

Peter was burning to ask what all these things meant but, with difficulty, he kept quiet as Al turned the page and threw out a question. "How well do you know Otte?"

"Jim? Not a great deal. Geoff's known him for years and my wife said Meg seemed very taken with him."

"He's the one who sent you the e-mail."

Peter sat up sharply. "Is he, by God! How does he know so much about it?"

"Because he was there."

"There...", Peter struggled unsuccessfully to find words.

"On the beach at about the time Meg died."

Peter's face was pale with crimson spots over his cheekbones. "You mean he had a hand in it?"

His voice was suddenly too loud. Al held a finger to his lips. "Easy, Peter. Hear the rest of it before you get mad."

Peter, feeling a little foolish, sat back and waited.

"Jim called me Tuesday and we met early next morning. He's lying low but your partner persuaded him to talk to me and suddenly I'm getting somewhere. At one o'clock in the morning of the fifth Jim picked up a package at sea and delivered it to two men on Smugglers Beach. From his description, one of the men was Giorgio Fermi so I figured now would be a good time to talk to him. The staff at his car company stonewalled but my guess is they haven't seen him for some time, probably since the fifth, and they're worried. They know there's something up."

"So why don't they go to the Police?" Peter's anger flared once more and the question came out before he could stop himself.

Al shook his head. How little regular citizens knew of Giorgio's world. "Because they prefer their legs the shape they are."

"Sorry, naïve question."

"That's OK. It's a limbo dance. It's tough for decent people to get down low enough," Al said sympathetically.

And what about you? Peter wondered, paid to confront monsters, how do you stay decent?

More coffee and a couple more pages are turned. "It doesn't take too much digging to find the other guy on the beach that night, a second-rate career criminal called Nick Angelino, and with a little persuasion he takes me to Giorgio, or what's left of him." He snapped his notebook shut. "That's where your money went. Shall I tell you what I make of it all?"

"Of course."

"I'll start with what we know, or can guess at. Somebody, some powerful organization, arranged to import something into the US without Customs paperwork. They recruited Jim Otte to make the pick-up and Giorgio Fermi and Nick Angelino to man the beach. The job was scheduled for the fourth because the local police are stretched that evening. Your daughter was killed, probably by Fermi, because she happened on the scene. Then Giorgio panics and tries to make the murder go away. He blackmails his brother, threatening to tell Ma about the Josie affair. Alberto panics too – seems it runs in the family - and dumps her the next day. I guess if push came to shove he wanted to be able to look his Ma in the face and deny everything. Then brother Giorgio does the one thing that could make his situation worse. He opens the package and dies of curiosity. What goes around comes around," Al concluded with evident satisfaction.

"Hmm… That's impressive work, Al. Now tell me what we don't know."

Al fuelled himself with coffee. "Too much, and it's all the important stuff. What was in the package? Where is it now? And most important, who's running this operation? Who's powerful enough to get the package brought from God knows where; smart enough to plan even for Giorgio's double cross and rich enough to fund the whole operation? Nobody I've spoken to so far has any idea who these people are."

As the questions piled up, Peter's mind strayed back to the hard fact that undermined the foundations of what he was doing - 'nothing will bring her back'. Helen had voiced it on the plane, urging him to turn straight round and get the first flight home - 'revenge is for fools'. But from a very young age, especially from childhood battles with his father, he'd learned that once he'd settled in his mind what was right, attempts at compromise led nowhere. He had to remove this obstacle standing between him and the remainder of his life.

He realized Al was speaking. "Hold on. Sorry, Al, I lost concentration. Where are we?"

"I was saying, we have an ace in the hole." With the air of a conjurer he produced from his wallet a piece of paper, carefully placed inside a transparent cover, and handed it to Peter. "You're an educated guy. What do you make of that?"

'That' was a photocopy - Al had shamefacedly handed over the original to Duane - of a page torn from a printed booklet of some kind. It was about six inches by four with the word 'Notes' printed at its head and 'Chrysler Corporation' along the bottom. One corner was missing, apparently nibbled away. In its center, hand written in clear script, were three words: 'Karistus Kümavereliselt Kuritegu'. In the lower right-hand corner there was a crude sketch showing a tree with overhanging branches and beneath it two stick figures, their arms around one another's shoulders.

"Where did you get it?"

"It was beside Giorgio's body."

"I see." Peter examined it then shook his head. "I'm no linguist but that's a peculiar language."

"And the drawing?"

"Well, it's hardly the work of an artist. Two men... no, two people, indeterminate gender, arms around one another's shoulders. Reminds me of Greek men dancing."

"You mean the words are Greek?"

"No, definitely not Greek. Could be Turkish, I suppose. Just a guess." With a rueful shrug he handed it back. "You think Giorgio's murderers left it?"

Al studied the note again although he and Mrs Hershey had spent so long poring over it the night before that he could have made a fair copy from memory. "I'd bet on it. And I believe it was left deliberately."

Peter raised sceptical eyebrows but said nothing.

"Look, it's a good lead, I can feel it," Al insisted.

Al's enthusiasm sounded genuine, but as Chairman of a technology company Peter knew about enthusiasm. The greater the enthusiasm the bigger the risk, he thought wryly. But then his specialty was laser optics not criminal investigations and besides, he liked Al and trusted his instincts.

"Alright, Al. Lets follow it up. What next?"

"Next I find somebody who can explain this," Al said as he returned the paper to his wallet.

"And then?"

Al was accustomed to clients wanting answers before he'd figured out the questions. "And then we decide what to do next."

"OK, sorry. It's in your hands. And thanks, that's good work. When will I get the typed copy of your report?"

"Well, if the word processor doesn't act up, a couple of days."

They shook hands and Al left, asking Peter to give him a couple of minutes start. Peter watched as he was swallowed up in the crowd around the doors and felt reassured. If he's not the man to crack this, then I'll give up, he thought.

Outside Al paused to let his eyes adjust to the bright sunshine.

To the right of the revolving doors, his one leg folded beneath him, a man of about his own age was sitting in the shade on the paved forecourt of the hotel, among the exhaust fumes from the limos parked with their air-conditioners running. His green beret, cocked at a self-confident angle, bore the Special Forces badge of a dagger and crossed arrows and the motto De Oppresso Liber.[14] On the sidewalk beside him a carefully chalked notice said: 'I gave a leg. What will you give, buddy?' The empty trouser leg was neatly rolled and pinned.

As he reached for his billfold, Al wondered how many oppressed this man had freed before the war took his leg away.

A drowsy black and white spaniel, its head resting in the man's lap, opened one eye, studied Al briefly, decided he was friendly and closed it again. The man's eyes remained firmly shut but Al knew he wasn't asleep, not with maybe twenty dollars in small bills and change in the box at his side. He selected a dollar bill then swore under his breath and changed it for a five. He moved on, betting himself the guy had never been anywhere near a war, then cursing his own cynicism.

[14] De Oppresso Liber. Latin = 'To Free from Oppression'. Motto of US Special Forces.

CHAPTER 22

Al strolled through the streets to Union Square, took a seat in the sun and got on the phone.

"Tiny, it's me."

"You don't say. What is it this time?"

"How are you on ships?'

"Sick."

"I need to trace a ship, probably docked in San Francisco in early July."

"And what would you want with a ship?"

"I need a Captain's autograph for my collection."

"Really!"

"Come on, Tiny. I gave you one scoop already. Like I told you, you're first in line, trust me."

"The last time I trusted a guy he stole my candy bar," Tiny grumbled, "But as it's you, for ships you talk to Reina Kaplan. She runs security for the port. The number's in the book. Whatever you do, don't get involved with her boss, a Polack, runs on vodka. But Reina's kosher, she'll help if anybody can."

Al was scribbling in his book. "And languages - how are you on languages?"

"I speak American. Never felt the need for anything else."

"I need somebody who knows about foreign languages."

"Any particular one?"

"That's my problem – I don't know."

"Then you want Paul Posner at Berkeley."

"He knows that stuff?"

"He'll have a rough idea, he's Professor of Philology."

Philology not being one of Al's strengths, the sarcasm was wasted. "Is that good?"

"It is if you want advice on languages."

"OK, thanks. And hang on, there's one more thing. That warehouse, where the body was found. I'd like to know who owns that too."

"Another one for your autograph book?"

Al pressed resolutely on. "Can you get straight back to me on the cell phone if you get anything? It's important."

"So you're making progress then? With your alleged murder."

"I would be if I wasn't yackin' to you."

Al could hear Tiny shaking his head.

"Jesus, PI's. I must've led a bad life in a previous existence. Give me your number. And don't hassle me, it aggravates my hypertension. I'll call you when I can."

"I won't hassle you," Al lied firmly.

"Enjoy your talk with Posner," Tiny concluded, in an odd tone which Al would come to understand soon enough.

He figured he could make the rest of his phone calls as well from home as anywhere and he'd found it good policy to show up often enough that his wife recognized him when he walked in the front door, so he recovered the Mustang from the Chinatown parking lot and headed for home.

When Tiny called back, Al and Mrs Hershey had just sat down to dinner together for the first time in three days.

"OK. Here's the good news. I talked with a realtor friend. The warehouse is owned by Jem, the artichoke man. Jem's owned it since it was a shed but sometime in May it was leased to a company in Hong Kong. Three year term, sight unseen, all done by fax and telephone and super fast, forty-eight hours flat. No questions, no price arguments, no screwing around. And there's something else. When they asked what it was wanted it for, to sort out the insurance, the Chinese guy suddenly forgot his English."

"Tiny, you're a genius. I'll love you forever."

"Not when you hear the rest of it."

"Go on."

"The Hong Kong company is just a dime-a-dozen outfit, a front. It's designed to keep our noses out and it works. Sorry, Al, dry hole."

"That's OK, Tiny, I'll work around it. Appreciate your help. I'll be in touch."

He cleaned his plate as he always did, but Mrs Hershey could see that his mind was elsewhere.

*   *   *

The following morning Al called the Port Authority and reached Mrs Kaplan. She sounded busy but Tiny's name worked its magic and she said she could fit in a short meeting at 1:30.

The office of David J. Kowalski II, Head of Security, was furnished for effect: rosewood panelling, concealed lighting and one wall with floor-to-ceiling bookshelves filled with heavy leather-bound volumes. A desk by the window overlooked a succession of piers stretching into the distance but the dominant feature of the room was a bank of sixteen TV screens built into the wall by the desk, each showing a sequence of images from security cameras.

Behind the desk a small neat woman in black trousers and white blouse stood up to shake his hand. She looked to be no more than forty but her hair was heavily flecked with grey.

"Reina Kaplan. Come on in. Have a seat." She gestured to a chair at the desk. "You take something? Coffee?"

"No thanks."

She noticed him glancing around the office. "Nice, isn't it? I hope it'll be mine some day. Right now I just get to use it when Mr Kowalski's not around."

The name was delivered with an edge that confirmed Tiny's observations on the man's worth. As she sat down the phone rang. She held up an apologetic hand to Al as she picked it up. "Kaplan." She listened for a few seconds. "I told you yesterday, a guy sleeps on the job here, he gets a career opportunity someplace else."

She listened patiently to what Al could tell was a stream of rising inflections of protest then, without raising her voice said: "You're not listening, Mitch.

I said the man has been dismissed. I want him escorted to the gate, right now. Is that clear?"

A short response then: "Thank you. Call me when it's done." She replaced the receiver, jotted a note on the desk pad and took a deep breath. "You need some help?"

"I need to find a ship."

She pointed to the television screens with a grin. "See one you like?"

"That's a neat set-up."

"We need it, believe me."

"I can see how you would. But my ship, can you help?"

"Well, let's see. What can you tell me – name, shipping line, port of origin…?"

"Sorry, none of those."

"Oh. Well, how about her destination?" But she saw the answer coming. "Mr Hershey, maybe you should tell me what you do know about this ship?"

"OK. I know that she dropped a package into the water two miles off Half Moon Bay sometime on or before the night of the fourth of July."

"And that's it?"

"Afraid so, ma'am."

She looked at him, head on one side. "You're a tough man to help. You'd better tell me what this is all about."

So Al told her just enough: Meg's death, her father's suspicions and the complicated procedure for recovery of the package.

Reina took all of this in then sat for while in contemplation. "OK…," she spoke slowly, thinking as she went, "The vessel had to come from overseas. You don't smuggle stuff from the US into the US. So she was an ocean-going vessel and she was very likely steaming into or, just possibly, out of a west coast port. Question is, which one?" She was running a forefinger slowly back and forth across her lips, oblivious of Al's presence, immersed in the conundrum. "Well, Half Moon Bay being so far north, the best guess would be here, the second possibility, Seattle. I can help with arrivals and departures here…"

She picked up the phone and dialled. "Hello, Kate? Reina. Look, how quickly can you get me a printout? I need a list of all vessels arriving or departing the first through the fifth of July. No problem? Good, thank you. I'll pick it up in a few minutes."

Al could scarcely believe his luck. "That's really good of you…"

She waved away his thanks. "It's nothing. The Computer Department costs plenty of taxpayers' dollars, it's good they should work for a living."

Pleased as he was, Al could see a nasty downside. "Suppose it wasn't San Francisco?"

"Then it was some place else." Reina smiled at his expression. "And yes, that does mean you have to work your way through the west coast ports, which is where Herr Mandelstam comes in." She got up, walked slowly along the wall of books, selected an encyclopaedia-sized volume and handed it to him. The spine read 'Mandelstam's Handbook of West Coast Ports 1991.' "You'll find the names of the security chief of every port from Chile to Alaska in there. Mention my name and they'll provide the list you need."

Al weighed the bulky volume ruefully but the indomitable Reina was still steaming full ahead both engines. "There is one other small complication," she went on remorselessly, "and that's the vessel's speed. Half Moon Bay is so little sailing time from here that differences in speed don't really matter. But if you take Seattle, for example, that's more than a thousand miles. The difference in sailing time between vessels has to be allowed for, OK?"

"As if this job wasn't complicated enough!"

She saw Al's face. "It's not so bad. If my list does it, you've got no problem. If it doesn't you'll just have to get the calculator out. It's no big deal, trust me."

Anything involving calculators was a damned big deal as far as Al was concerned but he didn't say so. It would be Mrs Hershey's problem anyway.

"Mrs Kaplan, I trust you, it's me I don't trust, not with this stuff." Al hefted the book. "It's going to be a long list," he said, hoping she'd disagree.

"You bet," she responded cheerfully then laughed aloud at his crestfallen expression and came around the desk. "Come on," she put a friendly hand on his shoulder, "it beats some of the stuff you PI's have to handle. Let's go down and get your list."

With the list, alarmingly long by the weight of the printout, in his hand, they went down to reception together.

"Hey, I really can't thank you enough," Al said.

"No problem. Just make sure I get the book back. Not that Kowalski ever opens it but he'd score a point if I lost it."

As they parted, Al turned back, recalling the way she'd handled the phone call. "Your name will be on the door one day," he assured her.

She was unconvinced but her smile was grateful. "Thanks."

Back in her office she stood at the window watching the ceaseless dockside activity and reflecting on the things she had decided not to mention – breakdown, serious illness aboard – which could throw a timetable out by days or even weeks. She wished him well. Her thoughts were interrupted by the secretary on the intercom telling her the trades union representatives were ready for the meeting. With a sigh she turned to the desk and pressed the switch: "Ask them to come in, please."

*　　*　　*

Al drove south on 101, Mandelstam locked with excessive caution in the Mustang's trunk. A strategic optimist and a tactical pessimist, Al saw a world filled with opportunities, every opportunity a tangle of problems. Reina had given him an excellent opportunity; there was a reasonable chance that her list included the vessel which had carried the package. But having a name on a list is an advantage only if you know how to recognize it.

After lunch he called Peter. "I've booked a meeting with the DA, tomorrow eleven o'clock." Al realized belatedly how presumptuous this might sound and backtracked. "I hope that's OK?"

"It's fine, Al, no problem." Peter was delighted to be doing anything; waiting for results was massively frustrating.

"Good. She'll be up in town so we're meeting at the Civic Center. How about we go together?"

"Fine. Can you pick me up here?"

"No problem. Is 10 o'clock OK?"

"See you then."

CHAPTER 23

In the elevator, Al made a point of warning Peter. "Listen, I know this lady. She looks like somebody's mother but don't be fooled, nobody elbows her off the sidewalk, OK?"

On the fourth floor, Al made his final pitch. "Above all, try to stay cool." Peter smiled. "I'll do my best." As they made their way along the corridor he added: "I just hope she's doing her job!"

In her late thirties, plump, fresh-faced and bespectacled, Deputy District Attorney Kristensen was new to the post. Her manner was coolly professional but Al thought she looked tense and apprehensive. She introduced herself and a young Hispanic man – something Ramirez - whom she described as 'one of my staff'. Then she got straight into it.

"How can I help you?"

So, no coffee, no pleasantries, OK, Al thought, let's just do it. "You've read the report on the murder of Giorgio Fermi?" Al looked enquiringly.

"I have."

"So you will be aware that he murdered my client's daughter?"

Kristensen pursed her lips judiciously. "Do you have any evidence for that assertion?"

"Nick Angelino says he did."

"He has made a statement to that effect. Do you believe him?"

"Yes, I do. Sure, he's a thug with biceps for brains but I believe him."

"Have you considered the possibility that *he* killed Fermi? That all his talk about a package and a mysterious organization is throwing sand in our eyes?"

Al shook his head firmly. "He was so scared he almost crapped himself."

"Most criminals are scared of being caught."

"Not Nick. He was relieved to be caught. He'd seen his partner without a face and anyway, you have Jim Otte."

"Actually, Mr Hershey, that's part of my problem. I don't have Otte. Perhaps he's talking only to private investigators." She waited but Al said nothing. "Do you know where he is?", she asked.

Al met her gaze. "I have no idea."

The staring between them went on.

"But you will advise this office if he contacts you."

"Of course."

"Aside from the fact that you wouldn't want to obstruct my investigation, without Otte we don't have much to go on."

Al wasn't done with Nick's testimony. "What did you make of Angelino?".

"I haven't talked to him yet."

"You haven't interviewed the principal witness in two murder cases?"

Al regretted the words before he'd finished speaking. Ramirez cleared his throat and adjusted the crease in his slacks. He was about to speak until he caught Kristensen's eye.

"If I want lessons in my job we have a training department. What is your point?"

Suddenly she seemed rather less motherly. At the edge of his vision Al saw Peter's imminent explosion and got in quickly.

"Excuse me, I was out of line," he said deferentially. "But you do have a sworn statement testifying that the girl was murdered."

"People swear to things you wouldn't believe but that doesn't mean they happened."

Now the explosion could not be contained. Peter leaned forward in his seat and stabbed the air with an accusatory finger.

"So what you're telling us, Miss Kristensen..."

"Ms."

"Oh, I do beg your pardon, *Ms.* Kristensen." Peter's tone was larded with spurious politeness.

Al figured he might just as well sit back and watch the show.

"What you're telling us is that this is just another case to file under 'Too Difficult' and hope I'll run out of money or patience."

"No, Mr Gilchrist, that's not what I'm telling you," she said, with admirable patience. "What I'm telling you is what I know." She began counting on pudgy but carefully tended fingers. "One, a young woman drowned, verdict accidental death. Two, there are three men allegedly involved – Fermi, Angelino and Otte. The first dead, the second a career criminal, and the third missing. We are pursuing the investigation, Mr Gilchrist, but frankly we don't have much to go on and your daughter's death is not my only case."

Peter stood up. "Thank you for your time, *Ms.* Kristensen. I won't waste any more of it."

He turned and strode angrily out of the office.

Down in the foyer Peter paced ahead, burst through the swing doors to the street then, white with anger, turned towards Al as he caught up.

"Bloody bureaucrat! She doesn't give a damn about Meg or me or anybody or anything other than her damned career. 'We are pursuing the investigation'. What *Ms. bloody Kristensen* means by that is that she's sitting on her fat backside waiting for somebody to walk in off the street with the package and a signed confession."

Al, hands deep in his trouser pockets, listened patiently to this diatribe against officialdom that he had heard frazzled clients deliver a dozen times. When Peter paused he said solemnly: "I admit I'm just a mercenary but I am on your side."

Peter's anger subsided and he raised his hands in a gesture compounded of apology and frustration.

"Yes, you're right. I'm sorry, Al. It's just…"

"No problem. You're right too, but so is she. Sure she's trying for the White House but she's a young woman sitting behind a very big desk. She has to put the taxpayers' dollars where there's something to work on and a reasonable chance of success. In her eyes, your daughter's case doesn't qualify. She has a bundle of cases, we have just the one. You like chowder?"

"Clam chowder? Well, yes, I do rather."

"Then let's go get the best chowder in the world."

As they crossed the street to collect his car, Al threw a histrionic arm in the air and, speaking in a fair imitation of Peter's public school delivery, exclaimed: "Oh, I do beg your pardon, *Ms. bloody Kristensen.*"

And despite it all, Peter laughed aloud for the first time since his daughter's death.

*   *   *

"So is it the best chowder on the coast or what?"

The Mustang, on top form, had whisked them across town to San Francisco's Pier 39 at startling speed. The restaurant was all natural wood, crisp napkins and Swedish cutlery. Above the bar an engraved glass sign read: *'Neptune's Palace – Since 1974 Fine Dining in the World's Favorite City'.* From their table overlooking the choppy waters of the Bay, they watched the sealions relaxing noisily in the dock. At the next table a young man in shorts and T-shirt, Nike clad feet up on a spare chair, was noisily eating pretzels while his heavily tattooed female companion immersed herself in *'Body Modification International Magazine'* and drank beer from a bottle. 'Fine Dining', Peter thought, a little ungraciously.

"Actually, you said it would be the best in the world."

Al shrugged cheerfully. "To Bay area folk, this coast is the world. But it's still great chowder, isn't it."

Peter thought it was rather heavy on the corn-flour but didn't say so.

Al took a connoisseur's sampling of chowder, set down his spoon and breathed a contented sigh.

"Where's Tallinn?"

Peter raised an eyebrow. "It's in Estonia – the capital, in fact."

"And Estonia is…?"

"On the Baltic."

Al pondered this new but unhelpful fact. "That's Europe, right?"

"That's right. Why?"

Al took out his notebook. "I faxed the message to Professor Posner at Berkeley – another gem from Tiny's address book - then I rang him. Jesus, Peter, I don't know whether he's the smartest man in the world but he sure comes tops in obnoxious. First, there was the voice problem, Henry Kissinger with laryngitis. Then he gives me a load of college-boy stuff I couldn't follow and anyway wasn't the point, then he demands to know why didn't I ask some woman at UCLA who is *the* expert in Baltic studies or, if it's *that* important, ask in Tallinn, gives me a crap translation, balls me out for wasting his time and for an encore, he hangs up on me! Listen…" He consulted his notes. "'The words on your card are in the Estonian language, a member of the Finno-Ugric group'"[15], he read solemnly. "I had to ask him to spell that."

"I see," said Peter, who also had never heard of the Finno-Ugric group. "And the translation?"

Al continued reading, "The Professor said, 'Three words devoid of context do not permit of accurate translation but it is apparently concerned with crime and penalties, possibly also with blood.'"

Peter thought about this. "And the sketch? Did he comment on that?"

Al grinned. "Oh, he commented alright. He said, and I quote, 'I'm a fucking philologist not a fucking art critic'. Then he put the phone down. I didn't think professors used that kind of language."

"Well, language is his specialty."

"Is it ever!" He turned a page. "OK. So next I tried the consulate. I got some PR woman who must have learned her Estonian in Arkansas; she was even less help than the Professor. And when I asked her about the sketch her only comment was 'A trifle crude, don't you think?'"

He returned the book to his pocket. "Look, Peter, I think it's time to review this investigation. Maybe it's going nowhere…"

Al stopped, caught unawares by Peter's expression. Although they'd met only three times, he thought that he knew the man pretty well. He saw him as intelligent, smooth, something of a charmer. The outburst over the DA's

[15] The Finno-Ugric group of languages includes Finnish, Estonian and Magyar (Hungarian).

performance he'd judged to be largely calculated, but suddenly he was seeing a different man, stony-faced and hard-eyed, a red flush over his cheekbones.

"No reviews, no re-assessments. There isn't going to be any 'stuck' in this investigation. Is that clear?"

Al felt like a raw lieutenant up before the CO. "OK, you're calling the shots." He was piqued at his own failure of judgement and he let it show in a cheap reply. "I can spend the rest of my life on this if that's what you want."

"What I want is to know who killed my daughter and why. Then we'll stop. Tell me what's next."

Al was pleased to move on. "Well, there are two lines of enquiry, one's hard work and the other's a big gamble."

"Tell me about the big gamble."

"I go to Tallinn and see if I get lucky with the sketch."

"And the hard work?"

Al explained Reina Kaplan's suggestion. Peter's reply was instant. "Good. We do both. When can you leave?"

"As soon as I can get a flight."

"And you have somebody to do the hard work?"

"Oh, sure," Al replied, wondering what it would cost him to persuade Mrs Hershey. He played idly with the cold remnants of the chowder, his mind turning to his boyhood and his father's brief posting to northern Germany. They had lived in married quarters on a sprawling US base with shops, church, school, sports center - small-town America on Lüneberg Heath. He had left it only three times in twelve months. "You know," he said, thoughtfully, "I've never really been to Europe."

Peter was staring silently at the Pacific.

CHAPTER 24

The Hotel Reval is a twelve story black-glass tower ten minutes walk from Tallinn's Old Town. It is the post-Communist era's first attempt at hospitality; the building is Western capitalist, the staff Soviet offensive. Along with the crystal chandeliers and marble-floored foyer, the amenities include scowling service, trades-union rigidities, incomprehensible English and, all these notwithstanding, blatant soliciting of tips.

Al sat sweating in his room, the vaunted air conditioning produced only belching noises and a trickle of water down the wall, staring gloomily at his notebook in which he had written 'Library', 'University', before exhausting his ideas.

Normally he, that is to say Mrs Hershey, would have made thorough preparations for such a trip but he had yielded to severe pressure from Peter and caught the first flight. Now he gazed forlornly at the result. He was alone on his first morning in a strange country, speaking not a word of the language, having no contacts and no meetings arranged and a list of two possible sources. Experience had taught him that such problems were best addressed by placing an exorbitant sum in the hands of the concierge. He headed for the foyer.

The desk was manned by a small, stocky, bustling Russian ex-commando stranded like so many others when the Soviet navy pulled out of its Paldiski naval base. He spoke poor Estonian and erratic but enthusiastic English and for US dollars he would do anything, not short of arranging or even inflicting grievous bodily harm.

"Captain!"

On arriving at the hotel Al had assumed that he had been spotted by a fellow serviceman but soon realized that the concierge addressed all Americans older than thirty-five this way.

"You are very good here in my hotel?"

"Very good, thanks." Uncomfortable truths were not part of Al's strategy. He laid the photocopy of the KKK message on the desk, placed a five dollar bill alongside it and started with an easy one.

"Can you help?"

The Russian stared at it blankly. "Make more? Business Center," he offered, pointing across the foyer.

"No, I don't want copies. I need to find…"

A smile spread over the large features. "Ah! Is club. Whiskey, pretty girl… good time, eh?" He wrapped his thick arms around an imaginary girl and made grotesque kissing motions.

"No. It isn't a club. It's a…" Al tried to find a description this bizarre man could recognize. "It's like a business card." He took out the card he was using for the trip – Mr Al Hershey, Hershey Finance Inc. "This is my card. This, me. OK?"

The Russian nodded. Al pointed to the KKK photocopy and was struggling to phrase a suitable question when the manager's voice came over his shoulder.

"Hans van Ost, sir. I am the manager. Can I help you?"

Al quickly discovered that this man was the only professional among the hotel's staff. He was courteous, Dutch, fluent in four languages and actually trying to help. Twenty minutes later Al left his office, stomach warmed by a glass of good bourbon, with a list of contact names and a feeling of optimism. Now he could get down to work.

*　　　*　　　*

The following Friday, all optimism evaporated, he sat disconsolately in the departure lounge of Tallinn International, skimming through the notes of the most unproductive two days he'd ever spent as a PI. The History department of the University, the Historical Society and the Central Library had offered wildly differing interpretations of the text and none had the slightest idea of the significance of the sketch. He'd broken one of his own sacred rules and booked himself out of Tallinn without first calling his client.

The PA system broke into his gloomy thoughts, booming something in Estonian then, in English: "Urgent message for Mr Albrecht Hershey, passenger for Frankfurt. Mr Hershey to the Information Desk, please."

The desk clerk handed him an envelope. Inside a typed note read: 'Estonian vessel on Seattle list. Freighter 'Three Lions', Baltic Star Line, left Tallinn Saturday June 13th. You owe me. Hurry on back. Barb.'

When, an hour later, he re-entered the Reval's foyer, the concierge, wise in the ways of men, greeted him without surprise. In his room, he threw down his carry-on bag and seized the phone. When Mrs Hershey answered she began by complaining that it had been the worst job she'd ever had to do, bar none. He told her she was the finest compiler of lists in the state of California and asked her to marry him. She pointed out she was already married and was expecting her husband home at any minute to take her on a promised trip to New York and signed off by telling him she had no more time for silly expensive telephone calls and to be sure to keep a proper record of expenses and just because this was their first client who didn't argue about the cost of the job, there was no excuse for sloppiness.

*　　*　　*

The Sepps' flat was on the edge of Tallinn's Old Town. When he had been given the job of Head of Security for Baltic Star, Margus had chosen the block because it was an easy stroll down Pikk Street, through the medieval gate with its Fat Margaret tower, to his office in the docks, but it hadn't a whole lot more to recommend it. In the glory days of the Hanseatic League the building had been the town house of a German merchant, a brilliant symphony in cobalt-blue and white topped by a steeply raked roof of scarlet tiles but now, battered by the centuries, a crude conversion and decades of Soviet maintenance, it stood faded and sad in the late afternoon sun. Leida hated everything about it.

Al waited for a response to the bell for apartment 16, wondering why the clerk at the Baltic Star Shipping Company's office had been so nervous when he made his purpose known.

Before he could announce himself, a woman's voice, bright and much too welcoming, came from the tinny speaker and the front door latch snapped open.

The elevator gates had been wired shut – the Soviet alternative to repair. The stairs were dusty and smelled of boiled cabbage. The door to the apartment was ajar and as he reached it, the same voice called out more bright, unintelligible phrases.

He stepped inside but left the door wide open. The room was larger and more pleasing than the building promised. The deep polish of the dining table, the fine pendulum clock on the mantle-shelf, the pale lemon walls, all looked fresh and cheerful. A capacious leather armchair gleamed in the sunlight slanting through a small window.

"Mrs Sepp, I'm Al Hershey."

From the kitchen came a crash of breaking crockery and a single word which was new to Al but the sentiment was familiar enough.

Leida Sepp appeared at the kitchen door, wiping her hands on a towel; she was small and slim, her pale, tired face illuminated by large, lustrous eyes. She stared at Al awkwardly, trying unsuccessfully to capture a few loose fair hairs that had escaped the tight bun tied on top of her head. There was an awkward pause then she returned briefly to the kitchen, reappearing minus the towel and her apron. She still didn't enter the room but stood at the door, again playing nervously with her hair.

"I thought..." She was clearly expecting someone else. "Margus not here. Come more late."

Al spoke slowly. "His office called him. He will meet me here. I'm sorry if I frightened you."

Before she could reply, they heard a heavy tread on the stairs. A momentary look of fear crossed Leida's face. "I get coffee," she said, and went quickly back into the kitchen as Margus entered the room.

"Mr Hershey?" Apart from luxuriant black hair, tumbling in ringlets about his face, Margus was medium in everything else and easily forgettable. His face was flushed, he was perspiring and the smell of tobacco hung about him.

"That's right. It's kind of you to see me at short notice like this but I'm not in town long."

"What you want?"

Al offered his legitimate business card. "Do you think we might talk in private?"

Margus took the card and examined it. "What is this about?"

Al moved closer and lowered his voice. "Better we can talk man to man."

Margus was staring, suspicious and uncomfortable, but he called brusquely to Leida and the kitchen door was closed quietly. Margus sat at the dining table and Al, uninvited, sat opposite.

"So what Mister Private Investigator Hershey want with Margus Sepp?"

Al explained as simply as he could the circumstances of the deaths of Meg and Giorgio. Margus stared in silent truculence.

"I'm hoping you might have some idea what could have been in the package."

"How I know?"

"Well, the 'Three Lions' is a Baltic Star Lines ship, isn't it?"

"We have many ship."

"But the 'Three Lions' was the only one in the area around the date the girl was murdered."

While Al was speaking, Leida came from the kitchen with a tray of coffee. Margus spat something at her in Estonian and, with a fleeting, panicky glance at Al, she put the tray on the table, mumbled a reply then, snatching her handbag from the sideboard, left the flat. Waiting until the door closed behind her, Margus turned on Al.

"Look, Mr American spy. I tell you. I have not idea what you are talking here. 'Three Lions' my brother ship, not FedEx. He don't carry packages, just cargo like it tell on ship paper. OK? So you get to hell out of my place and go spying at somebody else."

He stood up clumsily and leaned across the table, pushing his face into Al's. A cup toppled, spilling coffee over the bright wood. Al stood up too, backing away. The last thing he wanted was physical confrontation. "OK, Mr Sepp, if that's how you want to play it. I'm on my way. Please thank Mrs Sepp for the coffee."

His hotel was less than a mile away and Al set off strolling through the afternoon crowd, reflecting on Sepp's drunken hostility. He had gone no more than a hundred yards when he heard steps behind him.

"Please, Mr American. Please."

Turning he recognized the hunched and frightened figure of Leida Sepp. "Yes, Mrs Sepp. What is it?"

She clutched at his sleeve, glanced quickly over her shoulder then whispered:

"You will see church, Oleviste Church?" She stood on tiptoe and reached up with one hand then placed her hands together, fingertips pointing skywards. "Big needle."

Al started to say he had no time for sight-seeing then quickly switched to: "Of course. Thank you. What time is best to visit?"

"Time? Oh, evening service... tonight, seven o'clock. Thank you." She turned, half ran a few yards, turned back: "Thank you," she repeated, and hurried away.

Back in the flat, Margus drank two cups of coffee then placed a phone call.

*   *   *

Leida's 'big needle' was the fine, copper-green spire of Oleviste - St. Olaf's – Church, a feature of the Tallinn skyline visible from his hotel room.

Determined to make the most of the little spare time he had in a city he did not expect to see again, Al set off at five-thirty for a slow stroll through the Old Town, reaching St. Olaf's at seven.

The service was beginning as he slipped into the dark-panelled gloom of the church and stood against a side wall where he could see the door and the backs of the sparse congregation – mostly women, all middle-aged or older, all shabbily dressed. As the strains of the opening hymn died, Al tried and failed to locate Leida.

He was wondering, uncomfortably, whether Margus had prevented her from coming when he caught sight of her at the far end of a row, not a dozen yards from him. When the short service was over, she stayed, kneeling, head bowed over her clasped hands until the congregation had shuffled out leaving only a pale-faced young girl threading her way through the pews tidying the cushions, before she stood up, looked nervously around and gestured to him.

She led him into a side room, closed the heavy door and leaned against it, eyes scanning the gloomy recesses like a trapped animal. She had released her hair to sweep in a wave obscuring the left side of her face.

"He must not know, Mr…"

"It's Al. And I understand."

She fumbled in her pocket and produced a crumpled sheet of paper. Smoothing it with quick, nervous gestures, she held it out to him. "Is this girl?"

Al was surprised to see a handbill for a Tallinn night club, 'The Panoraam'. It featured a picture of the lead artist, a singer billed as 'The Swinging Swede – Miss Eva Bergstrom', a tall, slender blonde in a low-cut dress clutching a microphone, her eyes closed, her head thrown back, apparently in full voice. In one corner there was a hand written number: a telephone number, Al assumed. Leida plucked at his sleeve and repeated the question. Her breathing was rapid and shallow and there was rising panic in her voice.

"Please… this girl?"

Al took her gently by the arm. "Mrs Sepp, you'll have to help me. I don't understand."

Without warning, her knees buckled and had he not caught her, she would have collapsed. He half carried her to a stone bench set into one wall, eased her down and sat beside her, still holding her arm.

"This girl, the singer, who is she?", he asked, as much to keep her attention as in expectation of an answer. She took the paper back from him and stared at it then slowly raised her eyes to his.

"She is not killed girl?"

And now he realized what she must have overheard of his conversation with her husband. "Killed? No, of course not. Look…" He took Meg's photograph from his wallet and showed it to her. "She was English, she was killed in California."

"California?" The handbill slipped from her grasp and fluttered to the floor as she took the photograph from him. After studying it carefully, she returned it. "You not take him away?" It was more a despairing appeal than a question.

"I'm not a policeman, Mrs Sepp. I can't take your husband away. I'm just here to ask some questions."

She nodded. "Questions," she repeated.

Al retrieved the handbill. "Where did you get this?"

She looked at it as though it were unfamiliar. "Get?"

"Yes. Did you go to the club? Did you see her there?"

Smiling faintly at the idea, she shook her head. "Was in car."

"Which car?"

Suddenly the story spilled from her in a series of short, barely coherent sentences and Al needed to concentrate hard to piece it together. It seemed that a few weeks previously, Margus had, against his normal routine, dressed smartly and gone out for the evening, returning in the small hours. After three consecutive nights of this he had told her he would be away on business and was gone for two weeks. She had assumed it was a woman and when, on his return, she searched the car and found the picture of the singer, she was certain. When Al asked her how Margus had explained his behavior, fear flickered in her eyes and she said she had not asked. Did she know where he had been? Yes, according to the stamps in his passport, Germany. And the exact dates? Yes, as women so often can, she gave them without hesitation. He had left on June 1st and returned on the 13th – he'd been away for her birthday, June 4th.

"Thank you. I have one more question, please."

"Is for girl?" She pointed questioningly to Meg's photograph.

"Yes, it is."

Having described as simply as he could the events in Half Moon Bay, he showed her the photocopy of the message. Her dark mournful eyes flashed immediate recognition.

"You know what this means, Mrs Sepp?"

"Yes, yes. I know it. But..." She began to sob uncontrollably.

"Look, Mrs Sepp, maybe I should take you home..."

"No, no."

She was close to hysteria.

"Easy, easy."

He put an arm around her shoulders and held her until at last she was able to grope in a pocket for a handkerchief, wipe her eyes and sit up. She gestured as if asking for the bill in a restaurant.

"You have... for writing?"

Al produced his notebook and a pen. She took them with sudden firmness of purpose, wrote very slowly and deliberately then pressed the book into his hand.

"You tell from Leida." As she stood up her hair fell away from her face and Al saw the fresh bruise staining her cheek. "Jaakob very good man."

He made to rise but she pressed her small hands on his shoulders, bending to fix him with a look of fierce desperation.

"Stay, please! Follow after." At the door she turned. "You good man, Mr Al," she said earnestly.

Putting the handbill in his pocket, he waited until he heard the ponderous creak of the outer door then walked slowly out from the cool of the church into the warm evening air. He could hear the faint, hurried clicking of high heels echoing back across the cobblestones of the empty street.

CHAPTER 25

The concierge studied Leida's note at length, the effort ploughing deep furrows of puzzlement in his brow far beyond what its three short lines seemed to warrant. He carefully smoothed the paper as though its creases presented an obstacle to understanding. At last, as Al was contemplating the possibility that the man could not read, a huge grin spread across the hard-worn face and he raised a triumphal arm.

"Captain, is easy. You know where Toompea?"

Al didn't even know *what* Toompea. The Russian ran a calloused, disappointed hand through dense greasy hair.

"OK." He pulled a folder from beneath his desk and took out a badly photocopied street map. Stabbing it with a tobacco-blackened forefinger he started afresh. "OK. Here Pikk Street. Walk here..." To aid Al's comprehension he walked two fingers along the map. "...until Sweet Tooth... is café... very good." He smacked his lips, showing yellow teeth, and rubbed his large belly appreciatively. "Now after one hundred meters more, a thin street is name Saiakang... mean White Bread. In old time was all... make bread..." He looked for help.

"Bakers?" Al ventured.

"Ah, bakers, yes. Bread bakers. Now is touristical things. After twenty meters until..." A raised black finger signalled imminent arrival. "...big door. Has fish..." Again the appealing look but this time Al too was stuck until the little man made energetic banging gestures.

"Knocker..." Al guessed. "So people know you're outside?"

"Yes, yes... is knocker... big fish knocker."

"So I knock on this door?"

The concierge looked at him in derision. "Knock? Why knock? Turn handle.

Push. Door open. Is garden… much trees. Biiiiig trees." The short arms arced expansively as he stretched the adjective. "Very nice. No tourist. General don't likes tourist peoples." Vigorous shooing gestures. "He sweep out," he concluded decisively.

*   *   *

Beyond the gate with its promised big fish knocker, the tiny brightly-painted wooden house glowed jewel-like in the shadow of graceful rowan trees and frowning Stalinist apartment blocks. Al's peripheral vision caught a slight movement behind a lace-trimmed curtain before the door opened to reveal the man known throughout Estonia, although he had never been a regular soldier, as the General.

"Yes?"

Tall and heavy-set he stood stiffly upright looking down at Al with the wary, searching look of one with few visitors and many enemies. Al wondered why he had been addressed in English; was he really so obviously American or was he expected?

"Jaakob Oidsalu?"

"I am he."

Al blinked. Was this going to be a re-run of the Professor Posner conversation? He offered his legitimate business card. "Mr Oidsalu, I'm Al Hershey. Mrs Sepp suggested you might be able to help me. I've come on behalf of the parents of a young English woman murdered a few weeks ago in California."

At the mention of Leida's name, Jaakob's wariness evaporated and he stepped back, gesturing Al to enter. The cheaply furnished living room was dominated by a rather rickety bookshelf crammed to overflowing, almost entirely with paperbacks, the majority in English. More books lay on the dining table along with an ancient portable typewriter, a half finished page in its carriage. Jaakob gathered up still more books from the single armchair.

"Please sit down, Mr Hershey. Anyone sent to me by Leida is most welcome;

she is my niece but is like a daughter to me. I see her often, now that she and her husband have moved here to town."

Al seated himself rather precariously on a tired wooden dining chair.

"At my age, one welcomes anything which enables one to feel of use but I fail to see how a decaying Estonian who has not left his homeland for thirty years can help in so distant a matter." The smile was broad and the accompanying shrug eloquent. "California to me is a fairy tale written by Walt Disney."

"Well, sir…," Al began.

A giant, dismissive waft of the hand.

"Mr Hershey, please, even when I commanded men in the forest, they called me general but never sir. My name is Jaakob."

"Very well, Jaakob." Al did his best to copy the old man's pronunciation – yack-ob. "Then it's Al."

The old man nodded gravely. "Please continue, Al."

"Well, sir," Al began again, "it's a long story…"

"Excellent! At my age life is mostly stories. And as for length, you have read the novels of Charles Dickens?" Al hadn't. "I doubt your story is as long and I have read them all, some several times. Please go on."

So, slowly and carefully, watching the old man, trying to ensure he grasped every detail, Al described what he knew of the two deaths, ending by placing the Estonian message on the table. "I need to find out who left this message on Giorgio Fermi's body. That is why I have come. I hope very much you can help me. I've had no luck here so far."

The old man made to pick up the photocopy then changed his mind and simply leaned forward, studying it for a long time. At last he sat back, slowly stroked his silver-white hair, sighed and stood up. "Coffee." It was more of an order than an invitation. From the tiny kitchen Jaakob continued the conversation. "Were you a soldier, Mr Hershey?"

"Yes I was."

"A real soldier, who killed people?"

"Yes, sir, that's what I did." Al waited. The only sounds were the clatter of cups and the rising note of the kettle.

"And were you good at it?"

"I survived."

Another long silence.

"I was to be a teacher of English. My father explained that whatever would happen with the Germans and the Russians, English would be the language of the future."

Now Al understood the old man's extraordinary command of English. And again he waited.

"Did you ever look into the eyes of a man as you killed him?"

"Yes."

"And it affected you?"

"Yes, it did," Al responded.

"You were ashamed?"

"I was nineteen. We had been told the enemy were sub-human."

"In the forest, we had to discover it for ourselves."

'Forest'? Al wondered which forest and when? Who had been the old man's enemy?

Jaakob reappeared carrying two cups. He passed one to Al and stood over him, looking down.

"And if your enemy was already helpless?", Jaakob asked.

"The men I killed were ready and able to kill me..."

A slight figure in black pyjamas bursting through the tunnel's false wall, the click of a jammed weapon then the double bark of Al's nurtured Browning and in the brilliance of the muzzle flash the pain and incredulity on his smooth, child-like face as he was flung, arms flailing, to die in the dirt of the tunnel floor.

Jaakob, too, lapsed into silence gazing at images of long dead comrades in his cup, considering how much of their secrets he could reveal to this stranger. When at length he looked up, Al saw he was out of luck again.

"Mr Hershey, each morning I walk to the square, I take a cup of coffee, I exchange banalities with acquaintances, I come home to work. I read no newspaper, I have no television, my wireless is for music. I left your world some years ago." He gestured around the small room. "My work is my life. I regret I am unable to help."

Part of being a good detective is knowing when to press, when to keep talking and hope, when to quit, and when to go for a return match. Al decided to play for the return. "I understand. But please, may I ask that you take a little time, think it over. Then maybe we can talk tomorrow?"

But Jaakob was shaking his head sadly.

Al took a photograph from his wallet and held it out to the old man who looked at it, warily at first, then intently.

"The young woman... she is the one who was murdered?"

"Yes."

"And these are her parents?"

"Yes."

"That is a terrible thing."

"Yes, sir. So you see why I need your help."

Jaakob spread his hands in resignation. "Mr Al Hershey, you are a very determined man. The young woman's parents are fortunate to have your services. I will think it over but I hope you will not be too disappointed if nothing comes of it."

Al shook his head. "If I couldn't handle disappointment, I wouldn't be in this business. What time tomorrow?"

"About 10 o'clock, the Old Place, near the square."

Back at the Reval the concierge called from behind the desk.

"Good speak General?"

Bad speak General, Al thought, but he waved and nodded encouragingly. Maybe good speak tomorrow.

In his room Al sat trying to write up the day's events, his mind returning to the formidable old man. Warriors of his vintage were rare. It would be good to spend leisured time with him, to compare wars, talk of things civilians could not understand. With regret he turned to his work; it would not happen, he knew.

CHAPTER 26

Jaakob's 'near the square' covered a lot of territory and the Old Place proved difficult to find. Al completed an unsuccessful circuit of the bustling square with its jumble of timbered, pastel-colored Renaissance houses, brash new cappuccino bars and 'ethnic' restaurants, then asked a woman carrying shopping bags who looked at him blankly. Finally, in desperation, he tried a pizza bar where between the waiter's Italian and Al's Spanish, directions were communicated, together with the puzzling observation that the Old Place served excellent Kalev but that tourists were not welcome.

The café, it turned out, was a bare fifty meters from the square but down a twisting, cobbled street entered through an archway almost hidden behind a kiosk selling tourist trinkets. Although the building was dated 1795, the Gothic facade with its ornately carved wooden door and mullioned windows suggested a medieval chapel. Inside the atmosphere was heavy with the scents of coffee, strong tobacco and old wood. Two narrow shafts of sunlight from almost-closed curtains at the arched windows shone brilliant blue in the smoke-laden air. The half-dozen tables and their benches, the bar, the walls, the beamed ceiling – everything was made of the same rough-hewn dark wood burnished with age.

Jaakob sat at a corner table next to the bar. By his side on the bench-seat there was a battered briefcase, and on the table, with leather binding cracked and fading, lay a book, which he absent-mindedly fondled as one might a small animal. The only other customer was a man in a black leather cap and workman's overalls hunched shortsightedly over a newspaper and puffing on an enormous wooden pipe which gave out such volumes of smoke that at times the smoker merged into the background. At the sound of the door opening he waved a hand to cut a window in the fug, peered cautiously through it at Al then, apparently satisfied, returned to his reading, the fog reconvening comfortably about him.

Behind the bar a man in a striped apron placed both hands on the edge of the counter, leaned forward belligerently and said something in Estonian that sounded unwelcoming. Before Al could attempt a response, Jaakob gestured to him: "Al! You found us then. Come, sit. What would you like?"

"I believe I'd like to try a Kalev."

Jaakob snapped out something in Estonian and the barman grunted acknowledgement and disappeared behind a curtain.

"You like Kalev?", Jaakob asked, intrigued.

"I don't even know what it is. It was recommended."

Jaakob nodded. "Kalev is a type of chocolate."

Al's heart sank.

"It has been made here in Tallinn for two hundred years. We Estonians supplied it to the Tsars."

Al gestured towards the bar. "Does he greet all his customers that way?"

Jaakob smiled. "Only foreigners. He's owned this place since the sixties. Somehow when the Soviets collectivized everything, he was overlooked."

"They missed a good man!"

"Ah, Al, you must not prejudge." He wagged an admonitory finger. "Jaan is a patriot, he has a good heart."

Goodhearted Jaan reappeared, scowling, with a small silver tray bearing a bar of dark chocolate, a spirit stove, a copper pot with a long handle, a silver jug of milk and a cup, saucer and spoon. The tray was set down and Jaan left without a word.

"The idea is to heat the milk," Jaakob explained, "then melt the chocolate and stir the hot milk into it."

"Maybe I could have a regular coffee?", Al suggested.

"Al, I am offering you a new experience. Here," he drew the tray to him, "allow me; there is a certain technique. Jaan claims the recipe was handed down to him through the generations but in fact he invented the whole thing himself one winter in the seventies when business was especially slow. It was what I believe you would call a marketing wheeze?"

"A gimmick. 'Wheeze' is a British word." A Peter word, in fact, Al thought.

"Of course, a gimmick. Hmm... gimmick," he savored the word. "I like that. It sounds... duplicitous."

He began by breaking the chocolate into neat squares then poured the milk into the pot and set it on the stove. "In the square," he observed, swirling the milk gently over the flame, "there are now places they call coffee bars." As the milk was about to boil, he poured it back into its jug and began feeding the chocolate into the pot, tilting it slowly back and forth over the flame. "I understand they use an apparatus which blows steam through their chocolate." He shook his head. Now the whole bar was molten. Still gently rocking the pot, he began slowly to add the hot milk. "Estonians, who have made the finest chocolate in Europe for generations, now manufacture their drinks with a steam engine."

Watching the old man's measured, deft movements and intense concentration, Al glimpsed something of the young man who had risen to the informal rank of General.

With all of the milk added, he took the spoon and stirred the liquid rapidly for half a minute then poured it quickly into the cup and slid it across to Al. "A strange place, this new world, is it not?"

Al nodded agreement and apprehensively tried the drink. He was not one for sweet things but he had to admit this was special, its sweetness cut with a strong undertone of bitterness from the very dark chocolate. He was about to express appreciation when Jaakob spoke.

"When I was a young man in the forest, I learned to sleep even in the snow-covered branches of a tree and still sleep comes easily to me. But last night I slept little. I have spoken with Leida. The young woman's death has upset her. She senses you are a good man and advises that I help you. Please let me look again at your message."

"Certainly." Al took out the photocopy and handed it over.

The old man studied it silently. "'Karistus Kümavereliselt Kuritegu'". He repeated the words several times, savoring them, smiling to himself. "Ours is a strange language, Al, a linguistic playground. You know we have no future tense?"

Al didn't.

"Maybe it's because we have never really been certain that we have a future." A wry smile from the old man. "Foreigners expect that it will be similar to Russian, or maybe to Latvian or Lithuanian, but it is not."

Al groaned inwardly. What was it about the Estonian language that made otherwise normal people begin a lecture whenever it was mentioned? He hoped this version would be both shorter and more helpful than the one he'd endured from Posner.

"It's quite similar to Finnish and to Magyar. It is in fact a member of…"

Al could see a Finno-Ugric coming.

"…the Finno-Ugric language group."

Jaakob, warming to a favorite theme, saw or perhaps heard Al's gritted teeth. "Al, please forgive me. You did not come to Estonia to be battered with linguistics." He picked up the paper. "So… we have a message, a slogan. 'Karistus'… that is a penalty; 'Kuritegu' is a misdeed or an offence. Together they mean a penalty for an offence."

"Like a traffic ticket, maybe?", Al suggested disgustedly, his disappointment obvious. Then he saw the mischievous gratification on the old man's face.

"On the other hand…", the grin broadened as he paused for effect, "'Karistus' may also mean punishment or prison sentence. And 'Kuritegu' may mean crime."

Al nodded wryly. He'd been caught out by this subtle old man. "So maybe we have 'punishment for a crime'?", he suggested.

"Just so. And…", another dramatic pause. Cheated of the opportunity to complete his lecture, Jaakob was stretching out his brief drama. "…we have 'Kümavereliselt' which means 'in cold blood'."

"So… 'punishment for a crime in cold blood'." This was becoming interesting. "But the sketch, what does it mean? Above all, who wrote the message?"

"Ah," Jaakob responded, taking up his book, "for the answer to that question I must take you back to very sad days." He finished his coffee, his mind drifting back in time.

"Before the war, Anti, my father, was Professor of Military History at Tallinn University. He was a brilliant man, generous, perceptive. He would warn his students that they would suffer the curse of Cassandra: to see history coming and be ignored. When the war came, in all Estonia, only he could write the record. It is my final task to translate it into English. Until recently I have had to work in secret," he smiled a wistful smile. "Our Soviet masters would, of course, have destroyed the manuscript as they destroy everything that does not accord with their view of the world. Now maybe I will live to see the work complete."

He took from his briefcase a crudely bound typewritten document. "This is a copy of what I have translated so far. As I presume your time is short I have marked some passages which you will find especially relevant. Perhaps you will read it and meet me again tomorrow. Then I will tell you the remainder of the story."

Al took the typescript. "Thank you, sir… Jaakob. I appreciate your help and I do understand how difficult this has been for you. I will of course read it this evening. Would 10 be OK?"

"10 would be perfectly OK," Jaakob smiled as he returned the unaccustomed slang. "The café by the apothecary."

CHAPTER 27

Al stopped briefly to eat a rather good pizza in the restaurant where he'd obtained directions - *'Our pizza is best not in Italy'* - before returning to his hotel room and hanging out the *'Do not disturb'* sign. Then he stretched out on the bed and began to read. The journal told, in horrifying detail, the story of the rape of Estonia, first by the Nazis then by the Soviets, how those determined to resist or simply too frightened to stay in the towns and villages, came together in the depths of Estonia's forests to fight, and how Anti Oidsalu, Professor of Military History at the University of Tallinn, came to lead the Forest Brothers and to write their gallant but ultimately hopeless story.

Al located Jaakob's first marked passage:

'November 3rd 1941. Forest.

Endel Vanaveski, son of the Bishop of Tallinn, arrived today, brought by a charcoal-burner from across the valley. He said that yesterday he had heard bursts of firing for several minutes and found the boy, apparently uninjured but only half-conscious, a few hours later. The news of firing is ominous – there are rumors of mass arrests of townspeople. God help them and all of us. The boy appears calm but there is a fever in his eyes. I fear for him.'

'November 5th 1941. Forest.

For two days the boy has said not a word, now suddenly he tells us everything. Despite all we have seen and heard, we can scarcely believe his story.

His father, a fine man but unworldly, had concealed the Christ in the crypt. The senior officer in Tallinn, SS Sturmbannführer Roth - I note the name in the hope that one day he will be called to account - brought the Bishop, his wife and their elder daughter Maarja into the church. Endel followed and concealed himself among the roof timbers.

The father was ill, a problem with his lungs, and could scarcely stand. It was all very civilized, no threats. Through an interpreter, Roth asked him to hand over the carving of the Christ. The Bishop had prepared a story. He said the Brothers had the carving in the forest but claimed he did not know where.

Roth just looked him in the eye for a few seconds then, coolly unfastening his greatcoat, took out his pistol and shot the daughter dead. She was ten years old. Then he repeated the question. The father being unable to speak, his wife directed the soldiers to the hiding place of the carving.

Incredibly, worse was to follow. According to the boy's story, about a hundred people from the town, including his remaining family, were arrested the next day, marched into the forest and machine-gunned. As far as he knows, he is the only survivor.

When he had finished his story, he demanded a pistol, saying that he intended to go into the town to kill Roth. He was perfectly calm and fully understood that he would almost certainly be caught and killed. He simply said that his only wish was to give his life to avenge the murder of his family. Of course, I refused.'

Two months later the journal described how the partisans had learned that Roth was to travel to Tartu for a meeting of senior officers. Mustering every man he could find, Anti had ambushed the armored column, killing many Germans and capturing Roth, injured but alive.

'January 6th 1942. Forest.

Following the Council's decision we took Roth into town before dawn this morning. I had intended killing him myself but the boy, whom I could not in justice prevent from joining the party, demanded that he do it. I have never seen such determination. I believe he would have struck me had I refused. I offered him my own weapon but the comrade who took Roth in the ambush was carrying Roth's own pistol and the boy used that. It was chilling – the muzzle an inch from Roth's face, unhurried, saying nothing, no gloating, nothing. Stepping on an insect. Then he took a paper from inside his shirt and left it on the body. It looked, as best I can reproduce it, like this:'

Al turned the page, gaped in astonishment, sat up and, almost involuntarily reached for the telephone. It was only when he heard a rather bleary-sounding Peter that he was appalled to realize it was four in the morning in Half Moon Bay.

"Oh, shit! I'm sorry, Peter. I forgot the time difference..."

Recognizing the voice, Peter woke up fast. "No problem. What is it? Where are you?"

"I'm still in Tallinn. I've stumbled on something incredible."

Now Peter really was awake. "Go on."

"Well, I can hardly believe it myself but I'm looking at the original of the KKK message. Peter, it's fifty years old."

"Fifty years... I don't follow."

"Well, Oidsalu's given me a translation of a war journal written by his father..."

"Hold on," Peter interrupted. "Who's Oidsalu?"

Al took a breath. "Good question – sorry, Peter. He fought the Nazis and the Russians here back in the forties. I'm getting a bit carried away here. Look, it's all far too complicated to explain right now and I don't fully understand it myself. Can I call you later, when I can make some sense of all of it?"

"Of course. We're desperate for news. Call me any time – and that wasn't a joke, I mean any time, OK?"

"OK, I'll get back to you."

Al put down the phone and began skipping pages, looking for the next marked passage. He found it on the last page:

'March 23rd 1942 Forest

News from the station. A friend there has given us details of an SS special train, leaving Tallinn tomorrow evening, transporting what they've stolen from all over Estonia. We plan an attack to recover what we can – especially the Christ. He says it is in a special crate addressed to 'Pohl,

Berlin'. Our friend is a good man, reliable. Where would we be without his kind? Tomorrow we attack the station.'

And here the journal ended with a single line in a different, much less mature hand:

'March 26th 1942 Forest

During the night my father died in mother's arms. The struggle continues.'

*   *   *

Hauptmann Gerhard Seiler was cold, tired and irritated. Loading was running late and the station was already dangerously dark. He cursed his luck. The east was a disaster, Estonia was lost, the fanatical Austrian Corporal was destroying the finest army in the world. And loading stolen goods onto trains was for railway officials not fighting soldiers.

The explosion came as the last half-dozen crates were being loaded. Everyone hit the ground. For a few seconds, time was suspended; the echoes of the explosion died away. From a warehouse at one end of the platform ragged yellow flames and black smoke rose straight up into a windless sky. The Hauptmann twisted onto his side to free his holster and drew his pistol. Rifle fire was coming from a gap in the fence a hundred yards beyond the tracks. For a few seconds Seiler hesitated, weighing probabilities, but even as he was getting to his feet, Unterfeldwebel Erdmann, his second in command and second self, was already running towards the front of the train screaming:

"Up. Get up, you bastards. If this train isn't out of here in thirty seconds I'll personally shoot the driver. Thirty seconds!"

Obergefreiter Johannes Klieg, an ox-like man of criminal stupidity, slower to his feet than the others, took a crisp boot in the ribs. "Get up Klieg. Take six men, check out that fence."

In the cab the civilian driver, scared half senseless by the explosion and Erdmann's threat, threw open the throttle. A cloud of steam erupted from the engine. Its driving wheels spun, screeching, then took hold, sending a tremendous shock along the train. *Oberschütze* Erich Baumann, just three days past his eighteenth birthday, struggling to close the doors of the rearmost wagon, snagged his sleeve on the locking bar, was flung to the ground and towed along the platform. As the train gathered speed he began to slide writhing and screaming towards the platform edge. Despite frenzied efforts he was unable to free himself and before anyone could get to him he was dragged over the edge. There was a hideous final shriek as the wheels passed over him. The train snorted angrily into the distance, leaving his comrades to contemplate the bloody remnants of young Baumann.

From a signal gantry Seiler's carefully positioned heavy machine gun began firing measured bursts, its tracer rounds drifting lazily across the open ground, innocuous until they struck home, tearing up turf, mowing down small trees, splintering the yard's stout wooden fencing. Soon the hammering of the machine gun was joined by the rattle of small-arms fire and the crump of grenades as Klieg's troop took what cover they could and began exchanging fire with the invisible enemy.

Abruptly, as though on a secret signal, the firing stopped. Now came an eerie silence broken only by the crackling of burning timber and the loud whispers of the frozen, field-grey figures. A minute passed. Klieg, as brave as he was stupid, raised his head, peering for a view of his enemy, then, seeing nothing, stood up, silhouetted against the bright glow of the fire. For several anxious seconds his men waited but there was no more firing. Klieg's little group picked themselves up and moved cautiously forward, hoping for a prisoner or at least a corpse or two but, taking their wounded with them, the Brothers were already heading back to the forest. In the rearmost wagon, *Der sitzende Christus* had begun its long and hazardous journey to Pohl, Berlin.

CHAPTER 28

Having experience of Jaakob's sketchy directions, Al left the hotel early. Arriving at the café with time to spare, he chose an outside table, ordered a coffee and took his chance to play the tourist. He had traveled to almost every state in the Union, from magnolias and river-boats in New Orleans, to Douglas firs and snow-shoes in Maine; the army had shown him all he wanted to see of Southeast Asia, but he had seen almost nothing of Europe and he drank it in. A fierce sun slanted into the square. On the shaded side, the buildings merged into a seamless gloom of earth colors; opposite, the facade of pastel greens, blues and pinks shimmered in the heat. High above, seagulls wheeled and screamed, black against the cloudless sky. Immediately facing him a freshly-painted sign read, 'The World's Oldest Apothecary Established 1422'.

Tension drained out of him; it was like that deep first drag on a joint after a combat patrol. Usually he was quick to feel uncomfortable when relaxing on his client's nickel but in this place, centuries older than his America, it felt nothing but good. All it lacked was Mrs Hershey to share his enjoyment.

A young woman in peasant costume approached, carrying a tray of cheap jewellery. When Al shook his head she pouted and, undeterred, moved closer. Before he could deal with this determined intruder, Jaakob appeared and spoke to her in staccato Russian. Still unfazed, she kissed Al on the forehead and moved on to the next table brushing against his knees with a smile as she passed. It was the professional smile he had last seen on the face of a Saigon child prostitute, to be replaced by a venomous scowl and a scream of 'you plenty cheap Charlie' when he turned down her offer.

"You speak Russian?" Al asked.

"Many of us do."

"What did she say?"

"She said that you are a very sexy man and she would like you to take her home with you to Hollywood."

"Hollywood?"

He smiled at Al's innocence. "It is the only place in America she knows," he said, simply. As Jaakob sat down Al asked with a straight face: "What will you have? A Kalev?".

"Ah, Al, you should know better than to… pull my leg, is it? Only the Old Place can make Kalev. A coffee, please."

For a while they sat in silence, watching the kaleidoscopic life of the square, Al giving Jaakob time. They'd almost finished their coffees before the old man spoke. "You have read the journal?"

"I have, thank you." He passed the typescript across the table. "Your father was a remarkable man. I would have liked to meet him."

Acknowledging the compliment with a nod, Jaakob began elaborating Anti's story. "He had worked out the plan for the attack on the station in much detail." He shot a questioning glance at Al. "You have seen such plans?"

"Some."

"So you know how little they guarantee."

"Some plan is better than no plan."

"And his plan was good but those Nazis were too strong, too well-organized and their commander was a professional. My father was hit in the thigh by a grenade fragment. At first we thought it was not serious but…" he threw a haunted glance at Al, "…we had only aspirin. The wound became infected. There was talk of removing the leg but my father would not allow it. That night my mother said he had asked to see Endel and me. He told us to look after her and all the womenfolk. Then, when he was almost too weak to go on, he pulled us both to him and made us swear before God to track down the carving and keep it safe until Estonia was free and it could be restored to the church. At the end only my mother stayed with him. He died early in the morning. He is buried in the forest in an unmarked grave, like too many of our comrades."

He finished his coffee, turning away a little, then resumed.

"I shall never forget the grip of his hand on my arm and his last whispered words to us: 'Pohl, Berlin. The name, remember the name: Pohl.' We heard later that SS-Obergruppenführer Oswald Pohl was hanged by the Allies in 1951." He smiled thinly at Al. "Thanks to the British. They captured him as he tried to escape from Berlin, I believe."

"And the Christ? What became of it?"

An odd, puzzled smile came over the old man's features. "Ah, now there we have a most strange story."

Their waiter, seeing that Jaakob had finished his coffee, was hovering a respectful few yards away and at a nod from the old man came to refill their cups.

"War is terrible but it has rules; the Nazis above all had rules. But near the end, when the cause was lost, survival was the only rule and chaos the result. There was a rumor that, like others of those Nazis, Pohl had sent money and stolen art works to South America, preparing his escape, but I could not confirm it. I came to believe that the carving was in a Swiss bank vault or sealed up in a Thuringian salt-mine. Of course, I never gave up hope but I could not see how it could be found except by chance. It seemed to me like a lost symphony of Mozart, buried in a library. I could only hope that anyone who stumbled on it would know the worth of the discovery. That was until four months ago when the Archbishop of Tallinn – he is the head of the church in all Estonia - called to see me. His visit was most unexpected and made in great secrecy. You must understand, Al, that he and I are acquainted, but never before had he called at my home."

There followed a long silence, Jaakob idly running a fingertip around the rim of his cup. "He had received a strange telephone call. A man, offering to return the Christ for the sum of one million American dollars. The Archbishop was inclined to believe that it was a hoax except for this." He took from his briefcase a single sheet of paper and laid it in front of Al.

It was apparently a page copied from an art catalogue which read as follows:

Item:	Wood carving
Title:	'Christus sedens' (Der sitzende Christus)
Date:	1493
Artist:	Stoss, Veit c. 1450-1533
Nationality:	German national (b. Nuremberg)
Material:	Dark wood
Size:	45 cms (height)
Provenance:	1493 Commissioned Heinrich Schenck of Tallinn, Estonia
	1493 Consecrated Church of the Holy Spirit, Tallinn
	1943 Reclaimed for the Reich
	1943 Berlin apartment, SS-Obergruppenführer Pohl
	1944 Paraguay villa, SS-Obergruppenführer Pohl
Estimated value:	US$1,000,000?
Remarks:	Value uncertain due to the unusual nature of the piece.

Al gave a low whistle. "A million bucks!"

"Indeed. If the document was intended to add credibility to the claim, then it succeeded."

"But why did the church come to you, Jaakob?"

Jaakob drew a deep breath. "Again, I regret I must take you on a journey into my past."

Al gestured to show this was not a problem.

"You will recall the boy – I should better say the young man – Endel? Well, he left the forest in 1950."

Al's surprise showed.

"Ah, Al, do you think our war ended in 1945? While the allies had their celebrations – VE Day, were they not called? – we were still in the forest being hunted by the Red Army and the thugs of the NKVD…"

"NKVD?".

"I beg your pardon, Al. I forget that we are of different generations.

They were the Soviet Secret Police, now known as the KGB."

"Thank you. Sorry to interrupt. Please go on."

"As I said, in 1945 we were in the forest. Endel was still with us, a leader, of course. We all knew that my father had told him that he should leave Estonia before it was too late, take the flame of our freedom to the new world and keep it burning there. And always I was urging him to go. But always he refused, he was needed, he said. Then, one day in 1950, quite suddenly and without a word – that was always his way – he was gone. I believe he had finally decided the battle was lost and he could do more for the cause from abroad. For several years we heard nothing until, in 1956... do you say out of the sky?"

"Out of the blue," Al corrected.

"Of course, out of the blue. I received a letter. He was living in New York. After that we corresponded often. He wrote long letters, most interesting, about his life in New York, his successes in business... Later, it was 1970, there was the first mention of a woman, Francesca – a beautiful name, I thought. She was very young, Spanish, a translator at the United Nations. They were to be married but something bad happened. He wrote a short note, no details, just that he must leave New York at once and he would write when he could. Then nothing for almost a year, until he telephoned to tell me that he was in hiding from dangerous men and not to try to contact him. Nothing of his fiancée; he never mentioned her again."

"Did you ask what became of her?"

"One does not ask a man like Endel such a question."

Al nodded, acknowledging the reproof. "And this letter also came from New York?"

Jaakob spread his hands in a gesture of sad resignation. "This was a desperate man. From the time he left New York I received only telephone calls, irregularly, every few months."

"But you can contact him?"

"In an emergency, yes. There is a procedure." He clearly was not about to reveal it.

Al made to steer the conversation back to the Archbishop's carving. "So how..." But Jaakob was already there.

"In recent years it seems Endel has become both wealthy and powerful. He has made large donations to the church here and has helped a number of my countrymen find work and make a life in your country."

"So the church was hoping he would pay the ransom?"

"Not exactly. Of course, the church does not possess such a sum but first they wished Endel to determine whether the offer was genuine."

They were out of their depth and just wanted somebody to get their carving back, Al thought. And Endel was that somebody. So far, Jaakob's story raised more questions than it answered and shed little light on his own investigation but Al had long ago learned that his work, when it was not simply collecting evidence for a divorce suit, was like hunting down the pieces of a jigsaw puzzle without sight of the picture. When life handed him a new piece, he knew enough not to reject it merely because he couldn't yet see where it might fit.

"So you used the emergency procedure?"

Jaakob nodded.

"And what happened?"

"Endel telephoned me. I was to ask the Archbishop to give my number when the caller rang back. If he then called me, I was to request a meeting, here in Tallinn. Endel's instructions were extraordinarily precise, a certain bar, a particular table, I must sit facing the square. I protested that only a fool would attend such a meeting but Endel said if I told him 'no meeting, no deal' then he would come."

"And he was right?"

Jaakob smiled a pale smile. "As always. So the meeting took place a week later. As instructed, I told him the money was available but we must have proof that he could deliver the carving."

"Proof?" Al asked.

"It was to be a photograph of the carving together with the current edition of the Wall Street Journal."

"I see. And he agreed?"

Jaakob shrugged. "He was extremely angry but he was left no choice. He said I would have the photograph in three days."

"And the photograph, did you receive it?"

The old man spread his hands in a gesture of bewilderment: "I have heard no word since, not from Endel, not from the German."

"The German?"

"Ah, yes. The man I met was German, or at least a native German speaker."

"So the carving is still in German hands?"

"It would seem so."

Of course, Al thought, Endel's method was brutally simple. Maneuver the man into a meeting and he'll lead you to the carving. Only a truly desperate man could have been so reckless.

For the record and to avoid a procedural argument with Mrs Hershey, Al quizzed Jaakob about the German speaker but obtained only the hardly helpful information that he was, as Jaakob put it, a perfect Aryan aged around forty. Al wondered what proportion of the combined populations of Germany, Austria and Switzerland would fit that description.

Another street vendor approached, a small, heavily moustached man dressed in a white cotton shirt and baggy peasant trousers, an ivory-handled curved dagger thrust into his belt. He was dangling a fluorescent green furry spider from an elastic string, but catching Jaakob's eye he veered off.

Al looked at the notes he had made while reading the journal. "The weapon used to kill... what was his name... Roth? It was a Luger?"

"A Luger 9mm. And yes, Endel kept the gun. It was his trophy. He still had it when he made his escape."

"It was a 9mm parabellum round that killed Giorgio Fermi."

Jaakob was silent, massaging his brow with a weary hand. At length he straightened in his chair and beckoned a waiter. "More coffee?"

While the cups were refilled, Al pressed the point. "The bullet, the message...there can be no doubt that Endel killed Fermi."

The old man looked at Al over the rim of his cup, still silent. Then, after a long pause he spoke with his earlier firmness of purpose.

"And now you are seeking the words to ask me to help you find him...", a statement, not a question, "...and I regret I cannot. If you will permit me, I will explain why."

Al waited.

"First, a very practical matter. I doubt very much that anything I could do would help you. It is now twenty years since I had an address for him. But more important I still do not believe that Endel has the carving." The old man's jaw took on an obstinate set. "I can see no possible reason for him to steal it."

"Most people steal stuff because they can't afford to buy it."

"Endel is not most people. He is extremely wealthy."

"He told you that?"

"You are a great cynic, Al," Jaakob complained. "As I have said, he has sent me hundreds of thousands of dollars for the church, for hospitals. He is most generous."

"Did he tell you how he made the money he hands out so generously?"

"Business. He gave no details. It was part of his secret. I have long hoped that he would one day start a business here in Estonia."

He was rubbing his chin thoughtfully and Al paused, wondering if there would be more.

"Indeed, I have sometimes wondered whether this has already happened..." he murmured then his voice trailed off. Al noted the half-formed thought but decided not to pursue it, for the moment at least. Then Jaakob resumed but on a new tack. "Everyone is starting businesses." He gestured disdainfully around the square. "In the new Estonia one may buy anything – even a lime green spider."

"You disapprove?"

"My approval was not sought."

There was a silence. Al was trying to concentrate but the warmth of the sun was soporific and he felt his eyes closing. He was tired and realized he had been on the road – the damned trail as Mrs Hershey called it – for too long.

"Of course," Jaakob mused, "the silence is disturbing…"

Al glanced at him questioningly but the old man's gaze was turned inwards. Seconds passed. Through half-closed eyes Al watched a couple of seagulls squabbling over the remnants of a pizza.

"…but he is a busy man with many responsibilities. There have been many long silences."

Al waited, watching Jaakob struggle, trapped between harsh evidence and decades-old comradeship. Abruptly the old soldier sat up, shoulders back, a defiant light in his eyes. "He is my friend, a man of honor," he said, with dignified finality.

"Of course." This was certainly one for a return match, Al thought. "I have a proposal. If I can bring you evidence that your friend has the carving, then you will help me find him?"

The old man looked at him for a long time, staring the unpalatable decision in the face. "Al, we, too, are men of honor." He offered his hand. "We have a deal."

Al stood up and they shook hands. "We do indeed, sir… Jaakob. Thank you for your help. I will be in touch." He turned to leave then hesitated. "There is one other thing. It concerns Leida…"

Jaakob's eyes widened.

"When I met her, in the church, there was a bruise…" He held a hand to his cheek. "… here. You understand?"

Jaakob nodded sadly. "I understand. Margus is not a good man but… she absolutely refuses to allow me to intervene. Perhaps you have seen such things?"

Al nodded. "Too often." Raising a hand in final salute, he left the old man to his memories and returned to the Reval to write up his notes and consider his next step.

CHAPTER 29

"Peter? It's Al."

"Hello. Good to hear your voice. Where are you this time?"

"Still in Tallinn, but only just. I'm packed and ready to go."

"Where to next – Moscow?"

Just in time, Al stopped himself asking why he should want to go to Moscow. "Oh, yeah, I mean no. New York. I've managed to get a direct flight."

"You have something?"

"Yes."

Peter waited in vain for amplification. "Alright, Al," he said, patiently, "I'll take the bait. What have you got?"

A brief pause then, "I know who wrote the message."

Peter listened to Al's story for twenty minutes and cross-examined him for ten more before he reached the conclusion Al had already acted on: Vanaveski must be found and there was only one place to start looking.

Al hated New York. Living there for six months when he first came out of the service had taught him that too many smart, successful people crammed into too little space was not a formula for a comfortable life. On the other hand, he'd met Rick.

1981, Al's first year of life as a Vet, a bad life, he was discovering. Of course the fear had been left behind but with it had gone the unique bond between men who live with that fear and in its place came isolation. He'd learned what all Vets learn, that civilians are endlessly inquisitive, that combat can be described but not communicated, that a stranger with a marine haircut, drinking alone, can be construed as a challenge. 'How come you don't talk to nobody, man? You too good for us folks?'. There'd been too much drinking and too many fights.

~ CHAPTER 29 ~

On that first civilian evening in New York, he had drifted around Times Square feeling like a displaced person. He'd spent the first six years of his life in Puerto Rico speaking as much Spanish as English, then his father's work as civilian translator for the Army had taken the family to Germany where, in a stay of only one year, he'd learned some German, although not as much as his father had wanted, the first sign of a rebellion against parental authority, which would culminate on his seventeenth birthday when he enlisted in the Marines. His first experience of the continental US was boot camp at Parris Island, South Carolina. And now, his service life over, his parents divorced, his father dead, his mother and sister living in Ireland, he was homeless and alone.

To escape Manhattan, he'd dived into the subway system, crossed the East River to Brooklyn and emerged at random in what he would later discover was New York's Polish quarter.

He'd found a suitably despondent little bar where he'd just settled down with a beer when angry voices erupted from the back room and a young man appeared, staggering rapidly backwards and crashed into his table, hurling the beer to the floor.

Without a glance at Al, he recovered his balance and was on his way back to where he'd come from until Al took his arm and requested a replacement. The young man refused belligerently and Al was forced to hit him.

Having been drawn into whatever was going on; he entered the back room and was treated to a bizarre sight. Cheered on by the bystanders, a rotund but still agile man in his fifties was holding a man half his age in a savage arm-lock and using him as combined shield and battering-ram to fend off repeated attacks from two other young men, one wielding a knife. With the help of Al and the barman, peace was quickly restored.

Over a drink, the older man, known as Rick since his name was an unpronounceable Polish form of Richard, explained that the dispute had begun when one of the four young men had loudly asked of no-one in particular just who grandpa thought he was to wear a Marine Corps T-shirt.

During the ensuing extended drinking session, Al learned that Rick was a second generation immigrant whose parents spoke only Polish and lived in northern Minnesota – 'Oh sheet, Al baby, it voz so cold even ze dog peessed in a pot'. At fourteen, he left home to escape 'ze cold' and his father's belt, learned a form of English on the streets of Chicago for a while – 'Nice town ven ze vint don't blowink' – then joined the Marines figuring that while boot camp might be a bitch, the chances were it would be located somewhere warmer than Chicago. In the Corps, he'd lived tight and saved enough to make the down-payment on a house. Discharged in San Diego, he'd set off for New Orleans but the worse for vodka, he'd caught the wrong train, which explained why his B&B was in Brooklyn. Al crashed there for what was left of that night and had since never stayed anywhere else in the city, although he knew that when Mrs Hershey claimed her trip to the city, he would need to find somewhere considerably less basic.

*   *   *

Fifteen hours after leaving Tallinn, straight from the airport, Al's taxi was taking him down Brooklyn's Manhattan Avenue and, with theatrical speed, he was in Poland, shop signs in Polish, window displays of dolls in folk costumes, brightly-colored sandals, painted wooden eggs, portraits of the Pope, jars of preserves, dried mushrooms, and other more obscure imports. Bakeries displayed babkas, enormous round breads, and khruisciki, frothy pastries smothered in powdered sugar. Restaurant signs listed mysterious delicacies - klopsciki, golabki, kaczki. Al drank it all in and, as they drew up outside the unprepossessing little B&B, he celebrated his return by handing the surprised driver a ten dollar tip.

The euphoria was short lived. His trip to the local Station House the following morning was a disaster. Faced by a martinet of a desk Sergeant with a chip on his shoulder and no time for pain-in-the-ass PI's, his usual diplomacy deserted him and he came close to ending up in the cells. He excused himself with the argument that New York did that to otherwise nice people. Then the local telephone directory got him as far as the Estonian

Embassy, where an unusually helpful woman on reception suggested the Baltic-American Association, and there he struck gold. The Secretary, a tall, cadaverous man with a smoker's cough and a card-file memory said yes of course he knew Mr Vanaveski, in those days everybody in the Association knew him. Would have made a good Chairman but nothing would persuade him to join the committee. Then after that dreadful business in… when was it now…? Oh yes, 1971, he'd simply disappeared.

Over coffee in the Association's cafeteria, Al got the full terrible story, expanding on what Jaakob had told him.

Vanaveski had been engaged to a young Spanish woman he'd met at a reception given by the Association. At that time, he was the owner of a successful import-export business based in a rough neighbourhood near the docks. His fiancée had been warned never to go to the office after dark but one evening in late 1971, Vanaveski, not having turned up at the restaurant where they were to meet, she drove there.

What exactly happened next wasn't clear but the girl was found the following morning on waste ground only a block from the office. She had been raped and strangled.

Vanaveski's lack of reaction amazed everyone. Immediately after the funeral, he resumed his long working hours and continued spending his evenings in the Association. Nothing seemed to have changed, except that he became even more silent and intense.

Then, three weeks later, without explanation, he paid off his staff, cleared his office and disappeared.

Next day, the body of one Antonio 'Tony the Snake' Rastelli was found on the same waste ground. He'd been shot, rather nastily, as the Secretary remembered it. In Al's experience there was no nice way to get shot but he kept the thought to himself.

Rastelli had been a mafia enforcer whose technique with lead pipe or knuckleduster was widely admired. He was always well supplied with willing young women but even his fellow Sicilians, not noted for their sensitive attitude to the opposite sex, had complained about his treatment of the unwilling few. Of course everybody knew who had killed him and why, but the investigation was hampered by locals spitting and walking away when Rastelli's name was mentioned.

As to Vanaveski's present whereabouts, the Secretary couldn't help. Maybe he went back to Estonia, he ventured, adding fervently that in Vanaveski's shoes, he would have done the same. Maybe he was dead; back in '71 there were plenty of Sicilians happy to help with the arrangements.

Fifteen minutes of scanning the microfiches in the local library archive of the New York Daily News filled in the details. The gangland slaughter of the late sixties 'banana wars' had reduced the shock value of mafia killings and shuffled the story to the inside pages. The coverage was quite detailed, however, and in one edition included portraits of The Snake, before - an NYPD mug-shot - and after - from the ME's file. Al wondered what women had seen in him even before he was shot. Then, buried among this routine report of a routine killing, one headline brought Al up short: 'Killer's Kalling Kard'. The story described a printed card found pinned to the dead man's jacket. A much enlarged, grainy photograph showed Al the now familiar inscription 'Karistus Kümavereliselt Kuritegu'. There was no mention of any attempt at translation nor any explanation of the sketch in the corner. Al sat back and studied the screen in astonishment.

Back at Rick's that evening, Al called the Beach House. Helen answered the phone.

"Hello."

"Hello, is Peter there? It's Al Hershey."

"Hello, Al. This is Helen. Peter said you might call, he's out in the boat. How are things in New York?"

"Interesting, Mrs Gilchrist. What time can I reach him?"

"A couple of hours, but you can talk to me."

Helen waited for and heard the brief hesitation and the slightly exaggerated agreement which followed.

"Oh… yes, of course I can talk to you. It's about the note left on Fermi's body."

"Yes, I gather you found one in Estonia too."

"Yes, in Tallinn. But now I've found a third."

"A third? Really? In New York?"

"Yes. And just like the others, a criminal, shot dead. It was back in 1971."

"Good heavens. Are we looking for a serial killer then?"

"Well, that's three we know of. The bad news is that Vanaveski left New York right after that murder and vanished."

"So what do you plan to do now?"

"Not too sure. I'm waiting to hear from a friend in the Senate. I'm hoping that he might help me track down the carving."

Helen privately considered Al's pursuit of the carving a waste of effort but had said nothing, even to Peter. "You have friends in high places."

"One friend. He was my CO in Vietnam."

"How can he help?"

Al hesitated. "He has contacts… in the Intelligence community."

Helen had been simply making conversation until these answers roused her curiosity, but even as she was framing her next question she sensed that Al had said all he wanted to on the subject.

"I see. Well, let's hope he can help. I'll explain all this to Peter. Will you call back if there's anything new?"

"Of course."

"And do take care of yourself. There seems to be an alarming number of dead bodies accumulating."

"I'll do that," he assured her. "I don't plan on adding to the total."

*　　*　　*

That evening was spent eating and drinking around Polish Town with Rick, so Al was not at his sharpest early the next morning when Senator Thornton called to confirm that Pohl had been tried and hanged after the war.

His Paraguayan bolt-hole had been appropriated, presumably with all of its contents, by another senior Nazi, one Richard Glueks, aka Josef Brandt who had been used briefly by the CIA in the late forties but had proved of little value and his file had been closed in 1949. It was not known whether he was still in Paraguay or even still alive. Sensing Al's disappointment, Thornton offered to provide an introduction to 'someone senior' in the Paraguayan security establishment who would be able to provide more information. Al hesitated, conscious that he was leaning pretty hard on the relationship with Thornton, but accepted the offer because without it he was stuck. After putting down the phone he reflected that even with it he may be equally stuck but he reported the news to Peter as positively as he could.

His last call was to his wife who responded to his enthusiastic story of progress by reminding him to buy fresh shirts and underwear and to be sure to keep up to date with his written reports. Four hours later, he was on board a United Airlines flight bound for Paraguay.

CHAPTER 30

"Peter, come and take a look at this."

Helen's voice had the slightly abstracted tone Peter was accustomed to hear when she was deep in thought. Reluctantly he rose from the comfort of the balcony recliner and joined her in the study. "Good Lord, what's all this?"

He was looking at a large white board fastened to Geoff's study wall and covered with photographs and other documents, all annotated with jottings in Helen's hand. Along the top a horizontal line was drawn, with tick marks, dates and hand notes – a timeline of events.

"Oh, it was talking to Al the other day gave me the thought. He's a good man on the ground but I get the feeling that systematic analysis isn't his forte. Take a look at the three messages." Helen was pointing to three photocopied pages, which Peter recognized as the copies of the KKK messages sent to them by Al via Mrs Hershey. Helen had pinned them alongside one another and stood, arms folded, studying them with great concentration. Peter looked at them for a while, unable to raise any real interest.

"Are you seeing something I don't? We've been over this several times."

She said nothing for a while and Peter was close to his admittedly low limit of patience when she said: "Why is the second one printed?"

He looked at them again. He had of course previously noted that two of the messages were handwritten while the third was on a printed card but had not considered it important. "No idea. Does it matter?"

Before Helen could reply they heard Geoff's car. Grateful for the chance to interrupt a conversation which seemed to be going nowhere, Peter went through to the lounge to meet him.

"Good day? Anything of interest?" he asked, hopefully.

"Not bad. Usual stuff… Oh, that Italian guy rang, Milan…"

"The one who claims he can make cheap violet lasers? Crackpot, I thought."

Geoff was taking off his shoes. "Oh, Jesus, that's better. Crackpot? Oh, well, probably. But he's offering a demonstration. His office, next week."

"A demonstration?" Peter perked up.

"Yes. I'm booked to go Wednesday."

This was a surprise. It was long established ILT practice that any significant business opportunity would be followed up by them both. In the first few months, Peter had made a solo trip to Singapore to negotiate a patent licence. It had been a mess and from that day they always made deals in tandem – one to talk, one to listen, as Peter put it.

Geoff held up a hand. "And before you start, no," he hurried on, trying to prevent Peter working up an argument. "There's no way we can leave Helen on her own. And where is the lady?"

Beneath the jocularity of Geoff's manner there was a dullness, which stopped Peter before he began - the Milan trip would be only a token exercise. Since Meg's death they were all living through an extended intermission, each struggling to cope in the hope that real life would some day resume. At first, Helen had slipped into apathy. She'd scarcely left the house since they'd returned to Half Moon Bay and would spend hours sitting on the balcony, gazing along the coast towards Smugglers Beach. It had been only yesterday that, for no apparent reason, she had asked Geoff for the white-board, collected the file of Al's reports and thrown herself into a frenetic burst of study far into the night.

Peter had vacillated between the intense anger that had driven him to start the investigation and an odd, lotus-eating life totally out of character, sometimes lounging by the pool reading and drinking endless cups of tea and coffee, sometimes taking Geoff's new boat for wild, high speed rides up and down the coast. To make it interesting, he would especially seek out the big waves of the Mavericks, the area off Half Moon Bay known to professional surfers as the most dangerous on the planet.

Geoff's refuge was work. Whether at the house, in the California Street office or on the road, he worked non-stop unless eating or sleeping. His previous high-rolling life-style had ended on Smugglers Beach and he had no interest in trying to revive it. Even his treasured cruiser he left to Peter or her mooring.

Peter believed, although the others did not, that uncovering the whole truth of what had happened on the beach was an essential part of the process. Now, suddenly, it seemed that Helen might be coming to the same view.

"In the study," she called. "And you're right. Peter and I have an agreement – no work for a month. Come and see this, Geoff. I'm sure you'll get the point."

With an enquiring look at Peter, Geoff headed for the study. "Point of what?"

Peter followed, to find Helen still in the same pensive pose.

"Why is only the second message on a printed card, Geoff?"

But Geoff had stopped at the study door. "When did you do all this? I only got you the board last evening. Have you been up all night?"

"Yes, well, some of it. Is anybody going to answer my question or am I surrounded by dummies?"

Geoff crossed the room to stand next to her. "OK, I'll have a go. What was the question again?"

"Stop it, Geoff. You know perfectly well."

Helen saw at once what Peter missed – the flash of pain on Geoff's face. For years, this had been Meg's phrase in response to his teasing.

"Alright. Well, the question of premeditation crossed my mind."

"Exactly, premeditation!" Helen seized on the word. "He planned two of the killings but not the other."

Peter joined them. "Two? Which two?"

"The first two, of course," Helen replied.

"Hang on. I can see that the printed card on the New York body shows premeditation, but the first one was scribbled on a scrap of paper. Look at it."

Helen was shaking her head impatiently. "Yes, it was, but that was because the boy had nothing else. He was living in a bunker in the woods, wasn't he? But it was premeditated alright. Then he took from inside his shirt a paper and left it on the body.' Remember? The war journal?" Helen led them through the logic of her argument. "Of course, the third message was scribbled down too, but it was written on a page torn from the Owner's Manual of the victim's Jeep. Hardly premeditated."

"Yes, you're right," Geoff was shaking his head, irritated with himself. "How come I didn't see it before?"

"Which means Fermi's killing wasn't planned," Helen added "and there's something else. The first two killings....," she corrected herself, "... the other two killings we know about..."

"You mean there may be more?" Peter interrupted.

"Why not? But the first two we know about were both revenge for the murder of a woman or a girl who had been close to Endel."

"Whereas the latest," Geoff spoke slowly, thinking as he went, "was for that damned package. There was no woman involved."

"Yes there was," Peter said.

The significance of his remark stopped the conversation. They looked at one another in silence until Helen found words. "Yes, but the Fermi killing couldn't have been on Meg's account."

"It could, if the killer had known what happened on the beach," Geoff suggested.

"Apart from Fermi, we know there were two other men on the scene," Peter said.

Another thoughtful silence.

"Angelino and Jim, yes." Helen said. "But why would either of them use a fifty-year-old message from some place they've probably never heard of? I think there was someone else there." She looked at Geoff then at Peter, eyebrows raised in enquiry. Then, as nobody offered an answer, she turned away. "I'm going for a shower. If you can manage between you to start the barbecue without setting fire to the balcony, then I'll fix dinner – shrimp and tuna. We can talk later."

After Helen had left the room, Geoff went behind the bar. "What with

Milanese crackpots and forensic arguments, I need a drink. You?"

He poured them each a whiskey.

"There's something I haven't told you," Peter began.

"Something that wasn't in the written report?"

"Yes. Al told me on the phone from New York that Jim admitted to him that he intended to kill Fermi." As he spoke, at the rear of his mind he was wondering where Al was at that moment and if he was making any progress. What little he had heard of Paraguay was not reassuring and he hoped things were under control. In fact, as Peter was consoling himself with the recollection of Senator Thornton's support, Al was driving out of the remote desert township of Filadelfia on his way to a meeting at the ranch of a certain Herr Schneider. He did not at all feel that things were under control.

"Well, most of us have threatened to kill somebody at some time but..."

Peter was shaking his head. "No, not like that. Al said he was serious, really serious."

Geoff swirled his whiskey, ice chiming musically against glass. "Hmm. Well, while we're doing our True Confessions, Jim's been in touch."

"I guessed as much."

"Did you now! How?"

"Oh, a man on the run, you're an old friend and there's the work."

"All true. But he called today to say he's turning himself in."

"Not before time," Peter said.

"Indeed not. I offered to go with him to talk to the police."

"Generous of you."

"Not really. I feel I owe him. But I'm not the best person to do it."

"Oh?" Seeing what was coming, Peter was non committal.

"Come off it, Peter. You're her father. Who's in a better position to support him?"

"Support? With the authorities here? After what passed between me and that Kristensen woman, I'd be his 'Go directly to jail' card."

Geoff took a drink. "We'll argue that out later. Let's get the barbecue started.

I could use a shower too."

The barbecue was lit, the balcony unscathed, the dinner excellent. They chatted and argued into the small hours. Two bottles of a rather good Napa Valley red made the conversation more fluent but the logic less coherent until finally they went to bed, having raised more questions than they could answer.

CHAPTER 31

Helen thought Jim looked decidedly better. Since he'd arrived at the beach house that morning looking like an escapee from Devil's Island he'd had a shower, eaten his first decent meal for weeks and changed into jeans and a T-shirt of Peter's. Now, even in the drab Station House interview room with its Nile-green walls and sickly fluorescent lighting, he smiled at her, looking relaxed and confident. She was pleased to have convinced Peter and Geoff that she should be the one to accompany Jim; it was what Meg would have wanted.

They had been waiting only a few minutes when the door opened and a man in his forties was shown in by a uniformed policewoman. He was slightly built with small features, crisp black hair neatly cut and pale eyes behind rimless glasses. He wore a dark business suit, white shirt and college tie. Moving slowly and methodically he placed his briefcase on the metal-framed table and turned to Helen, hand extended.

"Good afternoon. Paul Scharf, of Montgomery, Kahn and Scharf. And you must be Mrs Gilchrist." His voice was unusually soft, his speech as steadily methodical as his movements. Could this slow-moving man really be the fearsome courtroom operator Geoff had described?

She took his hand. "Good afternoon." She turned to Jim. "Jim, Mr Scharf is the lawyer who handles Geoff's affairs in the US."

The men shook hands.

"You come highly recommended, Mr Scharf." She realized her incredulity was showing and she saw that Scharf had detected it too and that it amused him.

"I'll do my best not to disappoint you," he said, with a minute smile. Then, to Jim, "Mr Hughes has given me an outline of the situation on the phone but can I hear it from you before we talk to the police?" Without waiting for Jim's reply he sat down at the table, took a legal pad from his case and turned to a fresh page. Jim moved to sit alongside Scharf but was redirected with a gesture. "Sit opposite, please, Mr Otte."

In ten intense minutes of searching interrogation, Scharf covered three pages before laying down his pen and sitting back with an encouraging smile.

"That's good, thank you. Now, here's how this will work. The detective's name is Freeman, Captain Freeman. He and I have met many times. Watch me and take your lead from me. He will begin with great affability but he is intelligent and ruthless. Answer his questions truthfully but as briefly as possible. Volunteer nothing, avoid elaboration. You will find that occasionally he will fall silent after you have given an answer and you will feel the need to say more. Don't. He'll try to needle you – keep your cool, your anger puts him in control. If he asks inappropriate questions, I will deal with them. If he tries to put undue pressure on you, I will prevent it. The law lays down strict rules for these proceedings; Freeman and I know them perfectly but he will bend them just as far as I allow him to. Is that clear?"

Watching Scharf operate, Helen began to see that the soft speech and slow deliberation were mere professional affectations. Jim hesitated, looking uncomfortable.

"Mr Scharf, I appreciate your advice and you know a lot more than I do about this sort of thing but I came here voluntarily to tell the police everything I know about Meg's murder. All this tactical stuff just isn't necessary."

Scharf sat, staring at his notes for a while before standing, slowly removing his jacket and placing it over the back of his chair. Then, plunging his hands into his trouser pockets, he began to pace the room slowly, looking down at the floor. At one point he stopped and seemed about to speak then the slow walk resumed. At length he said: "Will you excuse me for a minute?" and again not waiting for an answer he left the room. Jim and Helen exchanged puzzled glances but neither was willing to say anything. In a minute or so the door opened and Scharf looked in. "A minute of your time, Mrs Gilchrist?"

She looked at Jim who nodded and she rose and left the room with Scharf.

In the corridor she recognized Duane Zimmerman's bulky figure. With a brief nod to Scharf he took her by the arm, to her mild irritation, and led her into a back office. The only occupant, a civilian clerk, looked up curiously when they entered.

"Give us some privacy, huh?" Duane said and the clerk, seizing his cigarettes, left without a word for his unexpected smoke break. Duane propped himself against the door. "Mrs Gilchrist, what I'm going to say puts my pension on the line, so we're strictly off the record, OK?"

Puzzled, Helen nodded her agreement. "If you wish."

"Good." He took a big breath. "Scharf tells me Otte's come here figuring that if he just lays it all out then he'll be OK, at least as far as your daughter's murder is concerned. Right?"

"That's right, yes."

"Look, let me tell you about the guy who'll do the interview. His name is Freeman. He's Captain of Detectives. He's the youngest Captain of Detectives in Northern California and he didn't get there by good luck. He's smart, he works hard and takes no crap... excuse me."

Helen smiled at the apology. "So are you saying Jim would be unwise to tell him the truth?"

Duane sighed – 'the truth is my shield!'. How many innocents had he seen convicted on that basis? "I'm saying it's an imperfect world. Why give the system the chance to make a mistake? Telling the truth is fine; telling a lawyer is safer, trust me."

Helen's instinct was to resist this advice. From the day of Meg's death she had entered a world in which all her assumptions about the way society worked had been called into question.

"But surely, with Angelino's testimony, there can be no doubt as to how my daughter died."

Duane shook his head. "Angelino's a career criminal facing 10 to 20 and desperate for a plea bargain. Freeman puts in the good word and maybe Nick gets five and he's out in three."

Helen was appalled. "You mean this Freeman person would bribe a witness to commit perjury?"

Again, the shake of the head. "Who said anything about perjury? With respect, Mrs Gilchrist, you believe Angelino because you want to believe him, because he gives you the man who killed your daughter. But think about the beach that night. It's dark, he's in the water struggling with the package, suddenly somebody's screaming, a fight's started, maybe it's the police. He panics. It's tough to be sure who did what to who? An hour in the interview room with Freeman, and Angelino won't be sure himself. You see how it is?"

And Helen, sadly, now was beginning to see only too well. Duane straightened and reached for the door handle. "I have to go. You will think about what I've said?"

"Of course. And I appreciate what you're doing for us, I really do."

He escorted her back to the door of the interview room where, with a hand on her shoulder, he gave her a very searching look and left saying no more.

*　　*　　*

It took Helen some effort to make Jim see the wisdom of Duane's advice but in the end, he was cornered by logic and gave in just as the door opened and a shiny-faced young policeman put his head around the door.

"Captain Freeman will see you now, Mr Scharf."

Helen was encouraged to note the deferential tone.

"OK, thanks."

The young man waited, obviously expecting them to follow him, and was disconcerted when Scharf made no move.

"Please tell the Captain we'll be there in just a minute."

"Oh, er, right. In his office then, er, you know the way, sir."

"Yes I do."

The officer closed the door and Scharf turned back to Jim.

"One last thing. Remember, today is just the start of the process. If Freeman sees sense, then it stops here but if he chooses to push it, he has to make the case to Kristensen."

"Kristensen? And he's on my side?"

"She. She's the DA, and she's too smart to take sides."

Helen noticed Scharf's first non-professional smile and how much more human it made him look.

"She just weighs up Freeman's case and, as I see the evidence, kicks his butt out of her office, not because she's anybody's friend, but because losing's not good for the career." He turned to Helen. "This will take a couple of hours, more if Freeman's got a hangover. I guess you'd rather not wait in here?"

Helen smiled. "Not really. I'll get some fresh air. "She took one of Peter's cards from her handbag and wrote her cell phone number on the back. "Perhaps you'll call me when you're finished."

"Of course." He pocketed the card. "And don't worry, Freeman's tough but he's not a fool. My bet is it ends today."

"Thank you." She turned to Jim as she left. "Good luck."

*　　*　　*

At the door to Freeman's office Scharf offered a final word: "Once we're in there, I'm the referee not a combatant. I'll stop the low blows and the knees in the groin but it's 'defend yourself at all times'. OK?"

Jim smiled, a confident smile. "Don't worry, Mr Scharf, you keep the fight fair and I can take him."

Freeman's office was icily functional, tidy desk, coat stand with a lightweight suit jacket on a hanger, executive swivel chair and a small conference table with six chairs. A twin-cassette recorder was set on a shelf, its microphone on a stand on the table.

Brandishing the promised affability, Freeman came from behind the desk to greet them. He was broad-shouldered, deeply tanned with a well-trimmed moustache, his dark brown hair just beginning to grey at the temples. He exuded authority.

"Paul! Good to see you. How's the family? Jean well, I hope." Having received

Scharf's ritual reply he turned to Jim. "Mr Otte, hi. Appreciate your coming in." He led them to the conference table. "Please be seated, gentlemen. Coffee?"

Coffee was brought by a young woman who smiled shyly when she caught Jim's eye. Then Freeman got down to business.

"OK. You understand that I will be recording this interview?"

Jim nodded and Freeman switched on the machine.

"2:35p.m. Monday, August 17th 1992, in the office of Charles Freeman, Captain of Detectives. Present, are Freeman, Mr James Frederick Otte and Mr Paul Scharf, lawyer for Otte. This interview is in pursuit of my investigations into events in the early hours of July 5th, 1992, culminating in the death of a young English woman, Miss Megan Gilchrist."

Elaborately casual, he sat back in his chair and turned to Jim with a comfortable smile. "Right. That's got the record straight, now the easiest thing would be if you would just tell me what happened that night in your own words."

With a practiced sigh, Scharf made the first of many interventions. "That may be the easiest for you, Chuck, but that's not how we prefer to proceed. Why don't you put your questions to Jim and he'll do his best to answer?"

Freeman, who had also played out this drama innumerable times, shook his head sadly. "Well, that's your client's privilege, Paul. It'll drag the proceedings out some but I've got all day." He turned to Jim: "Let's see if we can agree on a starting place, shall we? You were on the beach known locally as Smugglers Beach in the early hours of July 5th last, is that right?"

Jim was nodding but Scharf got in first again: "Sorry, Chuck, that won't do either. My client absolutely was not on the beach at that time or any other time on that date."

Freeman affected surprise: "My information is that he was, indeed, on that beach at the time in question."

"Then your information is incorrect."

There was a silence. Jim thought to clarify the apparent misunderstanding then remembered Scharf's advice and kept his mouth shut. Scharf sat, hands folded loosely in his lap, immobile, eyes on Freeman. At length, the Captain leaned slightly towards Jim.

"Then where were you at that time?"

"I was on board my boat, just off Smugglers Beach."

"I see. And what was your business there?"

"I was delivering a package."

"At one o'clock in the morning?"

Again Scharf jumped in: "My client has already answered the question."

Freeman proceeded smoothly: "And what was in the package?"

"I have no idea."

Freeman sat back as though astonished. "You don't know?" Then, catching Scharf's eye, "OK, counselor, he already answered that too." He paused, studying his fingernails. "Alright, Mr Otte, if you don't know what was in this mysterious package you were delivering in the middle of the night, you must know who it was for."

"Sorry, Captain," Jim was beginning to get into the game, "but I don't know that either."

"I see. So you planned simply to dump this valuable package…"

"Hold it." Scharf was off his mark in an instant. "What evidence do you have that the package was of any particular value?"

"OK, strike 'valuable'."

A nod from Scharf and Jim was free to answer. "No, my instructions were to hand over the package to someone on the beach, that's all."

"Who?"

Scharf again: "The question is ambiguous. Who what?"

For the first time, Freeman showed a trace of asperity. "Who was going to be on the beach to receive the package?"

Scharf nodded to Jim to answer.

"I don't know."

"Hmm… So, this package. Where did you get it?"

"From the sea."

"It was floating there and you just happened on it in the dark..."

"Come on, Captain." Scharf protested. "We agreed - you ask questions, Jim answers them. That isn't a question."

"How did this package come to be on board your boat?"

After ten exasperating minutes, Freeman had extracted the details of the radio device and how Jim had used it to recover the package.

"I see. Clever," he said, mostly to himself. He appeared to reflect on the ingenuity of this procedure for some time before consulting his file and looking once more at Jim, now with an expression Scharf had seen before and didn't much like. He selected a sheet.

"I am now referring," he said for the benefit of the record, "to a copy of a complaint filed on h September 17th 1987 by a Mrs Kathryn Otte, an address in Palo Alto."

Jim let out an audible gasp as Freeman continued: "That would have been your wife, would it not?"

Jim nodded, unable to reply.

"The witness is nodding his assent. It seems you assaulted her, knocked her unconscious, in fact. Do you make a habit of attacking women, Mr Otte?"

Scharf reached across the table. "Before we go any further, might I see that, Captain?"

"Of course." Freeman passed the document over and Scharf read it slowly, giving Jim time to recover his composure to the point where, as he was about to protest, Scharf held up a silencing hand.

"Two points. First, the complaint was voluntarily withdrawn, second, it has no bearing on the present investigation."

"And third," Jim's anger would not be silenced, "she attacked me, God damn it, with a kitchen knife! She was out of her mind. She tried to castrate me. She was in court..."

Now Scharf interrupted. "In court – ah! Well no doubt the Captain has the details of those proceedings in the file, also." There was a silence. Scharf looked enquiringly at Freeman. "Captain?"

"Not at this time."

"So you've investigated the complaint against my client but not the violent assault that occasioned it."

Another silence. At last Freeman spoke: "Interview halted at three eighteen for a comfort break." He switched off the tape. Then to Jim: "Would you give us a couple of minutes, Mr Otte? Anna will get you a coffee or whatever."

"Sure, no problem."

When Jim had left the office Freeman stood up. "Look Paul, at this rate we'll be here all night. Maybe you could ease up a little, eh? Cut me some slack?"

To Scharf, this was a tactical victory and he hadn't any intention of easing up. On the other hand, he didn't want to wreck a good working relationship with a fellow professional.

"I agree it's hard going Chuck, but you know perfectly well you can't make a murder charge stick so what are you left with? Smuggling? Smuggling what – an unknown quantity of unidentified material? You really want to run that by Kristensen? How about we just call it even?"

Freeman shook his head in exasperation, part real, part for the gallery. "You guys! How come I never get to win one?"

"You've got a short memory, my friend. What about the so-called rape last April? I bust a gut for that guy and the sky fell in on the poor jerk."

"Hey, he was guilty."

"Not as guilty as you made out and you know it."

Freeman shrugged happily. "Jury's decision."

"How about we don't trouble a jury with this one?"

With a show of reluctance Freeman conceded. It was a decision he had tentatively reached when he'd first read the file, but he hadn't made Captain of Detectives by being a quitter.

C H A P T E R   3 2

Alone in the elevator, Al worked on deep breathing exercises; the flight and
six hours of Asunción had wrung him out.

In an outer office on the twentieth floor of the Bureau of State Security, Al's
papers were studiously examined yet again, this time by a myopic desk-bound
youth who looked as though he had only recently learned to read and found
the task burdensome. His eyes blinking rapidly, he looked from Al to the
papers several times, glanced at the bodybuilder in combat trousers and khaki
T-shirt standing arms folded by the door, then at last reluctantly handed back
the papers and with an insolent jerk of his head, invited Al to proceed. A door
labeled 'Jefe de la Seguridad' slid open as he reached it, admitting him to the
secretarial office of the most powerful man in Paraguay. When the Senator
said 'someone senior' he meant it, Al thought.

From behind a desk, a woman – only the blouse gave her away – reached out
a hand: "Papers."

Al took a deep breath. She had the face of a concentration camp guard and she
was playing at home. He also recalled the earnest pleading of the ambassador
who had reached him by phone just before he'd left for this appointment. While
assuring him of the embassy's every support, he had also, distaste for amateur
diplomacy evident in every word, urged him to avoid any 'unpleasantness'. On
the other hand, the honor of the Marine Corps was at stake.

"My papers have already been examined three times. You have received a
letter of introduction from the U.S. State Department. Please tell Captain
Ortega I'm waiting to see him."

The stare between them lasted a long time, but when Al saw her lips
compress he grinned inwardly. She picked up the phone, buzzed and said in
rapid and colloquial Spanish:

"Sir, the big mouth gringo who made such trouble at Immigration refuses to show his papers. Shall I let him in?"

The inner door slid open and her lips disappeared altogether as she put down the phone. She said in English: "You can go in."

Al was heading for the door when he threw over his shoulder in Spanish: "If the crooked jerk hadn't changed his mind about the $100 Immigration fee, the big-mouth gringo really would have made trouble." Never miss the chance of a cheap shot, he thought, as the door closed behind him.

Captain Rafael del Rio de Ortega, known, in view of the extraordinary extent of corruption over which he presided, as 'chupaplata', 'sucker of silver', was an exquisitely fastidious man, fated to live in a disorderly and sordid world.

At twenty-one, the young Ortega's Paraguayan education complete, the profits from his father's property development business had smoothed entry to a prestigious US business school which, although providing little relevant knowledge, would have given him a patina unavailable south of the Rio Grande.

He was packed and ready to leave when a newly-built Sao Paolo high-rise collapsed, taking with it a dozen workmen, a high-ranking official of the Brazilian government and a good part of Ortega senior's assets. The cost of a satisfactory outcome of the official inquiry broke the Ortega bank leaving the boy with an unforeseen requirement to earn a living.

Showing a speed of decision, which was to be his hallmark, he joined the Security Service on a 'fast track' designed for applicants of exceptional zeal and competence. Twenty years later the track had reached its terminus in the office of Head of Security, and its youngest ever incumbent had become the J. Edgar Hoover of Paraguay, knowing everything about everyone. From his villa among the orange groves of Yaguarón via the armored Lincoln to his office suite, like an infant without an immune system, he moved in an aseptic bubble.

The Captain came from behind a surprisingly modest desk, empty save for a telephone, a leather blotter chased in gold and a pair of white kid gloves laid with meticulous precision one on the other, to offer a manicured hand.

"Mr Hershey, a pleasure indeed, sir."

He spoke lightly accented English in a silken voice which made Al want to spit on the carpet.

"It is not often I receive visitors from your country, particularly bearing a letter of introduction from so..." He pondered a selection of adjectives appropriate to describe the US government department responsible for relations between impoverished Paraguay and the most powerful nation on earth, "...distinguished a source. Please be seated."

He was a small man, an inch smaller than Al and six inches less around the chest but he carried no spare flesh and looked as though he ate little and exercised hard. The tailored white uniform was devoid of ribbons or decorations of any kind. His head was rather too large but the swarthy face was handsome and youthful and behind tinted spectacles his hard black eyes missed nothing. He looked what he was: intelligent and dangerous.

"I appreciate your time, sir. I know you must be a very busy man so I'll come straight to the point."

Ortega waved a dismissive hand. "A privilege to be of service to your country, sir, truly a privilege." He took a file from a desk drawer and drew from it a letter. "Your State Department tells me you are interested in an item belonging to a German national, now deceased – Richard Gluecks."

Knowing that Gluecks would have been ninety-two years old, the news of his death came to Al as a small disappointment but no surprise.

"May I enquire as to your interest in the deceased?"

Before leaving for Paraguay, Al had discussed with Thornton how to handle Ortega's questions. The private investigator's first rule when asked about a case should be to tell the truth to avoid being proved wrong subsequently. With some misgivings, Al followed this rule now, though without mention of Gluecks' CIA connection which in any case had long since ceased.

Ortega's response seemed encouraging. "I see. Well, I am pleased to say that I believe I can be of assistance. There is a file on Herr Gluecks but I doubt that it would be of value. However, it happens that there is another German national still living who knew Gluecks extremely well from the time he arrived here. His name is Schneider. If you wish I can arrange a meeting."

Thornton's briefing for this visit had included a strenuous warning that the country was corrupt in general and that the Head of Security, in particular, was a psychopathic liar, so the better the news from this duplicitous man, the less Al trusted it.

Nonetheless, he said yes, that would be enormously helpful. Ortega picked up the telephone and asked the secretary to send in Señor Mendes and within seconds the man appeared. He was in his fifties, gaunt, stooping, grey-haired, grey-faced and visibly terrified. Told to sit without being introduced, he perched on the edge of his chair and placed a folder on the desk.

Speaking excellent English in a dry, high-pitched voice, he explained that he was Head of Archive for the Internal Security department and that he had, on the instructions of Captain Ortega – his voice dropped at the mention of the name – produced for the visitor a short biography of Herr Martin Schneider. Moreover, Herr Schneider had been contacted and had agreed to a meeting on the proviso that it be held at his ranch which, Mendes explained, was in a remote desert region known as the Chaco, some three hundred miles to the west of Asunción.

When Al observed that he would be happy to pay Schneider's expenses if the meeting could be in Asunción, it was explained that it was not a question of money. Schneider was almost eighty and a strict Mennonite – an extreme Christian sect akin to the Amish, the grey man added for Al's enlightenment – and would on no account leave the privilegium, the Mennonite community lands in the west of Paraguay. Adding that a sketch map and directions to the Schneider ranch were included in the file, he passed it quickly to Al as though it were contagious. Before Al could ask any questions, the grey man, to his obvious relief, had been dismissed.

*   *   *

Later that afternoon, directed by the hotel's rose-scented Head Porter, Al made his way to the pandemonium of noise, diesel fumes and squabbling humanity which is the Terminal de Omnibus Asunción.

He eventually located a clerk, a gnome-like native of the aboriginal Lenguan tribe hiding behind a dirty glass window, who spoke a mix of his native Lengua, horrible pigeon English and odd phrases in Plautdietsch, a bastard derivative of German almost entirely unintelligible to Al. The resulting conversation confirmed his surprise at how many locals spoke little or no Spanish.

After much bad-tempered dialogue, he gathered that the three hundred mile journey via the Trans-Chaco Highway to the Filadelfia junction would take seven hours, and that he could expect to get a lift to the town from the bus stop in one vehicle or another. The clerk also claimed that the next bus would leave at seven the following morning. Partly reassured, Al returned to his hotel for a heavily-spiced dinner and a night disturbed by dreams of Mrs Hershey's cooking.

The clerk, as soon as Al was out of view, had telephoned an unlisted number given on a poster bearing a copy of Al's passport photograph which that morning had been issued by the Interior Ministry to all car rental outlets and all ticket clerks in this, the capital's only bus station serving the Chaco.

CHAPTER 33

Well before seven, armed with water bottle, cheese, smoked meat and hunks of chipa, a kind of yucca bread, he was back at the depot and had located the forlorn and sagging bus. He boarded and after some thought, took a seat at the rear alongside a door optimistically labeled *'Salida de la Emergencia'*. According to Al's brief experience of Paraguay, in what seemed the likely event of an accident, this would either fly open or jam solid but he still felt better having it accessible. At seven forty-five the driver showed up, opened the hood and began fiddling with the engine. At eight thirty he thrashed the bus into gear and the journey was under way. As the bus entered Avenida Villa Hayes, a black Land Cruiser slipped into the early-morning traffic and took a place a few hundred yards behind.

Al settled as comfortably as the seat and the bus suspension allowed and read again the tourist leaflet provided by the hotel. He learned that he was traveling along the Trans-Chaco highway, the one paved road in the Chaco, and the busiest - a vehicle passing every few minutes. Moreover, his destination was a region the size of France with a population of only sixty thousand. But least encouraging of all was the startlingly, frank observation that 'The Chaco is a synonym for adventure and excitement, combined with certain risks. Persons not attracted by adventure will dislike the Chaco and they would better desist from a visit.'

He disliked the Chaco already. Considering the adventure and excitement, not to mention certain risks life had already provided him, he would indeed have preferred to desist from his visit, but according to the Security file, Herr Schneider had entered the Chaco in 1932 and not left it since. Al had found something troubling about the grey man's mechanical repetition of this formula. 'Herr Schneider will be pleased to welcome you to his home near Filadelfia.' He had used precisely those words three times as Al had pressed for a meeting in Asunción. He returned the leaflet to his pocket. The more often he reassessed the situation, the less he liked it. There had been nothing good about his brief visit to the Bureau of State Security. Ortega's oily politeness, the groveling terror of his subordinate, the reclusive Herr Schneider being a close friend of the reclusive Herr Brandt. Al sighed, shuffled deeper into the seat and thought of home.

It turned out to be the most tedious journey of his civilian life. Of the four human passengers, Al was the only one unable to sleep and the hours dragged by.

There was one brief flurry of excitement caused by Boris, a gross, pink skinned, pig-like creature with foul breath and six inch tusks, which had been asleep when its wicker cage was manhandled aboard at an unscheduled stop an hour out of Asunción.

Al had christened the 'pig' Boris because its fiercely whiskered red face reminded him of a drunken and violent Russian husband in a divorce case he'd unwisely taken on soon after hanging out his shingle. Boris, wakened when the bus struck an especially large pothole, instantly unleashed a storm of screeching, snorting and desperate scrabbling to break free.

As the animal weighed some two or three hundred pounds, Al figured that should it succeed, only the Browning would prevent it from destroying the bus, but the owner, a great, sweating hulk of a man with a Pancho Villa moustache, quelled it by the astonishingly simple technique of scratching behind its ears with a length of bamboo, apparently carried for the purpose.

In seconds, with a final snort, it slumped back to sleep and tedium was restored. The only other incident of note came about three hours into the journey. More from a need for stimulus than for nourishment, Al broke out his iron rations and ate a slice of dry, salty cheese accompanied by a torn-off hunk of dry, salty bread and washed down with a mouthful of lukewarm water. Mrs Hershey would have been appalled.

It was four o'clock when the bus shuddered to a halt at the Filadelfia junction. The driver kicked out viciously across the aisle to waken an elderly Lenguan woman asleep in the front seat. Without a word, she got up, retrieved a heavy canvas bag from beneath the seat and clambered painfully down the steps. Al carefully negotiated the caged and still sleeping Boris and exchanged the suffocating heat of the bus for the furnace of the Middle Chaco. Without hesitation or a sideways glance the woman hoisted the bag onto her shoulder and set off along the dirt road which led, arrow straight into the shimmering haze, to the town or perhaps to the end of the world.

Al guessed the temperature at around a hundred degrees and he could feel the air sucking the moisture from his nose and throat. As the bus lurched and rattled its way towards Bolivia, absolute silence drifted slowly over the dismal landscape. It was a silence he knew from the seconds before a VC ambush when the jungle noises die as the sounds and smells of men and weaponry take over and the natural world holds its breath. Fighting the warrior's instinct to hurl himself flat, Al crouched slightly and looked around.

To the horizon in all directions the dust-covered view was undifferentiated; thorny scrub, squat, sturdy trees and cactus covering gently rolling hills. He could not see the only item which would have been of interest to him, the Land Cruiser parked among the brush a mile down the highway, its passenger studying him through binoculars.

"It would be easier here," the driver urged.

The passenger, older and less enthusiastic, said nothing.

Minutes passed. Already parched, Al wondered whether his water would run out and he'd die of dehydration before anyone showed up.

He thought he heard a sound, an engine, revving hard, then it was gone. A rustling in the brush behind him had him reaching for the Browning but he turned to see a pair of bright eyes beneath a cactus. He pointed a finger at it, made a pistol shot noise and it was gone, seeming to vanish instantaneously, translated into another dimension.

Gradually, the engine noise re-emerged - a vehicle, moving rapidly in a cloud of dust towards the road from about a mile to the north.

He had a momentary vision of Cary Grant in 'North by Northwest'; all that was lacking was the crop-dusting biplane.

And then the vehicle arrived, a panting, decrepit pickup of seventies vintage, braking hard and late but without locking its wheels as it came to a halt alongside him. The dust slowly cleared and he found himself looking into the wild blue eyes of the most fearsome and irascible man he'd ever seen. A voice rumbled around the cavernous chest and emerged from the ginger forest of the face. It spoke no language Al could recognize but was clearly directed at him.

"Excuse me?", he responded politely.

"Ah sayed, are yous wantin' tae gang tae Filadelfia?" the ginger one repeated, articulating more carefully.

After a few seconds thought, Al guessed at an appropriate reply: "Oh… I sure am. Are you going there?"

"Ah am if ye've gort the fare. Twenty dollars, ma wee mon." The 'r' sounds rolled on endlessly.

This was Al's first lesson in Chaco economics – the pedestrian pays the driver's asking price, no argument. He swallowed his pride.

"OK."

A large, freckled arm was thrust towards him from the pick-up window. "If ye'd kindly pay me first," the voice boomed, adding, with a surprisingly apologetic tone, "Ah'd no wesh tae engage in an argument aboot money."

With Al's twenty secreted about his capacious person and Al installed in the passenger's seat, the giant Scot floored the throttle, dumped the long-suffering clutch to spin the pick-up one hundred and eighty degrees in its own length and they were off, trailing a storm of dust and exhaust fumes.

The driver's wild eyes, added to the bravura start to the trip, made Al's pulse race nervously. In Vietnam he had often been the victim of this style of driving by young men with nothing to lose, but he quickly saw that the Scot was no boy racer. He handled the clumsy vehicle with finesse, controlling lurid slides on the track's occasional corners with seeming ease. Al began to relax. As the sound and fury of their departure faded, the Land Cruiser turned off the highway and began unhurriedly to follow.

Hamish Babington McMurdo, unasked, told his surreal life story. He had been born in the far north-west of the Scottish highlands where the locals are yet to forgive the English for the slaughter at Culloden in 1746. Brought up in a fishing village with an unpronounceable Gaelic name, his boyhood had been dominated by appalling weather, the Presbyterian Church and his father's temper.

When he was aged six the family had moved to 'the south', meaning Glasgow, where his father had taken work in the shipyards, joined the Communist Party and quickly risen to prominence in local politics. Hamish, violent and quarrelsome, had been in trouble with both his father and the authorities almost as soon as he could walk.

By the age of fifteen and already six feet tall, he was thrown out by his father and told to join the army - 'them'll pay yez tae fight'. Taking him at his word, Hamish told the recruiting officer he was seventeen and joined the Black Watch where he just made it through basic training before the army realized that he was a bigger danger to their own than to the enemy and awarded him a dishonorable discharge, launching his career as wanderer and seeker after trouble.

When a man died after a bar-room brawl – 'et was no me as started it, ye ken' - a quick dash to New York kept him ahead of the Glasgow police.

Later, Northern California introduced the energetic Hamish, bizarrely still a virgin, to the pleasures of mind-altering substances, sitar music and eager young girls, but another hasty exit was required when one of the girls turned out to be even younger than she'd claimed.

Two years hunting and trapping in the Alaskan wilderness, his first and last encounter with extreme cold, prompted a trip to Mexico where he'd worked as a horse-wrangler, then to Panama as bodyguard to a drug baron and at last, ten years ago, to Paraguay and the Chaco where violence was the only law, and where for the first time since his boyhood he felt at home.

"An' yersel'. Wit are ye runnin' frae?", Hamish asked. By his primitive reasoning, those who came to the Chaco came only because they had pressing reasons not to be somewhere more congenial. So Al, feeling an odd warmth towards this raw and simple giant, told him how, in pursuit of a murder enquiry, he was making this unlikely trip to meet an ancient German who could perhaps give him another piece in the puzzle.

Hamish was silent for a while then, with a quick sideways glance at Al, asked: "An yon Schneider Ranch. Juist whaur es it?"

Al described the fifteen kilometer journey from Filadelfia exactly as in the directions he had been given.

"Is that richt?", Hamish mused. He thought a while then added: "Ah wush yae weel o' it. Hoo d'yaez plan on gittin' there?"

When Al hesitantly suggested a rental car Hamish bellowed with laughter.

"Rental is it? Why mon, they fowks is Mennonites."

He saw Al's questioning expression. "Leuk, ye ken the Amish?"

Al allowed that he kenned the Amish well enough.

"Weel, the Menonnites es the Amish wi' the fun teken oot. Ye'd mebbe steal a car but ye'd no rent ain."

And he went on to offer to take Al himself for the 'raisonable wee sum' of fifty dollars.

But this time, Al wanted to travel alone and after some persuading, Hamish allowed that a Herr Jenkel had an elderly but carefully preserved Ford station wagon, which for religious reasons, he could not rent but would lend for an appropriate donation to the church.

Looking back, Al would realize why the loquacious Hamish was silent for the remainder of the journey but at the time he was puzzled by it.

Still following, a mile or so behind, the young driver of the Land Cruiser was uncomfortable. "How come we have to make ourselves targets?"

"What?"

"The suits, this big city car. Every hick for a hundred miles knows we're here and who sent us."

The older man exploded. "Look shithead, who gets to choose? I don't like this place. I don't like you. I don't like killing Americanos – it makes trouble. But the boss says we go in loud so the fuckin' Christians know they don't get things all their own way. So here we are, suits, Land Cruiser… we're in uniform, get it? You got a complaint, see the boss. Now shut the fuck up and drive."

In fact, the semi-autonomy enjoyed by the Mennonites of the Chaco caused Ortega extreme irritation. Formally, there was nothing he could do about it; what the lawyers called the privilegium had existed since the twenties but once in a while, he would run some high profile operation on their front lawn just to show that he could. This was one of those times.

CHAPTER 34

After an unexpectedly comfortable night in a small pension in the town, Al was in the Ford and on the road at nine. The route worked out exactly as it had been described; at nine thirty Al slowed as he reached a clump of bottle trees and quebracho shrub two hundred meters off the track on his right. As carefully as he could, he eased Herr Jenkel's prized possession across the scrub and halted, engine running, where the trees began. He was uneasy. He had seen not the faintest trace of habitation since he'd left the edge of town and this place felt all wrong. He switched off and listened: nothing, not even a breath of wind to stir the vegetation. More from habit than necessity, he eased the Browning in its holster then climbed down from the high-built Ford, closed the door quietly and stood, waiting, listening; still nothing. He took a deep breath and set off into the trees.

It took only five minutes to cross the trees and establish what he had half known since leaving Ortega's office – there was no Schneider Ranch, at least not where it was alleged to be. He had been set up.

Drawing the Browning and releasing the safety, he headed back the way he had come, moving as swiftly as the rough undergrowth permitted. At the edge of the trees he stopped. A black Land Cruiser was parked alongside the Ford.

"Do not turn around, Señor Hershey", said a voice behind him.

And immediately, "two against one, señor", said a second voice, also behind him.

For long seconds he weighed the odds; two of them, professionals, weapons drawn, behind him and probably in cover. Cursing his own stupidity he lowered the Browning.

They were chillingly calm. There was no unnecessary violence as they took the pistol, resetting the safety before pocketing it, cuffed his hands behind him and one ahead, one behind, both out of kicking range, steered him back into the trees. With death so close he was surprised at how he felt – no fear, just irritation at being so easily duped, a terrible pang of sadness when he thought of his wife and a sudden dazzling awareness of the sights and sounds around him, the way he'd felt when on furlough in Thailand he'd made his never again experiment with LSD.

The shot came quite unexpectedly, while they were still walking. Now gripped by fear, Al felt his stomach contract but his warrior's brain was still functioning. The shot came not from either man's pistol but from a high-powered rifle, very close. Behind him, he heard gurgling sounds and as he threw himself flat he twisted around to see the man behind buckling at the knees, blood pumping from a gaping wound in his neck. His companion in front panicked, started to run, firing blindly as he went. He had covered not a half a dozen yards before a second shot cut him down with the same fearsome neck wound. Relief flooding over him, Al struggled to rise until an enormous shape loomed from the trees and he was lifted to his feet like a child.

*　　　*　　　*

"Ah kenned fine yae wair on a hidin' te naethin'". Hamish's eyes glistened with excitement. "There's nae hoose in miles o' here and the ainly Schneider's an auld biddy back i' the toon."

Al, fully recovered thanks in part to a couple of mouthfuls of excellent whiskey from Hamish's flask, was seated in the dusty pickup. Hamish sat next to him, one calloused hand lovingly stroking the burnished stock of an old but well-oiled Winchester 30.30 lever-action, the Hollywood cowboy's weapon of choice from Tom Mix to John Wayne.

"An' when ah seed they twa corbies I thocht tae masel it'd be guid tae gang efter, tae try ma luck."

Adrenaline had scrambled what little intelligibility was normally available from Hamish but through patient interrogation Al eventually deduced that, realizing that a trap had been set, the warlike Scot had seen an opportunity.

When Al had turned down his offer of transport he had waited on the edge of town until first Al and then Ortega's assassins had passed. He'd followed. And the rest Al knew.

"And the bodies?"

Hamish grin was full of relish. "The beasties'll tek care o' they fellas, richt enough."

Indeed, Al thought, as they would have taken care of him but for Hamish's Winchester.

"How much," he asked, "would it cost for you to drive me to Asunción?"

Not easily fazed, Hamish took his time over this one. His answer was surprising. "Naethin' at a'."

He explained that his half hour's work that morning, assuming Al had no objection, had netted him an almost new Land Cruiser worth more than his total earnings in the preceding five years. Al wondered whether associates of the dead men would try to reclaim the vehicle but given the location, the terrain and the opposition, success would be unlikely. Besides, as Hamish pointed out, in the car theft capital of South America it would be cheaper, quicker and decidedly less hazardous simply to steal a replacement.

"How soon can you get me there?"

Hamish looked at his watch, thought briefly and decided. "Ef we leave noo - three o'clock."

"Then let's go."

Several minutes later, as they bounced and rattled south-east across the open scrub, Hamish clearly intent on cutting off the Filadelfia corner, a pang of guilt struck Al.

"What about the station wagon?"

"What aboot it?"

"Well, is it safe, left out there?"

"Et's under ma protection!"

And, Al thought, in the Chaco that's as safe as it gets.

*   *   *

The more confident the target, the easier the hit. Twenty-four hours of observation plus a few discreet enquiries among the street people revealed that this target's costly protective veneer was paper-thin.

Eight a.m. Tuesday, Café des Chansons, Avenida La Paz, Asunción. A black limousine, parked in a restricted zone, stands directly outside the entrance to the café which, according to the notice on the door, is closed. A passing policeman salutes the car. A young woman in tight black leather skirt and scarlet off-the-shoulder blouse, high heels clicking briskly, breasts swaying interestingly beneath the satin, approaches the car. The occupants, two broad-shouldered young men in grey uniforms and mirrored sun glasses, exchange glances. One says something and they laugh. She approaches the car, unlit cigarette in hand. The driver lowers his window and the girl steps up close to the car, leaning forward, presenting her cigarette to be lit, her cleavage to be admired. There is a brief exchange then, both tasks completed, the window slides shut and the girl, cigarette aloft between scarlet-tipped fingers, disappears into the crowd. A dozen yards on, with a grimace, she throws the unsmoked cigarette into the gutter.

Inside the café, Captain Rafael del Rio de Ortega has heard the café door open. This apparently everyday event puzzles him. He has a longstanding arrangement with the proprietor: in return for accommodating treatment of his tax affairs, the Café des Chansons opens to the public only after the Captain has left. Moreover, the Department of Internal Security pays two armed men to sit outside for an hour to protect this comfortable arrangement. He lowers his Wall Street Journal in time to see the compact figure of the man he had five days earlier ordered to be killed, stride swiftly to sit at the table immediately behind his.

"Keep reading, Captain."

Ortega's cool arrogance turns instantly to panic. Ashen-faced, he looks about wildly, disbelieving. How can this be? Where are his men? He starts to rise but a strong hand on his shoulder prevents it. Something jabs him painfully in the spine.

"The newspaper – keep it high."

Hands shaking, Ortega obeys.

"That's good. Now listen carefully. If I'd come for revenge you'd be dead already. The two you sent to kill me aren't coming back. If you want to try again, I'm on a United flight departing at two o'clock but be aware that the ambassador knows the whole story. He will have a man watching my back and the State Department will not accept 'mysterious death of American citizen'. You follow me?"

Ortega, half paralyzed with shock and fear, can only nod.

"I'm prepared to forget the attempted murder charge. All I want is what I came here for. Your driver will deliver the Gluecks file to the embassy for my attention before noon. Agreed?"

Another nod. Ortega, greedy, vicious and arrogant, is at the last, pragmatic. Behind him, pistol in hand, sits a confidant of ambassadors and senior senators, the killer of professional assassins and one who has passed through his elaborate and expensive defenses like the invisible man. For once, the Captain fights down his machismo instincts and takes the soft way. What does this dusty file on a dead Nazi matter? He finally manages to form words.

"Very well."

"Good. Let's go."

He persuades Ortega to his feet, holsters the Browning and together they step out into the morning bustle and pale sunshine of Avenida La Paz. With a smile and a genial slap on the captain's shoulder, Al turns and under the astonished gaze of two about-to-be-retired bodyguards, walks off into the crowd. An hour later, a young woman, a scarlet blouse beneath a nun's habit, two hundred American dollars in her money belt, boards a bus for Sao Paulo, home and safety. She'd never liked the chambermaid's job anyway and the manager's hands had been too busy for her comfort.

*　　*　　*

The file was delivered to the embassy at eleven thirty and brought to Al in a secure conference room provided by the ambassador; the Senator's name had a long reach. Al's concern was how much Ortega had dared to remove, whether perhaps the box contained nothing but blank pages. It was numbered 5 and titled 'Brandt (Gluecks) 1985-1992'. So he had only the most recent entries.

Inside the half empty file he found a dozen or so documents and four audio cassettes. Closer examination showed that six of the documents were minutes of internal meetings covering a variety of subjects, Brandt getting no more than a passing mention in each. The rest were transcriptions of the audio tapes, all in rather rough German, the most recent being a record of a meeting on the 27th of February between Brandt and someone described only as 'German Visitor'.

Astonished that Ortega's men had overlooked such a prize, Al began reading eagerly and then realized why they had not removed it. The transcription consisted almost entirely of paragraphs of odd words interspersed with a trancriber's comments - 'unintelligible' or 'inaudible'. Such disconnected, complete phrases as existed, as far as Al's German went, made little or no sense. A painstaking half hour of study of the text left him baffled and irritated. It seemed Ortega had had the last laugh.

He called Mrs Hershey to vent his frustration. Being accustomed to receiving such calls when he was traveling, she listened patiently but without comment, then told him Senator Thornton had telephoned twice sounding concerned and asking how things were in Paraguay, thereby confirming her own fears. She greeted his assurances that everything was under control with disbelief and demanded to know when he'd be back. He told her 'soon', which she also declined to believe. Not much buoyed up by these exchanges, he called Washington where Thornton came out of a meeting to speak to him and detecting his dispirited tone, pressed him for details. Told of the problem with the tapes, he slipped back into CO mode and more or less dragooned Al into agreeing to express the file to Washington for forensic examination.

Al's big mistake came in his call to Peter. Straightforward as usual when reporting to a client, he described in full the drama in the Chaco.

CHAPTER 35

In the beach house, the gloomy after dinner silence was broken by the telephone. Helen, sitting arms wrapped around drawn up knees, started; she never answered a telephone at any time if anyone else was available and she would have let it ring until the mechanism wore out. Peter and Geoff looked at one another, neither moved.

"It'll be Al for you," Geoff said.

"It's your phone."

The phone trilled on. Helen, feeling as though she were playing in a Bunuel movie, suddenly pounded with her fists on her knees and screamed: "For Christ's sake, one of you answer it."

Startled, Geoff reached for the phone. "Geoff Hughes." He listened, then held the instrument out to Peter, "Al, calling from Asunción airport."

Peter took it. "Hi, Al. How are things? Where are you headed?" He listened for two or three minutes. Helen watched the bad news register on his face. "Hold on," Peter seemed to interrupt. "What do you mean, trouble?" He listened then again broke in. "Let me get this straight, Al. What does 'attacked' mean? You mean physically?"

Then he listened for a long time, incredulity showing on his face and in the movement of his free hand. "OK, I understand. Just give me a minute." He allowed the hand holding the receiver to drop to his side. The others waited expectantly for him to tell them what was going on but he said nothing, just stared into space for half a minute or so before resuming the call. "Al, you there? I want you to come home, OK? Today. Now – the next flight out." It seemed Al was protesting but Peter broke in one last time, his voice hard. "Al, listen. It's over. Just come home."

He put the receiver down, crossed to the bar, poured himself a very large measure of whiskey then returned to his seat. "They tried to kill him," he said dully.

There was a stricken silence. Helen spoke first. "Kill Al? Who?"

"The Paraguayans."

Helen stared, puzzled. "Which Paraguayans?"

"The police."

"Don't be silly. The police don't go around killing people."

"They do in Paraguay." Peter described the events in the Chaco, reducing Geoff and Helen to incredulous silence.

To buy thinking time, Geoff poured himself a drink too. "God, it's hot in here." He stepped onto the balcony and stood staring out at the moonlit Pacific.

"I'm glad," Helen said at length. "I mean, I'm glad you've put a stop to it. I never wanted you to do it in the first place."

"You told me," Peter responded.

"What did he say when you told him to quit?" This was Geoff from outside.

"Oh, stuff about it being part of the job, wanting to see it through, all that macho thing."

"Hold on, Peter, Al wasn't the one who died out there," Geoff pointed out. "He can take care of himself, he was a Marine."

"I don't care if he was a Field Marshal, he's a civilian now and I'm not prepared to see him become a dead civilian."

Geoff was standing in the doorway. "No consultation required?", he asked, acidly.

"None," Peter replied, without rancor.

"There was no need for consultation, Geoff," Helen said. "Peter started the investigation and now he's ended it and I'm pleased it's over."

Geoff advanced into the room and stood over Peter's chair. He was flushed with anger. "Well I'm not," he shouted. Then, as suddenly as it had come, the violence was gone. Geoff moved away, put his glass on the bar and turned to face Peter across the room. He was pale, controlled, but no less angry. "And

I can explain why I'm not. I should have explained a long time ago."

Helen had seen these two, her husband and her closest friend, argue more or less amicably over business and technical issues countless times. She had thought she'd seen it all but there was something in Geoff's tone that filled her with foreboding. This, she knew at once, would be no ordinary altercation.

"Do you remember when we first met?" Geoff wasn't interested in an answer. "It was the University Chess Club. You breezed in, impeccably casual, full of charm and self-deprecation; 'Peter Gilchrist, how d'you do? I'm new this year. Wondered if I might get a game…'. Get a game! You were first board on the University team inside a month. And that's how it always was. Rowing, Leander Club, parties in the Eaton Square flat. Then it's Finals and you're cramming like mad, trying to make up for the rowing and the parties. I'm working pretty hard, too, but I'm thinking 'just watch the lucky bastard sail through'. But no, it seemed life was fair after all – it's a Third – Certificate of Generalized Incompetence, old Braithwaite called it. And mine's a First, top honors. Hallelujah!"

Peter looked across at Helen but she was hunched over, staring at the floor.

"So, time to join the world. Me with my glittering prize, planning my successful career: big corporation, bit of research, senior position, my name on a couple of patents, wife and kids; 'one of each, aren't we *lucky*, darling?' – expense paid trips to places I couldn't have afforded, to give papers nobody reads and it would all end in a generous pension, sunset in Surrey, honey for tea, and a Golden Labrador.

And I'm thinking 'poor old Peter, all that panache and a miserable Third – where's he going with that?'. And guess what? We've not even gone down and you've got me in a corner at another party. 'How would you like a job in my start-up company, City money, interesting work – lasers, your specialty, old chap – good salary and ten percent of the equity?' And even while I'm taking your arm off, I'm asking myself 'How does he do it? Who gives two million quid to a playboy with a Third Class Physics degree? And then, silly old Grammar school boy, I get it.

It's dinner at the Club with Bertie bloody Wooster[16], 'Young Gilchrist? Oh, of course. Know your father, member here, decent chap, very sound, Chairman of the Royal College of somethin' or other isn't he? And this idea of yours – lasers, is it? *Jolly* good – technology's the thing these days. Keep up with the times, what? How much d'you say you'll need?'"

Geoff took a deep breath. The longer this went on, the more contained and sardonic his tone became. He was beginning to enjoy himself.

"And there I was, decent, hard-working, best Physics graduate of the year, absolutely no bloody money and even less hope of raising any. And that was when it finally dawned and I've had the taste of it in my mouth every day since. I was born with a Second Class ticket and the only way I'd be traveling First was as your valet. And you know the best part? Bertie bloody Wooster was right! Look at it..." He gestured around the expensively furnished room. "...it's been twenty years, First Class all the way. Company's floated, worth... just what is it all worth this week, Peter?" But still he wasn't interested in the answer. "Mostly, I just keep my eyes tight shut and enjoy the ride but once in a while... Do you remember that dinner at Claridges? Merchant banker, some takeover thing and you took me along in case he brought a whiz and I could terrify him, but the old idiot came alone and looked me up and down, through a monocle for Christ's sake. 'Hughes... don't think I know a Hughes... which school was it? Oh, can't say I know it.' He was the ticket inspector, you see, Peter. 'There seems to be some mistake, sir' which means 'what's a nasty little grammar school pleb like you doing in First Class?' And tonight you did it again. Consultation? Sorry, old thing. My bat, my ball, my rules."

And it was over. Geoff's twenty years of angst had been spewed out in two minutes. With a despairing look at Helen, he went back out onto the balcony. Peter and Helen sat in uncomfortable silence, avoiding each other's eyes. Before they could speak Geoff was back. "Sorry, Helen, but I think we should have been consulted and I think stopping now is a mistake."

Peter was about to stand but Geoff was in his way and he could see that

16 Bertram Wilberforce "Bertie" Wooster is the wealthy 'hero' and narrator of P. G. Wodehouse's Jeeves stories. A minor British aristocrat and member of the idle rich, he always appears alongside his highly intelligent butler, Jeeves, whose genius extricates Bertie from numerous awkward situations. [adapted from Wikipedia.]

physical contact was not a good idea. Trying to keep his voice level he said:
"Look, Geoff, Meg was my daughter and it was my investigation."

"I tell you," Geoff's voice had a stern intensity, "if she'd been my daughter I'd
never have quit." He turned away suddenly calmer. "I just think we should
discuss it, that's all."

"OK. Let's do that," Peter was still convinced he'd made the right decision
but, bewildered by Geoff's tirade, was trying to mollify him. He drained his
glass and got up for a refill. "Anybody?", he asked, holding up the bottle. They
both declined.

"Well," he said, returning to his seat, "the way I see it, there've been enough
killings. Al, from what I gather, and it's a safe bet he gave me the quick
version, came close to being another. I've always said time and money were
not an issue but I didn't reckon on more deaths. So that's it. Enough. We tried,
it didn't work out." Ever the tactician, Peter moved to consolidate his two-
against-one position. "You can see that, can't you, darling?"

But Helen had been rethinking. "I'm not sure. I admit I was against the idea
at the start. I just couldn't see the point... it wasn't going to bring her back."
She stopped, gathering her thoughts. "But now, it's all different. Al's such a
good man and he's making progress... it seems wrong to give up now."

Peter's whiskey went down the wrong way and it took a glass of water and a
flurry of over-energetic backslapping by Geoff before he could respond to this
reversal of thinking. He was too flabbergasted to be really angry.

"Wrong to give up now? For God's sake why?"

"I don't know. It's just how it feels."

"But Al was almost killed."

Now it was Geoff's turn to play the tactical game. "Hold on. It sounded to
me like he was arguing to continue. I agree with Helen. As long as Hershey's
willing, I say press on."

Peter was mute. His success in business, as in chess, was due more than
anything to his ability to see around corners the opposition hadn't even
noticed; to be caught flatfooted like this was a novel and upsetting experience.

He knew intuitively that to concede was his only reasonable course but it took his brain a little time to formalize the decision.

*   *   *

Al sat alone in the icily air-conditioned conference room, wondering what he should do next. At length he determined on a gamble. He would press on, express the tapes to Thornton, say nothing to Mrs Hershey and delay leaving Paraguay for twenty-four hours. When he asked himself how long this could go on, his answer, through clenched teeth, was 'as long as I feel like it'.

He tracked down the young Third Secretary who'd been given the job of looking after him, gave him the file for immediate despatch and arranged a camp bed in the Duty Officer's room. He was sitting on the iron-framed monstrosity, finishing a diplomatic coffee and smoked salmon sandwich when the phone rang and he grabbed it. It was the call he had been fairly confidently expecting – Peter, slurring his words slightly. He put down the phone and punched the air. After just forty-five minutes out of work, he was back on the case.

The following day, as United's 747 began its steep climbing turn away from Silvio Pettirossi airport, Al stretched out in the Business Class seat, all that had been available at short notice, sipped his complimentary champagne and looked down at the arid landscape with relief. Never again, he thought. But then, with a stab of affection and regret, he thought of the quarrelsome Scotsman to whom he owed his life. Hamish was a warrior, a rare man who lived by his own rules, a man whom Al understood and admired. He raised his glass in silent toast, sorry they would not meet again and that he would probably never know what a corbie was.

CHAPTER 36

Seeking later to understand how he had been so easily caught a second time inside a week, the only excuse Al could find for himself was that the excitements of Paraguay followed by twenty-four hours traveling had dulled his senses. He had dumped his bags in the room and not stopping even to open the waiting FedEx package, the tapes from Washington, he assumed, set off to stretch his legs before bed.

Being even more sparing of clients' cash than he was himself, Mrs Hershey had booked him into an anonymous, three star hotel in the heart of Nuremberg's club land. It turned out to be a long way from Bowen's apartment but he'd learned early in his investigative career that complaints on such matters resulted only in an invitation to make his own arrangements.

The street outside the hotel was ill-lit and narrow. Made for it, he reflected later. It was no more than a hundred yards to what looked and sounded like a main street and he was half way there when he heard the tap, tap of the stick and saw the blind man coming towards him. He turned slightly to give him room to pass, feeling the stick tap gently against his leg. At the very last instant his training tried to help as he detected the faint sound of a step behind him but he had scarcely started to turn when the first blow fell…

*   *   *

"Herr Hershey. Sie hören mich?" A woman, leaning over the bed.

Darkness. The rasp of his own breathing.

"Herr Hershey. Können Sie Ihre Augen öffnen?"

Can I open my eyes? I guess so, ma'am… Dazzling light. A huge white form towering over him. He tries to fend it off but sickening pain overwhelms him.

The last thing he recalls as he slips back into unconsciousness is the tapping of the blind man's stick.

The next morning, having discharged himself from the hospital against medical advice, he was back in his hotel room, fighting off nausea, calling Bowen to apologize for the delay to their meeting and rearranging it for that afternoon.

*   *   *

Al's ribs ached and his legs wobbled as he climbed the steps to press the intercom for the top floor flat of a large house in a tree-lined street close by the University. He would be irked if the Professor failed to come up to Thornton's glowing recommendation.

"Ja?"

"Professor Bowen? Al Hershey. We spoke this morning."

"Ah yes, Mr Hershey. Hold on."

Brisk but arrhythmic footsteps on the stairs, a shadow at the spy hole and at last the sound of a chain and the door was opened by a bulky, rumpled man in his sixties wearing very elderly English brown corduroy trousers and a green woollen sweater draped about him like a peasant shawl.

"Do come in Mr Hershey. Sorry about the Peeping Tom impression but I find paranoia keeps me healthy." The huge, deeply gnarled hand gripped hard. "Please follow me and do watch the last flight, couple of loose boards. Don't believe all they tell you about German attention to detail."

Al struggled to keep up as the big man limped upstairs with surprising speed, talking energetically as he went.

"I've been looking forward to meeting you. Never met a real gumshoe... do they still use that term? Probably went out in the fifties." Four flights up he ducked slightly to enter an attic room. In contrast to the Professor's unruly appearance, his study was mathematically neat. "Take the armchair."

Bowen eased himself into a kneeling position in an oddly-shaped chair fashioned from artistically curved steel tubing and padded black leather. "I'm

stuck with this Scandinavian contraption, I'm afraid. Bit of a back problem."
He sighed. "Fell from a library ladder – never was good with heights." He
leaned backwards painfully, running his hands slowly up and down the back of
his ribs. "But never mind me... how are you? The Embassy said you'd had a
bit of an accident. You fall off something too?"

Al considered playing down the attack but decided it would be better for the
Professor to know the truth. "Diplomatic language. There was nothing
accidental about it, I was attacked. Professionally."

Bowen's reaction was interesting, not the usual explosion of surprise and
distaste of those for whom violent assault is what happens to others, but a
narrowing of the eyes and a measured response: "Were you? Please describe
what happened."

"Well, I can't tell you much. It was in the street outside my hotel. There was
a man with a white stick, I was struck from behind then the serious beating
started, boots plus a blunt instrument of some kind, the medic said. The white
stick was probably a diversion. Neat."

"Neat indeed," Bowen agreed dryly. "They might have killed you."

"Not this time. They put me in hospital but if they'd wanted me dead they'd
have put a couple of bullets in my head. This was just a polite enquiry."

"Enquiry?"

"Somebody wants to know if I give up easy."

"And do you?"

"Professor, those guys gave me more injuries in sixty seconds than I got in
sixteen years in the military. That's not a good way to get me to give up, you
have my word on that."

Bowen looked at Al thoughtfully. "Then they may yet wish they'd paid the
extra for the bullets."

Al took out his notebook. "Would you mind if we get started? I'd rather not
have a late night."

"Of course, but just one more question, if you don't mind. How did they find
you? You were hardly off the plane."

"I was wondering that. It seems these people have connections both in Paraguay and here. In Immigration, most likely."

The Professor nodded slowly. "Yes, that would fit." For a moment he seemed to want to say more but didn't. "Right. To business. What is it you need?"

"I'm trying to trace a carving, fifteenth century German, a figure of Christ stolen from the Church in Estonia."

"And how do you think I can help?"

"Well, I know that it was among a collection of stolen art sent to Paraguay in 1944 by a senior Nazi called Pohl. Pohl didn't make it to Paraguay, but his collection fell into the hands of another Nazi who did. He went by the name Brandt, but my information is that his real name was Gluecks. According to his Paraguayan security file, just before his death in February this year, following a visit by a German national, the entire collection of stolen art works was secretly shipped back to Germany. My problem is the trail ends there. There's nothing in the file to identify the visitor or to tell me where to start looking for the collection." Al took an envelope from an inside pocket. "This is a surveillance tape of Glueck's meeting with the visitor and the Paraguayans' idea of a transcription. I couldn't make much sense of it but the tape's been cleaned up electronically. I was told you might be able to help."

"Yes, I had a call from Washington, no less. Senator Thornton, can't say the name means anything but he sounded…"

"Like a Commanding Officer?" Al suggested.

"Ah, I see. Well, I'll do what I can. Let's have a listen, shall we?" He cast his eyes quickly over the transcription then put the tape into a studio-standard cassette player and ran it once through. When it ended he said: "A pretty rough tape and the Beethoven accompaniment doesn't help, but it's very interesting. An elderly chap with magnificent articulation. Old school… Northerner. Prussian aristocracy, that would be Gluecks, alright."

Al was about to speak but the Professor held up a hand and ran the tape again. Altogether he ran it four times, during which he sat – knelt, rather, in his contraption – perfectly still, eyes closed. At last he got up, seized a pad from his desk and began to pace back and forth in the confined attic space, scribbling frenetically, muttering in a mixture of German and English. Finally he threw the pad onto the desk, rubbed his hands and turned to Al enthusiastically.

"That is a priceless historical document, Mr Hershey." But the enthusiasm evaporated as quickly as it had appeared. He sighed and looked troubled. "Don't envy you, though. Unpleasant sort of a fellow. Wouldn't be surprised if he arranged the 'polite enquiry' as you call it."

Al looked blank. "But he's dead, sir."

"Dead? Course he's not... Oh, I see. Sorry, cross purposes. Not Gluecks – that is his real name, by the way. No, I'm talking about the chap who's got your carving."

Al gaped. "You mean you know where it is?"

"M'dear fellow, of course. All there on the tape. Edelmann's your man."

"Where does it say that?"

Bowen took up the Paraguayan transcription. "Look here." He pointed to a line which read: 'eine Geschichte von einer Gruppe der edlen Männer'. That translates as 'a story about an organization of noblemen'. Precisely the kind of faintly plausible rubbish emanating from some of these ultra-right groups, but it's quite wrong. What Brandt actually said was: 'ein Geschenk von Amtsgruppe 'D' zu Edelmann'. Now, that translates as 'a gift from Department 'D' to Edelmann'. You see?"

"And this makes more sense?"

"Oh, perfect sense. Department 'D' was the SS department responsible for Concentration Camps. In 1942 it was run by one SS Gruppenführer Richard Gluecks. He was Chief Inspector of Camps from 1939. Escaped May 4th '45 from a British naval hospital near Flensburg on the Danish border. Into the rat-line, no doubt."

"The rat-line?"

"ODESSA's escape route for senior Nazis."

"ODESSA? You mean like the movie?"

The Professor's laughter rattled the attic beams. "Good Lord, you Americans! ODESSA was made in Germany not Hollywood. The name stands for *Organisation der ehemaligen SS Angehörigen*, that's the Organization of Former SS Members. It was started in 1944 when a few of the more perceptive Nazis realized the game was up. They got together with the money men, Krupp, Thyssen and the rest, to organize an escape route, the rat-line as we came to call it. And the one thing they weren't short of was money. They had around four billion dollars in stolen gold bullion in friendly Zurich banks and there's a lot of it still in Nazi hands today. It's the Fourth Reich's war chest."

"I see. And Brandt was the name Gluecks used for his escape?"

"So it appears. Gluecks was certainly too prominent for his own good in 1945."

"And Edelmann? Where does he fit?"

"Ah, my old friend Der schwarze Baron – the Black Baron. That's what they call him around here and with good reason." He paused, scratching his head reflectively. "Well… there's good reason for the 'black' but the 'Baron', now, that's different. He's less of a Baron than I am. My maternal grandmother was a distant cousin of the Duke of Marlborough. Der Baron seems to have elevated himself about five years ago. Helps with the… what do they call it these days? Public Relations, I suppose."

Al was tired and sore. He interrupted Bowen's musings. "Where is he based?"

"His home is in Berlin but his organization, that's The New Templars, is based at Schloss Edelmann near a village called Erden about thirty miles northeast of here."

"Ah, Templars. The file did say that Fiedler represented a religious order."

The Professor smiled. "A religious order! Edelmann would really enjoy that. He's the founder of The Order of the New Temple, Templars for short. Ostensibly it promotes the preservation of German cultural inheritance but that's a front. Anything Nazi is illegal here so they have to box a bit clever, but they're Nazis alright. They'd be stoking the ovens right now if they could get away with it. That's why I'm here. There I was in Cambridge, very comfortable thank you, a sinecure teaching Goethe to a lot of youngsters who thought Birkenau was a ski resort, when I began hearing things from friends in Germany, plans to re-establish Germany as cultural leader of the world, in plain terms, the Fourth Reich. Well, they built the third one in the thirties while everybody stood and watched so I thought I'd better get over here and do something." He stopped abruptly and admonished himself. "Enough of that! Is there anything else I can help with?"

"A couple of things. First, have you actually met the Baron?"

Bowen shook his head. "I work better from cover, you see. Can tell you his age though - he'll be forty-six on the 11th of November... Armistice Day. Ironic, yes? And I can show you a photograph." He selected a file from one of several cabinets, took from it a newspaper cutting and handed it to Al who studied the thin, bloodless face carefully.

"Thanks." He returned the picture. "And these... Templars. Where do they get their funds?"

"Ah, that brings us back to ODESSA. I can't prove it but I'd bet my pension against a bottle of the Dean's sherry that there's ODESSA money involved."

Al was having difficulty focussing on his notes but he managed to ask "I don't suppose you could tell me the name of Brandt's visitor, could you?"

"I can, as a matter of fact. He introduced himself as Karl Heinz Fiedler. Another Northerner, much younger man, thirty-five to forty-five, I'd say."

Al put away his notebook and looked around the room. Apart from the essentials of everyday living, it was a workshop dedicated to an obsession. "You seem to live for this work, Professor. Is it worth it?"

The question was slightly flippant but the response was grave: "Don't be fooled by the ageing dilettante performance, Mr Hershey. I'm not playing a game. I detest living here. I don't like the food and I can't stand the climate. But I'll probably die here because I can't bring myself to ignore violent, perverted men like Edelmann - Himmler without the power. He must be taken seriously."

"I understand, Professor. And I'm sorry if I gave you the idea I see this as a game. I spent four years and lost some good friends in Vietnam fighting fanatics; I'm on your side."

Bowen smiled, stood and extended a hand. "I never doubted it. Good luck with your search."

With difficulty, Al levered himself out of his chair to grasp the large hand. He enjoyed the company of this man who, like himself, had volunteered for a dangerous and unpleasant duty. But aching everywhere and feeling a little dizzy, he had simply run out of concentration. "Professor, you've been more help than I could have hoped for. I'm in your debt. Would you mind calling a taxi?"

In his room Al just managed to undress before collapsing into bed where he slept for almost twenty-four hours.

CHAPTER 37

At nine on Friday morning, feeling much more like himself, Al called the Baron's office.

"Edelmann Engineering, Guten Morgen."

Al had decided to use English, on the grounds that he could be more irritating and more memorable than in German. "You speak English, ma'am?"

"Of course."

"Then let me talk to Herr Edelmann, please."

"Who shall I say is calling?"

"My name is Stoss."

"Baron Edelmann is at this moment not available, Herr Stoss. Perhaps you will leave a message?"

"OK ma'am. Just tell him that Veit Stoss will meet him in the Jagdhorn Weinstube in Wendelstein at ten o'clock tomorrow morning."

"Herr Edelmann has an engagement tomorrow."

"He sure does. Like I told you, the Jagdhorn, ten o'clock."

"Excuse me, Herr Stoss…"

"Just give him the message."

There was a frigid silence then: "I will give your message to the Baron."

"I'm sure you will, ma'am."

*   *   *

Al had studied every tourist brochure in the rack in the hotel foyer to choose the location for the meeting. 'To be sportive, to take a cure or just to find back to yourself within the nature – Wendelstein is the perfect place for this goal,' boasted the guidebook. And the Weinstube Jagdhorn, tucked away in the woods above the village, a sleepy little tourist trap an hour from Erden, was also a safe place to meet unpleasant people with a tendency to violence; at this hour it was quiet and strangers would not go unnoticed. Al had chosen a table adjacent to the emergency exit.

As he sat sipping a rather pleasing pale beer, he could see the main door and through a small leaded window, the parking area under the pine trees.

At a few minutes before ten he picked out the big BMW as it turned off the track. The moonfaced, powerfully built driver was obviously muscle but Al noted a slight awkwardness as he clambered from behind the wheel. The passenger, clearly not the Baron, was equally obviously the brain, tall, compact and lithe, with blonde hair curling at the nape. His pale-colored suit, black leather document case and something about the way he moved combined to remind Al of a gay rights lawyer he'd recently tangled with and his dislike was reflexive and intense. When the pair of them entered, moonface went to the bar, ordered a beer and took up station at a table by the door; the other stood in the middle of the room looking around with slow deliberation until, Al, catching his eye, he came over.

"Herr Stoss?" He remained standing, stiff, almost at attention.

Al switched on his good ol' boy bonhomie. "That's me, buddy. Pull up a piece of bench and take the load off, why don't you."

"Thank you." Disconcerted by Al's approach, he examined the bench with distaste before perching on its edge, made to put his case on the table then changed his mind and held it on his knees.

"Your message gave no indication of the nature of your business," he said reprovingly.

"And you've given me no indication of the nature of your name."

The German flushed. "I beg your pardon." He took out a monogrammed leather case and handed Al his card.

The name on the card was Gunther Neubauer. Al affected not to understand the remainder of the contents. "What's that in American?"

"I am Head of Security for the Order of the New Temple. Baron Edelmann has instructed…"

Al shook his head slowly. His brain had caught up with his instincts about Herr Neubauer and he chose to let it show. "I don't give a flying fuck about the Baron's instructions, pal, I don't talk to office boys."

Neubauer's face blazed scarlet and the pale blue eyes glittered with anger.

"I assure you…"

"No you don't. You nauseate me."

Al stood up abruptly. The lawyer jerked backwards on his seat. Al was moving as he spoke: "Tell the Baron same time tomorrow and," a gesture across the room, "no goons."

Al moved fast and was in the car-park before moonface had extricated himself from behind his table. Walking steadily towards the hire car, he heard the stomping tread then felt the big hand on his shoulder, yanking hard to turn him. Unresisting, Al spun on one foot and in the same movement kneed the man in the groin. In an instant, the once threatening bulk was rolling among the pine needles of the carpark, a writhing, retching wreck. Al's still bruised body protested at this explosion of effort but despite the stabbing pain, it was wonderfully satisfying.

*   *   *

Twenty-four hours later, Al was at the same table when the Baron arrived at the wheel of the BMW, parked, marched across the car park and slid into the warmly welcoming little Stube like a shark into a children's pool. His face was long and sallow, the high brow emphasized by the oiled, flattened-down black hair. The dark, narrow eyes beneath thin, low set brows, were coldly intelligent, the fleshy lips pale and devoid of humor.

He crossed unhesitatingly to Al's table, sat down and began speaking without greeting or delay. His voice was a high tenor, quiet but sharp with crystalline articulation and almost no accent. With a little practice and less perfect grammar he could have passed for a native English speaker.

"You are a violent man, Mr Hershey. An ambulance was required. The man is in hospital. There was really no need…"

"There was every need," Al interrupted. "Now that you know I am serious, we can talk."

As though Al had not spoken, the Baron said, "I understand you served in Vietnam. A Sergeant of Marines, were you not?"

"I was."

"Indeed. And quite unscathed. One establishes long lasting friendships in war. So useful in later life. How is Colonel Thornton?"

"The Senator was very fit the last time I saw him."

"And influential."

At the bar two English tourists, stern hill-walkers by their lean bodies and monstrous backpacks, struggled to communicate with the barmaid.

Edelmann eased back in his seat and folded his hands in his lap. "Do you have any conception of what you are involved in?"

Al said nothing. In the background the Englishmen plunged ever deeper into a morass of incomprehension.

"For an American, you are remarkably taciturn. No smart retort? No anti-German joke?"

"I'm waiting for you to quit demonstrating your superiority so we can get down to business."

The German's eyes narrowed. "Very well. You called the meeting. What is it you want?"

"It will speed things up if you tell me exactly how the carving was taken."

The Baron studied Al thoughtfully. "Do you know how important that carving is to me?"

"I know that if the German public finds out how much taxpayers' money you and your closet Nazis in Intelligence are spending chasing after it, it'll bring down the government."

It was an unexpected shot and Al saw it strike home.

"Why should I tell you anything?" A trace of petulance in his voice.

"Because you want the carving and I can find it."

"But you don't work for me, Mr Hershey."

"I work for the highest bidder."

"Indeed. Such cupidity...curiously uplifting." He laced his fingers together, staring down at his hands. "But if you know who has it, why do you need me?"

Al played his best card. "Did Herr Fiedler enjoy his visit to Tallinn? It can be unpleasantly cold there even in April."

No amount of Teutonic self-discipline could conceal the Baron's astonishment. He jerked upright, began breathing quickly, struggling for control.

"Ironic, isn't it?" Al continued, "that Fiedler, the trusted aide, the hero who rescued the carving, should try to steal it."

It had all been solid so far but now Al was almost out of ammunition. He threw in his best guess at what had happened next.

"But all he did was to lay a trail back to its hiding place in the Schloss and so the unbelievable happened. Somebody lifted it right from under the noses of your guard dogs. It must have been something of a shock."

The Baron had regained control of himself but the joints of his clenched fingers showed white.

"Yes, a severe shock. I admit it." He drew in a deep breath as he reached a decision. "Mr Hershey, I underestimated you. You are correct in every respect." He paused, searching for a way to begin. "It was a girl..." The full lips tightened with distaste and Al realized the man was homosexual. "...a tart. She seduced one of my security staff and obtained a copy of his keys and the pass code for the alarms. When he was on the overnight watch she drugged him, walked in, took the carving and left. She even reset the alarm so that when the dolts arrived next morning and found the guard unconscious it was several hours before it occurred to them to check the premises."

"Describe the girl."

"Very tall, dark. Late twenties. Expensively dressed."

"How did she make contact?"

"She was a waitress at a Nuremberg club where the guard used to drink at weekends. Picked him up, slept with him then moved in. Three weeks later it was all over and she hasn't been seen since."

"She took only the carving?"

"Yes."

"Stolen to order."

"As you say."

"And when was this, exactly?"

"The twelfth of June. A Friday."

Al sipped his beer. Of course, they calculated on getting the whole weekend start. "And the guard. I take it you no longer employ him?"

The Baron's response was offhand. "The last I heard of him, he was in hospital."

Al bit back his anger. "Is there anything else I should know?"

"Nothing."

Al got to his feet.

"What do you propose to do now, Mr Hershey?"

"I propose to find the carving, Herr Edelmann. And you?"

The Baron stood up too. "I will watch and wait."

Al had gone only a few hundred yards down the dirt road when the BMW, traveling very fast, passed his hire car, showering his windscreen with stones and mud. As the wipers struggled with the mess, Al smiled. In his line of work, really good days were few.

CHAPTER 38

The thing about Stockholm, Al learned as soon as he stepped off the plane, was that things worked. The taxi from the airport was clean inside and out, and its driver's English was more than adequate. The hotel receptionist's cool smile was tailored to dispel any prior notions about Swedish girls and her English was as flawless as her appearance. In his room the doors to the shower cubicle ran so smoothly and clicked shut with such precision that he opened and closed them several times, first to be sure it wasn't a fluke, then just for the tactile pleasure. Al wondered whether it was all the cleanliness and precision that made the people so desperately serious – or was it the other way around?

After he'd showered and changed into one of the new shirts he'd bought at the airport, he still had a couple of hours to kill before the 'Blue Moon' opened. He found an isolated table in the coffee shop, ordered an espresso and a ham croissant and set about reviewing his notes. He'd been moving so fast he was sure he knew more than he realized and so it proved.

He turned to what he'd written in the Tallinn square and heard again the old man's precise English telling the story. He shuffled the pieces in his mind, adding what he'd learned at such cost in Asunción and Nuremberg, plus a few practiced guesses and he could at last fashion most of the picture. Yet, without Endel, the picture was worthless and without Jaakob's help he had no place to start looking.

The 'Blue Moon' was one of a clutter of bars and clubs crammed into Stockholm's Old Town. Al crossed the carpeted foyer to the Sinatra Bar, threaded his way through the almost empty tables and took a seat near the small stage.

It was 8:30 and there were three other customers. At the table nearest the door, a middle aged woman in a pale pink jacket and matching plastic boots, who looked as if she could be from Wisconsin, was nursing a beer glass. She looked speculatively at Al as he passed. At one end of the bar, a twentyish blonde with black eyebrows and fingernails to match sipped moodily at an electric blue concoction in a melon-sized glass. At the other end a man with a Cossack hat and a well-nourished beer gut was engrossed in a porno magazine. Behind the bar a ponderous ex-heavyweight-hopeful in a tight, plum-colored jacket polished already spotless glasses.

Al ordered a beer and settled to wait. The place slowly filled up. At around ten, three men in tuxedos appeared on the stage and began setting up an electronic organ, drums and bass. Al disliked electronic instruments and the trio were appalling. They opened with a reasonably competent version of the predictable 'Blue Moon' but it was downhill all the way from there. They took 'Sweet Georgia Brown' so fast the drummer couldn't keep up, then launched into 'My Funny Valentine' too slowly with the bass player firmly on the wrong chord most of the time; in the middle section - 'Is your figure less than Greek?' the organist, vibrato working overtime, was using chords Richard Rogers hadn't considered necessary.

At last it was over. The organist took the microphone and, ignoring the absence of applause, thanked the ladies and gentlemen very much indeed and began his spiel.

"And now the moment you've all been waiting for."

That's certainly true, Al thought.

"The wonderful lady with the velvet voice, Stockholm's Queen of the Blues, I give you, ladies and gentlemen..." as his voice reached a scream the drummer threw in a snare drum roll and the PA speakers howled enthusiastically... "the one and only – the Swinging Swede – Miss Eva Bergstrom!"

Al knew something about the blues and given the quality of the warm-up, he was prepared for anything except what followed. Eva was about thirty, tall, blonde and beautiful. In a fitted white, strapless cocktail dress she was effortlessly stylish and she sang the blues with a growl straight out of the Mississippi Delta she knew only from the movies. Al was entranced. Accompanied by her own keyboard player, she swung through half a dozen jazz standards, ending the set with a version of 'Miss Otis regrets' that sent a shiver down Al's spine. As she stepped from the stage and sat down at a corner table with a 'Reserved' notice, the applause was enthusiastic. Al gave her a couple of minutes, then went across and sat at her table. In the mirror behind her head, he saw the bartender, right hand in the plum colored pocket, step out from the bar.

"Whatever he's got in his pocket, he won't need it, Miss Bergstrom. If you don't want to talk, just say so and I'll leave."

She studied Al steadily then caught the barman's eye and shook her head almost imperceptibly. He returned to his polishing but Al knew he was being watched.

"He's mean and not too bright but he takes care of me." She gestured around the room. "A girl needs somebody..."

"So why did you stop him?"

"I can see you're not going to make trouble."

"How can you tell?"

"You've got nice eyes."

Al said she had nice eyes, too, and he figured she wouldn't make trouble either. She laughed.

"You sing real well. Can I get you a drink?"

She shook her head. "Not while I'm working."

Al liked her at once. She looked terrific, she was talented and she sounded genuine. He didn't much like what he had to do, so he gritted his teeth and jumped in before he got to like her any more.

"I visited Tommi in hospital. The left leg doesn't bend too well and he's not as young as he was but he'll survive."

She was devastated. The color drained out of her face and her mouth fell open. There was no hope of bluffing it out and she knew it. She hesitated, glancing back and forth from him to the bar then slumped in her seat. Al went to the bar and got her a double brandy, ignoring the barman's scowl. She gulped at it, the glass chattering against her teeth. Brandy trickled from the side of her mouth, unresisting, she allowed Al to mop it with his handkerchief.

"Look, I'm not here to make trouble. I just need your help. Trust me, please."

He took the picture of Meg from his wallet and slid it across the table. She looked down at it dull-eyed.

"This young woman was murdered on a beach in California six weeks ago. She was twenty-two years old."

The girl looked at Al blankly. "I don't understand. Who are you? Why do you show this to me?"

"Because she was murdered for the carving you stole."

"It's not true." But he could see that even as she spoke, she knew. She stared at the photograph then looked up at him despairingly. He said nothing. "Say it's not true."

"I'm sorry."

In the mirror, Al could see the barman leaning on the bar, eyes on the girl.

"I'm investigating her murder. I need your help."

She was staring at the photograph "What was her name?"

"Meg."

"She's pretty. Did you know her?"

"No."

"Then why are you doing this?"

"Her father asked me to find out why she was killed."

"He's a friend of yours?"

"No, it's my job." He opened his wallet to show his PI's licence.

She drained the brandy and held up the glass as a signal to the barman then sat, mute, gazing blankly across the table until he brought it.

"You got some troubles, Miss Eva?" He was massaging his right fist with his left hand and eyeing Al hopefully. She shook her head and he turned reluctantly away.

"So you do this for the money."

"Yes."

"Like you'd do anything?"

"Not drowning young women."

She shuddered. "Is that how...?"

"Someone held her under until she was dead."

Al watched her working out that she had no choice. Then she spoke slowly, in a monotone.

"It was in here. About three months back. He sent his card to my dressing-room. Nils Petersson, address in Malmo. The message said how would I like a job in Nuremberg. First, I thought he was after the usual but he said he worked for the government recovering stuff stolen during the war and I could help and make good money at the same time. I normally only take bookings through my agent but I was pretty desperate. The money's good here but it's unreliable. And there was an advance... not much but it paid the rent."

"So there was a real job, singing?"

"Oh sure. A good job. A club in the Old City. Big, flash place. They get top artists... it sounded like a chance. And I like working in Germany, I speak the language pretty good."

"And the rest of it?"

"He said that there would be a guy, German, a regular. I was supposed to let him pick me up and get his keys. Then Nils would do all the rest..." She ran a weary hand through her hair, "I should have known..."

"It turned out to be not so simple?"

"You could say so. First, I had to go and get stuck on the guy." Her face twisted in pain. "Poor Tommi... He shouldn't have been in that job. Oh, he was big and strong and everything, but he was too decent. He should have been married, kids, all that. He said he wanted to marry me, the big dummy. They beat him up, those Nazis?"

"Yes."

"I knew they would. Nils said they'd never figure out he was in on it but I knew Tommi. He couldn't hide anything, especially not from those swine."

She muttered something to herself, something violent-sounding in Swedish.

"So what happened?"

"You mean apart from me falling for Tommi? It was too easy. I borrowed his keys so Nils could get a copy and I got the code for the alarms from his wallet. He wasn't supposed to write it down but he couldn't remember it and they said if he set the alarms off once more he'd be out of a job."

"So who actually went in?"

"Me. It was the Friday, Tommi's week on night-shift."

"Can you remember the date?"

"Oh, yes. It was the 12th."

"Of June?"

"June, yes."

"OK. Please go on."

"Right, well, Nils had given me some stuff to put into Tommi's flask of coffee. Around two, I rang the security office from Nils' car. When there was no reply I used the key and the alarm code and just walked in. Nils had given me a plan of the building and I found the carving right where he said it would be. I put it in a holdall and left."

"And you set the alarms on your way out?"

"Yes," she said. "Nils said that was very important."

"The carving. How big was it?"

"Oh, about...", she looked around, then pointed "...about the size of that snare drum. But solid, quite heavy, solid wood."

"And the plan of the building, what was that like?"

"Like?"

"Well, was it just a sketch?"

"Oh, no. It was a proper thing, thick paper with blue lines... with measurements and stuff, you know? It made it real easy to find the room with the carving."

An architect's drawing; these people have contacts, Al thought. "So you walked in, got the carving and locked everything up after you?"

"Sure. Nils said that was important. He said with any luck they might think Tommi had just got sick and we'd have more time to get clear. It seemed to work."

"And then?"

"Nils was waiting in the car. He seemed to be in a terrible rush, kept on looking at his watch. It frightened me, the way he drove. He dropped me at Berlin airport and gave me a ticket for Stockholm."

"What was the car?"

"What? Oh, it was a Volvo estate car. Nice color... kind of midnight blue."

"Miss Bergstrom, I'm almost done. I just need to know anything you can tell me about this Nils. Can you describe him?"

"Oh, nothing special. Medium height, very tanned, the outdoor type."

"His hair?"

"It was dark, long curls, sort of boyish. He had a nice smile but a hard look, could be mean, I think. Oh, and he smoked all the time, horrible black things, Russian. I could smell it on my clothes for days."

"And he was Swedish."

She looked surprised. "Swedish? Oh, no. He was Estonian."

"How could you tell?"

She smiled. Al thought how much better she looked smiling.

"His accent - horrible. I've done a couple of gigs in Tallinn, that's where Nils heard me, at the Panoraam, so I know the sound." She looked at Al, childishly anxious. "Does that help?"

"It helps very much."

She reached across the table; long slender fingers dug into his arm "Are you going back to Nuremberg? Will you see Tommi?"

Al shook his head. "I'm afraid not." He caught her expression. "And you shouldn't either. Don't even call. Tommi tried to put them off the scent – said you were a waitress, not a singer. And they're looking for a brunette. You changed your hair?"

She nodded.

"OK. So that gives you a chance but they don't give up. If they find you, dying won't be the worst of it. You understand?"

For a while she stared down at the table in silence then, without looking up, she said: "It wasn't going anywhere. But he was a sweet boy."

Al could see that she was in a private world, unheeding. He took her by the wrist firmly enough to make her wince a little.

"Look, Eva, you must understand. These people will kill you if they find you."

He was hissing the words, his voice harsh with urgency, but part of his attention was on the barman who had left the bar and was crossing the room, hand in pocket as before. Time to leave. Al stood up and watched the big man advancing, purposeful, unhurried. Al glanced back at Eva but she wasn't going to help this time. He sighed inwardly, wondering why he hadn't just left a minute ago, no trouble. Now the barman was some ten feet away and his hand was out of his pocket. Catching the dull glint of brass across the knuckles of the hefty right fist, Al made his calculations.

On the plus side, the guy was overweight and in poor shape, too much of the 'and one for yourself, Oh, thank you, sir, just a small one'. On the other hand, he was a head taller and a sack of potatoes heavier than Al and from his stance and the untidy arrangement of his features, he knew what happens in the loneliest time after the bell goes. It seemed that, whichever of them was left standing at the end of it, a good many drinks, tables and guests would be upset along the way. He decided to play safe and took a firm step towards the oncoming heavyweight, opening his jacket carefully to show him the Browning.

The guy stopped dead, his eyes narrowed, fixed on the pistol, not a common sight in the bar-room rumbles he was so practiced in. Not giving him time to think, Al held up a hand – of thanks, of warning, whatever - and headed for the door as swiftly as he could without running. To his immense relief the barman was happy to let him go. The thought of even unholstering the weapon in this remote place where his firearms permit and PI's licence were so much waste paper, turned him cold. In the cab, he took a few deep breaths and threw a silent thanks to whichever Nordic God had the crap duty of looking after visiting detectives. He was headed for his hotel and an appointment with a cold beer.

A glass of Swedish lager later, he checked the time difference and called Peter.

*   *   *

"Peter? It's Al. Are you free to talk?"

"I can be. Just hold on."

Peter covered the mouthpiece. "Turn the music down, Helen. It's Al."

Helen pointed the remote control and Wagner faded to inaudibility.

"OK, I'm listening. Where are you?"

"Stockholm, at the airport. I've talked to the girl."

"The singer? Jolly well done. How did you find her?"

"I got lucky. I saw a handbill for a club where she'd worked. Fortunately the security guard she seduced gave them a false trail, said she was just a waitress. Anyway, let me bring you up to date. She was the one who actually took the carving from Edelmann's headquarters but the job was organized by a man called Margus Sepp. He's Head of Security for Baltic Star Lines in Tallinn and, by the way, his brother is captain of the Three Lions."

"Is he, by Jove! So it's a family affair."

"Well," Al's professional caution intervening, "there's no direct evidence the carving was ever on board the Three Lions but if Eva's telling the truth then, driving hard, Margus could have arrived in Tallinn with the carving in time to catch his brother's ship before she sailed on the Saturday, that's June 13th."

"Indeed." Peter was running with the argument. "And, thanks to your wife, we can definitely place the Three Lions off Half Moon Bay three weeks later."

"Sure we can." Al took up the running. "And soon after, an unidentified package was picked out of the water and off-loaded on Smugglers Beach."

"And to top everything, somebody kills the pick-up man and leaves a fifty-year-old message on the body," Peter went on.

"And the weapon, it was a World War II German officer's pistol," Al concluded.

There was a silence as they pondered this bizarre sequence of events. Then Peter asked: "So what happens next?"

"I go back to Tallinn for another talk with Jaakob."

"I thought you'd got all you could from him."

"Not quite. I made a deal."

"A deal?"

"Yes. If I do a favor for him, he'll catch the guy behind all of this for us."

"Hold on, is this a joke or…"

"Sorry, Peter, that's the last call for my flight. Be in touch."

There were in fact two hours before take-off but one of Al's small indulgences was, as he described it to himself, 'keeping a little something in the bank' when reporting to clients.

*　　*　　*

Jaakob rose slowly from his armchair and made his way to the kitchen, running his hands up and down the small of his back. The heavy silence was broken only by the sounds of coffee making. As Al had presented the evidence gathered since their previous meeting, he had watched the old man's expression change from interest to concern, to anger and finally, as the truth forced itself upon him, to despair. The coffee was brought in and Jaakob was back in his chair before he spoke.

"I knew it already, of course. In the square. I'm sorry, but I just could not…"

"The apology isn't needed, sir. I was a soldier, I know how you must feel."

The old man was shaking his head. "No, Al, excuse me but you do not know. It's not simply a matter of an old comrade. My father was dying when Endel and I swore the oath. What he has done cannot be forgiven."

Jaakob's heavy frame shifted restlessly in his chair; coffee slopped over the rim of his cup and ran over his hand but he seemed not to notice. "After my father, he was the best of us."

Al waited, hoping not to have to ask. At last he was rewarded.

"Very well, Al. I will help you find him although truly I have no idea where to begin." He shook his head wearily. "He became invisible in 1971."

Al knew the extent of the Mob's reach. "With Rastelli's friends after him, his choice was invisible or dead." He rolled his almost empty cup back and forth between his palms, staring down into it, muttering to himself. "But there has to be a way."

When he looked up, he saw Jaakob shaking his head and smiling at him like an indulgent father. "Ah, Al – you Americans, you bring us fast food, loud music, a piece of the moon. You think everything is possible. And you, you are a hands up man, yes?"

Al smiled too. Jaakob's errors of language were few but always good value. "Hands on."

"Of course, hands on. You believe that because you want something, there must be a way to get it."

"I think you just showed it to me."

"I did? How?"

"Would you say Endel is also a hands-on man?"

"I would say so, yes."

"What does he do if he's threatened?"

Jaakob looked surprised. "I would say he mostly does the threatening."

"Supposing…"

Jaakob considered. "Well… you could say Roth was a threat… and maybe the man in California also…"

Al nodded. "So he doesn't delegate important tasks?"

"I told you, he was praying the Brothers would bring back Roth alive."

"Yes, you did tell me that," Al said. And, after a little thought, he proposed, to Jaakob's sorrowful agreement, how Endel, invisible in America, might be persuaded to show himself in Estonia.

CHAPTER 39

PART 4

1st – 9th September 1992

ENDGAME

"Buy me a drink?"

She was very young, small, dark, exquisite and so elegantly dressed that for an instant Margus wondered if she really was just a lonely girl looking for company in the hotel. He shook his head. "Another time."

She smiled her regret and moved on. Behind him, he heard her receive an enthusiastic reception from two loud Americans who were already comprehensively drunk. With a little finesse she would get her drink and her fee for nothing more than a bedtime story.

The digital clock projected onto the wall flicked over to midnight. In disgust, Margus finished his drink. He'd waited too long and spent too much. Leida had probably fucked up the message, stupid bitch. When he got down from the bar stool, the furniture seemed to be shuffling about rather more than when he'd arrived, and it took concentration to find a route to the door. Behind him he heard one of the Americans bellow an order for a bottle of champagne and wondered what the girl's cut would be. In the two acre foyer he waved away the concierge's offer of a taxi and stepped into the street. The cool air steadied things somewhat and he set off, demonstrating his sobriety with a firm and deliberate tread. Back in the foyer a heavily-built man of around seventy carefully folded the house copy of a Russian daily newspaper, replaced it in the rack, put on his overcoat and followed Margus into the street.

The first stretch of the walk home was brightly lit, the restaurants and bars still bustling with Tallinn's post-Soviet mix of tourists, local entrepreneurs, marketing consultants, politicians, snake-oil salesmen and working girls. The new Estonians; Margus hated their wealth and fast talk and condescending looks almost as much as he'd hated their Soviet predecessors.

It wasn't until he'd left the main street and the only light was from occasional curtained bedrooms, the only sound his own footsteps echoing from darkened house fronts that he realized he was being followed. Careful not to change pace he fingered the clasp knife in his jacket pocket. He wished he'd brought the pistol but he wasn't very good with firearms and could never find a comfortable way to carry them. He kept walking, straining to pick out the following footsteps. How many? Surely not, only one? He'd take his chances with one. Then he remembered The Crane. It was a rough bar, a base for cheap whores, pimps and third division gangsters, all Russians. No decent Estonian would go near it but to Margus it would be a haven and not three hundred meters away. It was time to run.

"Margus."

The voice was behind him. He stopped, turned and peered astonished into the blackness.

"Over here." The voice came from a narrow entry between two disused warehouses. It sounded familiar but he couldn't place it. He took the knife from his pocket, snapped it open and held it in front of him. Its cold, solid feel gave him confidence as he crossed the street and paused at the entry.

"Who is it?"

"Come out of the light. We need to talk."

Excellent Estonian but there was something peculiar, he thought. Could it be a Russian? Still the identity evaded him. Tightening his grip on the knife he took a step into the darkness. "Who is it?"

He had only a split second to sense a presence in the darkness before something smashed into his forearm with paralyzing force. He heard the knife clatter to the cobbles as a hand took him by the throat, squeezing, thrusting him backwards, stumbling for balance until the back of his head hit the stone wall and set his world spinning. His one good arm clawed the blackness, desperate for something to strike at, to hurt, some way to damage this invisible monster throttling his life away. He had almost lost consciousness when the crushing pressure on his throat eased, allowing him to gasp a few desperate lungfuls of air. The presence bore in on him. Something hard was pushed into his ribs and he was propelled deeper into the darkness, unresisting as a child, until he was wedged into a doorway invisible from the street. A click, a blinding light in his face and questions.

"How much did he pay you?"

The question came at Margus down a tunnel of pain. 'Pay you'? Pay for what? He wanted desperately to say something but he couldn't get words to come. Then suddenly he knew the voice, the anonymous voice which handed out promotions and issued orders on the telephone. His stomach heaved and he was spun away until the vomiting stopped then dragged back into the light beam.

"How much, Margus?"

"Boss, I, nothing…"

"Fiedler, Margus. How much did he pay you?"

Fear and pain were threatening Margus's grip on reality. In a flash of dreadful clarity he realized this man was prepared to kill him. With a supreme effort, he forced some sense into his words.

"The Kraut? I haven't seen him… not since I followed him to Erden."

There was a long pause. Margus could feel the man's eyes on him but he was gradually sensing that he had been believed, that at last his terrifying inquisitor was satisfied.

"Alright Margus. I believe you. But don't ever forget. You got your job because of your father. I told you then: loyalty, as it was in the forest, loyalty before everything."

The light moved away a little, the gun withdrew from his aching ribs.

"One last thing – you tell no-one about our talk, understand?"

Euphoria swept over Margus. He wanted desperately to show his gratitude. He fumbled into the darkness, desperate for some human contact.

"Sure, Boss, sure. Look, I…"

The first blow took him low on the ribs. He groaned as pain and surprise hit simultaneously. "But…"

"That wasn't about Fiedler. That was about Leida." Another savage blow to the body dropped Margus to his knees. "If you ever strike her again, I'll kill you." The third blow smashed into the side of his head. "And stay off the drink."

Then there was only a silhouette, large against the lights of the street, before the cobbles flew up and struck him in the face.

*   *   *

Back in his hotel room Endel stretched out on the bed, grim-faced. He, of all people, the master strategist - set up. The words of a great player and philosopher of the game came to his mind: 'The blunders are all there on the board, waiting to be made'. There was no doubt that Margus, on the edge of death, had told the truth. And the stolidly loyal Captain Sepp didn't know enough to be a threat. Which left only Jaakob and no matter how he analyzed it, it made no sense. Certainly Jaakob was a formidable warrior and no ordinary man, but he lacked the imagination to concoct a trap like this. At last, still fully clothed, still lacking an explanation, he lay, drifting in and out of sleep, dreaming, remembering.

'To the Church. Remember, both of you – to the Church. Swear you will never give up.' Anti's hoarse, desperate whisper and death grey features dragged him, panting, sweating and dishevelled, back to wakefulness. It was two-thirty a.m. For a while he lay, battling to shake off the memories, then he picked up the phone and requested a taxi. At last, swaying with fatigue, he made his way to the bathroom.

Half an hour later, re-energized by a shower and a miniature of vodka he entered the waiting taxi, his entire life focussed to a single point of purpose.

*   *   *

Earlier that evening Jaakob's telephone had rung.

"Jaakob? It's Leida."

He picked up her flustered tone.

"Yes, child. What is it? Are you alright?"

"Oh, yes. No problem… well, I'm not sure."

Jaakob's anger rose. "Has Margus…?"

"No, no," she cut in swiftly, "he's not home yet. He'll be at O'Toole's." Margus had recently added to his list of vices a taste for consuming great quantities of Guinness at a newly-opened so-called Irish bar in town. "A man's been here. Looking for him… well, he asked for him but I think he came to see me."

"To see you? What man? Who was this?"

"I don't know. A large man, large like you. In an overcoat. Not young."

"Like me, also, eh?"

"Maybe not that old." He heard her smile and was relieved. "He was strange, Jaakob. He asked questions."

"Questions?"

"Yes. About me. And Margus. And…"

Suddenly she sounded lost. Jaakob waited.

"I answered them," she ended, apologetically.

"He forced you?" Jaakob asked, already knowing the answer.

"No," she said, decisively. "Not at all. He was… quiet. Thoughtful. Like my father was. But not a man to be lied to. You understand?"

And Jaakob understood perfectly.

"He left two messages. For Margus, to meet him later."

"Tonight?"

"Yes, tonight. Eleven o'clock in the Bristol Hotel." She laughed nervously. "If he stays in O'Toole's much longer he won't be able to find his way there."

Jaakob was thinking hard. "You said two messages."

"Yes, two. The other was for you. He said to tell you that he will call tonight as soon as he can." Then, before Jaakob could respond, he heard the alarm in her voice. "Margus is back. Bye, Jaakob." And the line was dead.

*   *   *

When he came, it was as Jaakob had known it would be, the Secret Police knock in the small hours. Still fully dressed, Jaakob opened the door within seconds and caught the surprise on Endel's face.

"Jaakob, old friend."

Endel reached to embrace the old soldier but Jaakob silently stepped back, holding open the door. The room was the same litter of books and papers it always was, except that the dining table had been cleared and on it were placed two glasses and a bottle of vodka. Jaakob sat, gestured to the other chair and filled the glasses. The only light was from the fire. Endel took off his coat, laid it carefully over the armchair and sat opposite Jaakob at the table. He took up his glass and raised it in salute: "The Brothers," and drained it.

Jaakob sat motionless, expressionless, his glass untouched. Endel flushed at the brutal insult. He held up his empty glass.

"May I?"

Jaakob slid the bottle to within reach. Endel filled his glass, picked it up, stared down into it.

"I've spoken with Margus." He swirled the oily liquid, watching reflections of the room pirouette across its surface. "There won't be any more trouble." He ran the fingers of his left hand across the damaged knuckles of the right. "He won't harm her again."

Jaakob pushed away his untouched glass and sat back, big hands flat on the table. Endel shifted in his chair. He looked around the cheap room, groped among his memories for something, some shared experience that might ease the tension, coax some response from the implacable monolith opposite. No words came.

His stiffening joints moving awkwardly, Jaakob drew a revolver from his pocket and placed it heavily on the table. Oil gleamed on black metal. Another link to their past. Endel tried to recall how many times he'd seen that weapon fired, how many it had killed.

Jaakob leaned forward, eyes fixed on the visitor. "Why?"

This was the fatal question Endel had feared since the moment he had decided to take the carving for himself. And now here it was. In a heartbeat he considered and dismissed the possibility of making a deal – Jaakob of all people did not make deals. So here he sat, in the stillness and the flickering firelight, wondering whether his oldest comrade would seek to avenge his betrayal and whether he could summon up the will to resist.

CHAPTER 40

Helen, reading on the balcony, heard the sound of a car at the front, then Peter answering the door. After a short conversation he came through from the lounge.

"Who was that?"

"What a damned peculiar chap."

He handed her a sheet of paper. It was a letter on printed stationery. "It's Vanosivich's driver with this. And he's waiting for an answer, damn it. What do you make of it?"

She read:

Wednesday 9th September

Dear Mr Gilchrist,

I would be pleased if you would come to my home this evening at eight p.m. to continue the fascinating but inconclusive struggle of two months ago. I would prefer it if you would come alone. If it would assist, my car is available to collect you and for the return journey also.

Sincerely

Stefan Vanosivich.

Helen grimaced. "This evening! The man's absurd... an ogre."

Peter took the letter back and studied it in silence.

"You won't go, I assume."

Still gazing at the letter Peter was wandering back and forth abstractedly.

"Peter!"

"What? Oh, yes, of course I'll go."

*   *   *

At the gates of the estate, Peter lowered the window of Geoff's Lincoln but before he could reach for the bell a floodlight came on, illuminating him for the security camera and a voice said: "Please drive right in, Mr Gilchrist. You can park at the door – two hundred yards on your right." And the light and speaker were switched off. The greeting was polite but the abrupt procedure irritated Peter and he was ready for a confrontation when the front door was opened by a middle-aged man in dark trousers and a bottle-green butler's jacket who greeted him with a disarming smile. "Good evening, sir. Please come in. Mr Vanosivich is in the study. This way."

The ecclesiastical silence was broken only by the polite squeak of the butler's well polished shoes as Peter was conducted across the hall and up a broad flight of stairs to a green baize door. The butler knocked and Stefan's unmistakable voice called them to enter. As the door opened Peter was greeted by the aroma of coffee and the music of Bach.

"Mr Gilchrist, sir," the butler announced gravely.

The room was large and rectangular with a desk in a bow window. Apart from the fireplace, the door and one large window, bookshelves covered the walls from floor to high ceiling. Stefan switched off the music and came from behind his desk to meet Peter, hand extended. "Mr Gilchrist, welcome. It is very good of you to come at such short notice." He gestured to a pair of armchairs on either side of a low table. "Please be seated. Will you take something – coffee, a drink?"

Peter shook the proffered hand and sat down. "Coffee, please."

The butler busied himself at an Italian coffee machine set incongruously on an ebony and gilt table. Stefan took the other armchair. Peter saw no board or pieces, no preparations for a chess game and found himself unsurprised.

"I must apologize, I have brought you here under false pretenses." He waited, expecting some response. Peter said nothing.

"I do not propose that we play chess, not this evening, not ever."

And again a pause, Stefan watching his guest with a strange intensity. The silence persisted until the butler had served coffee and left the room.

"You do know who I am?"

And in that instant Peter did know. His suspicions had started the moment he read the letter of invitation, had grown as he drove to the meeting and now he was certain. And in the way of these things, with the knowledge came surprise at how long his blindness had persisted. He nodded slowly. "Yes."

"And you hold me responsible for your daughter's death?"

To the very instant of the question, Peter had had his answer clear and unambiguous. Now, facing the reality, he equivocated. "Ultimately, yes."

Endel, Peter saw, recognized the uncertainty and allowed himself a sad wisp of a smile. "So do I," he responded. For a while he stared down at the floor, appearing to be reconsidering this admission until he murmured to himself 'Indeed, so do I'. Stirring himself from this introspection he met Peter's eye. "So you expect me now to excuse myself."

Again, Peter's answer seemed to shape itself. "I expect you to explain."

Endel nodded. After a pause, whether for effect or in preparation Peter could not discern, he began speaking with studied rhetoric, in the manner of one addressing an audience.

"My name is Endel Vanaveski. I am Estonian. I was born in Tallinn in 1926, the son of the Bishop. Estonia is a small country, rich in history; a warrior nation, but we have a geographical problem." He gestured first to one side, "The Soviets," then the other, "the Nazis. A weasel between wolves. During the war…"

He broke off suddenly and sought Peter's gaze. "You are not a violent man, Mr Gilchrist?"

"No." Peter's response was instinctive, then he recalled uneasily the primal need for damned retribution which had overwhelmed him when he first heard of his daughter's death.

"Neither am I."

A bold claim, Peter noted, from a man who had left a trail of at least three corpses across a hemisphere.

"Yet," he resumed his address, "violence has followed me since I was a boy."

He sighed in resignation.

"When the Nazis first came to Tallinn they had a list of things they wished to steal. At the top of the list was a famous carving of Christ which belonged to the church. My father had arranged for it to be hidden and when he refused to tell them where, they shot my elder sister." He paused. "Through the head." Another pause. The enormity of the crime seemed to squeeze the detail from him drop by drop. "In the church." He hurried on as if to prevent comment from Peter. "That was on the first of November 1941. It was very cold, even for our winter. On the 2nd, my father's fifty-fifth birthday, they came at first light, two truckloads of troops, stamping, yelling, battering down doors."

His mouth tightened in a grimace of hatred. "The officer sat there in the staff car with his greatcoat collar turned up, looking on while his men kicked and beat old people and children as if they were herding pigs."

He had abandoned the declamatory style and was speaking quietly, personally, to Peter alone.

"When they'd got us all into the square we were marched into the forest. My father was ill, his lungs were very bad, and my mother was almost carrying him, I had my little sister Tia by the hand. We were ordered to stop in a clearing. It was quiet, not even birds - there were always bird sounds, even in winter, but not that day. When the firing started everyone panicked, began running."

He shook his head, saddened and puzzled still by the recollection.

"It was as if they were blind, not even knowing where the firing was coming from. My parents were carried along by the crowd and I lost them, so I dragged my sister through the snow to where the trees were thickest. At first I thought we would make it but she was hit. I knew at once she would die but I kept running – to hesitate was to die with her. Two of them came after me but they were slow and clumsy and poor shots. Once I got to the river I knew they'd never find me."

In an unchanging monotone he went on to describe being picked up, half-frozen, from the river bank a mile down-stream by a charcoal burner who lived deep in the forest and taken to the partisans – the Forest Brothers as they came to be called, and how, for many years he had lived and fought with them.

"It was a hard time but also a good time. When the shooting begins one learns the truth about a man, and Anti, our leader, was the best of the best." He drew a breath, smiled a little. "We had small victories, ambushes, raiding supply depots, you know the sort of thing."

Peter did not know. He realized that this man had lived in a different world.

"For a while, we killed more men than we lost but..." He shrugged, a token of submission to the inexorable power of overwhelming force.

"We all knew the war could end only one way. Life without hope burns a man away," he placed a hand on his chest, "from the inside. So I left."

He made it sound like walking out during the first act of a bad play. Peter wondered what the reality had been.

Still showing faint surprise, as though he had made the discovery only yesterday, Endel explained that in America, where the fighting was with words and lawyers, the rules he had learned at such cost in the forest still applied. The man who looks you in the eye without fear and without hostility makes a good friend or a dangerous enemy, anger corrodes judgement, profit goes to the man who runs against the crowd. And he'd been lucky. His first job in the new country had been as office boy in a shipping company, not because he had any interest in ships but because he'd seen a 'Vacancy' sign in New York docks in the window of a place with an air of calm that reminded him of Anti. So he'd run the errands and made coffee and kept things neat, all the while watching and listening and remembering. And then one day he'd heard someone in the manager's office speaking Estonian, the first time he'd heard his language since saying goodbye to the fishermen who'd smuggled him past the Russian patrols two years earlier. The speaker was Maart Laar, the owner of the company, visiting from head office. They'd talked at length. Laar had listened to his story and described how he too had recognized the relentless futility of the war, and had left in 1946 to join cousins in Canada.

"Soon Laar moved me to headquarters, not to make coffee but as his aide." His delivery was suddenly brisk, energized by the excitement of recollection.

"At first I was just answering the 'phone, keeping the files tidy, making notes at meetings but within a year Maart left the day-to-day running of the business to me. What times we had, traveling, meetings, negotiations…", another quick, nostalgic smile, "…and terrific rows; the old man was a tough character."

Endel waved a hand around the comfortable room. "I owe everything to Maart. For seven years he taught me how to manage men, to make a deal, to make a profit. But most of all he taught me that I would never get rich working for someone else." He smiled. "He was right. A few months later, I bought a broken-down shipping company to try my luck. When I told Maart, he nodded, smiled, shook my hand and wished me well."

Carried along by the narrative, Peter listened to a story of business life that he understood well enough.

If the Laar years had been hard, Endel's first years on his own were immeasurably harder. For three years he'd worked all day every day. On day one he'd called the fifteen staff together and told them how the old days of hopelessness had ended, how his own commitment would be absolute and how he expected nothing less from them. And he'd ended by inviting anyone who could not or would not join his crusade to clear out. Four had taken him at his word, leaving the meeting without discussion. Two more had fallen out within a week and another two a month later, one suffering from nervous exhaustion. The others, the Magnificent Seven they'd called themselves, had stayed on to become part of the legend of the newly-christened Baltic Star Line and of its proprietor who never slept, never broke his word, never forgave an enemy and never lost a deal.

Endel shrugged, a little defensively. "Foolishness, of course. But a man must live up to his legend."

In 1971, when he had accumulated a sizeable fortune and life was less frenetic, to the amazement of the staff of Baltic Star he announced that he was to be married.

"The legend had not allowed for a woman. I myself had not allowed the possibility. Apart from my mother and sisters, no woman before Francesca had been worthwhile." He shook his head. "I should have known the gods would intervene." He rose and took his cup, still not yet half empty, to the coffee machine. Now behind Peter, he continued. "It was a week before the wedding. We were to meet at a restaurant. I was late. She came to look for me at the office, a bad part of town, close to the docks. The next morning her body was found not a block away."

He returned to his seat and set down the replenished cup.

"When the police came to tell me, it was as with my sister in the forest, I could not allow time to grieve. It was easy for me to find the man, all the dock people knew him. As soon as I had dealt with him, I left New York. Not from choice; I liked the town, such intensity, a town crazy for money, but violent men were looking for me."

At first he had wanted only sufficient money to protect himself from men of violence, to ensure that he would never again be at the mercy of a man in a greatcoat but once this had been achieved, money ceased to concern him. He'd never wanted it for itself and he despised those enslaved by the pursuit or even worse the consumption of it. The deal was his raison d'être and his life became a quest for worthwhile opponents. He also was waiting for the chance to extend his business to the Baltic States.

"The collapse of the Soviet system was of course inevitable – Marx was a good revolutionary but a third-rate economist; the question was whether I would live to profit from it, then suddenly Gorbachev flung open the door."

Always anonymous, by telephone and messenger, he had lured Margus Sepp, son of a forest comrade, away from the family farm to set up the Tallinn office which would at last make the reality of Baltic Star Line accord with its name. But even as the Baltic business boomed he began to feel uneasy. At first it puzzled him and he hated it, then he understood it and he hated it more. Facing the super dilemma of the super-rich: what is worth buying to the man who can buy anything, he'd found a solution which was worse than the problem. The only thing he coveted was subject to the unyielding embargo of a sworn promise to a dying leader.

"And your greed caused my daughter's death."

Endel nodded sad agreement. "For twenty years I have lived quietly here, without family, without friends. Then, a little time ago, I met an extraordinary young woman. I had hoped perhaps to be a friend to her. But within a fortnight she, too, was murdered, a death for which I was myself partly to blame. It seems that it is not wise for young women to become close to Endel Vanaveski. It is not possible to convey to you how much I regret it."

While the narrative continued Peter had listened, unthinking, impassive, but now, in the silence, an image of great savagery filled his mind. Howling with animal rage, he sees himself battering an anonymous victim with a heavy implement until, blood soaked and sated, he collapses exhausted. This image had come to him first on the night following the discovery of Meg's body and had reappeared intermittently since, often as a grossly disturbing dream. But now, the victim no longer anonymous, the conjured image having become reality, the very idea of a physical assault on this sad man in his own house was absurd and repellent.

Endel remained silent. Was he waiting for a response or had he simply exhausted his narrative? Was he hoping for Peter to offer some comment, of understanding at least, if sympathy were too much to ask?

Peter tried to form a reply but nothing he could think of was other than inadequate. Just what is the correct form for the occasion? How should a gentleman respond when his host confesses his part in the murder of an only child? Could he simply leave? If finding a suitable reply was so difficult, why say anything? Only the combination of human failing and unhappy accident had brought him here. So, say nothing and leave.

And at last that was what Peter did. He rose, took a final look at the figure opposite, now hunched, head drooping, looking smaller, older, defeated, then left the room. By some below stairs clairvoyance, the butler appeared as Peter reached the hall, got to the front door first and held it open. Outside, damp air rising from the Pacific threaded strands of fog among the redwoods.

~ CHAPTER 40 ~

"Good night, sir. Do drive carefully, the fog can be rather nasty on the hill. Patchy, you know?"

"Yes, I know, thank you. Good night."

A few minutes later the butler was summoned to the study where he started to tidy the coffee cups.

"Leave that," Endel instructed and handed him a large sealed envelope. "That is to be opened at noon tomorrow." Then, for the first time in six years' employment, his employer shook him by the hand, and told him he could go to bed.

*   *   *

It was eleven o'clock when Peter arrived back at the beach house, scarcely conscious of having made the journey. He found Helen and Geoff in the study. Geoff was sprawled asleep in an armchair, Helen had moved the sofa to face her ever more complicated wallchart and was sitting, as so often recently, lost in thought.

"It wasn't chess then," she said, over her shoulder.

"I never believed it was, that's why I went." Peter replied, crossing to the bar. "Care for a drink?"

"No thanks."

"Geoff?"

Receiving no response, Peter nudged the armchair with his knee, forcing its occupant into grudging wakefulness.

"Drink?," Peter repeated.

"Sleepily, Geoff struggled to sit upright. "What? Oh, no thanks."

Peter reached for the whiskey, changed his mind and joined Helen on the sofa.

"If only Stefan weren't Russian…", she began.

"He isn't. He's Estonian. And he isn't Stefan. His name is Endel Vanaveski," Peter interrupted. "He's our KKK man." Peter gestured at Helen's white board.

"I see." Helen seemed unsurprised. It seemed that instinct had reached the answer a little ahead of logic.

"So what will you do now?"

"Do?"

"About Stefan… Endel."

"What do you want me to do?"

"Well, you could call the police."

"And tell them what?"

"My God, Peter. Tell them he's a smuggler and a murderer, to begin with."

"Hmm…"

"What do you mean hmm?"

"It's more complicated than I'd thought. Let's leave it until tomorrow. I will call Al though." Not wanting further discussion that night, he got up and went quickly to the phone.

As Al explained to Mrs Hershey, the call that ended what had been by far his biggest and best paying contract was also the most satisfying news of his investigative career. She gave him a congratulatory kiss before reminding him that, as of that moment, they had bills to pay and no clients.

Peter lay awake for a long time trying to work out why he had wanted to delay contacting the police.

CHAPTER 41

EPILOGUE

Thursday 10th September 1992

CHECKMATE

In Tallinn's Church of the Holy Ghost the packed congregation overflowed into the cobbled street. The sounds of the service, broadcast for the crowd outside the church, echoed from the medieval buildings, decorated for the occasion with Estonian flags of black, white and cornflower blue.

Inside, the congregation coughed and shuffled to their places. Jaakob took his seat nearest the pulpit steps and drew from his pocket a small, tattered book.

The Bishop's sermon was brief, his text, 'The truth shall make you free'. Then, after a long pause, he looked slowly around the crowded church.

"The first sermon in our language was preached in this church. For seven hundred years our people have gathered here to give thanks and to pray for God's deliverance."

For most of the Brothers, God's deliverance was too late. The Nazis came in 1940, the Russians left in 1991.

"In the old times, on their way to meetings, the town council came to pray at this altar, in God's sight."

You were only a child, Endel, when you killed a man before this altar, in God's sight.

"Our grain supplies were kept in the attic above our heads. Edicts were proclaimed here, taxes apportioned, agreements signed and trade transacted. For centuries the sanctity of the church has been a guarantee of honest dealing. But in all her long history there has never been a day like this. For we come to re-consecrate the sacred image, the Seated Christ, stolen by heathen, lost for half a century, and to honor the three men who ensured its safe return. Of these men, one is dead, one is far away; the other is here to speak to you now."

He descended from the pulpit and gestured an invitation to the old man. Jaakob, climbing with difficulty, ascended the narrow winding wooden stairs, passing between the carved figures of St. Peter and St. Paul and beneath the cornice with its text - 'God bless your entrance and exit both now and ever.' As he reached the lectern, a curtain in the chancel was drawn back and the afternoon sun streamed through the intricate stained glass of the south window trapping the carving in a shaft of brilliant yellow light. He set the ruins of the book on the lectern and looked out over the congregation in silence, his mind a kaleidoscope of fragmentary memories.

At last he began speaking. "I am, as you see, an old man. I had not thought to live to see this day."

He turned, stood silently gazing at the carving, then turned again to his audience.

"My father was Professor of Military History at the University of Tallinn. No longer young when the Nazis came, he joined the Brothers and wrote their story. In 1943 he was wounded while leading the raid on the rail station to reclaim the Christ from the barbarians. In hospital he would have survived but we had no medical supplies... At the end he summoned me and my friend Endel Vanaveski...

Fierce dark eyes scarcely changed by sixty years. 'Jaakob. Old friend.'

...son of the Bishop of Tallinn, and made us swear that we would never give up the struggle to find the Christ, to keep it safe and to return it to the church when Estonia became free.

'To the Church. Remember, both of you – to the Church. Swear you will never give up.'

He died in my mother's arms and lies in the forest with our comrades."

The old man paused, cleared his throat and went on.

"After the disaster at the station, the carving was taken to Germany. Then the

Russians came and for many years it seemed my father and the others had died in vain. One tyrant had been replaced by another. The Christ was lost, it seemed for ever. But Endel never tired of the search and, a few weeks ago, he recovered it for us."

When you stole the Christ you spat on my father's grave.

"It will for ever be the sacred duty of the Estonian people to care for it, to defend it against those who would again take it from us."

Jaakob cast a challenging gaze over the congregation, allowing his words to sink in. When he resumed his voice had an edge that seemed out of keeping.

"Endel, sadly cannot be here today. He asks your forgiveness for his absence."

Jaakob pointed to the carving, now glowing amber in the declining sun, seeming to pulsate with inner energy.

"As you see, my father's dying wish has been fulfilled. My task is complete."

He stood immobile for a long time, gazing out over the packed congregation. Then he raised an arm in salute: "Long live free Estonia."

*   *   *

As Jaakob was climbing the pulpit steps, half the globe to the west, California Highway Patrolman Fidel Santos Martinez stretched his lean frame, yawned and checked his watch. Six thirty. To his left the sun crept above the San Pedro Mountains. The air was warm already; it would be another hot one. He was not a morning kind of a cop and he wasn't pleased to have drawn this early patrol but at least it gave him the chance to drive a hot car. Recently this stretch of the 280 Freeway had been the scene of several major accidents, including a couple of fatalities and a special patrol detail provided the opportunity to try out the force's brand new Camaro, the only vehicle on the books capable of really high speed pursuit.

A characteristic growl heralded a lone motorcyclist, a burly figure in the upright, stiff arm position of the Harley rider, preposterous red beard fluttering in the wind, the back of his sleeveless denim jacket decorated with

Nazi double thunderbolts picked out in metal studs, his bare arms black with tattoos. He wore no helmet and according to Martinez' practiced eye was traveling at around 85 mph.

At school, Martinez' best subject had been martial arts and his knowledge of the SS or indeed of anything historical was negligible. However his street schooling had taught that him this insignia always spelt trouble and usually violence.

Martinez smiled the wan smile of the man who'd been here before. Time was, he'd have taken off after the biker with relish in the hope he might turn nasty but, older and tired, he now left him for the next man. Or the paramedics. Once he'd realized his promotion wasn't on anybody's agenda, he'd figured that he could afford to stop seeking out trouble and settle for what God sent him and still be a decent cop. These days, he reflected gloomily, he was fuelled more by Coke and Big Macs than adrenaline. At ten after seven he decided to try another spot and eased the Camaro out of the bushes.

As he joined the highway he saw a car maybe half a mile back. Gently allowing the Camaro to gather speed more or less of its own volition, enjoying the sound of the tuned V8, he took another look. The car was already on top of him and traveling extremely fast in the otherwise empty outside lane. A few seconds later it flew past him.

He swore under his breath. Unlike the biker, the driver must have seen him. What a way to start the day, a drunk, a lunatic or a junkie in a high-powered sedan. He floored the pedal, switched on the siren and put in a swift call for back-up. Then, shuffling deeper into the seat, he prepared for a long chase.

The target had taken a big lead and it felt like he'd been accelerating forever before he began slowly gaining. It was the highest speed pursuit he'd ever been in. Brake lights showed briefly when a lone semi drifted dangerously close to the outside lane but otherwise the driver seemed not even to ease the throttle. On sweeping freeway bends, the car would lean hard on its suspension and at times looked to Martinez to be in real danger of sliding off the road. The Camaro's tires were squirming under the g-forces too and he thanked God there was almost no traffic. The longer the pursuit continued, the more Martinez appreciated that this was no joy-riding juvenile but someone who understood as well as himself the subtle and dangerous art of high-speed driving.

They had just passed the astonished biker and Martinez was sparing a fraction of his concentration to wonder where his back-up was, when the big sedan, its speed undiminished, tires howling, dived at the last second across three lanes and onto the El Monte Road slip. Exploiting the Camaro's capabilities to the limit, Martinez managed to follow, then had to brake hard for the intersection. The sedan did not brake.

At the bottom of the slip it smashed through a fence, ploughed across the grass, took off over a slight rise and, still airborne and traveling at one hundred and fifty feet per second, struck a concrete bridge abutment.

Martinez, at that moment preoccupied with a Camaro straining to stand on its nose, was startled by the noise of the impact. When he'd finally wrestled the car to a halt at the bottom of the off-ramp, he gazed in stupefaction through a cloud of dust and flying débris at the crumpled remains of the sedan. He figured he'd pretty much seen it all, but it took several seconds before he was able to reach for the microphone and his voice was slightly unsteady as he reported: "We got an 11-80 just off 280 Southbound, the El Monte slip. It's a bad one."

He clambered from the Camaro and sprinted across the grass then halted a few yards short. According to the characteristically precise factory specification, the Mercedes S-class sedan is two hundred and three point one inches long; this one had been reduced to about half that in a few tenths of a second. Wisps of dust or maybe fuel vapor drifted from the wreck. Going cautiously closer, Martinez thought maybe the driver had been male and bald-headed. He could see no sign of any other occupants. "Tell the ambulance not to hurry," he thought.

Back in the Station House Martinez swore on his mother's eyes that the guy just drove straight to the accident but when his report talked of a 'death wish', the Sergeant chewed him out for this unsupported allegation.

*   *   *

In accordance with his long-standing will, the driver's entire estate passed to the Estonian church. Under the terms of a recently added codicil, his remains were buried in the small, neglected cemetery of the Northern California town of La Honda. The headstone, incorrect in every important respect, is Endel's final deception:

Stefan Vanosivich
Born Moscow 1930
Died traffic accident, California 1992